CW01432262

The Rune House

L. J. Hutton

ISBN 9781792915321
Published by Wylfheort Books 2012
Revised edition 2018

Acknowledgements

Many thanks are due to Dr Philippa Semper for introducing me to runes and expanding my knowledge of Old English – any mistakes are mine alone, as is the fictional arcane use the runes are put to, which is a far cry from her academic rigour. I owe Mary Ward many thanks for reading the first drafts and commenting on them, and hope that she isn't too disappointed with the occasional piece of artistic license.

Also, thanks to Dave and Chris Vale for their encouragement. To Teresa Fairhurst I owe much, for providing me with laughter and sanity breaks.

My husband and my lovely lurchers have kept body and soul more or less intact, and this couldn't have been written without them.

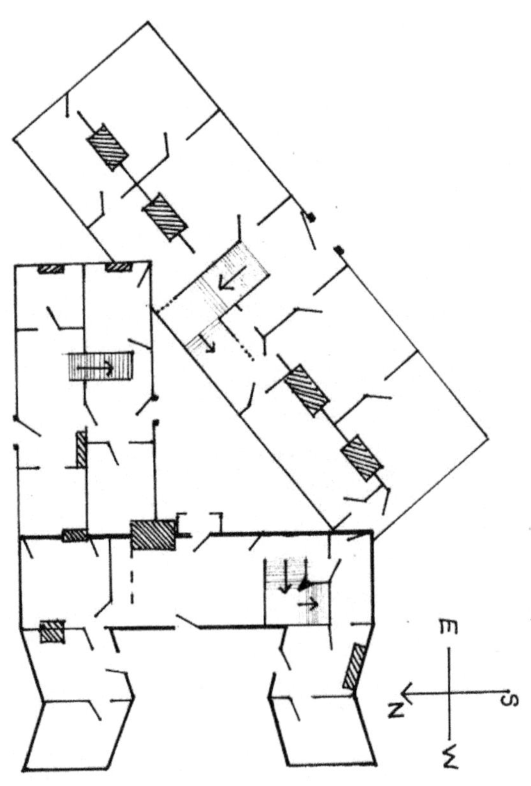

Weord Manor School

Blest is Ffreuer: how sad it is tonight,
After Elfan's death,
......
Though war may rage in each region,
We care not, our side won't be slain.

Ffreuer from the *Helledd Saga*
Taken from *Medieval Welsh Poems,*
Ed. & trans. by Joseph P. Clancy,
Four Courts Press, 2003.

Prologue

The Welsh Borders,
October, The Year of Our Lord 1574

The four workmen kept glancing nervously at the lowering sun as they worked. They were infilling the timber frame on the new house as fast as they could, but the work was still taking longer than they would have liked.

"There's somethin' creepy about this place, don't tell me there isn't," Sam Turley muttered for the umpteenth time that day, as he wove another elder bough into a space between thick oak timbers.

"I ain't arguin' with yer Sam," Amos Trevithick's voice drifted down from the ladder above Sam's head. "I done built many houses, but none like this 'un."

"Humph," Sam snorted with little conviction. "I thought you Cornish folks were used to ungodly things like fairies and pixies. Wouldn't a' thought it would've bothered you!"

"Don't you go maligning things you know nothin' about, Sam," Amos' burly son, Ezra, chastised him mildly. "I ain't sayin' that the Otherworld doesn't touch ours a bit more closely in Cornwall than in other places, but we ain't in Cornwall now and this ain't like anythin' we've ever come across either."

"What I still don't understand is why he insisted that the last timber of the frame had to go in on midsummer's day," fretted Thomas, the final member of their group, as he trimmed more elder for Sam. At the height of the building work the two Cornish carpenters had been supervising half a dozen more travelling journeymen in order to complete the work to their employer's precise schedule, but now they were gone again leaving only these men. "Smacks of something heathen to me! Why couldn't he just leave things be and go to church like the rest of us? We ain't had no religious troubles in these villages yet, and we don't want none either!"

"He surely got everyone off the land pretty smart as soon as the frame was done, that's for certain," Amos agreed. "And why stop work until after midsummer if he's in such a hurry for it to be finished? I ain't arguin' with yer that it was to do some strange ritual, Sam, but we don't know what he done any more than you."

"That's right," Ezra said pointedly to the suspicious Sam, as he hauled a bucket of daub over to him. "The fey should be treated with respect. Don't mean you ain't a Christian just 'cos you keep your eyes open and go careful about your business. Anyone with any sense don't go dabblin' in things they don't understand and can't control. Folks like us know it's dangerous to go around those places where the fairy folk've been seen on certain nights of the year, and back home no-one with any brains would go payin' them a visit on midsummer night of all nights. That's just askin' for trouble! God-fearin' folk like us keep well away."

"Aye, but he's one o' yours!" Sam retorted, not to be so easily quashed.

"The man comes from Cornwall!" Ezra growled in frustration, as he now climbed the ladder and handed his father more wooden pegs for the roof frame on the last wing. "It's a big county, Sam! As big as Herefordshire! I ain't never even *heard* of the place he's supposed to come from! We ain't all like him. He's travelled all over the place – to foreign countries an' all

– how do you know he ain't brought them strange rituals back from some ungodly heathen place?"

Amos and Ezra had been surprised to be hired by Doctor Nathaniel Parker to come to the Welsh borders to build a house for him, but work was work and not always easily come by. Why the strange doctor would bypass local craftsmen was a mystery, especially as once they'd arrived, they'd found that the local carpenters hadn't even been asked. Perhaps it was because the house was like no other that they'd ever worked on, and the doctor wanted no local interference with his grand plan.

It had seemed straightforward if a little unconventional at first. The doctor had courted the daughter of the local knight, Sir Timothy, and as part of the marriage arrangement had acquired a substantial plot of land on which to build her a house. The locals all agreed that Sir Timothy doted on his only child, Margaret, and he must have thought himself lucky when the doctor had asked for some of the poorest land on the estate rather than prime farming land. But then the doctor didn't need to farm for an income, so maybe that was why he'd chosen the picturesque fold in the great ridge which loomed to the west of the rolling acres of ploughed fields and pasture. The land around here was rich and fertile, but there was a reversed D-shaped plateau of highland in a crook in the course of the River Wye, which was steeply edged and heavily wooded. The curve of the 'D' faced west, following the sweep of the river, while the straight edge formed the long ridge facing east, and it was here that Dr Parker had decided to build.

The plot certainly had its charms, and on a practical note there was a good natural well with plenty of clear spring water. However, those involved now wondered whether the doctor had wanted outsiders for the main construction so that his soon to be father-in-law wouldn't be able to influence the design. All the local craftsmen lived on Sir Timothy's land, and without his continued approval would find work hard to get. So if he'd chosen to make his views known, they'd have been heeded and acted upon. Maybe it was out of the way, some folk now wondered, precisely because the doctor had known he wouldn't always be around to supervise things for most of the time, and so he'd chosen a spot where no-one could see what was happening. The villagers who lived in the isolated hamlets nearest to it were hardly experts in grand houses, so if none of the local gentry came past who was to say if it was right or wrong?

Yet now it was clear for all to see that the house was anything but ordinary, and now it was far too late to change without the whole place being taken down and started again. Something for which none of those working on it had the authority or courage to do. The men shook their heads in disapproval at all things foreign, and hurriedly worked the last bucket of daub for the day, gathering their tools up and heading for the tiny village alehouse as the last of the light faded.

"It's a funny lookin' place, that's for certain," Sam confided in his friends as he drained his tankard beside the fire in the alehouse.

"What I don't understand is why he wanted them funny shapes in the bracing wood between the main timbers," Amos fretted. "I told him, 'I ain't guaranteeing that it'll be as strong as if we done it the normal way,' but he wouldn't have it. Thank the Lord they'm only on the single storey bit 'cos I ain't got the learnin' to work out how to do that and still make two floors stay standin'! I don't want the responsibility of killin' one of his posh friends if it falls down!"

"Maybe it'd be a good thing if the cursed place did fall down!" Thomas muttered softly, and received sage nods of agreement as they all refreshed their pints.

"They're not funny shapes," said a slightly breathless voice from the door, coming in at the end of the conversation. Billy the woodworker from the next village bustled in and shut the door firmly against the late autumn chill. Nodding to the innkeeper, he paid for his beer and then came to join the cluster of workmen by the hearth.

"Where you bin all day?" challenged Sam. "We could've done with you comin' and workin', not gallivantin' off someplace. We'll never get it done at this rate!"

"Oh, stop moanin' Sam!" Thomas said firmly. He peered at Billy through the gloom of the weak candle light. "What's up Billy? You look all flustered."

"Aye, and well I might!" Billy replied with an air of triumph. He looked round to make sure all the hamlet's men were listening. "I bin to Hereford!" he proclaimed and had the satisfaction of seeing that he'd caught everyone's interest, including the farm workers who'd only seen the place in passing. "A few years ago, I done some work for the cathedral on some of the buildin's they own, ye'see? And the Dean was real pleased with what I done, so I thought I'd go and see if he could help – him bein' learned and all that."

He held up a rolled sheaf of paper which all the builders knew contained the plans to the house and the instructions for the design.

"I went to him and asked if he would take a look at this stuff. I told him it was some work I'd been asked to do what didn't seem right. And as it was odd, I wanted it checked over to make sure I weren't doin' nothin heretical, like."

The others nodded their approval of his ploy. Although Queen Elizabeth was now safely ensconced on the throne of England, everyone remembered only too well the huge religious upheavals of earlier in the century – if it wasn't exactly known first hand, nonetheless it was still within the lifetime of the elderly or their parents. First the endless chaos of the queen's father as he'd divorced or disposed of one wife after another. Then his son Edward VI had persecuted Catholics on an unprecedented scale, and when his oldest sister Mary had succeeded the pendulum had swung back the other way, and it had been the Protestants who had been in fear of their lives.

Not that such events had had much impact on the more isolated parts of the country like this, but everyone had heard about them and worried. The old king had purportedly had spies everywhere. As a result, most ordinary people walked very carefully around the niceties of religious observance, mostly following the lead of whoever the lord of their local manor was. But it paid not to take things for granted, and so Billy's course of action was accepted as prudent rather than paranoid.

Making a sweeping glance around his audience Billy went on.

"Well once I explained that we was all a bit nervous, he was most obligin'. Said it was the right thing to do." He paused for the murmured obligatory acknowledgement of his foresight and acumen.

"But what did he say?" an impatient voice from the back demanded.

With a frown at the interruption of his moment of superiority, Billy made his pronouncement.

"They'm *runes*!" he declared with a flourish.

"Runes? What's runes?" asked an irritated Sam.

"All of it!" Billy declared triumphantly. "That funny shape of the house? That's a rune! That's what the Dean says. That's why the two end pieces are at those funny angles. And those odd shapes of the bracing pieces you kept worryin' about Amos? They'm runes too!"

"But what *are* runes?" fumed Sam, annoyed that he had to show his ignorance in front of his mates.

"They'm an old alphabet from the days afore William the Conqueror," Billy said with a conspiratorial wink.

"So they'm witchcraft?" someone said in a tremulous voice from behind him.

Accusations of witchcraft were just about as bad as it could get. The Protestants and Catholics might hate each other, but they all had it in for those who practised the arcane arts, and differences would be buried in a heartbeat if there was even a hint of a witch to be burned. But Billy shook his head.

"No, no, the Dean says that they ain't nothin' like that! Seems that they appear on old grave stones and the like. Might even be from the Roman times, some of 'em."

"Aye, but didn't the old parson say those Romans were funny buggers," the brewer said, coming round to join in the conversation with his customers. "Didn't they worship all them strange gods and make 'uman sacrifices and the like? They weren't no Christians from what I remember of the sermons he gave us. That fella Pilot was a Roman weren't he, and we all know what he done!"

"Well the Dean says it's all right from what he's seen o' this," Billy said firmly. "So now I can go ahead and make all these carvin's of *runes*..." he rolled the word again with relish "...on the staircase, like what the doctor ordered, with a clear conscience!"

"Well thank the Lord for that!" another of the workers said with relief. "Good on yer Billy! That were good thinkin' goin' to the Dean like that. Put's all our minds at rest that does. I ain't ashamed to admit I been havin' some sleepless nights frettin' about that strange place, but now I can stop worryin'."

The men drifted off congratulating the smug Billy, leaving Amos and Ezra to make their way to the tiny room at the back of the alehouse which they were renting for the duration. Once inside the sanctity of their room, though, Ezra leaned in to his father and whispered softly,

"Pa, I still don't like this, I don't like it one little bit!"

"No, son, me neither."

"Did you notice that Billy didn't say that the Dean could actually *read* that stuff? Knowin' what it is ain't the same as understandin' it, is it? We still don't know what it is that them letters say, do we? And now it turns out that Billy's goin' to carve more of them on the inside!"

"I know," Amos agreed, his voice carrying his concern even though in the darkness Ezra couldn't see his face. "All these layers of words! They worry me! If it was passages from the Bible, why aren't they in words normal folks can read? Ain't nothin' wrong these days in havin' stuff in English, but if he wants to show off, why not have it in Latin like any other Christian soul? Why go for some strange writin' even the Church don't understand?

"We done that place down by Falmouth two year ago, you remember? Where that chap had the psalm verses writ in paint on the wooden ceiling? Looked real smart it did too! Not that we could make out the Latin any more than old Paul who painted it could, but we knew what it was 'cos the rector came to check the spellin'. But that were a job like any other, and none of us lost any sleep over it. This job makes the hairs on the back of my neck stand on end every time we go there, and it's gettin' worse. T'weren't ever good, right from when we put the base-plate timbers down in that funny pattern, but the closer it gets to bein' finished the worse it's becomin'!"

"And another thing," Ezra said fearfully. "Have you noticed when it's goin' to be all finished on the outside? The end of this month, that's when! Who wants a house completed for All Hallow's Eve? The night of the dead?"

"Aye, and it's called somethin' else in the old ways," Amos said with a shudder. "Do you recall Granny Wicks sayin' it were called Samhain? Poor old crone near got burned for a witch, too, for talkin' about such stuff an' all! I can still hear Parson Trewin rantin' on about it bein' an old druid's feast – somat about the time of death and rebirth for them as turned away from the right path and the Lord. He fair put the willies up me for goin' near them stone circles!"

Ezra chuckled. "Us lads stopped playin' on the moors for weeks after that! Scared us to death he did!" But he swiftly lost his merriment again as his father said,

"What I wonders is, what's goin' to be born out of this?"

"You think it really is somat heathen?"

"Mebbe? But I see'd enough pictures in church windows of folks burnin' in hell to not want it to happen to us!"

They both shuddered, and Ezra wrapped his thin blanket a bit closer around him as he said,

"What say you we make sure we're out of here by then? I reckon by the time the last of the daub is in, there won't be any need for us to stay on. Won't be any work for the likes of us. It'll all be for fine carpentry like Billy does, and fancy plaster-work on the inside."

"I say 'aye' to that!" Amos answered with relief. "Yes son, you're right, there can't be more than a couple of weeks work left for us. It'll be cuttin' it fine but we should be able to be on the road a good couple of days before the thirty-first. We can take our time goin' home, and then start that nice new farmhouse for young Mister Petherick. Lord, but I'll be glad to get back to normal work again! Houses made like runes! Whatever next!"

Chapter 1

Worcester
The present day

The day had started off indistinguishable from the many that had gone before it, and afterwards, Merlin Roberts realised that he could never have dreamed how much it would change his life. Inevitably, with a name like his and his Celtic heritage, Merlin was known to his fellow police officers as the Welsh Wizard, no matter how un-wizard-like he looked. In a desperate attempt to avoid his nickname sticking, he'd managed to get most of his colleagues to call him Robbie to his face. But as he was the one person with a real knack for record keeping and with the computers – apart from the boffins who programmed and maintained the things – the 'wizard' bit had unfortunately stuck. Having only just scraped into the force back in the days of minimum height requirements, and with a small but noticeable middle-aged spread beginning to form, Robbie was hardly anyone's image of a wizard, and he'd long ago realised that he was hardly built for pursuing villains on foot either. Instead, he'd created a nice niche for himself tackling a job that most officers tried to avoid at all costs – the old paperwork.

With the ever-rising pressure to improve the quota of solved cases, someone high up had had the bright idea of letting Robbie loose on the files which hadn't made it into the computer, to see if any of those could actually be connected to ones on the system which had been solved. A string of burglaries successfully laid at the feet of a known felon, already convicted, could still mount up to a nice number of closed cases, even if some of them were twenty years old. It looked good in statistics, and that was what the government wanted the police to produce – comforting figures that they could throw at the public to demonstrate that things weren't going to hell in a basket during their period in office.

Whatever the motivation was behind the move to his own office in the county headquarters, it made no difference to Robbie. What he thoroughly enjoyed was delving into the past, and often he got so engrossed that it was only the cleaners coming around at night which made him realise that he'd worked on far beyond the rest of the office staff. His diligence had already paid off in terms of solved old cases, thereby giving the accountants the idea that they were getting value for their money out of the project.

So Robbie's contract had been made permanent after twelve months and he'd settled in with relish, until seven years later when his tidy world was now being disrupted by the announcement of a new arrival. His heart sank into his boots when he was summoned to the Superintendent, and was told that he was having someone assigned to help him.

"I don't need any help, sir," Robbie protested. "Half the reason why this works is because, with only one person working on the files, I'm not missing things because they've gone across someone else's desk. Someone who hasn't seen the other half to make the connection."

"I know Robbie," his superior sympathised. "And this is no comment on your work." He sighed and then seemed to come to a decision to tell him everything. "The fact is Robbie, we're in a bit of a pickle. The man we're sending you ...well, the truth is, we don't know what else to do with him."

"Oh great!" Robbie muttered in bitter despair. "Thank you very much ...sir."

Superintendent Williams had the grace to look slightly sheepish. "I know, it's a real backhanded compliment, isn't it, but hear me out please. His name is Alaric Drake – only for God's sake call him Ric."

"Alaric? Where in heaven's name did that come from? Parents Tolkien fans by any chance? Sounds a bit elvish to me!" mused Robbie with weary resignation, indulging himself in a rare fit of sarcasm as the only way to vent his disgust. "He's not a bloody hobbit is he?" Clearly he was going to get this help, like it or not.

"Now then, Robbie," the Super' chided him with a faint smile as he checked the file. "He's in his early forties, but Tolkien was published by the time he was born, wasn't he?"

"Oh yes," Robbie confirmed with a sigh. "*The Lord of the Rings* led to a lot of people taking an interest in Anglo-Saxon things. And lots of hippies learning elvish and that sort of stuff. More in the late sixties, mind you, but might be about the right generation if he had young parents and they were a bit ahead of the masses in catching on to all that. A bit grim saddling your kid with a name like that, though. He must have suffered at school!"

"I'm sure he did," Williams agreed, "because he's always been what the charitable might describe as driven – others would say that he's got a skin like a rhino, and doesn't care who he offends. He started off in West Yorkshire on his home turf, and was soon making quite a name for himself. Then he transferred to the Met and did the same. A very successful officer who could've risen even higher if he'd had a bit more tact.

He certainly had a high success rate, and he's nothing if not a real tough nut who doesn't crack under pressure.

"The trouble was Robbie, the life style ultimately even got to him. However well he handled the stress mentally, his body didn't keep up. He's had a major heart attack and had stents fitted. So they can hardly put him back out on the streets. But he's a highly commended officer – many times over! – and his face has been in the press. It would be different if he was willing to take retirement on health grounds – let's face it, most of us would be after a scare like that – but the awkward bugger wants to carry on working! The men right at the top don't want bad publicity if he starts complaining too loudly – decorated officer thrown on scrap heap, that kind of headline in the gutter press!"

"No, I'm sure they don't," Robbie conceded. "So what you're telling me is that he's got to be found a desk job, and it's in my office?"

"Pretty much," said Williams sympathetically, wishing there was a way to soften the blow for the odd little detective he couldn't help but like. "They're moving him right out here because it's quieter and he'll be less in the limelight. Not many snooping tabloid reporters out here to spot him. As for why you, they've tried putting him in with working teams in the Home Counties already, and he keeps trying to take over their investigations. It's bloody difficult because he can pull rank over a lot of them – he's even been an acting DCI in his time – and they find it hard to ignore him. It's not easy running a case with the famous DI Drake staring over your shoulder at every step.

"On top of that, the heart attack saved his life in the most bizarre kind of way. While he was lying in A & E, with paramedics jumping on his chest, some villain he'd upset chose to plant an incendiary device in his flat. It went off in the small hours, and the Fire Chief said that had he been at home he would've been dead from the smoke even before the flames got to him. Someone knew what they were doing! That's why there's another worry if he attracts publicity, and why the powers-that-be want him as far from the south-east as they can get him. The man's refusing to lie low, but his life's in danger."

"That Drake?" gasped Robbie, struggling to reconcile what he'd heard with the thought of a man he would soon have to be in close proximity with. "Blimey, even I've heard of him! ...Heard of that fire too! I just never thought much about what happened afterwards."

"Mmmm, ...so you begin to get the picture. We desperately need you to take him under your wing, Robbie."

"That's hardly going to be easy, sir," Robbie protested. "He outranks me too! What am I supposed to do if he starts ordering me about? How's that any diff..."

Williams held up a hand to stop the flow of protests. "...We thought of that. Drake's been told in no uncertain terms that this is his last chance to stay on the force. Mess this up and he'll be forcibly retired, like it or not. He's been told that this is being viewed as a secondment, and for the purposes of his working on this project you are the expert, and he's to follow your lead. In fact, I do believe that words to the effect that 'the Met can't spare men just to guard some arrogant copper who hasn't got the sense to get his head down,' may have crossed his governor's lips!" The Super' smiled at Robbie. "We have every confidence in you! Just be yourself, ...you know, fatherly towards him."

"I'm not that bloody old!" Robbie protested vehemently. "I'm not turning fifty until next year! I'm certainly not old enough to have a son in his forties as well!"

"Sorry, Robbie," his boss apologised hurriedly, realising that he'd put his foot in it, and that actually Robbie was younger than himself, and not the other way round as he always tended to think. It was just that Robbie was such a stolid, bookish sort of chap that he seemed older in his ways. "No offence intended, ...honestly! It's just that you're seen as someone stable enough to cope with him. You're highly thought of, you know. The Chief Constable asked for you personally. This isn't a case of putting him with you because it's out of the way, and if he messes up your work it doesn't matter. It's more that having him on current cases would be even worse. Try your best to get him to settle into this job. It'll be hard work, because temperamentally he couldn't be more unsuited to desk work, but it's the only way he can stay working. And if he causes trouble then he'll be out on his ear, hero or not, but at least it'll be up here where it's all quieter – in every sense!"

"You don't want much, do you?" Robbie said resignedly, recognising when there was no point in fighting those above him. "I'll do my best, sir, but on this occasion it might not be enough."

His worst suspicions were surpassed on the day that Ric Drake walked in through the door. It opened with a crash, causing a small landslide of files from off the top of the nearest filing cabinet, and before he'd registered who was there, Robbie let rip as he dived for the sheaves of paper coming out of covers.

"Careful, you sodding idiot! It's taken me three days to get those in order! It's not the bloody Wild West in here! Try coming in without slamming things about, why don't you!"

"Oh deep, bloody, abiding joy! The king of the paper clips," a deep, Yorkshire voice drawled, and Robbie looked up to see DI Drake towering over him with a sneer on his face. Drake wasn't conventionally handsome by any means, with nondescript mid-brown hair and eyes, and what looked like a permanent sneer, but he certainly had a presence which went beyond the fashionable smart shoes and suit.

"Ah, ...it's you." Straightening up, Robbie put the files down on the floor where he hoped they couldn't get further disrupted. "Sorry, that wasn't the welcome I'd planned." He held out his hand. "I'm Merlin Roberts, Robbie to you."

Drake looked down at the extended hand, and for a moment Robbie thought he was about to turn on his heels and leave there and then. Instead, the newcomer seemed to almost physically bite back a retort he was about to make and struggled to contain himself, then after a couple of seconds took Robbie's hand and shook it.

"Ric Drake," he said tersely, putting emphasis on the first name as if daring Robbie to comment.

Instead, Robbie waved him to the second desk they'd managed to shoehorn into the opposite corner of the office the day before, and then went to the windowsill where the kettle sat.

"That's your desk, and I'm sorry about the lack of space. I'm sure you're used to an office of your own, but out in the sticks they don't run to such luxuries for the likes of us." *There*, Robbie thought, *that makes it sound like it's just normal round here to have a broom cupboard for an office, not that you've been demoted.* He turned and forced a smile. "Tea or coffee?"

Drake sank into the swivel chair and leaned his elbows on the desk, burying his face in his hands. It took him a while to answer before he said "Tea …and strong if that's possible."

"Strong enough to stand the spoon up in!" answered Robbie cheerfully, dumping a tea bag into a second large mug beside his own. The cheerfulness was all on the outside, though, and inside he was desperately wondering what on earth he could do to summon up even the most basic interest in his work out of this man, let alone the enthusiasm he himself felt. The days could turn out to be very long indeed at this rate.

The first two months were every bit as hellish as Robbie had feared. Drake would turn up every morning late and sit morosely at his desk, spending most of the day staring out into space, barely going through the motions of shuffling papers. However, Robbie was nothing if not patient, and he instinctively realised that the worst thing he could do would be to push Drake – or worse, complain to his superiors. Clearly Drake was waiting for him to start preaching the gospel about filing systems, or try to force confidences out of him, which would have given him an excuse to be confrontational and leave, with the blaming going on Robbie and not himself. Instead, Robbie just got on with his job.

The turning point came when Drake asked him about where he could find cheap housing, instead of the B&B he'd stopped in so far.

"I'd have thought on your pay, you could have your pick of houses round here," Robbie said in surprise.

"Not with the amount of alimony I have to pay!" Drake snapped back bitterly.

Robbie didn't enquire further, but it confirmed something he'd begun to have his suspicions about. Walking through the offices, he'd heard various comments about Drake; and along with the expected variations on 'arrogant bugger', there had been others. One of the clerical staff had muttered something about 'fashion victim' to one of the sergeants, who'd responded to the effect that Drake's fashion sense seemed to have stuck ten or twenty years ago. 'Would've thought he could've afforded some new stuff if he could buy what he's wearing in the first place', another had commented.

All of which had made Robbie look at his new colleague again. Even someone as fashion unconscious as Robbie then saw that there was something not right. Yes, Drake's clothes were beautifully made, but on closer inspection they'd also seen a great deal of wear. And the smart shoes might well have been top of the range – or even handmade – when new, but they'd seen an awful lot of repairs, which Robbie spotted when Drake had parked his feet up on the desk one day, as if trying to emphasise his boredom. All of which made Robbie wonder whether Drake took such good care of his appearance because he couldn't afford to replace things, rather than out of vanity. Yet the man was hardly approachable enough for Robbie to instigate any inquiries, and he'd kept his suspicions to himself.

However, Drake now evidently felt the need to talk to someone at last. "The first ex-wife is up in Yorkshire, knocking off the biggest crook in the building trade up there, but she won't move in with him let alone marry him. Not that *that* could happen until he divorces his wife! Every time I think she'll find someone else and get off my back, she always goes back to him, and I'm still stuck shelling out for her fifteen years later!"

"That's rough," Robbie sympathised. "A long time to still be having to pay for a choice you made when you must've been very young."

"Too bloody young!" growled Drake. "Should never have married her, but you know what it's like when you're barely out of your teens – you think you know everything! We were just a couple of kids and the flame burned out inside of a year. We stuck it out for five years until I moved with the job, and then I left her the house, breathed a sigh of relief, and stupidly thought that would be that."

He paused, then seemed to come to a decision to carry on. "So that's number one. Can't say I have the same excuse for number two, who I suppose some would say I married on the rebound. But then I honestly thought – in my stupid, smitten way – that it would work."

God, he's bitter, thought Robbie. *I bet the police psychologist could have a field day with him, ...wonder if it started with the mother who gave him that awful name? He certainly doesn't seem to like women much.* But Drake was still talking.

"I was already with the Met when we met, so she knew what the job was like. I couldn't believe it when she said she'd expected things to change once we were married. What did she think I was going to do? Go to the brass and say, 'sorry I can't work the big cases 'cos the missus wants me home for tea'? That lasted for two years, until I came home in the early hours one night to find her shagging some Polish sailor she'd picked up in a club, on one of her nights out with the girls."

"Bloody hell! What did you do?" asked Robbie, fearing the worst, given what he'd heard of Drake's temper from the gossip on that, which was also doing the rounds of the building.

Drake grunted, but looked up to meet Robbie's gaze. "Luckily, my mates had just dropped me off after a stakeout, and the driver was still stopped and trying to light-up 'cause his lighter wasn't working. So they saw the Pole coming out through the bedroom window, and me following him, trying to beat the shit out of him. They pulled me off him before I killed him. Then they took him off and shoved him back on his bloody boat. They covered my tracks for me with some cock and bull story about me surprising a burglar when the brass noticed my bloody knuckles. Good job no-one asked further, 'cause it would've been harder to explain how he was thieving stark bollock naked!"

"No, you don't get many of them," agreed Robbie with a chuckle.

"So then we come to the last fiasco, the luscious Lucinda! God knows what I was doing there. Thinking with my bollocks, that's for sure! Jesus, you should have seen her back then! Legs up to her armpits, the biggest blue eyes, and a cleavage so deep you'd need a mountain rescue team to get you out. Why I ever thought she'd fall for a bloke over ten years older seems daft now, but I did. Well for six months I bought into the dream before I found out it was a nightmare, and I'd married the local bike! Seems the DI's pay was all she'd ever seen in me. These days she's running a tattoo parlour in Camden, with a transvestite Jamaican and a Serbian rent boy! Lovely combination, eh? And the best of it is, it's my fucking money that pays for the rent on the sodding shop!"

Drake leaned back in his chair and laced his fingers behind his head.

"So that, my friend, is why I need the cheapest bloody flat that this back end of the universe can offer."

Robbie was stuck for words. What a catalogue of disasters! Maybe Drake had brought a fair amount of it down on himself, but he did seem to have been more than usually unlucky. "What about kids? Got any of those?" he asked, almost dreading what the answer might be.

"The last two didn't hang about long enough for that," was Drakes waspish retort. "And Angie at least had more sense than to get pregnant, 'cause she wanted to be shot of me as much as I did her. Thank God! They've taken me to the cleaners enough as it is! I'd be in a bloody dog kennel if I'd had to shell out for kids as well!"

Then he suddenly looked at Robbie and the wedding ring on his left hand, and went on the attack in what Robbie guessed was a cockeyed method of self-defence. "What about you?" he demanded. "Missus? Kiddies? Cosy semi with the Volvo on the drive and the Labrador in the back?"

"Dead," Robbie said flatly, and saw Drake sit up in genuine surprise looking stunned.

"Bloody hell, mate! Sorry," he said, clearly not so selfish as to not recognise that he'd gone a step too far, and was genuinely contrite, which prompted Robbie to feel like he should explain.

"It was a long time ago," he said wearily. "I was working in South Wales, and we were up to our ears with a missing kid's case, everyone on overtime – much like that current case the Oxford lads have got on the go at the moment. We'd had a long hot spell, and then that night the weather broke and we had one of those good Welsh torrential downpours. Our house was on a bend on a real nasty one-in-four hill.

"It wasn't anyone's fault. There'd been a petrol spillage earlier that no-one had noticed, and with the heavy rain it turned the road into a skating rink. The driver of the milk tanker didn't stand a chance once it started to slide. There was nothing for his tyres to grip on, and he went straight down the hill and into our front room. He was killed as well. The tanker didn't stop until it embedded itself into the wall between us and next door. Jean and the kids died instantly."

"Christ Almighty!" Drake gasped, truly appalled, and for the first time Robbie saw behind the mask of indifference Drake had worn until then. "God, I'm so sorry. ...How many kids?"

"Two, a boy and a girl. Claire and Peter." Robbie rummaged in his desk and produced a faded and battered framed photo of a typical happy family group on the beach, which he held up for Drake to see. "They wouldn't have known a thing. That's the only consolation. We'd only been in the house two months, and we'd just bought a pair of new sofas because we could get one of them into the bay window. Claire and Peter were sitting on it watching telly, and Jean must've been handing them their Horlicks before bedtime. The full force of the initial impact took them all out instantly, the coroner said. The curtains were closed so Jean didn't see it coming, even though she was facing it, and anyway we were getting used to the constant headlights in the window.

"Witnesses said the driver was practically standing up trying to get the brakes to work, but then we'd heard nothing but brakes on that hill all the time. Do you know the sad thing? If we'd stayed in the rented miner's terrace up on the top of the hill, they'd still be alive, but Jean was desperate to buy that house. It was everything she'd ever wanted, and she'd never asked me for anything for herself. How could I refuse?"

The contrast between Robbie's marriage and his own bitter experiences clearly affected Drake, because his tone lacked its usual bite when he asked,

"Is that why you're here?"

"In the West Mercian force? Yes. ...I couldn't face

living in the Valleys after that. This was ideal because my parents were still alive then and getting on, and had retired to the Gower, so I was far enough away from my old home to not be reminded every time I turned a corner, but close enough to be able to visit them regularly."

"And you never thought to try again? You know, marry."

Robbie gave a little shrug. "Not really. I suppose it would've been different if I'd ever met someone I really liked, but I don't go to the sort of places I'd need to go to meet women – or at least the kind of woman I'd want to meet. I'd been with Jean since we were sixteen, and for the first few years after they all died, I was too shell-shocked to even think about it. Then after that, there didn't seem much point."

"So what do you do in this hive of culture of an evening?" Drake teased, with some of his normal cynicism returning, but obviously trying to be more approachable than he'd been so far.

"Don't you knock these county towns," Robbie said with mock severity, trying to lighten the mood further. "Quite the hot beds of vice on a Saturday night, they can be! As for me, well I got interested in history. Joined a few history societies at first, but found that most of them were filled with people who wanted to know what great-uncle Albert did in the war. The stuff I was interested in was much further back. Medieval and things."

"Bloody hell, don't you go cross-eyed with all that reading?" Drake snorted in disbelief. "Couldn't you find something a bit more exciting to do with your weekends than burying yourself in more dusty old books?"

Robbie tutted and rolled his eyes in mock desperation. "DI Drake, you may have come up from the Smoke, but you must be the most culturally ignorant bloke I've ever met! History isn't all about sitting in the reading room of the British Library, reading ancient tomes by dry old Victorian writers, you know! If you must know, when the weather is half way decent I often get the boots on and go walking. There are lots of old castles and forts around here to go and look at. And yes, I do do a lot of reading, but some of it's done sitting outside a nice little pub on a summer's evening after a good steak and chips!"

A quiver of a smile lurked around Drake's mouth, and Robbie realised that he'd finally broken the ice with his newest colleague.

"I've even done a couple of archaeological digs, you know," he told Drake, pretending to puff himself up a little with mock superiority to keep the humour going. "It's surprising how much you learn on one of those. A lot of the time it's not so very different from some of the scene of crime stuff, but most of the archaeologists will answer your questions, unlike our lot!"

"God help me, I'm incarcerated in an office with a budding Tony Robinson!" Drake groaned, but with a new twinkle in his eye. "Put the kettle on quick before you start getting your trowel out!"

After that conversation, things improved dramatically between the two of them, and it was only a couple of days later that Drake first expressed interest in a case which Robbie had dredged up from the archives. At first it was slow going, but soon Drake began to grasp what Robbie was trying to do and joined in, if only because he was bored beyond belief without anything else to do. He also seemed to regain some interest in life, because the dreadful pallor with which he'd arrived in the depths of winter slowly changed into a healthier colour with the coming spring, and he put on some much-needed weight. He even joined Robbie on a couple walks on the nicer weekends, and despite being a fish out of water in the open Worcestershire countryside, seemed to enjoy himself in an odd sort of way.

Inevitably, one day the conversation turned to cases which had lingered in their own memories. For the first time, Robbie saw Drake helpless with laughter as he regaled him with the tale of how the accomplice in a string of rural murders had turned out to be a farmer's prize pig, which had eaten the evidence. The detectives had called the local vet out to destroy the enormous sow, but then no-one had been able to face the idea of eating it, knowing that it had previously consumed the farmer's two wives, a man from the village, and another woman. The offer of free sausages from the grateful community had never looked so unappetising! In turn Drake dug up a few hilarious moments of his own, but in the process, Robbie learned that the one case which haunted Drake was a missing girl from back in his Yorkshire days.

Consequently, on that fateful day when he answered the phone, he knew straight away that trouble was afoot. On the other end of the phone a strong northern accent asked,

"Is Ric Drake working with you?"

"Yes, ...yes he is," Robbie answered. "Why? Do you need him for something?"

"I think you'd better stick around," the voice told him. "We've just heard that Helen Fisher's body has been found. I thought I should let Ric know, but we heard he'd had a heart attack and left the Met, and it's taken us a day or two to track him down. Has he heard yet?"

"No, ...no he hasn't," Robbie replied, feeling his own heart sinking into his boots. He'd begun to get quite attached to his surly companion, for all his brusque mannerisms, and he had a nasty feeling about what this was going to do to Drake. However, the man himself was now looking up at him with curiosity, and Robbie held the phone out to him.

"It's for you."

Drake got up and strode to Robbie's desk, but Robbie held the phone back. "Sit down," he told Drake gesturing to his own chair.

"What?"

"Sit down. It isn't pleasant news."

Drake dropped into Robbie's chair with a perplexed frown and took the receiver off him. Robbie himself went to the kettle and switched it on, but kept his gaze on Drake's face. There was a brief pause then Drake greeted the officer on the other end of the phone,

"Michael, you old sod! How are you?"

A slightly longer pause followed as the unseen officer must have been relaying the reason for his call, inciting Drake's response of, "...What? ...Really? ...Oh God! ..."

There was a long pause while Drake listened further to the caller, during which he slumped further down in Robbie's chair. Even Drake couldn't disguise his distress at the news, and his face disappeared behind his spare hand for a moment. But even as Robbie hurriedly placed a steaming mug of strong, sweet tea in front of him, Drake sat bolt upright.

"Where? ...Are you sure?" He gestured to Robbie for a pen and paper, and then began to scribble rapidly in his appalling handwriting. "Thank you, Michael. Thank you, I owe you one. ...No, don't mention it, mate. Bye."

He dropped the receiver back down with a clatter and looked up at Robbie, his eyes shining.

"Are you OK?" Robbie asked, wondering if Drake's heart was going to take this excitement. His own First Aid skills were distinctly rusty, and he mentally sifted through the rota for the more competent men he knew were in the building, and who were likely to answer calls for help.

"I'm fine. Never better!" Drake declared to Robbie's relief, then seemed to subside a little, "...I think. ...They've found her Robbie, they've found Helen."

"I know. Your mate said to hang around because that's what he had to tell you."

"Ah. But did he tell you where?"

"No."

"She's here! Or at least not here, as in Worcester, but not far away. Just over the county border near a place called Much Marcle."

"Good God!" Now it was Robbie's turn to be astonished. "How on earth did she end up here? I thought you said she went missing in Rotherham?"

"She did." Drake sat back and took a swig of tea, and for once Robbie just dumped his files on the floor to perch on the edge of the desk beside him. "The alarm was raised when she didn't come home from school one day. Nice kid from wealthy parents and only twelve. Not the type or the age to go running off with a boyfriend, and with the money the family had there was always the danger that some scumbag had seen the chance for a ransom."

"But there wasn't...?"

"Nah... Not a whiff of kidnapping, and the parents were in bits. They'd lost their oldest daughter a couple of years earlier, you see. She'd been at some posh school over this way and just disappeared. Helen had been at a different boarding school, but as soon as that happened her parents had hauled her straight back home and sent her to the local version – still not your average comprehensive school, though! They weren't too impressed with the police as it was, since the plods over here hadn't found a thing out about where the oldest one went.

"The Chief told them things would be different this time, with the cream of the West Yorkshire force on the case – read me the bloody riot act over it too. Find her, he said. No excuses, turn every rock, wring out every informant, do what you have to, just find her. Except we couldn't. I couldn't!

"God, Robbie, I've never known another case like it," he said, reliving the memoires. "We turned the district inside out. No-one saw anything, nobody heard anything, and we found nothing. No sign of a struggle. No reports of a lone girl walking away from the area. Not so much as a perv' in the vicinity. You wouldn't think that in a town the size of Rotherham, with so many people around, that a little girl could just disappear, but she did. It's not the biggest place in England. I could've understood it more if it'd been in Sheffield, or Leeds, where she'd have just been one more kid on the street, but it was like she'd just vanished off the face of the earth.

"In the end we got one tiny clue. A girl a bit like her was seen catching a local bus into the centre, and going into the main bus station. We questioned every driver, but nobody saw her boarding a bus out of there. Time-wise the best – or rather the worst – probability was the express bus to Manchester. And of course, once ...if ...she got there it was open season as to what might've happened to her. Prostitution, drugs, and God knows how many routes out to other big cities and out of the way places. We thought of them all.

"At the time I did wonder if she'd gone to try and find her missing sister. The two of them were supposed to be very close. But the drivers saw nobody getting onto a bus of any kind, let alone out this way. I even came down to Hereford to get the locals moving down here."

"Why Hereford?" Robbie asked.

"Because that posh school her sister, Suzanna, disappeared from was over here, that's why. A school in a big old house out in the sticks near Much Marcle!"

"Where they've just found Helen?" guessed Robbie, aghast.

"Bingo! Well done, Doctor Watson!" Drake declared, chinking his mug against Robbie's in a mock toast.

"But how on earth did she get down here?" Robbie struggled to make the connection. "You said you checked all the buses, so I'm assuming you checked the trains too."

"That we did," Drake pronounced with great firmness. "Checked, double-checked and triple-checked! The only thing which always worried me, and kept me coming back to the coaches, was the baggage holds. In the bus station she could well have crept inside one of those big spaces under the seats.

"When the drivers pull into a stop, they have to open the hold from inside the bus, you see. The hold door would've lifted up before the driver got outside, plenty of time for a nimble little girl to scramble out and be gone before she was seen. The Chief was obsessed with her being seized near to home, but I've never shaken off the feeling that she left intentionally, and that it was only when she was far away that something happened which she didn't expect."

"Of course," Robbie mused, "yes plenty of time for that. If she went of her own volition there'd be no struggle or anything for anyone to witness, and if she got off at a stop rather than a major bus station she could've been out of sight in no time. She must've got lucky and spotted someone going to a place she knew ...saw a luggage label or something, so she knew the bus would be stopping and the hold opening. ...But of course, for you there'd be no trail if she didn't even speak to anyone."

"No, that's what I suspected. What's been bugging me for years, Robbie, is why we never heard of her after that. You'd think that someone would've spotted a kiddie wandering around in the open on her own. I've had nightmares where she meets some dirty old man who drags her off into the bushes, and then does away with her. But then where was the body? For years I kept an eye out for every child's body that turned up, wondering if it was her, but it never was."

"So how did she get found this time?"

"Carrie Lewis," was Drake's blunt reply.

Carrie Lewis had had the police turning every blade of grass in the area since she'd gone missing from her home in Oxford a week ago.

"Carrie Lewis? Here?" Robbie couldn't imagine how that had happened either.

"Apparently some dog handler who normally works Dover docks, checking for illegal immigrants, was up here on holiday and went out for a run," Drake elaborated bleakly. "His dog buggered off into the bushes and wouldn't come out, so he went in to investigate and found Carrie's body. They're breaking the news on TV tonight. Apparently they're arresting her stepfather any time now. He'd supposedly gone to collect her grandparents from the airport, but not so surprisingly never turned up there, which is why it's been kept under wraps. They didn't want him alerted that they were on his trail.

"Anyway, the forensics have been all over the site like a rash. They stripped the bushes down branch by branch and then the dog goes loopy again and starts digging at the ground, so they dug down and that's when they found Helen."

"Bloody hell!" It wasn't often that Robbie swore but this seemed the only response. "What were the chances of that happening? I suppose there's no connection between Carrie's stepfather and Helen?"

"None at all, apparently. Just sheer coincidence that poor little Carrie should be dumped only feet from where Helen had been buried all those years ago."

"I'll say!" Robbie said with feeling. "A fair few coincidences, in fact! At least the Oxford lads have got their man, though. Not that that's much consolation for her family." Then a thought occurred to him. "How did they know it's Helen? It's a bit quick for pathology results, surely? And what about Helen's family?"

"There was a bag with a couple of books with her faded name in, and one of those school name-labels in her coat apparently, although it's barely legible. So the locals rang Rotherham to double-check, and someone went and dug the file out. From that, the description of a St Christopher and a watch were matched too. As for her family," Drake shrugged, "I think I'm the only one left who cares. Both lots of grandparents are dead now, and the mother took an overdose a couple of years afterwards. Poor woman couldn't cope with losing both children. I think the old man remarried and went to live in Marbella, or somewhere like that. There was an aunt, but God knows where she is these days."

Robbie looked at the expression on Drake's face and came to a decision. Drake needed to be able to put this behind him after all these years.

"Come on, get your coat," he told Drake.

"What?"

"Get your coat! ...Don't you want to go out there and find out how it all ended? I know my old Honda's not the kind of hot motor you're probably used to tear-arsing around London in, but I think it'll make Much Marcle without falling apart!"

For a second Drake sat in stunned surprise, then leapt up and dived for his coat.

"Time we got out a bit more, anyway," Robbie said with a twinkle in his eye as he pulled his battered waxed jacket on, in stark contrast to Drake's tailored black overcoat. "Where did you say this place was?"

Drake snatched the scribbled piece of paper off Robbie's desk as he followed him out.

"Some old manor house near Marcle Hill, on the way to..." He had to peer harder at what he'd written, "...Fernhope? Is there such a place?"

"You mean Fownhope? Oh yes," Robbie replied cheerily as they left the building. His car was only around the corner, and getting in he grabbed a road atlas off the back seat and dropped it into Drake's lap. "You'd better have this ready. I'm guessing we'll be on some very minor roads to find this place. What's it called?"

Drake angled the paper to the window and held it at arm's length.

"Would you like my reading glasses?" Robbie asked with tongue-in-cheek innocence over Drake's vanity about wearing glasses in public.

"Bugger off!" Drake muttered back, but without malice, far too pleased after all this time to be getting out and doing something like proper police work to take offence. "According to Michael it's called Weord House. That's right, it was Weord House School that Helen's sister went to."

Robbie twitched the car in his surprise. "Really? Weord?"

"Something wrong with that?" Drake asked, alert to the change in Robbie's tone.

"No, I suppose not," Robbie answered cagily, edging the car out into the traffic on the main road. "It's just that that's another way of spelling wyrd," he spelt it, "and they're both Old English words – that's Anglo-Saxon to you uncultured types – meaning fate, ...chance, ...fortune. It's where we get our word 'weird' from." He chuckled at Drake's astonished expression. "One of those things which has stuck in my head, you see. I came across it ages ago when I was reading something on the Anglo-Saxons and it's stayed with me ever since."

He sighed and shook his head as he turned off to take a short cut and avoid the building traffic queue. "It just seems odd, that's all, someone in effect calling their place Fate House. Or even Weird House, if you see what I mean. Not the kind of name you'd pick if you knew what it meant – and the original owners must surely have known, even if latterly it's kept its name more by chance than anything."

"Well I'll leave such arcane things to you, my old Welsh Wizard," Drake said dryly, "although it's another nasty coincidence given what's gone on there. It's not been such a happy fate for Helen and Carrie, ...and I do hate bloody coincidences!"

Chapter 2

January, The Year of Our Lord 1575

Billy's hand trembled as he rubbed the oil into the wood watched by the sinister Doctor Parker. By his side Sam stood holding the pot for him, and Billy could tell he was every bit as unnerved by the doctor's presence. Neither of them could explain it, for Doctor Parker was all pleasantness in his manner to them, even going so far as to compliment them on the quality of their work. Maybe it was because Billy had let slip the fact that he'd found out about the runes that the doctor was favouring them with his company more and more.

At first his explanations had seemed reasonableness itself. He was an antiquarian, he told them, a man fascinated with history and the past. So much lost over the years which needed to be retrieved before it all disappeared forever. A wealthy friend of his, he informed them with great condescension, went around sketching ancient churches and their sculptures, many of which had already suffered irreparable damage after centuries of weathering. He himself enjoyed searching through the libraries in great houses. Good King Henry had done the nation a favour, he told them proudly, for by dissolving the monasteries, he'd allowed many objects and documents to come into the hands of men with enough learning to do something with them for the common good, instead of mouldering away in the hands of monks. The latter word being said with much disgust and disdain! Why, hadn't he himself quite recently found an ancient herbal in the language of the Anglo-Saxons? Just imagine that! What cures might there be in such a book?

Now, though, Billy and Sam were wondering whether it wasn't something more like curses which the book had contained. At Christmas the doctor had married Lady Margaret, and the poor girl had already started to look pale and distracted. Luckily, with the house still inhabited on a daily basis by craftsmen, she couldn't be expected to move in, and so she was still living over a mile away with her father. What would happen, though, in a week or so's time, when the soft furnishings arrived and she could take up residence, was the source of great concern for most of the tenants on the estate. Lady Margaret was well liked by all, and it was even rumoured that Sir Timothy was regretting ever allowing the union to take place. Not that he could now have the marriage annulled without some good evidence, and the doctor was clearly too cunning for that to be easily found.

"Excellent, gentlemen, excellent," the doctor declared, reminding them only too well of his vigil. "All ready for the feast of Imbolc tomorrow! Perfect!"

Billy wiped the last newel post, and then stepped back with Sam to see the doctor gazing up at his new staircase in raptures. Imbolc? What on earth was that? Both locals looked at one another in worried bemusement, but could do nothing except let the doctor get on with building his strange home.

The house was orientated east-west, with an imposing porch looking east towards the valley and Sir Timothy's land. It was on the rear, west side that two peculiarly kinked wings protruded at either end of the long building – the wings which had been the source of Amos' concern months ago. The staircase where they currently stood, however, was south of the central great hall and separated it from the kitchens, which began with a housekeeper's room beyond the stairs from which the kitchens proper were accessed in the south wing.

Windows in both the external walls on the ground floor, and above it on the first, let plenty of light into the stairwell, illuminating the huge mural which covered all the staircase walls. Another outsider had been brought in to do those. A strange Italian artist who'd spent days working his paints into the final skim of damp plaster as it was applied to each wall. So those paintings weren't on the walls, they were part of them. And what paintings!

A fantastic landscape of wooded groves was populated with every imaginable animal and bird, which alone would've been fine if a little old-fashioned. These days someone with the money to build a new manor-house wouldn't be expected to spend it on an outdated medieval nature scene. What made this one stand apart, however, were the figures. These were no noble medieval ladies picking fruits in the garden, attended by courtly gentlemen playing instruments, or jousting, as would befit even a very late medieval wall-painting.

Instead they seemed to come from a far, far earlier time. The men wore ringed mail byrnies, and helms which had nose guards and cheek protectors, and carried deadly looking spears along with swords broader and shorter than the standard late-medieval court rapiers. Nor had they any of the studied elegance of courtiers under the Lancastrians or Yorkists from the previous century. Rather, they had the air of men who had seen brutal battles with far older enemies.

Not that the ladies were any more appropriate to the scene, either. Instead of elegant gowns decked with embroidery, these women wore dresses of a single hue, and their hair was bound in braids under simple bands, rather than ornate head-dresses. Some of them even carried hunting bows and had hawks at their wrists.

Even the artist had seemed unnerved by what was appearing from under his brush. Often he was heard muttering gloomily as he came in each morning and surveyed what he thought he'd painted the day before, only to apparently find something very different staring back at him. He was clearly glad that time only allowed for him to paint the three walls which followed the first flight, then along the window wall which included the stairs' turn, and the second flight to the first-floor landing. And the day after he finished, he was already gone when the locals got up in the morning, never to be seen by any of them again. That too had caused a good deal of worried speculation.

For his part, Billy had never been so glad that the walls adjoining the stair treads were wood panelled up to a height of four feet, matching the panelling on the ground floor beneath the stairs. That at least was reassuringly normal, for no-one wanted their prize display decorations dirtied by the passage of people brushing against them as they went up and down. But in this instance, Billy had been very glad of the separation from the figures appearing from under the painter's brush, as he'd followed him to remove specks of paint from the wood. It was hard to explain to anyone who hadn't seen the paintings, but Billy felt that if ever he reached out and touched one of the figures, they in turn would reach out of the plaster-work and pull him into their strange world, and he would become just another flat little ornament on a wall and cease to exist in the present. The one person who really understood his qualms was Sam, but there were others who'd done bits and pieces of work who had found it equally unnerving to walk past the walls. Most especially old Moses Jones, the Welsh master glazier, who'd spent many days with Sam making the intricate windows throughout the house.

The house wasn't that big, but on the imposing east front there were two large windows at ground level to either side of the front porch, and five more evenly spaced above along the jetted upper storey. At the back, there were only two much smaller ground-floor and three first-floor windows in the main block, because of the presence of the wings. But then both of the inward angled rooms, which at ground-floor level made the wings, had a small window next to their external doors which exited onto the back courtyard, and windows above them on the upper level. On the upper floors there were large windows on the outward facing walls, for these wings each had only one room.

Beyond them, the strange single storeys returned at an angle on the ground floor layout to complete the odd shape. Both these single level rooms had very meagre windows, for only the servants went there, but their roofs were looked down upon by windows in the end walls of the first-floor rooms which joined them to the main house. The whole thing made a shape which looked something like

at ground floor level, but meant that many of the first-floor rooms at the back looked into one another.

"By Dewi Sant, I've never known such a place!" Moses had muttered darkly as he'd worked.

"Well might you call on Saint David!" Billy had agreed. "We need all the help the saints can give us in this place."

"Well you wouldn't get me spending a night in this place for anything!" Moses said with conviction. "Look at it! It's like the whole bloody place is spying on itself! You couldn't even go out to the privy without someone knowing you were going! No, give me my little cottage any day. Nice and snug in the winter it is. Not enough chimneys in this place! ...Brrrr! I'm freezing and I've got my thickest winter coat on! Your poor Lady Margaret'll be lucky if she lives through a winter in here, and I wouldn't fancy the chances of any babe surviving long in this frozen hole either."

Not being given to frequenting the great houses of the area, and not expecting an employer to light fires for mere workers in an uncompleted house, Sam and Billy hadn't noticed this until Moses pointed it out. But once he had, it was clear that although there were two big chimney stacks at each end of the main house, the central rooms were going to be very cold indeed. It seemed that the doctor had been so preoccupied with getting the proportions right on the outside, and his fancy schemes within, that he'd clearly forgotten some of the practicalities. The great hall didn't have a hearth anywhere.

"He's either going to have to put a chimney in on the inside and up through that nice new roof, or he'll have to put it in on the courtyard side," Moses pronounced with all the authority of his craftsman status. "Can't put it on the front now, because the windows and the main door are in the way!" With the unspoken codicil that he wasn't about to start altering his windows for anyone.

"I bet he won't, though," Sam said darkly. "He was so particular about this shape – it had to be to his exact measurements – he won't want it messed about with."

"Well I bet most of the local gentry won't be visiting often, then," Moses declared prophetically. "They'll come once, freeze their refined behinds off, and never come again! It's that thin noble blood, see? And the silly clothing," he added sagaciously. "No stamina! Can't take the cold like us, see? Hate being cold, do your nobles. A few years ago, a couple of houses I put lots of windows into, like this place, I got called back to recently – to take the glass out of some of the panels and put wood in instead, would you believe! Too cold in the winter, see? All that glass, lovely in the summer, but you've got to have plenty of fires and fire wood, and good chimneys that draw, to keep rooms like that warm once it gets dark and cold."

However, when Billy had tentatively mentioned the absence of fires to the doctor he'd been dismissed with an airy wave of the hand. Clearly the doctor believed he knew better than some grubby yokel, and they never mentioned the subject again.

Now Moses had packed up his tools and gone home, just as Amos and Ezra had done before, and Billy was getting a very bad feeling again. Amos and Ezra had made their excuses and gone the day before All Hallow's Eve, to much leg-pulling by the local men. Yet Billy now wished he'd listened more to what the Cornishmen had been trying to warn him about. He hadn't been involved, of course. Like any good soul he'd gone to church on All Saint's Day, and the night before he had gone straight home from work to his bed. But those whose homes looked up the valley reported that in the depths of All Hallow's Eve night the new house had been lit up with candles, and someone with a lantern had been seen going from room to room.

But even if they hadn't heard that in the evening in the alehouse, Billy and Sam could have told anyone that something had changed the minute they returned, and walked into the courtyard on the morning of November the second. There was an almost tangible lurking presence about the place that hadn't been there before, and both of them had spent days jumping at shadows and looking over their shoulders. Slowly they'd become re-accustomed to the place, but just the mention of another of the doctor's feasts was enough to give them the jitters all over again.

"What's he going to be up to this time?" Sam whispered fearfully to Billy, as they trudged back down to the village that evening. "He's building up to something, as sure as my name's Sam. What's this feast that goes on on the first of February?"

"God only knows, and I'm not sure I want to," Billy answered, even as he lifted his hand to draw Sam's attention, "but I don't like the look of that."

Coming up the hill out of the village was a pair of heavily laden drays pulled by teams of heavy horses, and on one was what could only be a large tester bed.

"Heaven preserve us, he's moving in!" Sam gasped. "In the depths of winter and with no servants hired! Poor Lady Margaret!"

"We have to tell someone," Billy said, making a decision. "The reeve! We'll tell Reeve Baldwin. He's got the authority to be able to go to the big house, and Sir Timothy will listen to him."

Sam stared at him in a moment's doubt but then nodded, and the two of them altered their course and set off across the fields towards the reeve's house. Like most reeves, Simon Baldwin was hardly a popular man amongst the villagers, but at least he was respected and thought to be fair. On this occasion he was just sitting down to eat when the pair of dishevelled workers appeared at his door, but by the state of them he could see that it must be important and invited them in. By the time Billy and Sam had finished telling him of how cold and damp the house still was, and yet the bed was going in, Simon's brow had become a worried frown. Without further ado, he sent them home and donned his coat for the walk up to the manor.

Sir Timothy was somewhat perplexed by the arrival of his reeve at such a late hour, but conceded to his request for a private audience. Simon had no wish to be melodramatic, but it was hardly possible for him to speak with his master in the manor's parlour when the doctor was sitting by the fire as bold as brass. By the time Simon had finished, though, Sir Timothy looked as worried as Simon had ever seen him.

"Are they sure about this?" Sir Timothy asked Simon. "Are these men reliable? I can hardly challenge my son-in-law on the word of common men if there's any chance they're wrong."

Simon sighed. "I'm sorry sir, but yes, I am sure – if only because I don't think either of them are learned or imaginative enough to be able to cook up a story like that about this ritual, or feast, by themselves. And I would certainly take their word about the state of the building. Both are good at what they do, and I trust their assessment. If they say it's still far too damp to move things in, then it probably is. And they came to me not for any reward for themselves, but because they were genuinely worried about Lady Margaret being made to live there."

"Well she certainly won't be living there, I can assure you!" Sir Timothy told him heatedly. "Not yet at least! I no longer have the authority to prevent her ever living with that husband of hers, but I can insist that she wait until fires have been lit in the place for a week or two, and it's been thoroughly aired and warmed through."

Then he realised that he'd said far more than he'd intended to in front of someone who was, after all, not much higher than a paid servant. The problem was that he really wished he'd never agreed to let Margaret marry the man. The doctor had come to visit with a glowing reference from an old friend in London on the pretext of looking at some old papers, and in those first weeks he'd enchanted them all. It was only as Sir Timothy had got to know him better that he'd begun to have his suspicions that things were not all that they'd first seemed. But by then it was already too late. Margaret was besotted with the man, and Timothy could never refuse Margaret what her heart desired.

Only now Timothy could see that even Margaret was beginning to have her doubts. Maybe it was whatever had passed between them now that they shared the same bed. He'd tried to believe that it was only a sensitive girl's reactions to her marital duties, and wished his wife was still alive to ask more delicate questions of her. Yet now it didn't seem so likely that that was all there was to it. Margaret was becoming positively clinging where he was concerned, becoming agitated at the merest mention that he may have to leave to attend to business outside the estate. It was almost as if she was becoming frightened of her husband – and now this! It looked as though Nathaniel Parker was trying to get his wife moved out while Sir Timothy was in Hereford tomorrow, and Timothy growled and kicked the log in the fire basket in anger. No, he would not let this happen.

Marching back into the parlour, he confronted Doctor Parker.

"I understand you already have a bed and furnishings going into the house – you can't possibly mean to move in so soon?"

"But indeed I do," Nathaniel Parker replied smoothly, without batting an eyelid. "I can scarce wait to share our lovely new house with my wife!"

The colour drained from Margaret's face at this, and Timothy realised that she could have known nothing of it, which gave him even greater resolve.

"Good God, man! You surely can't intend to move my daughter in with February barely in, ice on the ground, and when there hasn't been so much as a fire lit in a grate yet!"

"Nonsense, Sir Timothy," Parker countered with false good humour. "The house is excellently built, it will soon warm up."

"Not soon enough!" Timothy growled back. "I absolutely refuse to let you take my daughter up there until the place has been aired for at least a week, and you have servants there to attend to her needs."

The mask of urbane politeness began to slip as Parker saw his plan being undermined. "If you'll forgive me for saying so, Sir Timothy, Margaret is now my wife and as such she will do as I say. You no longer have authority over her! I wish to celebrate the arrival of the new month in my house, with my wife! We've remained here as your guests for far too long, I see now. I should've moved Margaret out to lodgings in the city as soon as we were married, where she would've had to make the adjustment to married life much sooner."

In all of this Margaret herself had gone paler and paler, and now she slid to the floor in a total faint.

"God damn you, Parker! How could you be so insensitive? She's a refined girl of eighteen, not some hardened wench from the gutters!" Timothy spat at the other man, and bellowed for the servants who ran in and immediately began to fuss over Margaret. Parker took one exasperated last look at his wife crumpled on the floor, and stormed out without a word, slamming the door behind him.

During the night Sir Timothy came to a major decision. In a rare act for him, he ventured to the servants' bedrooms and roused them shortly after midnight. With great stealth, they were ordered to pack enough clothes for Margaret for a couple of weeks from amongst those clothes which were away from the bedroom his daughter occupied next to her husband. No matter if they were clean or not, that could be attended to after they were away, but under no circumstances was any noise to be made which might wake Doctor Parker. And since the servants neither liked nor trusted the doctor any more, they were only too willing to do as their master wished.

In the early hours he then had the groom prepare the small carriage which he possessed, and before the winter dawn had fully broken, he and his daughter were on their way. Not to Hereford as he guessed Parker would expect, knowing he should have gone there on business that day, but south to Ross. A message was sent to Hereford instead, apologising for his absence and rearranging his meeting. In the meantime, he was taking Margaret to his sister in Bristol where he knew she would be safe. Once there he intended to enlist his brother-in-law's help to get this marriage annulled, whatever the cost. Indeed, so worried was he, that he sent another message on ahead by a fast rider once they reached Ross, begging for an escort for them, for his brother-in-law was wealthy enough to keep several muscular retainers for just such purposes.

Meanwhile, Parker was in a towering rage. February the first and his wife was gone with her father, thoroughly spoiling his fine plans. Yet no matter how he raged at the servants he was met with sullen silence. Even when he struck them, they said nothing of where his wife might have gone. There was nothing for it, he finally decided, he would have to go ahead with the ritual alone. For there was no way that he could ride out, find them, and still be back at the house before the end of the day. And it must be today! The house was his great experiment, and having begun it at the midsummer solstice, and refined it at Lughnasadh, Samhain and Yule, he had to make the next move today on the feast of Imbolc. Nothing must be allowed to stand in the way. Quite where he would find the sacrifice he believed he needed was now problematic, but if necessary he might have to use one of Sir Timothy's plentiful sheep.

He fair flogged his borrowed horse the couple of miles ride up the hill to his house, and almost broke the key in the lock in his haste to get inside. Once there, though, the atmosphere washed over him and he felt calm returning to him once more. His own few servants had been sent up here last night and had followed his instructions to the letter, as well they should! All had worked for him for some time and knew the perils of crossing their master – unlike Sir Timothy's.

Unfortunately, they were so well trained that they had set off again the very same night, to bring more of the household goods here from where he'd had them stored in a warehouse in Bristol. Goods he'd collected over the years travelling in eastern Europe, a place which in this modern age was so much more accommodating to certain of a man's needs than the prim and proper place England had become. The

Tudors had done many things for the country, but a man like Parker found it stifling. Especially as the royal family's plotting and counter-plotting had agents riding all over the place these days.

Yet at forty-five he recognised that he couldn't go on living the itinerant life forever. He needed a base, a home where he could have all his interesting things unpacked and to hand to experiment with. And he'd had the idea for the house long before he'd found this backwater where he was sure not to be disturbed – not to mention a suitable victim in the form of Margaret.

Already the place was starting to feel familiar, with some of his many oriental rugs scattered across the upstairs floors. It would be even better once the rest of his belongings arrived, although many would be regarded as decadent or improper in their style by his new neighbours. Not that he intended to do much socialising. He reluctantly accepted that he would be subjected to visits by the surrounding gentry once they knew he'd moved in, but he had every intention of making sure that their first visits would be their last. It wouldn't take much, he was sure, to convince them that he wasn't the sort of person whom they would want to have mixing in their polite society.

For now, though, there were more pressing matters at hand. He went into the great hall and carefully unfolded a small book out of its protective oilskin wrapping, placing it on the mullioned window's sill where he had the best light to read by. Unpacking the bag he'd also brought with him, he set about making his preparations. There were diagrams to be made with salt upon the flagstone floor to begin with.

He'd thought about drawing them on, but the problem would then be how to erase them. The last thing he wanted was one of the local peasant girls he would have to hire to do the rough domestic work, finding the thing and inadvertently triggering it. The whole idea was to elevate himself to a higher plane of existence, not open the floodgates for every fool in creation to follow. Salt was much easier to sweep up once he'd done, if more expensive to acquire in the quantities he needed. He'd brought enough with him to avoid the inevitable awkward questions had he bought it locally, then had to buy even more for the regular household use only a week or so later.

He was so engrossed in measuring out the intricate pattern, preparatory to laying it out, that he failed to realise that someone else was in the house until he heard a clattering coming from the north wing. Incensed that someone would break into his beautiful house already, he stormed through the north parlour and flung open the door into the wing's first room only to see Sam in the one beyond wrestling with something.

"What are you doing here?" Parker snarled.

"Come for my mattock," Sam told him sullenly, annoyed at Parker's aggressive manner. "I left it here when I was trimming the elders for the in-fill, and then Billy says leave it in case we got other stuff to trim. But now I remembered it 'cos I need to do some hedging and come back for it. Only some fool's gone and dumped all these bits of crates on top of it! Ain't my fault if I'm making a noise! I'll just get the thing and go. I don't want your stuff, if that's what you'm thinkin'. Sam Turley ain't no thief! No I ain't! I just come for the tools o' my trade, and I'm entitled to them!"

And with that he turned his back on Parker, and began hauling away at the handle which Parker could now see was sticking out from beneath the crates his servants had evidently left there in their hurry to go and get the second load. Parker only hesitated for a moment, then picked up a heavy iron poker which had been left in the grate of the north parlour, ready for the fire which the servants no doubt hoped he would allow them to light. In short strides he'd crossed the wing's first room and entered the second, raising the poker above him as he made his silent dash forwards.

With one mighty blow he hit Sam across the skull, collapsing him forward onto the crates insensible. Parker checked Sam's pulse, and noted with satisfaction that although it was irregular, he was still alive. Working quickly, Parker found some rope and bound Sam tightly, then left him where he was while he finished the work he'd begun in the hall.

As the afternoon light faded Parker was ready and lit the candles which he'd placed about the house, all of them illuminating the different sets of runes which Billy had so innocently carved for him. In a serpentine procession, the runes began at the back door into the hall and went left, all around the dado rail to the front door, then on and around the walls to go up the staircase, finishing at the top newel post. When all the candles were lit, he went back to Sam who was still only semiconscious. Although Sam was only a small man it took all of Parker's strength to hoist him onto his shoulders and carry him into the hall. He couldn't drag him without disturbing the intricate lines and circles which now covered the hall floor, and he needed Sam in the centre of it.

Long after the early winter darkness had fallen, Parker went to the water pump in the yard and drew fresh water with which he carefully cleansed his hands, then came back inside and stepped up to the outermost circle, opposite to Sam's collapsed body. Reading from the book in his left hand, with a blackthorn wand carved with satyrs faces in his right, Parker launched into a long declamation. For over an hour he recited and chanted his way through page after page, desperately trying not to fumble the unfamiliar language and hoping that he was pronouncing it all correctly. As he recited, he moved to different points on the diagram where circles and lines intersected, sometimes touching the points with the wand, but always moving inwards until he stood beside Sam.

Finally, he got to the last page, and placed the wand on the floor, picking up the yew-handled knife at his feet that he'd left on the floor with a flourish. Lifting Sam's lolling head by the hair, he looked into the glazed eyes and brandished the knife before them. Suddenly the dazed Sam seemed to realise that the knife was for him and began to struggle, but Parker was too strong and too fast for him. As the church bell far below struck midnight, with one vicious swipe he plunged the point into Sam's neck and then drew it across his throat.

Except it wasn't as easy as he'd thought! The knife only cut the skin, and Parker had to saw away raggedly to make the deep cut. So much for finesse! Finally letting go of Sam, who was weakly making gargling sounds as he drowned in his own blood, Parker held the bloody knife up in both hands in a victorious salute and made his last declamation of the rite.

Exhilarated, he threw his arms wide and waited. And waited. But nothing happened. Absolutely nothing! With rising panic Parker picked up the book again and skim-read through it, frantically casting about for something he might have missed, but he'd done everything. His panic changed to fury, and he threw the book down on the windowsill and stormed out, his anger only fuelled by the realisation that in his haste that morning, he'd failed to tether the horse and that she'd gone back to her stable long ago, leaving him to walk back to Sir Timothy's for a bed.

He marched off, cursing his servants who had brought the bed but not the linen to go with it. Today had not gone to plan at all! And nothing angered Parker more than things not going to plan. Was it because it was a mere common labourer who had been sacrificed, rather than the noble Margaret, which had caused the rite to fail, or was it something else? Then he had an awful thought. Should the sacrifice have been a virgin? In which case he should have restrained himself with the dainty Margaret for longer, instead of indulging his animal desires.

As he stormed off down the path he failed to look back, which was why he never saw what happened next. In the flickering light of the candles one of the figures on the mural moved and stepped down off their horse onto the landing.

"Has he gone?" a voice from within it asked.

"Yes, my lady," the first replied, and stepped aside to allow a female figure to also step out of the painting beside him. Regal in her bearing, she glided down the stairs towards where Sam lay, his lifeblood running away onto the flags.

"Poor soul," she sighed, stepping into the circle, and reaching down to softly stroke his hair with a hand which seemed to glow with moonlight from within.

Behind her a tall, muscular man with long, dark, braided hair reached the bottom of the stairs and looked about him. The cloak which was flung back over his shoulder was clasped on the left by a large round brooch enamelled with fighting dragons, and his hand rested with light assurance on the hilt of the sword at his hip. Gesturing his attendants to spread out into the other rooms, he walked over to the diagram and peered down at it.

"What did he think he was doing?" he wondered aloud.

"My lord," one of the attendants spoke, gesturing him towards the book on the sill.

In feline, fluid strides the lord stepped to the window and read the pages which lay open. He snorted in disgust and gestured towards the door.

"Get rid of this thing! Take it outside and burn it! And find a broom and get rid of this monstrous thing on the floor!" He shook his head. "What kind of man would attempt to summon a thing from the Otherworld? He's taken charms from our time and perverted them to do the reverse of the protection they were intended for. Thank the Gods that he did his sign in salt and not blood, or we might be wading in our own here tonight!"

Meanwhile his lady still knelt beside Sam, her hand upon his brow. "This poor meagre life was being sacrificed through no fault of his own," she declared sorrowfully, looking up at her husband, "but he's not dead yet! We must act now or not at all."

"You wish to take him with us?" the warrior-lord queried in surprise.

"I do," she replied, "but not just on a whim, my love. Great wickedness has been done here tonight. We may yet have to fight to repair what has been set in motion, if only to save ourselves. In which case I feel we cannot simply stand back and allow this night to stay as it has fallen so far. We must begin to turn events back to a better course right now, or we may not be able to do it later. I sense that this night is a pivotal point – although it is beyond me to tell you exactly how – and we must use it while it lasts, or all we possess may be in vain if we cannot find another fulcrum to use.

"Even with our skills we cannot give this man back his life to walk here on this earth, any more than we once did. But his life does not have to end overwritten by murder in this place. If we remove him to our side, even if it's only for him to die there, I suspect we shall dilute the evil energy of this wicked attempt to summon something. Like us, he must now live beyond the portal."

"Are you sure we can do that?" her lord asked. "We ended up there through the druids' rituals going far astray. No such rite has been performed here, and in effect you would be taking the sacrifice through the portal. Whereas the souls who died sending us across the divide remained here in their correct time ...as far as we know."

The lady sighed and shrugged. "No, I'm not sure. But can you be sure that the evil one who left did not succeed in some measure in opening the veils between the worlds? Why else have we been able to come through on this night, when we've never been able to connect with our old world before? I feel something dire approaching even though it is some way off yet. And would you risk giving a demonic summoning a soul to feed off, to give it strength if one comes in here after we've retreated? Once we're back through the portal we have no idea when we shall next be able to connect with this world again. Much may happen in that time."

"Very well," the lord replied with a wry smile. "As ever, my love, your reasoning is impeccable, and you know I trust your foresight."

He gestured two of the warriors forward, who flung their woollen capes back over their shoulders out of the way, and bent to help lift Sam up. Another took hold of his feet and with great care they carried him up the stairs, like parents carrying a sick child. At the first landing they turned, and with a strange bending of the light stepped once more into the mural, the small scruffy figure of Sam incongruously cradled in the arms of the tall, fierce warriors.

One by one, the rest of the strange figures retreated back behind the portal until only the leader was left. As he finally stepped through, a sudden draught blew through the house as if a massive door had slammed shut in a gale, and as one all the candles in the house went out and all was darkness once more. Yet in the darkness something stirred. Over the spot where Sam's blood still puddled, a hazy shape took form. For a moment something solid seemed to reach out and what might have been a tongue lapped once at the blood. Nothing more, though, and it faded again although not quite completely, and seemed to drift towards the dark space amongst the roof beams like fading smoke. If Sam's blood was not sufficient to the task, nonetheless Parker's summoning had brought something to the house which had not been there before.

Under other circumstances the disappearance of Sam Turley might've been of greater significance, and have kept the locals in gossip for weeks, but for the villagers, greater things were afoot in the following days. For a start the hurried departure of their lord and master with his daughter, hotly pursued by her husband was more scandal than they'd had in years. But then the news came that Sir Timothy had been waylaid on the road, and had only been saved from certain death by the timely arrival of his brother-in-law with his armed men. It was said that it would be some weeks before he would be well enough to return home, but even that was dwarfed by the news that it was his wicked son-in-law who had done the deed. Even now the villain was languishing in Gloucester gaol awaiting the justice's pleasure, and good riddance the tenants all thought.

"We could've had him livin' amongst us! Imagine that!" Thomas said, as the estate families assembled outside the tiny chapel below the hill on the first Sunday afterwards, to discuss the goings on at the great house. "We'd none of us 'ave been safe in our beds!"

"Oh come on, Thomas," his elderly aunt reproved him. "What would the likes of the doctor 'ave to do with simple folk like us? He never even noticed us!"

"Ah! But that's the thing!" Thomas countered her with a knowing wag of his forefinger. "To the likes of men like him, we're so below them they thinks they can do as they like with us. We could've been slaughtered in our beds! Or been kidnapped and dragged off into one of the far fields for one of his strange rituals, only to be found with our insides on the outside!"

"Oooh, our Thomas! Don't be so disgustin'!" the elderly lady shrieked flapping her hands at him. "Tell him, Father, tell him!"

The humble cleric who ministered to this portion of the villagers' spiritual needs looked mournfully at his flock, who were all now waiting for his pronouncement. The parish church was in the distant main village, and that priest disdained to come to this meagre chapel, but for once it would have been good to have the full weight of the Church behind him. He cleared his throat,

"Indeed, ...indeed. A most worrying set of circumstances. We can only thank the Lord that worse did not happen here, and pray for Sir Timothy's rapid recovery."

A chorus of 'Amen's followed, but Billy was

straining to look over heads and behind people, and now spoke up.

"Well you might think Tom's being gruesome, but where's Sam? I haven't seen him in days, have any of you?"

Suddenly alerted to Sam's absence, everyone began to confer, and worringly discovered that no-one had seen him since the first of the month, when he'd told someone of his intention to retrieve the missing mattock. En masse the locals headed down the road to Sam's humble one-roomed cottage at the far end of the road. To their horror they found the fire long cold and food going mouldy in the cupboard, but no sign of Sam.

"We're goin' to have to go up there," Billy said with more courage than he felt about returning to the awful house.

Everyone turned to Simon the Reeve, who reluctantly squared his shoulders and led them off up the hill. In a long file, the occupants of the hamlet walked up the hill in their Sunday best, every one of them trying not to show how unnerved they felt in front of their neighbours. Yet when they got to the front door only to find it wide open, and the chill wind howling through the deserted house, wives unashamedly moved closer to their husbands, and strong men looked around to make sure their friends were nearby for support. Simon rapped his knuckles hard on the front door and called out, but nothing happened. With great trepidation he stepped over the threshold and entered the hall, only for the others to hear him exclaim,

"Oh my Lord! Oh, dear God!"

Hurrying forward, several of the leading men followed him in to find him staring at the pool of dried blood on the flagstones in the centre of the floor. For several minutes the villagers were all too paralysed by the discovery to move, but then Billy remembered Sam and his mattock and hurried through into the north wing. Moments later he was back with tears in his eyes, holding up a small pocket knife alongside the mattock.

"This was Sam's," he said in a weak voice. "He never went anywhere without it. He must've come up here."

"In which case..." Simon couldn't quite bring himself to say what they were all thinking, as everyone looked from the knife in Billy's hand to the blood on the floor. He shuddered. "We'd better search for him, I suppose."

The men split into two groups, with one group of four including Simon going into the north wing, while Billy went with three others into the south one. Within minutes they were back having found nothing, and so, bracing themselves, they ascended the staircase to search up there. Everyone stepped carefully around the strange carpets with their odd patterns on, but apart from them and the tester bed lying on the floor in its constituent parts waiting to be assembled, they found nothing upstairs either. In gloomy silence they filed back down the staircase, Billy trailing in the rear. As he got to the midway landing he looked out of the window, hoping in some vague way that he would see Sam's scruffy figure traipsing up the path with his usual shambolic walk.

Had he not done so he probably would never have looked at the mural as he turned to go down the last flight. But he did, and there in the foliage of one of the burgeoning bushes in the scene was a small face that hadn't been there before. A small Sam-shaped face! Billy involuntarily gasped and stepped back, and as he did so the face smiled and winked at him. With a strangled cry, Billy took to his heels and bolted out of the door to catch up with the villagers who were turning to go.

"You all right, Bill?" Thomas asked, seeing his ashen face, but Billy could only shake his head. However could he explain what he'd seen? Part of him wanted to take Thomas with him and go back into the house to look for the face, but the other part of him never wanted to set foot in the place again.

Chapter 3

The present day

Later, Drake's comment about too many coincidences seemed determined to haunt them. To their surprise their arrival at the investigation site was greeted with relief by the officers already there. Drake was eagerly questioned for the background on Helen's case, and while that was going on Robbie managed a quiet word with the senior officer, whom he knew vaguely from way back, to explain why he'd brought Drake out here. Yet even as they'd talked, another policeman hurried up with unwelcome news.

"You're not going to like this sir, but that dog's going barmy again!"

"Christ Almighty, not another body!" the detective inspector exclaimed in disbelief.

"Looks like it, sir. You'd better come and have a look."

Drake saw Robbie heading off down the hill with the others, and hurried to his side – trailing the two detective constables who had been taking notes of his recollections – as they were led past a tent covering the site where Helen had been exhumed. They were uphill of what had once been the formal gardens lying alongside the house, on the edge of what amounted to a small arboretum of exotic trees planted by some wealthy former owner. In the lee of a magnificent magnolia which was just finishing blooming, they saw the handler with his spaniel straining at its leash, and several white-suited members of the forensic team who'd gathered at the spot. Robbie nodded to one of the white suits, the leading pathologist Dr Carol Whitmore.

"Afternoon Carol,"

"Hello, Robbie! Didn't expect to see you here."

"No, neither did I! But my new partner led the original investigation on Helen Fisher and he needed to see it brought to a close."

Robbie's expression made Carol nod sagely. "Ah, I see! Mmmm... I could imagine that being a case which might creep under your skin. Well you've arrived at a strange moment, that's for sure."

However, their conversation was cut short by Carol being summoned forward to where a shallow trench was already appearing, and Robbie went to join the local DI and Drake over to one side. The dog handler was apologising profusely and his news made Robbie's blood run cold.

"I'm so sorry, sir," the man was saying, "but Betty's rarely wrong. You've got at least two more over here, and I think there are more in amongst the trees."

Poor DI Hobson looked stunned, as well he might. He was hardly equipped in terms of manpower to handle the sort of investigation this was turning into, and Robbie could see he was dreading the kind of circus it could turn into once the press got news of it. Drake was obviously thinking the same thing when he said with poorly disguised eagerness,

"Is there anything we can help you with? I doubt anyone would object to you commandeering us under the circumstances. It's not as though our case load is exactly pressing."

To Drake's chagrin, Hobson immediately looked past him to Robbie and seemed to breathe a sigh of relief.

"The Welsh Wizard! Yes... Yes there is something you can do! Get me everything you can dig up on this bloody house. Who owned it. Who lived in it. The names of anyone who's worked in it or on it lately. The lot! You're the expert on digging up the past, so dig for me. There's no point in me sending the lads out on a door to door for Helen Fisher – you covered that long ago, Drake – and until these new poor souls are uncovered there's nothing we can work on there either. So find out for me if this house has any secrets to give up."

"The house. Yes sir," Robbie said with genuine enthusiasm, even though Drake visibly cringed at the thought. "Come on, Sherlock! You're going to get your education expanded!"

Drake trailed reluctantly after him as Robbie set off across the neglected lawn towards the front of the house. On the gravel driveway, as Robbie gazed up at the frontage, Drake grumpily scuffed grass and mud off his leather shoes, which were already showing signs of not coping with the damp conditions despite the copious layers of polish Drake lavished on them to preserve them.

"Better bring those new walking boots with you tomorrow," was Robbie's chirpy aside, noticing Drake staring glumly at his feet, earning him something between a grunt and a snarl in response which he chose to ignore. "So, DI Drake, from your extensive knowledge, tell me what you see in front of you."

"It's a house," Drake said with heavy, disinterested sarcasm. "A bloody big house. Probably built by toffs who could've bought and sold my ancestors a hundred times over. So?"

Robbie shook his head in mock desperation and sighed. "That won't get us very far, will it? Now then, if you can get rid of that chip off your shoulder and look more closely, you'll find out a whole lot more. And by the way, the people who built this could've bought and sold my ancestors time and again over the centuries too, so stop looking so disapprovingly at me. ...*So* – as you put it a moment ago – what we have here, my dear Sherlock, is a Georgian frontage. Or if not Georgian then not far before it. When we were stood up by the trees, had you been observant, you would've noticed that there's a lot more of the building round the back, and that looks a lot different.

"You won't have seen much like this in your big cities, but out in the country it was much more common to tart a building up rather than tear it down and start from scratch. This big double-fronted effort was put up in front of an older building, and probably somewhere between 1700 and the early 1800s, because that's when this Georgian style was going around. What it wouldn't have had, though, are those two dirty great rusty, iron fire-escapes which are stuck on each end. They must be to do with the school you said was on this site."

At the mention of the school, Drake perked up and followed Robbie around as he began to explore the place. Clearly the police had already gained access to the building because the outer doors were all unlocked, and there was evidence from collections of crumbs on the entrance hall floor, in amongst the dust, that several officers had come inside to eat their sandwiches out of the biting wind which funnelled up the valley. Inside the front door, the elegant hall had a marble floor and an imposing staircase winding up past the first floor to the second. On either side of the hall were doors leading into the adjoining rooms, and beyond those, in line, were second rooms. By the look of it the nearest left-hand room had been the reception area, and the room beyond it the head teacher's office. At the back of the head's office they found a small door which was locked, but had the key left in it on their side.

Drake turned the key and had to lean his shoulder to the door but it suddenly moved, catapulting him through into the room beyond, and suddenly they were in a different world. Instead of the tall, airy Georgian rooms filled with delicate plaster-work and large windows, they stood in a low-ceilinged room of heavy dark beams. A huge chimney stood to their left and the only light came in through a small window to their right, which was so close to the Georgian extension as to be nearly useless. It was only a door standing open, opposite to the one they'd entered by, which gave them enough light to see by.

"Wow!" Robbie gasped in delight. "Look at this! Late medieval or early Tudor, I'd say."

"Bloody gloomy hole," muttered Drake disapprovingly, but Robbie was already exploring the room opposite.

"Aah…!" his voice came from beyond the door. "These are the kitchens that's why! And probably always were. This is the servants' area, that's why the builder wouldn't have bothered so much with windows." Then couldn't resist pulling Drake's leg as he reappeared. "You should feel at home here, this is where our ancestors would've been."

"Bugger off, little Welsh peasant!" Drake snorted, but with something of a return of his sense of humour, for which Robbie was glad. The appearance of more bodies seemed to have threatened to tip Drake back into his old gloomy ways, hankering for action, and Robbie wanted to jolt him out of it before he got too depressed again. But then a few minutes later he got a shock of his own as he explored on and found a door to the right and opened it.

"Good God!" Drake heard him exclaim and hurried through to where Robbie now stood, staring at the room's window which illuminated a beautifully carved wooden staircase.

"What is it?" Drake demanded seeing Robbie standing in open-mouthed amazement.

Robbie gave a nervous little laugh. "All joking aside, my cousin did the whole family tree thing a few years ago."

"Christ, is your whole family obsessed with the past?" demanded Drake.

"No, listen!" Robbie said impatiently. "I'm not joking! See this mark here in the stone? Well craftsmen often made their mark on important work. It was like a signature. A record of who'd done what. I wouldn't know most of them from Adam, but this one here is the one – and the only one – I do know because he's an ancestor of mine."

"You are bloody joking!" Drake exclaimed, stepping forward to peer at it more closely.

"No I'm not," Robbie said emphatically. "I couldn't forget him because our Sîan was so proud of getting back that far, she went round the whole family telling us all about him. His name was Moses Jones and he was firstly a master mason in Abergavenny and then, when these big mullioned windows took off, a master glazier. He must've travelled all around the place, although I would never have guessed he'd have come as far afield as this."

"Well, well," Drake muttered, "seems like I'm not the only one of us to be haunted by the past in this case."

Looking out of the window he could see that the

successive building works had created a gloomy triangular courtyard in the central space. From the back, the Georgian extension was much more roughly finished, but to his left making the other bar of the triangle, was the back of a pleasant homely-looking house.

"What do you reckon went on here, then?" Drake asked Robbie.

"Somewhere along the line they decided that this original house wasn't good enough, or too small, I'd guess," Robbie said thoughtfully. "Nothing odd about that, it happens all over the place. I'm no expert, but I'd say that north wing up there dates from somewhere around the Civil War."

"What? Roundheads and cavaliers, and all that stuff?"

"That's the one. Makes sense because that would put it somewhere like the 1650s or 60s, nicely after this bit was built but also well before the Georgian bit. It makes the current house a bit of an eccentric design once you get the Georgian wing added, but the principle is nothing out of the ordinary."

"This is a gloomy old hole, though, isn't it?" Drake said, turning back to the staircase behind them and screwing his eyes up to peer at the details in the half light.

"It wouldn't originally have been like this." Robbie reminded him, still staring out of the window at the layout. "When it was built don't forget that these windows would've looked straight down the valley. They'd have filled the rooms with light. It's a mark of how unfashionable this old part was thought later on that they blocked off the light with the Georgian wing, and relegated it to being the servants' quarters."

"Jesus! Look at those paintings on the wall!"

Robbie turned to follow Drake's gaze and saw a series of paintings going up the stair walls.

"My God!" Robbie breathed softly, "they're amazing!" He turned to Drake. "I know this doesn't mean much to you, but believe me, paintings of this kind of age almost never survive. They get whitewashed over or scraped off, and all that gets left to show that they were ever there would be some bits of paint pigment in the more inaccessible bits of plaster. It's one of the things the National Trust and people are always struggling to preserve tiny bits of. To have a whole scheme like this in some provincial manor like this is ...well, it's unheard of!"

Drake took a few steps up the stairs. "Bloody creepy thing to have on the walls, though. Look at all those little faces in the bushes! They're sort of only half there. You'd have thought this thing would've given the kiddies nightmares and someone would've covered it up."

"Maybe the kids didn't come into this part of the house, or they tried to cover it and the whitewash came off," Robbie speculated, spotting what looked like flakes of elderly whitewash on the wooden floor. "But you're right, the faces are unusual. They're not quite green-men..."

"...Green men! What the hell are you talking about now? Medieval Martians?"

Robbie tutted. "Don't be facetious! Green-men are those carvings you see on all sorts of old buildings. Usually, they're a man's face all wound about with foliage. Sometimes they even have leaves sprouting out of the mouth. They're all about re-growth and the power of nature. I rather like them, actually! I've got several books on them at home, and depending on the carver they can be quite cheerful and characterful." He pointed one face out to Drake. "The difference here is that these faces are looking through the greenery, almost like they're using the leaves for camouflage, but the plants aren't part of them like they are with a green-man."

"I'll take your word for it," Drake conceded with a shiver. "Anyway, however interesting they might be artistically, may I remind you, dear Watson, that we have an investigation going on. Let's see what else this place has to offer," and he stomped off leaving Robbie to follow.

They migrated into the Tudor great hall, with its huge fireplace in the east wall, and on into its north wing – Robbie pointing out that the fireplace had to be a newer addition, even as a frustrated Drake hauled him onwards. From the north end they gained access into the seventeenth century wing, and it was immediately clear that this must have been where most of the schoolchildren had lived. The two upper floors had every appearance of having been made into dormitories. Yet nothing gave them any clues as to what had happened to either Helen or her sister.

"We're not going to find anything here," Drake said with finality, expecting to have to drag Robbie out bodily.

But his colleague agreed without argument.

"No, nothing here at all. The best place for us to start will be the local record office, come on!"

The following day Robbie introduced Drake to the inner workings of the county record office, and they spent several days trawling the old records there and in the parish churches. Coincidentally, this work brought them another step closer, because working away from the office meant that Robbie wouldn't hear of not taking Drake back home at the end of a long day –

especially when they'd been out in time to make the long commute to get to Hereford record office for when it opened, and hadn't left until they were thrown out. On the first day Drake managed to thank Robbie and make a dash for it on the pretext of not hanging about in the rain.

However, what Robbie might have lacked in ambition he made up for in shrewdness, and in the morning, he was waiting outside when Drake came out, and so saw other occupants come out beforehand. That night Drake thought Robbie had driven off, and had left the door open to his dingy bed-sit as he went to fetch the bin bag to take outside. As he turned back, he found Robbie behind him with an unreadable expression on his face.

"I told you I was broke!" Drake snapped defensively, somewhere between annoyed and horribly embarrassed at being found living in such a place.

"Yes, you did," Robbie answered quietly, keeping his voice very neutral, "and maybe I should've listened a bit harder." He looked about the room, at the clothes in a bag waiting to go to the laundrette, and others hung off the old Victorian picture rail for want of anywhere else to put them. He was appalled that Drake was reduced to living like this. Arrogant bastard though he was, Robbie was certain that he didn't deserve this, and with that he came to a decision. "Come on!" He stepped into the room and picked up the laundry bag.

"What do you mean, 'come on'?" Drake demanded aggressively, totally on the defensive now.

Robbie turned to him and, deliberately keeping his voice quiet and even to avoid confrontation, said, "I meant, come with me." He shook his head. "You can't stay here." He struggled to find a reason which would let Drake keep some fiction of dignity, and returned to the clothes Drake was obviously so proud of and so desperate to keep nice, even if he would never in a million years admit that it was because he couldn't afford to replace them. "All these clothes'll be wrecked in no time with this damp. I've got a big front bedroom that never gets used except when my cousin comes down to stay once a year. You can have that. Even as a bed-sit it's bigger than this! You can pay me for your share of the bills and what you eat. I don't need rent, I bought the house outright a long time ago." And with that he turned on his heels and walked out with the bag, leaving Drake to follow him or run out of underwear and shirts.

It took no time to pack Drake's few belongings into the old Honda and drive across the Severn to Robbie's house – a between-the-wars semi on a quiet residential road on the west side. The front bedroom was sparsely furnished with just a bed and a wardrobe, but once the radiator was turned on it warmed up quickly. Having heard what had happened to Robbie's family it didn't surprise Drake that he wouldn't have wanted the front bedroom with its bay window for his own, and downstairs he clearly used the middle room which looked onto the back garden as the main sitting room. What Drake wasn't prepared for when he came back downstairs was the sight of the entire bay-windowed front room being lined with bookshelves, but at the end of a long and very wearing day Drake was past making comments. For him it was bliss enough to be allowed to take his time under a hot shower in a clean bathroom, and fall into a bed where all the springs were still intact.

It felt strange coming downstairs to greet a work-mate in the morning, but Robbie was so matter of fact about it that Drake decided to put off making any attempt to change things until after this case had been put to bed. By now they were on the third visit to Hereford, and at the end of that day Drake was wondering whether their involvement in the investigation would end quite as quickly as he'd thought. For Robbie had begun to unearth a trail of strange happenings. Under other circumstances they would've been of little interest to an ongoing police case, but while in the record office an archivist had come to find them to take a phone call.

Up at Weord House, Hobson sounded at his wits' end as he told Robbie about yet more new discoveries. Carol Whitmore had apparently examined the body which had been under excavation when they'd left, and pronounced it male and very recent. To the officers' confusion, once they'd got the male body to the lab it had turned out to be Carrie Lewis' missing stepfather. That, as Drake put it, was "a bit of a bugger," since it immediately threw the case into confusion and explained why the Oxford police had been unable to find him to arrest him. However, things got even odder when the lab was able to prove that while it was undoubtedly her stepfather who'd killed Carrie, someone else had done for him with a bow and arrow. Or rather several arrows, since Carol had found no fewer than ten entry wounds, and that there was evidence that the arrows had been ripped out once he'd been dead.

"And as if it wasn't enough that we seem to have some local vigilante on the loose," the harassed Hobson groaned to Robbie, "then we have to go and find another child where that fucking dog was going berserk! Except this one is so old that Carol said we needed a forensic *archaeologist* instead! Certainly over a century old anyway, and possibly even more. And speaking of twos, we still haven't exhausted Betty the bloody spaniel's possible body sites from when you were with us. H.Q. is starting to shit bricks over the expense! And that sodding dog has been back and is still finding more sites for us to uncover.

"I need to know what we're dealing with, Robbie, and urgently! If the family who owned it was some sort of nutty religious sect, illegally burying their kids in the garden, it would help to sort out what the hell is going on here. But more than that, if I can hand the remaining whole lot over to the county archaeologists as plague pits, or something, my governor might just get off my back for a few hours."

Robbie had offered what words of comfort he could, but pointed out that so far, they'd found large gaps in the house's history, and that in the end the news might not be good. He hadn't found any nutty religious sects, but the house was certainly out of the ordinary. When it had first been built the old building was named on the ancient land maps as Peorth Manor, 'peorth' being an enigmatic Old English word as Robbie was able to tell Drake just from memory. The change in the name seemed to have come somewhere between the start of the Civil War (when local records for the whole area got very sparse) and the period after the plague in the mid-1660s, after which they had a map showing it as *W*eorth Manor. Later still it had gone under a further transformation and become Weor*d* House.

That night Drake entered Robbie's personal library for the first time, to stand looking over Robbie's shoulder as he found a book on Anglo-Saxon magic, thumbing through to the page he was looking for.

"Here you are," Robbie said, pointing to a passage. "I knew I'd seen it in here somewhere. ...Peorth. It crops up in this poem, The Rune Poem. No-one knows what the word really means." He let his finger fall to the translation, quoting a piece, "...a source of entertainment and laughter in the beer-hall, ..." then his finger drifted on down to the footnote. "No satisfactory explanation, ...could be a chess piece, or a dice-cup, or a board game, or a musical instrument."

"Oh marvellous," Drake muttered, "how bloody inscrutable!"

Robbie laughed. "The Anglo-Saxons were very fond of their riddles and things."

"And what does that mean for us?"

"Haven't a clue!" Robbie responded cheerfully. "But it does seem a bit odd that the house starts off being called after a rune which went out of use centuries before the place was built."

"And what about what you said about the current name?"

"Yes, that's even odder isn't it," Robbie admitted with a frown. "When you said Weord was the name of the school, I thought it was a very rare case of an old name coming down the centuries unaltered – and believe me that's very rare indeed! But then to find the Peorth reference has totally thrown that theory out."

"So it's not that at all, is it," Drake said as more of a statement than a question, as he went and flopped into the chair behind the desk and stared up at the ceiling in thought.

"No, not at all. ...In fact, I find it downright bizarre that the house starts off with an Old English name, then slides into being called Weorth instead of Peorth and then goes *back* to the Old English Weord..." His voice drifted off and he reached for another book off the shelf and thumbed through it.

"What's that?" Drake asked, sitting up and trying to read the spine by twisting his head round.

"Mmm? ...Oh, this? ...It's a dictionary. Not your normal sort, though. It's by someone called Clark Hall, ...J. R. Clark Hall actually, and it's a dictionary of Old English..."

"...So Anglo-Saxon…?"

"...That's it! ...I've really only dabbled in Old English to be honest, Ric. That's why I've only got this paperback dictionary instead of the massive hardback one which you need a mortgage to buy. I started reading some of the poetry just out of interest after I got curious about the history. ...Well, it was when I started reading *Beowulf* that I saw what the original language was like, because I read an edition which had the Old English on one page and the modern translation on the opposite page." He reached out and pulled a slim grey book off the shelf and held it up for Drake to see. The outline of something which Drake guessed was a helmet was on the cover.

"And is this bloke Michael Swanton any good?" he asked Robbie as he peered at it.

"Must be since he was one of the leading lights at Exeter University according to the publisher's blurb," Robbie announced with an airy wave of his free hand. "But what I was coming to is that because of that I thought I'd seen the word or name 'weorth' before. Well I had... it's here in the dictionary! It's an Old English noun. Instead of the 'th' at the end it has one of those funny letters that looks like a 'd' with a bar through it, ...but apparently that's pronounced the same as 'th'."

"Hmm," Drake murmured coming to read over Robbie's shoulder at the entry which he was pointing at. "Bloody hell, that's a bit queer! 'Price', 'worth', or 'value' would be a bit odd for a house name if you knew what it meant, but I don't like the sound of 'ransom' as being one of the possible meanings, do you? Certainly not after what's been going on up there!"

Robbie sighed and slipped the dictionary back onto the shelf. "No, I don't like it either. But what puzzles me even more is why this Old English keeps on cropping up. Damn it, Ric, it was a language which went out with William the Conqueror!"

"What? You mean 1066 and all that?"

"Yes, I do. ...Well all right, maybe not straight away. I can't imagine everyone suddenly stopped speaking Old English in that year and suddenly started picking up on Norman French. That would be spectacularly weird! But it *was* long gone by the time this house was first built. I mean, even the first phase isn't really in the medieval period. There's no sane reason why someone should call it after some chess-piece or game or ...phfff, ...whatever…!"

He threw his hands up in disgust. "But just like you said about coincidences, I don't like the way that when the name changes it goes to something which just happens to be another Old English word. And then when you get it change a third time, and we're *still* using a completely archaic language ...well I don't think it's just by chance."

Drake wandered to the rain-streaked window, and stood staring out at the lamp-lit street glistening in the wet. He seemed mesmerised by the swishing of traffic going past until he squared his shoulders and asked,

"Is there *any* way that the name could be simple coincidence?"

Robbie rubbed his eyes and delved out an A4 pad from the desk drawer and some felt- tipped pens. He then went and dragged a couple of books off the shelves and went and sat back down again. After a minute flipping through the one he carefully wrote something on the pad.

Ƿēōrð

"What's that?" Drake asked coming to lean over his shoulder.

"That's Weorth written as it would have been done originally. That funny letter at the beginning is called a wynn, and we've got one of those curly 'd's at the end. An eth is what that's called. The wynn's pronounced like a 'w' even though it looks like a 'p' with the round bit stretched to be longer and the tail cut short."

"And does it all have some deep, dark significance?" Drake asked sceptically.

"Oddly enough, given the amount of dark goings on at the place, no. If it had any meaning at all, the wynn meant 'joy', which is about as far away from our events as you could get."

Drake groaned. "Hang on a minute, now you're making my head hurt! ...So this word which was 'Weorth', you might ...if you thought someone's handwriting was really duff! ...misread it and actually think was pronounced 'Peorth'?" Robbie nodded. Then Drake groaned again. "But we've found it was Weorth *after* it was Peorth, ...not before!"

Robbie sighed wearily. "I know. That's just it. ...I can't explain it, Ric. The other way round you might say it was just as you said. Someone misreading the wynn for a 'p', so 'W' becomes 'P', and it became Peorth House instead of Weorth House. But as you've said, it goes *from* being Peorth House and *becomes* Weorth. The only way that could happen would be if someone knew what a wynn was, and deliberately made the change – although God knows why. Some inscrutable idea of a pun? And all that about five hundred years after wynns stopped being used in the English language, if my books are to be believed. So you see what I mean, it defies belief that the change is just some slip."

Drake shook his head. "Too late at night for me to follow this academic stuff, mate. I'm sorry, I'm off to my bed. Explain this to me again in the morning. I might just get it second time around!"

However, in the morning it was still as bemusing. As Robbie drove once more to the record office, Drake sat in the passenger seat with the pad on his lap staring at what Robbie had written. In the end he took another slurp of the hot coffee which he was clutching in a thermos mug and rubbed his forehead with his spare hand.

"Bugger me, Robbie, this is bloody odd. The house goes from being called 'a chess-piece' or 'a game' or something, ...to possibly being called 'a ransom', ...to being called 'weird' or 'fate'! I don't like this, I really don't, and I'm not the superstitious sort!"

Robbie had to smile at that. Anyone further removed from being superstitious than Drake would be hard to imagine, and yet Drake had hit it on the head – the name was too horribly prophetic for anyone's comfort.

At the record office they were greeted with familiarity by the staff, who were becoming resigned to the appearance of these two odd policemen amongst them. Some of the ancient residents of Hereford, who seemed to have spent their lives in amongst the stacks, were less than delighted to have their sanctuary invaded, and even less so when Drake brusquely took over a table which one regarded as his personal space, in order for them to examine some house plans.

"We're jolly lucky this is here," Robbie murmured softly to Drake. "It's only in the modern era that you need planning permission and have to submit plans. They could have done loads of work and never had a scrap of paperwork left here for us to find."

The two of them pored over the faded plan.

"What's the date on this again?" Drake wondered, and Robbie squinted at the rather worn corner of the sheet.

"18… No I can't quite get those last two numbers."

Then he did a double-take and stood back from the table.

"What's up?" Drake looked up from his bent position at the strange expression on Robbie's face. Instead of replying immediately Robbie fished in his jacket inside pocket and brought out a piece of paper. From it he copied a shape onto an A4 notepad he had on the desk. "Does this look familiar?"

"Not really. Why?"

"Because it's the Peorth rune *and* the shape of the floor-plan of the oldest part of the school."

"Good God!"

"Yes, well, ...it is. Look, stand up and look down at the plans from a distance – you can do that even better than me being such a long-shanks! I wouldn't have made the connection without the name, although I did wonder why those back wings were at such an odd angle to the main body of the house. And I want to have another look inside that hall, because there was that old record we looked at yesterday, that said something about a local carpenter being paid to carve letters that no-one could read."

Drake rummaged in the file they had put all their copies into.

"This one?"

"Yes. ...You know, it's making me wonder now... Do you know, I think the person who built the first house might have come across some Old English writing but not really fully understood it."

"What makes you think that?" Drake wondered, as they went down to find the coffee machine, and somewhere they could talk without the black looks from the regulars delving into their families' pasts.

Robbie gathered his thoughts. "Well we all know the New Age lot in this day and age go in for omens and the like, don't we. But centuries ago they really believed in that stuff too. Omens, I mean, not crop-circles and aliens. So I'm wondering whether this builder, whoever he was, thought that he was building some kind of powerful symbol by having the house the shape it is. You know, summoning up guardian spirits and the like."

"I thought we were all Christian by then?" Drake said doubtfully. "I can't imagine that going down a bundle with the local vicar!"

"Oh we were definitely Christian, and by 1574 Protestant as well," Robbie confirmed adamantly. "We're not talking about some sixteenth century hotbed of paganism in the depths of the countryside! But as for the Church, well we're talking about a very small community. They'd probably only have had some priest who was largely paid for by the local big man in the manor way down the hill – hardly the kind of priest with the power to object to someone who had the money to build a place of the size of Peorth."

"So money talked even in the Middle Ages," Drake snorted cynically, "why am I not surprised!"

"People are people," Robbie reminded him. "It takes more than a few hundred years to change human nature."

By the end of the ninth working day, having been interrupted by the weekend, they'd exhausted every lead on the house itself, and drove the short way into the centre of Hereford for a drink. Parking by the leisure centre, Robbie led Drake over the old packhorse bridge towards the main streets. For an awful moment, Robbie thought he was going to have to drag Drake away from the concrete and chrome development called the Left Bank when he heard him say,

"That looks promising!"

But to Robbie's surprise Drake walked past the mercifully closed café bar without so much as a glance, and headed straight for the half-timbered Black Swan across the road.

"I'll get them," Robbie said as they walked in, still expecting to be asked for some dreadful iced lager, and anxious to secure himself a pint of real ale even if Drake wanted to pollute his taste-buds with chemicals. Yet again, though, he was surprised when Drake inspected the hand-pumps and decided to join Robbie with a pint of Hereford Pale Ale.

It was still early in the evening, and so they were able to secure themselves the small table in the window by the open log fire which was warming the area nicely.

"Ah, the joys of a proper pint! God, I don't envy the poor bastards doing the field work," Drake observed as he stretched his long legs out to warm his feet by the fire. The day was cool and dry, but the last two had been soaking wet with a bitterly cold wind, reminding everyone that spring was belatedly only just getting going. Robbie had just been thinking that such weather would hardly have made excavating any easier, when Drake broke his train of thoughts, adding, "I wonder how they've got on?"

"We'll soon find out when we go back up there tomorrow," Robbie replied, after taking an appreciative mouthful of the H.P.A. "I don't know whether it's going to help them much knowing that it was only a school after 1925, but I don't like the sound of what happened to the family beforehand."

As they'd trawled through the records, it had become chillingly apparent that throughout its history Weord House seemed to have lost people. The family who'd sold it to become a school in the 1920s had left after they'd lost three children at one go. Robbie couldn't explain to Drake exactly what was amiss with the report, but it just didn't read right as though the children had died naturally of an illness. Drake's initial scepticism had faded, though, once it became clear that there was no record of the children's deaths or burial anywhere in the area. 'Lost' was beginning to look like an accurate statement, rather than a euphemism for bereavement.

That had made Drake's skin creep as it was, but Robbie wasn't about to stop there. Hobson had asked for the background on the house and Robbie was always thorough. So much so that Drake had grudgingly been forced to admit,

"I wish I'd had a bloke with your commitment to background detail on my team back in the Met. We could've done with some of your determination to tie up every last thread. A few of the slippery bastards I nailed who had posh lawyers might not have got off so easily then."

Which was when Robbie's statement about human nature came back to Drake.

"Who'd have thought it," he said swirling the dregs of his pint and draining the last bit.

"What?" Robbie asked vaguely, having been lulled into comfortable peacefulness by the beer and the flickering fire.

"That there'd be so much villainy in a quiet little place all those years ago. You were right. Human nature doesn't change that much."

Robbie gave a brief laugh. "It never fails to surprise me the way we sanitise history. Personally, I blame Hollywood. All those glamorous epics! But real people get hurt, and real people die, and real people do the most awful things to one another. It doesn't matter whether it happened yesterday or five hundred years ago, the consequences still hurt."

"Well Hobson isn't going to be any too happy when you tell him what we've found." Then Drake paused and thought before asking, "What are you going to tell him? Will you give him the full potential body count?"

"I honestly don't know," Robbie said with a worried frown, as Drake got up and rummaged in his pocket for the money for another round. "The trouble is, we don't know whether all the people who seem to have disappeared have all been buried in the grounds, do we? I mean, some of them might've been doing the killing and just scarpered. Gone on the run. I don't want him looking for bodies that aren't there."

"No, the brass really wouldn't thank us for keeping a forensic team tied up for weeks only to find nothing. Quickest way to get us closed down too!"

That cheered Robbie immensely, in as much as it was the first open indicator he'd had from Drake that he considered himself a part of the project now. On the other hand, it didn't help him decide what to do, and perversely Drake was clearly going to defer to his judgement on this. When Drake returned with the pints, Robbie was thumbing through his notebook, but then seemed to reach a decision.

"I think all we can tell the folks on the spot, is that the whole place seems to have had a lot of unnatural activity over the years, and that they may well find several ancient corpses. But," and Robbie leaned forward and wagged the pen he was holding at Drake, "for the purposes of the investigation, we have a record of two more sisters being taken out of the school in the days before Helen's sister Suzanna disappeared, and that the head was annoyed that the father gave no explanation. And we can tell them that you've been on to your mates in the Met, and that it was a pack of lies that those two went home to London, because they were never seen again or registered in any other school in that area, and the address was false. Whether they went somewhere totally different is, of course, something that we can't tell. But we can say that the school records show that another girl left as well, and that the school tried to keep that very quiet, because she told her parents she wanted to leave because of an 'evil presence' in the dormitory at night."

"Definitely not good having the local kiddie-fiddler getting into the dorm' without being spotted," Drake said sardonically, getting a funny look from a couple walking into the pub past them.

"No, and you were right about the local lads being slow off the mark on Helen's sister's case. That should've been picked up back then. No wonder Helen's mom and dad gave your lot such a hard time. Mind you, if the school was hiding the records, it would've been hard for those lads to find much. We've been lucky that when it closed three years ago, the files all went to the Record Office for want of anywhere else to store them. We'd have been in the dark if they'd been destroyed or lost."

"Oh, Hobson is going to be a happy bunny when we tell him that he might have three from the 1920s, and maybe three more recent kids in the post-war period to find, too!"

"And that those are the only ones we can be certain about!"

"I've never worked a case like this," Drake said hovering between bewilderment and frustrated anger. "That bloody dog tells us we've got them popping up out of the ground like rabbits, but we've got an even longer list building of potential victims if only we could find the bodies! What was it you were blathering on about last night? When the fairies are supposed to have taken a human child?"

"Ah, changelings! But when that happened the fairies left one of their own in the child's place. These poor little mites just disappeared altogether." Robbie sighed. "I suspect the fairies would've been an altogether kinder fate than what we'll find happened to these kids."

Chapter 4

February 17th, The Year of Our Lord 1575

The next news to arrive in the village was not good. The infamous doctor had somehow got out of Gloucester gaol and was on the loose. But even that was overshadowed by the events of the middle of February. On the seventeenth the first indicator that something was amiss was an ominous rumbling like distant thunder. Except it wasn't the weather for thunder.

Out in a field Thomas was trying to mend a section of hedge which had suffered the attentions of an amorous bull trying to get at the cows in the next field. As he worked, he couldn't help but wish that he had Sam with him to help, even if Sam had been a surly and morose companion for much of the time. The only consolation was that he could just see Billy working away on the wood-shingle roof of a barn, repairing winter storm damage. It was hardly the kind of work to tax Billy's finer woodcarving skills, but a man couldn't afford to be picky about what work he did, and big commissions like the new house weren't so common that Billy could afford to be too specialised.

Thomas was just fighting another wand of field maple through the upright stakes he'd put in when he heard a distant yell for help. Looking up he cast about him, then saw Billy hanging on for grim death on the edge of the barn roof, his feet swinging over the long drop to the floor. Dropping his tools Thomas sprinted across the field, vaulted the gate, and raced across the other field making a slithering turn into the farmyard.

The ladder which Billy had been using lay on the floor, well out from the barn, and Thomas was just wondering how it had been flung so far out when the ground shook beneath his feet.

"Aaaagh!" Billy screamed as he slid another foot towards the edge.

"Hang on Bill! I'm a comin'!" Thomas called and, staggering to keep his feet, ran to the ladder and pushed it up beneath Billy.

With frantically scrabbling feet Billy found the ladder, and with Thomas leaning on the base for all he was worth to stop it sliding again on the shifting ground, Billy scurried down. As soon as Billy was down, Thomas let the ladder drop and pulled his friend away from the now wobbling barn.

"Jesus save us! Oh God! What's happening?" a terrified Billy cried.

"By Our Lady!... I don't know," an equally frightened Thomas replied.

Then as they made a drunken-like stagger out of the yard with an arm looped over each other's shoulders, he stopped stock still and, with mouth open in shock, pointed at the hill with a shaking finger. Billy was halted in his tracks and was about to protest when his glance followed Thomas' hand, and he too was suddenly lost for words. The whole of the hillside along the ridge above Much Marcle seemed to be shuddering and starting to move. As they stood in silent horror, they realised that they could hear other cries of alarm echoing along the normally quiet country valley, and then the distant bell of the main church in the village began to ring out in alarm.

"Dear Lord save us!" whispered Thomas in disbelief. "The whole hill's on the move!"

Without really thinking why, the two friends began to run towards the village, only to find the place in chaos when they arrived gasping from the long dash. Some were crying out that Judgement Day had come at last and that the gates of Hell would be opened, many of those hurrying to find solace in the church. Others feared for members of their families working out in the fields or for their livestock. Some even grabbed what they could and simply fled while they thought they still could, to the sanctuary of family in nearby villages. For the rest of the day the villagers milled in confusion and did what they could rounding up terrified livestock. However the sheep and cattle up on the hillside had to be left to fend for themselves, for it was far too dangerous for anyone to risk heading up there to find them. With the coming of night there was still no respite from the spasmodic tremors, and many folk were too scared to think about going to their beds, congregating in the church instead.

The only consolation was that the rumbling, shifting earth seemed confined to the hill and showed no sign of spreading out to encompass the whole of the Wye valley and beyond. For three whole days the ground grumbled and tumbled, finally stopping as unexpectedly as it had begun. For a full day the petrified local population seemed to collectively hold its breath, waiting for the worst to happen and it all to start up again. However, nothing of the sort happened and they slowly began to pick themselves up and started counting the cost. Miraculously no-one had been killed, but Kinnaston chapel which Billy, Thomas and Sam had attended had disappeared under the shifting earth, as had several sheep and cattle. To everyone's astonishment, Marcle Hill seemed to have moved under its own accord the best part of a quarter of a mile, so that it was hardly surprising that murmurings of witchcraft were rife. With everyone now congregating at the main church of St Bartholomew's in Marcle village, the talk around the ancient yew tree was of who was to blame for the misfortune which had befallen them.

It didn't take long for the strange doctor up at the new house on the hill to be seen as the prime culprit, and there was talk of trials and burnings if he showed his face in the village again. Once everyone's courage had returned it was decided that someone should go to see if the house still stood. It had always been a little out of sight even from the main street of Kinnaston, but those who'd since walked part the way up the hill claimed that it seemed intact. Once more Simon the Reeve found himself in charge of investigating things in the face of the continued absence of Sir Timothy, and so bracing himself for what he might find, he led a small contingent of the village men off up the hill again. To everyone's amazement the house seemed to be intact, although many of the windows had shattered and a howling gale now ripped through the rooms.

"T'ain't natural," someone declared from behind Billy as he peered in through an open window. "How come it's even standin' when the chapel was taken? 'Tis evil I tell you! Pure wickedness is this place!"

"Aye! The home of a male witch!"

"He should burn for his wicked ways and all who helped him!"

"Oye! You hang on there!" Billy protested. "You just remember, young Albert, that some of us worked on this place in all innocence. And afore you start throwin' accusations, just remember that I went all the way to Hereford and got the Dean to check on what we was goin' to do! So don't you go sayin' any of us was party to any witchy goin's on!"

"A wise and apt reminder," Simon quickly stepped in. He could see the way this could be going, and had no wish for his master to return only to find his estate and the surrounding ones tearing themselves apart with suspicions and accusations. "I'm reminded of Sir Timothy talking about a murder trial he was present at, where it was pointed out that the blacksmith who made the knife which did the killings could hardly be held responsible for the use it was put to later. Well, I think he would say the same about this. If the doctor put the place to bad use it was done without the knowledge of those who worked on it. And let's not forget that one of our number may have suffered in his innocence just for doing his job."

The memory of the still missing Sam sent shivers through the assembled men, but reminded them that they were all potential victims and that the outsider was the villain. To Simon's relief there was no further talk of blaming anyone in the village, and so the house was shut up as best as was possible under the circumstances, and left for Sir Timothy to decide what was to become of it.

Had they gone inside they would have been even more worried, for the observant amongst them might have noticed that the figures on the mural had changed positions. At the time when Billy had been hanging from the barn roof, those beyond the portal which the mural created had sensed another presence.

"What's that?" asked one of the coteries of senior warriors around the lord of the Elfael, as they all felt the ripple in the fabric of their world.

"Something evil this way comes," their ancient soothsayer proclaimed, limping into their greensward hall on his staff, milk-white blind eyes detecting undercurrents beyond the ken of the rest of them.

"What sort of evil?" their leader queried.

"Something that has been woken from the beyond, my lord Elfan."

The hall was as large as the one built by Amos, Ezra, and Billy, but this one was made of living trees whose branches had been interwoven to form the upper walls and roof. Around the lower trunks graceful woven hangings formed the lower walls, with high-backed, carved wooden settles in front of them to accommodate the many who regularly congregated there. At each end, open rope-strung stairs wound round larger trees to give access to chambers built on decks in the canopy above, and down one of these the lady who had rescued Sam now descended, speaking before she even reached the floor.

"Ah, so now it happens! Did I not warn you that the evil man may have unleashed more than he foresaw?"

"My lady Ferylt," the soothsayer acknowledged her warmly. "Yes, I fear you are correct. The right he performed opened the way for you, but also for something else. Perhaps we should have lingered longer and observed more when the portal first opened, for I fear that something was roused on that night and has attached itself to that location, or at least perceived that there was now a weakness at that point. And now something else has happened. Almost as if the veil between the worlds was a bladder – like a water skin – which since that night has had the evil force of the Otherworld dripping into it like water until, like a bubble, it has been stretched too far and has now burst. I do not begin to understand what is going on, but it feels as though the whole house through there is now some kind of open invitation. Yet I have no idea to what. I fear that it was the letting of human blood which made the difference."

"Is it my fault, then?" a quavering voice asked from one of the corners and the scruffy figure of Sam crept out into the light. He was having a terrible time adjusting to this new world he found himself in. For a start off he didn't feel as though he was quite here, even though he didn't know where else he would be. He had distinct memories of dying and of the strange sensation of being brought through the portal. The only way he could have described it was like being a cork being pulled the wrong way through a bottleneck. Something of the old Sam had definitely been left behind, but on the other hand he was fairly sure he was still alive. He had a permanent feeling of being slightly light-headed and rather disorientated, and so his first assumption on waking had been that he'd been abducted by fairies.

Yet previously when the talk had turned to the fae folk, as with Amos and Ezra, he'd always thought of them as rustic little folk who sometimes caused mischief. Tiny quaint characters who'd largely been driven off by the presence of the Church and its ministers, who could endanger livestock and small babies, but nothing much more substantial. Who lived in fairy circles, delineated by the rings of toadstools which appeared in autumn, and did a lot of dancing and merrymaking. It didn't help that even in his most drunken dreams he'd never imagined tall, dangerous people like these, who were quite adamant that they were definitely not fairies, elves, or any other of the fae beings he could think of.

They told him, once the language they used became a bit more familiar to him, that they had once lived in the same area of the borders as he himself had been brought through from. Sam couldn't be sure, but he had the distinct feeling that it was also something of a shock to them to find out how far the world had moved on from their day. This world seemed to be some kind of dream-time, and at first, they told him, they'd assumed they had come to the Summerland – the place where the dead went to in their traditions. However, they'd been worried to find that none of their ancestors seemed to be here, or any others of their kind, and had been forced to rethink their situation.

Their shift to this world from their native time had occurred after a major battle, which was just the last of many in a long running war against persistent invaders from across the sea. Elfan of Powys and his warriors had returned to their home to carry out the funeral rites for those who had fallen, accompanied by some of the filidh – successors to the ancient native druids and who were determined to resurrect some of the old rituals. Whatever rite they'd performed, it had been accompanied by the slaughter of the prisoners of war, and Sam was told that Elfan had tried to intervene to prevent it fearing reprisals, but it had been too late.

As the last throat had been cut the folk who now lived here had felt the earth move, had been knocked senseless, and they'd awoken on this side of the veil, permanently sundered from their home. Since then, no-one had died except in battle, but time appeared to have a strange quality to it and there had been few births. Nor were any of the new-borns quite as ordinary children should've been. However, none of them had had any idea that nearly a millennium had passed since their leaving, for they'd only glimpsed the real world on rare occasions.

Yet, they had had contact with some disembodied and mysterious beings in this world, who came and went with no warnings, and more recently they'd been drawn into battle to defend this, the only home they now had. As far as Sam could make out, the strange seer Seithmath had been here already when they'd arrived, but had attached himself to them as their guide or teacher, depending on how you looked at it. Unfortunately, Sam really couldn't work out who their enemies were, and he could only guess that it was some kind of demonic summoning.

On the other hand, he was sure that his own priest would think the same of Elfan and his people, and demand that they be exorcised. Not that he could imagine any of them being intimidated in the slightest by the ragged cleric from the chapel with his bell, book, and candle, or even the priest from the main church. Any encounters of that kind, he imagined, would result in the fearsome Elfael warriors staring at the ranting priest with bemusement and then carrying on regardless. Partly because they seemed far too solid to be driven out by the strength of prayer alone, and partly because the more he got to know them the more he found himself believing that they were fundamentally good people, if rather more warlike than anyone he'd ever had contact with before.

Now he found himself being kindly smiled down upon by the lady Ferylt as she said,

"Oh no, you could not be to blame for this. You were the unwitting victim, not the instigator. The man you spoke of used you."

"Doctor Parker?"

"Indeed. But as we feared at the time, he knew too little of what he was summoning. Have you been viewing the house through the portal as we asked? Has he returned."

"No, my lady," Sam was quick to confirm. "I ain't seen hide nor hair of him, or those servants of his who

Billy and me saw bring the cart up the hill." He summoned his courage for he feared he was talking out of turn expressing any sort of opinion. "If you don't mind me sayin', though, my lady, I reckon somethin's changed. Cos I saw my old mate Billy walkin' through the house with Simon the Reeve not long after I came here and you stitched me back together. If the Doctor had been there they wouldn't have got in through the door, let alone be walkin' about so free. I don't reckon he's been there at all since."

"Interesting," Elfan murmured, giving the nervous Sam a nod of acceptance, which felt like more of a reward than anything Sam had ever had in his life before, although he couldn't have said why. "So the Beast of Battle he summoned has manifested without further encouragement or incitement. What do you make of this, Seithmath?"

The old seer looked grave. "I fear it may be worse for being undirected, my lord. Had the one who summoned it been around to claim it, it probably would've had its energies focused on whatever gains the man hoped to make in his world. Ironically its power would then have been diluted, for even one such as this could not predict the actions of humans far removed from its sphere of influence."

"So if he made a lot of money and then wanted to buy a bigger house, even this thing couldn't help him if someone else then came along from far away, and with more money, and bought the place he wanted?" Sam gabbled hurriedly, hoping he wasn't overstepping the mark having just got the fierce lord's approval.

But the seer smiled benignly and spoke before Elfan had even reacted. "Indeed Sam, that's exactly the sort of thing I meant. The creature might well have expended much energy to little effect in such pursuits then. But without this Doctor person around, the creature has developed a will of its own. It's had time to become aware of how powerless many of the folk around it are." Seithmath's smile faded.

"It now has ambitions of its own and I fear, because of the ritual the Doctor used, it now has an awareness of us which it might never have had. Without a body for it to occupy its actions are probably limited at the moment in your world, Sam, but being essentially of the same matter as us it can attack us and make its presence felt. It now exists as a presence in your world if without physical form. Imagine a ghostly creation coming up through a rabbit hole from the Underworld into yours, because once it was drawn to the place it kept digging until the barrier fell through. I fear that this latest disturbance was triggered by its emergence into a world it was never meant to gain access to."

"Could it have sommat to do with the strange shape the house is built in?" Sam wondered emboldened by his success. "Billy said the Dean said it was a rune itself."

The Elfael exchanged hurried glances. "The house is in the shape of a rune?" Elfan double-checked.

Sam nodded, prompting Seithmath to ask, "Which one?"

"I dunno," Sam shrugged. "I got no learnin' in that sort o' thing." He picked up a stick and drew the peorth rune in the fire's ashes. "It were that one, though."

Seithmath peered at the shape in the dust. "An invitation to play ...how ambiguous!"

"Is it?" Elfan demanded. "Is that a good or bad thing?"

"Maybe both," Seithmath mused. "It could be open-ended. Indeed it might be the reason why we have suddenly found the portal from this world we were all cast into. But – and to me this weighs heavily on my mind – if it was done with evil aforethought, does that mean that it calls more strongly to the wicked?"

"And what of the attempt to kill Sam?" wondered Ferylt.

Seithmath nodded. "Indeed! ...In fact, that is an encouraging thought, my lady, for it may mean that only by violence and bloodshed was the whole thing able to be orientated to call only to the dark-hearted and the creatures of the night. As you rightly guessed at the time, my lady, by bringing Sam here we may well have averted or disrupted that action. We may unwittingly have ensured that the doorway was left open to all, rather than allowing it to become a locked door which only the evil presence the Doctor summoned could use.

"And the other good thing, I think, is that the man drew the summoning charm in salt, which would have turned the demonic essence to a different path. Had he made it in another material, or carved the diagram into the stones of the floor, we might already have come under attack or even have been overrun. I truly believe his ignorance has worked for us in that respect. And if, as you say Sam, he had you make the wattles for the house out of elder boughs then that too may have rebounded on him."

Sam's face creased in confusion.

"You think of elder as dangerous because it summons the fae," Seithmath explained, "but its true properties are of regeneration and rebirth. It's a healing tree, Sam, not one that can be turned to evil use ...and that may even be why you have been able to hold on to some shred of life once you passed through to our world. The house itself may be resisting the evil the Doctor tried to impose upon it."

"Then we must fight back," Elfan declared. "If we cannot expel it from Sam's world yet without further knowledge, we can at least deny it ours. How long do we have, Seithmath?"

"Not long," the seer replied. "You must watch the portal, for I feel that that will be the way it will come. At the moment it's as though we sit on one side of Sam's world, and the creature is on the other. It has to come through Sam's world to get to us, even though it's our distant world which it senses more strongly. And who knows what it may bring with it if it fully breaks free of its own realm and starts heading for ours? I fear it will not come alone, because if it gets control of our world then it will completely encompass Sam's. The evil ones will have a free rein amongst men unable to resist that kind of power."

Poor Sam was appalled. All his life he'd grumbled and argued with every one of his neighbours, but all of a sudden, he found that he cared desperately about whether they lived or died.

"Please sir," he asked with a quavering voice, craning his neck to look up at Elfan. "What will happen to my village if you chase this demon, this monster thing, out of the house? Will it die? Or will it just live outside instead? Can you stop it eating my friends, or whatever it does to people?"

Ferylt came and put a comforting arm around Sam's shoulder. "We can make no promises, Sam, and it would be wrong if we did because we don't fully know what it is we will be facing. But remember what Seithmath said, this thing will find it harder to attack your world unless it can find a flesh and blood host. And if it takes a host then we can hopefully kill it. But even if we can't do that, if we can drive this summoning back to where it came from, we can set a watch on your world, or at least as best we can through the only portal we have."

"Thank you, my lady," Sam said humbly, but nonetheless felt what he hoped was still his heart sink into his boots, when he thought of the homely villagers in the path of something which might yet overwhelm such mighty warriors as these.

So as Elfan prepared his warriors for war, Sam was only too willing to share guard duty with a couple of the younger Elfael, while their world periodically shook in synchronicity with the rumblings Billy and Thomas were witnessing. When the moment came, he actually saw nothing. Instead, he felt the tremors start again beneath his boots.

"What's that?" he asked the young lass to his right. "Is it the beast again?" She exchanged a glance with the youth beside her and then took off at a sprint which Sam couldn't hope to match. Even as she ran Sam could hear her calling, and moments later there was another pounding but this time from behind him.

"Quick! Out of the way!" the youth cried and grabbed Sam by the scruff to haul him to one side.

As Sam stumbled away from the edge of the portal, a stream of warriors, fully armed and wearing mail-coats, raced into view through the trees and two at a time leapt to the portal. From his viewpoint Sam saw them take the stairs or simply jump the stair rails to stream into the Elizabethan hall. Elfan was in the lead, and charged with his most senior men straight to the door, flinging it open so hard it slammed into the wall behind it. Beyond the doorway Sam could see nothing for a while because of the constant stream of warriors who followed their lord, but he could hear the most terrifying noises. There was a savage shrieking and howling, and the hammering of metal upon metal.

Behind him he was suddenly aware of a presence and turned to see Ferylt and her handmaidens standing there, all also clad in mail surcoats and carrying longbows. With great calm and dignity, they stepped down past Sam into the hall and went to the door and windows. Disregarding the expense of the window panes, the archers opened the windows they could, or broke the panes and leads out of the others, to give them gaps to fire through. With great precision they began to pick out targets and fire at them. What those targets were Sam couldn't see, but by the screams of pain they were hitting something.

He was about to ask if he could go back through the portal into his home world when he saw that several black presences filled the hall's doorway. As if the portal drew them the dark-robed figures headed Sam's way.

"Mearcstapan!" gasped the lad at his side fearfully, even as Ferylt and her archers turned and began firing at these new enemies who were now behind them.

"What are they?" Sam asked as they ducked down to avoid being shot by stray arrows.

"Those who live on the borders of this world," his companion hissed in his ear as they flattened themselves on the ground. "Maybe once they were as human as us, ...you know, one of the Cymry even if they weren't of our Elfael clan." He shrugged, "Now, ...who can tell? Seithmath says that they were but got seduced by an evil power. He says that some of its power is in them, which is why they can make sallies into your world. They haunt the moors and dark places looking for the unwary to trap and carry back to their master. What they do to them we don't know, but we've found the remains sometimes when we've patrolled our own borders. I was born over here, but those who came here say that the Mearcstapan are worse than ghosts, because ghosts are only the shades of ordinary humans. These are something much stronger and worse."

"Oh!" Sam gulped, rather wishing he'd never asked. These Mearcstapan sounded like the stuff of nightmares, but his guide wasn't finished yet.

"Normally they wouldn't attack us because we're too much of an even match for them in our homeland, and they like to have more of an advantage over their victims. Seithmath says we're now the same as them – unlike your folks – which is why we can fight them and you can't. ...Unfortunately they seem to have found something physically powerful to ally themselves to this time!" the lad called back over his shoulder, even as he drew his dagger and leapt through the portal to drive it into the throat of the only Mearcstapan to have made it to the stairs.

Without thinking, Sam jumped after him and followed him to the bottom of the stairs to where he could see outside. The world seemed to have gone mad. It was like a scene he'd once seen in a great stained-glass church window of suffering souls in hell. And in the centre was a black writhing shape which was lashing out at the Elfael warriors, who made dashes in to stab at it, and then retreat as another of their number distracted its attention in a different direction. To one side Elfan was fighting one to one with a leading warrior from the Mearcstapan, each of them having members of their own bodyguard fighting off any of the opposition who tried to get to the back of the duellists.

The Mearcstapan were altogether bigger than the Elfael and were ghastly to look at, seeming like some dreadful parody of human beings which had been put together piece by piece, but never properly finished off. Or maybe very old beings who hadn't died at their allotted time. They fought with an unrestrained fury with anything which came to hand, and carried on even with appalling wounds. Sam caught a glimpse of one with its arm hacked off, but using the severed limb to beat its opponent Elfael over the head with, while another, which at a guess was female, had one of the Elfael on the ground and seemed to be trying to wrench his head off by twisting it round even as the Elfael's companions hacked lumps of flesh off her with an axe. Nauseated, Sam looked away and searched for Elfan again.

If he'd seemed daunting to Sam before, he was positively terrifying now. Under his helm, the Elfael's lord had his long dark hair tied back in an intricate braid to keep it out of his eyes, which was just as well for he fought with an intense fury of the kind Sam had never seen before. Lightning-fast sword strokes were being rained on his opponent even as he blocked the other's blows with the buckler and dagger he held on his left. For an awful moment Elfan seemed to be losing ground as the Mearcstapan lord pressed home a particularly vicious attack, but then Elfan made a daring leap inside the other's guard and sliced him across the stomach as he danced past the oncoming blade. A mighty backhanded stroke to the Mearcstapan lord's back inflicted more damage, and Sam expected to see the Mearcstapan fall. However, he turned to fight on, although it was clear that he was now the weaker of the two.

Sam had been so engrossed in the duel that he'd failed to notice the rest of the fight until his young companion grabbed him by the arm.

"Look out, Sam!"

As the youth once again almost hoisted him off his feet, Sam realised that they were close to the manor door and that the strange beast was heading their way.

The roiling form revealed itself to be a huge crow-like shape, although what should have been feathers were more reptilian with tiny hooks along them, and seemingly able to attach themselves to those unfortunate enough to get too close to it. However, it appeared to have difficulty distinguishing between Elfan's veterans and those of the Mearcstapan, for even as Sam watched, one of its defenders got driven in too close to it by one of the Elfael and got entangled in a wing. With a soul-harrowing scream, whatever life it possessed was sucked out of the creature, who collapsed onto the ground moments later a withered husk.

Yet the reason Sam had been hauled out of the way was once again because the Lady Ferylt was not content to stand by and leave the desperate fight to her husband. She appeared in the doorway and, with two others of her archers, began to fire into the armoured tentacle-feathers of the crow. Sam could hear her repeating softly to herself as she loosed arrow after arrow.

"You shall not have the house! You shall not have the portal! You shall not have my world or the other's! You shall not pass!"

And suddenly Sam truly grasped that if the crow reached the hall, it would have the means to come fully not only into the world of the Elfael but also into his. The Mearcstapan were redoubling their efforts, but many of the Elfael ignored them and their own safety now to turn their backs on their ancient enemies and assault the crow's flanks even as Ferylt's archers attacked its front. Yet the crow was possessed of some fearsome energy, for no matter how hard it was assailed it still came on until it stood before the carved manor door.

As its wicked sharp beak came up to strike at Ferylt something snapped inside Sam. This lovely lady had saved his life and treated him with more kindness than anyone else had ever done, and now she was going to die to save his world and his friends. Without thinking, Sam grabbed the Elfael youth's long dagger and launched himself at the crow, plunging the blade into the swirling pool of blackness that was its eye as its head struck downwards.

Ferylt's cry of, "No Sam!" was lost in a thunderous explosion which knocked Elfael and Mearcstapan alike insensible. When the Elfael came to, it was to find themselves alone, and all evidence of the Mearcstapan gone. Elfan was hauled to his feet by his veterans and they sprinted to the door where Ferylt still lay unconscious.

"What happened?" Elfan cried in dismay at the sight of his beloved lady lying barely breathing on the still shaking ground. But the archers who'd been inside the hall couldn't tell him, and the two who'd fought right beside her in the cramped space were also still unconscious. His answer came as Seithmath limped his way down the manor steps leaning on the shoulder of another youngster to come and kneel beside Ferylt.

"It was Sam," he told Elfan. "My young guide here saw it. Sam saved her. He saved us all."

"Where is he?" Elfan asked, suddenly missing the strange little man who'd followed his wife with dog-like devotion ever since he'd been brought back with them.

"This time he truly is dead," Seithmath said regretfully. "But Lady Ferylt was right when she said he might yet have great importance. The Beast of Battle, the hooded crow Feannag, being of the same matter as us had great power over you and yours. Now I know who it was, I realise that you could only ever have achieved a stalemate, and that may have been at a terrible cost. When Sam tried to protect Lady Ferylt and made physical contact with Feannag it sensed the Middle world in him, and seized its opportunity to find its master who summoned it."

"Great God! Then we failed to protect Sam's world," Elfan lamented. "Evil is afoot there and they have no idea how to counter it!"

"No! Not necessarily. Take heart my lord! Sam's act was all the more potent because he'd unknowingly used his connection to Lady Ferylt to step into his own world while it was under the thrall of our powers and the portal's. Remember that it was only Lady Ferylt's power that gave Sam life – the gift she possesses only by virtue of having lived beyond the veil for so long where she's absorbed much of its energy. In his world he's already long dead. As the crow joined with him and made the leap fully into this Middle world, it must have assumed that it was getting a body it could inhabit there. Yet once it was there, of course, Sam would have been lifeless – especially as his connection to your lady was severed when she was knocked unconscious by the blast. All Feannag would have got would have been a lifeless corpse whose soul had fled. It can do nothing now until it finds someone new to work with, and even then – because it is again insubstantial – it no longer has the strength it would have had when the Doctor first summoned it. He needed to have bonded with it immediately for it to have massive power in that world. Now much of that power has dissipated. By bringing Sam through the portal Lady Ferylt brought the Feannag's doom with her, and Sam's courage did the rest."

"Then he should have a sending fit for one of our best," one of the veteran warriors said with respect.

Elfan nodded, but was still stroking Ferylt's hair. "Will she recover, Seithmath?"

"I think the sooner we get her back into our own world the better," the seer told him. "Please remember my lord, the last time I had any dealings with this sort of energy was many centuries ago, and no-one I know of has experience of the upper, lower, and middle worlds colliding like this. However, I sense no abiding evil in her, and I hope that her condition has everything to do with being too close to the blast when the fabric between the three worlds was ripped apart for a moment."

"Then let us get litters to carry her and her maidens back," ordered Elfan. "We must all pray that she recovers, and in the meantime prepare a funeral feast fitting for our fallen and for Sam as one of the veterans. It will take several days to complete, so we must hope with all our hearts that she is with us to celebrate the actions of the one who saved her and two worlds with her."

Chapter 5

The present day

When they drove out to the house the next day Robbie and Drake found a lot of very worried policemen. The team had expanded to include the county archaeologists, who were finding it more than a little disconcerting having to use their skills under the supervision of Carol Whitmore, and side by side with those members of her team unearthing far more modern remains. DI Hobson had set up an incident room on the ground floor of the second-phase building, and someone had got a much-needed fire going in its large hall grate, by which everyone warmed themselves as the pair gave him the news.

"The reason you're stuck with delving amongst the trees is because the Victorian owners were trying to cover up the bad rumours," Robbie started off.

Poor Hobson seemed to have aged years in a matter of days, and now fixed Robbie with the gaze of an elderly bloodhound. "Rumours?" he asked wanly, as though he almost didn't dare ask what was coming next.

Feeling some sympathy for the local man's plight Drake cleared his throat and waded in. "According to several entries in the local papers the place has a long history of strange sightings and none of the locals come up here after dark. The family who put the Georgian extension up had nothing but bad luck, and were reduced to poverty by the mid-1800s. They'd tried to sell the place on several occasions but no-one local would buy it. Then some bloke who'd made his money bringing coal up from the Forest of Dean decided he'd like a posh pad for his family. Pretensions of being one of the nobs instead of just some scabby little upstart, no doubt! So he buys it and then finds he can't get anyone local to work up here."

Robbie took over. "That's less of a problem for him because he just brings in servants from his other houses when he needs them. And with good Victorian industrial pragmatism, he decides that he'll simply get rid of the bad luck. If the locals have seen odd goings on up at the back of the house, then he'll just wipe the site out by planting an arboretum over the top of it. He called in an outside landscaper who created the gardens we see now. Apparently, while they were planting the trees, they came across the bodies of three men buried together. The assumption then was that it was a plague pit from the mid-1600s. They told the locals what they'd found, the bodies were removed, and it all seems to have gone quiet for a good sixty years."

He sighed. "Of course, that could be because there was no-one living here regularly over that time. The industrialist went on to bigger and better things, and by the start of the twentieth century this was just the country place the family came to once in a blue moon. The rest of the time they were in London for the season, or hobnobbing it at some country house party trying to climb even higher up the social ladder.

"The next change comes after the First World War. The younger surviving son seems to have been one of those poor souls who suffered severe shell-shock. He needed peace and quiet, and so he brought his family to live down here, instead of living with his remaining older brother in Surrey at what had become the family's new posh pad. Sadly he didn't live that long to enjoy it, and it's after that that things start getting nasty again.

"Apparently, it was quite a local scandal when, with her husband barely cold in his grave, the widow starts having a fling with the local bad lad. Only a year later they marry and he comes to live here with her and the four kids. The merry widow gets pregnant and then the oldest boy dies suddenly. We found the record of that, all right! He's buried in the big church over the hill, but apparently the locals were very suspicious, and someone tried to get the boy exhumed for a proper examination!"

"Good Lord! Wasn't that a bit unusual even back then?" Hobson asked.

"Very! But the cause of death had been given as him falling over the banister from the top floor of the Georgian wing and the two-floor fall killing him. Then the local undertaker got a bit pissed in the pub one night and started talking about how the boy had marks around his neck. Well, the locals start wondering whether the new man throttled his stepson, and then chucked him off the top floor to cover it up. Drake got this from the recorded evidence a group of locals gave to the coroner to try to get the boy exhumed. Unfortunately, the bad-lad – one Gregory Smith by name – was nothing if not wealthy by now, and the whole thing was hushed up."

"Rich bastard," Drake grunted in disgust, then having got Hobson's attention carried on. "The trouble didn't stop then, though. God knows, I'm not superstitious, but even I'm finding the coincidences more than a bit strange."

"Oh?" Hobson queried, seeing Drake's expression and beginning to fear the worst.

Drake gave him a sympathetic look. This would've been giving some of the hardened city coppers he'd known the creeps, and this poor bloke was rapidly heading out of his depth through no fault of his own.

"The thing is, then the other three kiddies from the first marriage disappear. And I really do mean *disappear*. Me and Robbie have trawled through every bloody death register in the area and those kids are buried nowhere in the county."

"Oh God!" sighed Hobson despairingly.

"Oh there's even odder to come! The merry widow is absolutely frantic by this time. All she has left is the baby by Gregory Smith. There's even a report in a local paper about her having to be restrained and removed from the main police station in Hereford because she was making such a scene there, demanding that the police find her three boys. The same report also says that the new husband, Gregory, tells the coppers of the day back there that the children all died of scarlet fever – which our resident wizard here tells me was a real child-killer in the days before antibiotics – and that she's just distraught. He seems to have got away with it by saying that they died when the family was away for several weeks, and so the kids had been buried in some seaside town – except we've already tried the record offices at the obvious ones and they aren't there either."

"The poor woman seems to have been dismissed as some sort of hysteric," Robbie said sadly. "Anyway, what's even odder is that all of a sudden only a week or so later Gregory Smith disappears, and the woman's family have to step in because she seems to have lost what's left of her mind. They took charge of the baby – because that had strange bruising which everyone thought was her losing the plot – and committed her to a mental home because she kept rambling on about the fairies having come for their revenge! That the fairies had killed Gregory! To cap it all Gregory Smith was never seen again and his body never found either – not that I think anyone looked too hard. He wasn't a popular man locally, and especially not with the local coppers for some reason we can't find out about. But they certainly didn't over exert themselves looking for him, and just put some ambiguous comments on his file and closed it."

"Bloody hell!" someone's voice behind them said, and Robbie and Drake realised they had the whole incident room's attention by now with the story. Back in his element, Drake turned to address them all, completely outshining Hobson without even realising he was doing it.

"Well that's the point when her first husband's family, who still officially owned it, sell this place to the people who wanted to open a school. At first it all goes quiet again – although the period of the Second World War is a nightmare in terms of the records, because kids were being evacuated out here from cities, with some of them only staying a few weeks and then going again. Through the fifties and sixties, the place positively flourishes, and seems to have been under good management. One or two odd claims of strange sightings in the late sixties and seventies, but nothing you couldn't put down to the older kids smuggling some weed in! These were rich little buggers, so they must've had money to spare out here with nothing to spend daddy's walloping big allowance on.

"Where it gets nasty is eighteen years ago. The school had been on a downward slide for some years. The Thatcher recessions meant that there were fewer kids coming here because the fees were pretty steep. By the early nineties the school was running at barely half its capacity, and dithering on the brink of insolvency. They weren't exactly in the market for enticing dedicated teachers, as you can imagine, and it seems to have been run on a shoestring with a few members of staff, and a handful of other odd-bods who did things like the cooking and cleaning. And that's where we come to Helen Fisher's sister Suzanna. What we didn't know back then was that Suzanna wasn't the only kid to go missing from this school."

A chorus of groans greeted this as the assembled officers all had visions of even more weeks digging through the grounds.

"I know, I know," Drake said, holding his hand up for silence and getting it with an ease that Hobson envied. Even the men who he'd had to fight to assert his own authority over when he'd been promoted were instantly in thrall to Drake's charisma. "The trouble is, we can't be sure what happened. We have a report – which was hushed up at the time – of one girl getting her parents to take her home because of what sounds like the local perv' getting in at night. Hardly surprising! Out in the sticks like this no-one would've noticed him shinning up the fire escape, and the windows are hardly secure either. On top of that, the staff seemed to have commandeered the posh rooms in the Georgian wing, while all the girls were upstairs above where we are now. The poor little buggers could've screamed their lungs out and the staff would've been hard pressed to hear."

"What's peculiar is that two more girls left," Robbie continued. "DI Drake has been in touch with some of his old colleagues down in the south, and the address they were supposed to have moved to is false. It just doesn't exist. They never went there or anywhere else as far as we can tell – not them or their father."

Hobson clearly felt that he had to get control of his investigation back before Drake took over altogether. "So what you're saying is that there could be another two girls out there in the shrubbery?"

"No three," Robbie corrected him, "because don't forget Suzanna Fisher."

"Oh crap," another detective said, suddenly diving for a grisly photo taken by Carol's team. "Do you think this could be those two girls' father?" He held up the photo of a far from recent corpse, but one which was equally obviously not from so long ago that it was in the province of the archaeologists. "We found him two days ago after Carrie's stepfather."

"If he is," Drake said, consulting his notes, "his name is Albert Walters, fifty-three years old, from the Wirral. Let's get in touch with the lads up there and see if we can get some dental records and stuff e-mailed down to Dr Whitmore. Suzanna Fisher went missing on the thirty-first of October 1990, and Walters took his girls away at Christmas of the same year under the pretext that they weren't safe here."

"Without knowing that they were never destined to arrive in London, I suppose it just looked like they went home for the holidays and never came back," one of the crime scene analysts observed from behind her laptop screen. "That's why the Fisher investigation never picked it up. It would just've looked like an overprotective parent."

"Is it always girls who go missing?" her colleague sitting next to her asked.

"No," Robbie was able to tell her. "The most recent ones are, because by then it was an all-girls' school. But the children in the 1920s were all boys, so I don't think it's exclusively a girl thing. Why?"

"Because we found a little boy that Dr Whitmore says must've died in the 1940s, or maybe the early '50s," the second analyst told him. "We weren't sure whether he was connected to the school or not, or maybe a housekeeper's child?"

"This is the list of kids we couldn't tie up with later records from that period," Drake said, producing a list printed from Robbie's computer. "That's the names and addresses that the school was given when they arrived. It was mixed back then."

The information sent everyone off making calls and checking information, but in the midst of the activity Robbie was standing stock still with a worried look on his face.

"What is it?" Drake asked him as they stepped back to by the fireplace and out of the way.

Robbie drew him into the next room to where they were alone. "Look, I know this may sound barmy to you but..."

"...But what?"

"Well Suzanna disappeared on Halloween and then the other girls go at Christmas. But we celebrate Christmas at that time of year because it coincides with the old pagan festival of Yule – the Church took over an existing festival because actually no-one knows just when Christ was born. But get this – those three little lads in the 1920s went missing in August – on the first – on the very day of the old feast of Lughnasadh."

"Are you saying that there *is* something pagan going on after all?" Drake hissed irately. "Because you've just told Hobson that there were no cults here!"

"No cults we ever found a *mention* of!" Robbie countered. "And anyway, he was thinking of some loopy twentieth-century bunch of nutters dancing round the oak trees at midnight and getting high. Or a group of innocents who'd fallen under the influence of some charismatic villain, who had them thinking they were heading for heaven here on earth while they did stuff no-one sane would entertain doing. I'm talking about something far older, and most of the time way less malevolent.

"It would be more like someone trying to resurrect a misguided idea of what the old feasts were about. And it's far more likely it would affect the bodies the archaeologists are dealing with anyway. But that doesn't mean there wasn't something ritualistic going on. I mean, what do you think? Do you just accept those dates as misfortune? Me, I think it's too much of a coincidence that these children are going missing on the pagan feast days, and not at random dates through the rest of the year as well."

Drake's expression got even blacker. "*Feast*? That's got a nasty ring to it! I do hope we're not getting in consumption as well."

"Good Lord! I hope not too."

"Well you'd better be very sure of the connections," Drake warned him, "because if you start getting Hobson all wound up over some witchy bunch dancing starkers round the bushes, we're likely to look a right pair of pillocks when it turns out to be just your average nutter on the prowl!"

However, their reputations were upheld when it transpired that the corpse actually was Albert Walters, saving the local investigating officers ages trying to track down an anonymous body. What disconcerted everyone was that he'd apparently died in the same way as Carrie's stepfather, Timothy Wiggins. Once again Carol Whitmore's report stated that the cause of death was multiple arrow wounds, but that no sign of the weapons remained.

A local archery club was contacted to provide samples of arrows to try to sort out what had happened, but Carol's team quickly ruled out modern sporting archery as the culprit. The next step was one of the archaeologists proposing that the wounds looked more like the kind of thing a medieval barbed arrow would make. Several experiments later it was confirmed – either someone involved in re-enactments or someone conversant with medieval weaponry must have done the deeds. However, matching such a profile with a name proved elusive, for no-one with the appropriate know-how had even been in the area at the time of both deaths – not even a visiting re-enactor – let alone possessing a motive.

As for the anonymous little boy, Drake and Robbie yet again found themselves in the archives, once the team had tracked down the easily identified and living boys from the World War II school register – although this time they also had the forensic team's descriptions as something to work with. On top of that another male body had appeared – the corpse Drake and Robbie had seen them working on alongside the archaeologists when they had gone to report to Hobson – which was probably of the Second World War period as well, and then that of another little boy. Red-eyed from staring at computer screens and files, Drake and Robbie were able to help confirm the identity of the man to the team by the end of the fourth day of the second round of hunting.

"He was dismissed from a school right down on the banks of the Thames at the outbreak of the war," Drake told the team assembled in the hall once again on the following morning. "He got lucky – if you can call it that. Without the war he would've found it impossible to get another post in a school after the report we found. Apparently, he was found in the suspected act of raping a seven-year-old boy and it was reported to the local police, but only a few weeks later the bombing started and it never came to trial. It seems he planted some of his papers on a body in a bombed-out building, so the London police thought he was dead – no blame there, too many dead and no modern forensics to help.

"He then came west and made the excuse that he didn't have any documentation because of the blitz. He was very clever, picking and choosing what to take and what to leave behind, so that no questions were asked. We know more about his dirty dealings than we might, though, because some years ago a chap came forward in response to one of those investigations about a children's home where there was a history of abuse. Sidney Claypotts, as this perv' was called, had worked at a children's home before the London school. But because it was only allegations back then, and there was no medical evidence to back it up, he got away with it. Which was why he wasn't banged up in a local nick when the bombs started falling."

"Do we know who the boys are?" Hobson asked hopefully.

Robbie rubbed his tired eyes wearily, having had very little sleep in the last forty-eight hours due to a trip to London for that evidence, before answering. "Well we can make a good guess. As luck would have it, we know when Claypotts' successor started work here, so at least now we have a time frame. Again luckily, most of the kids evacuated to the school were from Birmingham and have been accounted for, if only by numbers of kids brought down and then taken back." He made a relieved aside. "Thank God there were never the mass evacuations from the Midlands like there were from the south! We'd never have coped with that lot!

"Then we have the regular residents of the school, who were all older kids and therefore apparently not Sidney's type. That leaves a local boy called William Smith who went missing, but it was assumed that he went off with his father's family who were gypsies and therefore itinerant. The other candidates are Anthony Crump, a boy sent down to a rather dotty great-aunt in the village. He went missing, but was assumed to have been killed trying to get back to his family in Birmingham on the night of an air raid. Or Morris Solomon, a sad little soul who seems to have gone missing and not been noticed until his father got back from the war. His mother apparently went off with some other bloke and thought he was with her in-laws, while his father's family thought he was with her parents."

"God, you think that sort of thing only goes on nowadays," someone said in disgust.

Robbie sighed. "I know what you mean, but this bunch of idiots were a real feckless lot, trying to make a swift half-crown whenever the chance arose – that's the mother's family. The father's folks in all fairness did try to keep tabs on the boy, but it was hard when they were living in the East End and lost everything but what they were standing up in. It was the mother's family who sent little Morris down here to the school's cook, who was some friend of the family, and I suppose the father's family thought he'd be safer here than with them with bombs falling every night."

Carol had come back out to the site to check on progress and now looked up from the autopsy reports she'd brought with her.

"Going on the state of the first child's teeth and the like I'd guess that our first body is Anthony Crump," she suggested. "The gypsy boy would probably have had a better diet, living off the land when the other children spent their early years in cities during the end of the depression. Did your reports have anything in the way of a description of these lads?"

Robbie shrugged. "Nothing you could get excited about. Anthony is said to have been small for his age, which was about twelve, but could pass for nine or ten. Drake got that from a piece in the Birmingham Post for the time. It's possible that he'd had polio, although not badly enough to be really crippled by it."

"Ah!" Carol exclaimed. "Then he's the second boy we found! There was definitely some evidence of polio in his case. The other child wore glasses and they were still on him – looks like they were tied on originally. Must've kept losing them."

"Oh dear, well that makes him likely to be Morris," Robbie said sadly. "He too was said to be small for his age and wore glasses."

"I suppose it's too much to hope that William Smith really did just go off with the gypsies?" Hobson said faintly.

"Well so far we've not found another little boy, sir," one of the PCs said hopefully.

"Yes, but we've had seven bodies in almost as many days, not to mention the ancient remains our very own *Time Team* have already exhumed and are scrubbing up out the back," Hobson retorted with morose sarcasm.

"How many older remains have you found?" Drake asked straight out, getting a withering look from Robbie for his tactlessness.

Hobson just shuddered and it was Carol who replied,

"Well it all gets very interesting."

"Harrumph...!" Hobson snorted and walked away in disgust.

"Well it is!" she insisted to Robbie and Drake. "It's like whoever buried Helen Fisher, and Carrie Lewis and her stepfather, knew where the others are, because they're all in sequence. The only reason we got the first older body out of sequence was because of soil erosion making it more noticeable for the dog. But in terms of placement, it was off to one side of the others we had at first.

"Yet the more the archaeologists uncover, the clearer it's becoming that there's a definite pattern to these burials. All the modern ones are clustered up on the edge of the arboretum, as if the tree roots made it too difficult to dig further in. But they've surveyed the ground in amongst the trees, where they can, and it's starting to look as though there was a whole line of burials. We've had no sign of your 1920s family, but over on the other side of the first line of trees we've got eight male bodies..."

"Fuck me!" Drake interrupted in shock.

"No thank you, not right here," Carol riposted with a smile, drawing a shaky laugh from Robbie who nonetheless looked more than a little rattled at having so many new discoveries. "Don't worry," Carol continued cheerfully, "the archaeologists are quite clear on this lot. They're soldiers of the Civil War period, probably the casualties from some small skirmish in this area. Nothing we need worry about, although they're getting quite excited about them."

"Thank God for that!" was Drake's heartfelt response. "Bloody hell, no wonder poor old Hobson's got a face like a wet weekend. What a nightmare to have crop up in the middle of your investigation!"

"But what about that first odd body you found?" Robbie wanted to know.

"Somewhere in the middle, time-wise as well as geographically," Carol told them. "It's interesting that you said no-one lived here much from the 1850s to the 1920s, because that period's completely clear of remains. Our first ancient corpse is probably from around 1810 to maybe 1820. Do you have any likely candidates for him?"

Robbie dumped the thick file he'd compiled onto a folding table and sifted through sheaves of notes, but then shook his head.

"No. No adult males at all for that period, only a couple – no make that *three* again – children going missing."

"Ah, that's good," Carol said pensively.

"Good? What the bloody hell's good about that?" Drake demanded angrily, completely thrown by her response. "Poor Hobson's got bodies coming up like Hell's issuing day-out passes and you say it's good?"

Realising how it must have sounded Carol hurried to correct herself. "I'm sorry, that wasn't how it was meant to come out. No, it's rather that the forensic archaeologist and I were talking about this one, and we both agreed that it looked like the man was either very poor or had been living rough for some years."

"Oh I see!" Robbie suddenly caught on to where she was going. "So it actually makes more sense if he isn't attached to the family in the house!"

"That's right."

"Ah well... but in that case ...mmm ...I wonder if it actually could be connected to the disappearance of these children, although one of them is almost an adult by the standards of the day. You see the current incumbents of the house of that day were a childless couple. A squire and his wife. They appear to have invited the daughter of a poor relative to come and stay. The next thing we hear is that the family's employing a nurse for a baby. Now it could be the child of the lady of the house, but by that stage she's in her forties so it's unlikely when she's been childless all those years. The girl would be about fourteen..."

"...So young to have a baby but not impossible!"

"Exactly! Now Drake and I were wondering whether our Georgian squire was being a dirty old man and getting the girl pregnant behind his wife's back, so to speak? Because then a second baby appears only a year or so later – again according to the records of another wet nurse needing to be found. Then within two years both nurses are being dismissed with full references. Drake found a newspaper report that said that the girl had run off with a man who'd been seen lurking around the house. I wonder if that's your chap? You know, rough and ready but a better bet than an old and abusive relative, ...that sort of thing..."

"Could be," Carol agreed enthusiastically, "but he's more of an age to be her father than her boyfriend. Do you think he attacked her and the squire did away with him, then just buried him rather than face questions?"

Robbie suddenly froze and stared off into space.

"What is it?" Carol asked, and even Drake wondered why the faraway look was in his partner's eyes.

For a moment Robbie remained silent, then rummaged hurriedly in the file again before looking up with a triumphant glint in his eye.

"You might have been closer to the truth than you knew, Carol."

"Why?"

"You said this man was old enough to have been her father. I'm now wondering whether in fact that was *exactly* who he was! You see the reason the girl was there at all was because her mother died, and her father was a soldier who hadn't been heard from in some while. Well by your dating he could've been returning after the end of the Napoleonic War. After the Battle of Waterloo! Which was the summer of 1815 if my schoolboy history serves me correctly. There were huge numbers of soldiers who were just dismissed with no job or home to go to when the war ended, and many of them ended up living rough. And if he'd been with Wellington, fighting his way up through Portugal and Spain into France he would've been living rough for a good many years – or at least by modern ideas of living."

"Ah..." Carol breathed softly. "Yes, that sort of lifestyle would take its toll. Yes, I think you could be right, because Sylvia – that's our forensic archaeologist – said that he had evidence of old wounds, as though he'd been in fights a lot. We just thought of brawls, but it could well have been the result of hand-to-hand fighting."

"In which case," Drake chipped in, "he comes home from the war, can't find his family, hears his daughter's been shipped off to the wilds of Herefordshire and comes looking for her." He was nodding enthusiastically with Carol now. "So he gets here and finds the bastard's been screwing his little girl and is none too pleased, there's a fight and he gets killed."

"How did he die?" wondered Robbie.

"He was shot," Carol told them. "Which is odd now I come to think about it because that makes him the only one who is. Even those Civil War soldiers died of sword wounds and arrow wounds. That's one of the reasons the archaeologists are getting so excited, because by the Civil War they wouldn't expect arrows to be being used. They normally look for musket balls and the like."

"And..." Robbie tapped the page of his file, "it's interesting that, according to the death records, our squire died in 1815! Just right for dying from wounds from a fight with a returning soldier! The house passed to a brother's son, who was the one who eventually sold it to the industrialist from the Forest of Dean we told you about earlier. A son who, incidentally, they'd tried to interest in marrying our girl with the two babies. He refused, not surprisingly if he knew his uncle had been taking advantage of her before him."

"So we may never know the exact truth of what went on," Drake summarised, "but we're unlikely to be far astray if we think that this is a family feud."

"For our man, yes. But what about the girl and her children?" Robbie wondered. "What happened to them if her father came for them and then died in the attempt to free her?"

"Well she isn't buried with him, that's for sure," Carol told them. "And the archaeologists didn't just excavate the immediate grave, they went well around it because of the modern bodies we'd already found. They didn't want to miss something important."

"This case gets odder and odder," Drake said as they walked out to the cars. "It's all men and children, isn't it. I mean, it's not just the modern stuff, is it? It's this old stuff as well. The 1815 squire raping some helpless lass who thinks she's been orphaned and left to their mercy. And that 1920s family with the dodgy stepfather. Come to that, we've got Gregory Smith, the 1920's stepfather, and then lo-and-behold young Carrie Lewis and her stepfather, Timothy Wiggins. That's a very nasty coincidence, even if I can't for the life of me see what the connection could be, given there's over seventy years' gap between the two sets of deaths."

"I know what you mean," Carol said, unlocking her car door and depositing her files on the passenger seat. "And to crown it we have some remains which are of a child that are probably even earlier. The problem there is that the gardeners who put the trees in were probably the ones who broke up the fragile bones with their spades without even noticing. Those could be Civil War too, or even as a result of the plague in the mid-1660s, but they're too damaged to tell."

"I wonder what happened to the women?" Robbie mused.

"Jesus, don't tempt fate!" Drake warned him. "Remember what happened when I said there were too many coincidences? Now we're tripping over the buggers! Just keep quiet with your speculations or God knows what might turn up next!"

Chapter 6

October 31st, The Year of Our Lord 1575

Lady Margaret sat on the stairs of Peorth Manor and wept. The baby she cradled in her arms was no consolation to her, even though the little boy slept peacefully, blissfully unaware of the distress he was part of the cause of. Her elderly maid came in search of her and wrapped a heavy woollen shawl around the younger woman's shivering shoulders, coming to sit by her but saying nothing. What was there to say? In the course of one short year the lives of those in tiny Kinnaston had been turned upside down, and none more so than Margaret's.

When she and Sir Timothy had finally returned from Gloucester, everyone had hoped that he would recover fully from the beating he'd taken, and that they could put all the upsets behind them. But it wasn't to be. For a time, Sir Timothy had rallied and then unexpectedly, while walking out in his garden he'd collapsed and died. At the time no-one had doubted the doctor from Hereford who'd said that there'd been unseen damage to his head following the assault, which had finally weakened and then killed him. The estate had mourned for him and buried him in the family vault, yet within the week his heir's bailiff had appeared. Lady Margaret's distant cousin had declared his intention of taking up residence on the estate, and had no desire to have a lone and heavily pregnant relative cluttering the place.

Margaret was in an awful position. As a woman she couldn't inherit her father's estate and, with no brothers to inherit and protect her, her home had passed far down the family to the next male, whom she'd never even met. With Doctor Parker alive, even if he was now on the run and wanted for assault, she was technically still married, for Sir Timothy had never got round to having the marriage annulled.

Had she been widowed she could at least have hoped for a new proposition of marriage to provide a roof over her head, but now there was no-one she could turn to. Her connection to the family in Gloucester was through her aunt, and the uncle by that marriage (who'd sheltered them following the assault) clearly thought that he'd done quite enough for a girl who'd been foolish enough to get herself involved with such a rake of a husband. So when the cousin's men had turned up at her old home with the backing of the local justices, there'd been nowhere else to go but Peorth Manor, which legally was still hers even if she'd never wanted to set foot in the place ever again.

She couldn't find words sufficient to express the gratitude she felt towards the folk of her father's estate, for without them she had no idea how she would've coped. Instead, Simon the Reeve, finding himself out of a job under the cousin's new lordship, had organised the collection of certain items of furniture which he'd discovered belonged to the absent Doctor, and which had been abandoned by the Doctor's servants after the news of his arrest, along with bits that were unlikely to be missed from Sir Timothy's. The villagers had scraped together old carts and wagons to go and fetch the furniture, while Billy had done his best to repair the damage to the manor with Thomas' help. The great hall was a barren and cold place even in the summer, and in the end Margaret, and the small household she could afford on her tiny inheritance, had simply shut the door on it and all of the north wing. Instead, they had focused on making the south wing, with its servants' quarters, as pleasant as possible.

For all of August it seemed as though they'd succeeded. Simon and his wife took on the running of the place, while Margaret's old maid, Maud, had declared that nothing would drag her from her young mistress' side, and that if necessary, she would starve with her. In the face of such stout declarations Billy had felt he could hardly leave them to it, and so he and Thomas now shared what should have been the grooms' quarters over the small detached stable built into the hillside to one side of the main house – another place which had miraculously survived the landslide.

Even loyalty to Margaret wouldn't have got Billy to spend a night in the manor itself, but he'd managed to get some high-class work out of the patronage of the Dean of Hereford once more, and added his wages to the income of the tiny household. With some of the money he'd bought seeds, and Thomas had made a useful vegetable patch where an ornamental garden should have been. This winter would be tight but they weren't likely to starve just yet.

That was until September came around and an unexpected visitor had appeared. Out of nowhere the Doctor had turned up one afternoon to accost the heavily pregnant Margaret, while she sat in the sun on a little bench Billy had made for her in the shelter of the rear courtyard. Too terrified to even cry out, Margaret had been found still shaking hours later by Maud. It took much cosseting by the warmth of the kitchen range to get her to speak, but when she did the household were appalled. The Doctor wanted his house back!

Not to live in, because he knew that sooner or later word would reach those in authority of his return, and he would be arrested once more. What he wanted to do was perform his wicked ritual again, although the petrified Margaret couldn't begin to tell the others what that might be. All she knew was that he was demanding his book back.

The trouble was that neither she nor the others had any idea what the Doctor was talking about. Thomas was next to get confronted as he bent over the row of young winter cabbages he was tending too, and, being already down on the ground, found it impossible to defend himself when the Doctor went into a screaming rage and began belabouring him about the shoulders and head with a stout staff. Soon after, Thomas managed to stagger into the kitchen bleeding from his head wounds, but when Simon and Billy rushed out armed with cudgels the Doctor had already disappeared. Next it was Maud who got assaulted and shaken nearly out of her wits, and weeks later she still carried the bruises on her arms where he had grasped her.

Simon went to the new lord, Master Bertram, who grudgingly sent a couple of mounted men out to ride round the estate. However, it was clear that he thought it beneath him to get involved in what he saw as a domestic argument. If the man wished to beat his wife there was no law to say he couldn't, and Simon failed to make him see that the man had been responsible for Sir Timothy's death. No doubt Master Bertram thought the Doctor had indirectly done him a good turn by enabling him to have a living of his own, for that was the last they heard from the landlord who was supposed to protect them. It certainly made the servants wonder whether Sir Timothy's death had been quite as natural as they'd thought.

Mercifully the rest of the tenants took the news much more seriously, and to their credit tried to keep an eye on the place. On the Sunday after Maud's fright, they even went round the estate hunting for Parker – covering their activity from Master Bertram by saying they were checking fences and hedges. However, the Doctor seemed to have the luck of the Devil, for no-one saw hide nor hair of him.

Yet the next day he was back and threatening Simon himself this time. Clearly realising that Simon would be a tougher nut to crack he didn't attack Simon but threatened what he would do to his wife Sarah if he got in the way again. At the time Simon put on a brave face, but in the kitchen that night he admitted to the others that he feared the Doctor's ability to appear out of nowhere, for he couldn't possibly be with Sarah every minute of the day.

With Billy the only one not yet threatened it seemed impossible to deny the evil man what he wanted. So they came up with the plan that they would allow the Doctor the house and try instead to protect one another, and Margaret in particular. Parker turned up the next day and everyone simply walked out of the house and left him to it. For what seemed like an eternity they heard him crashing and banging through the rooms, and at the end he simply stormed out without another word to them. However, he appeared to finally believe them when they said they had no notion of any book, for it was never mentioned again.

Yet the upset brought other problems, for Margaret went into labour that evening, two weeks early due to all the strain and worry. Her agonies dragged on through the night and into the next day, despite the best efforts of Maud, Sarah and Nanny Wright, the local wise woman who had hurried up from the hamlet when fetched by Billy. The three men huddled miserably in the kitchen, praying when they felt able and sitting in tense silence when they couldn't summon the words. All feared that this would be the end of Margaret, but as the sun rose to noon on a beautiful crisp autumn day there came the wail of a tiny infant from the room upstairs and everyone breathed again. Against the odds Margaret herself was weak but otherwise seemed likely to make a full recovery.

It would be weeks before Margaret could go through the ritual of being churched – welcomed back into the arms of the Church following childbirth – but the next Sunday no-one wanted to leave her alone, and so they all stayed at home and prayed together. Later Simon made the long walk down to the main church and spoke to the priest to ask for prayers for intercession in the hope that that might offer some protection. The priest was a decent man who understood their worries and offered to come and pray with Margaret, an invitation which was swiftly accepted. He arrived the next morning and spent time praying with them all, but after he'd gone, they admitted in private that they felt no safer from the dreaded doctor than before.

A prophecy which proved true only too quickly. Not a day later Parker barged his way into the house through the kitchen door, Thomas hot on his heels from the garden, and swiftly joined by Billy brandishing the mallet and chisel with which he'd been working on a carving in the stables.

"I hear I'm a father," Parker purred malevolently.

"Lady Margaret has been delivered of a son," Simon said stoutly, "but you'll never be a father to the child while we are around," although he felt far from as brave as his words.

But Parker just laughed nastily. "You can't stop me, fool! I have a higher purpose than dangling some squalling brat from my knee. But he's mine and I will have him!"

With that he turned on his heels and left, leaving the household bemused and worried at what the mad Doctor was up to now. They didn't have long to wait. A terrified and ear-piercing scream from Margaret's room in the depths of that night brought them all running to her, even Billy and Thomas, having decided to sleep inside for safety's sake by now.

"He came to me! He wants to sacrifice my boy!" Margaret howled hysterically. "He wants his blood on All Hallow's Eve!"

"May the Blessed Virgin save him and us," gasped Sarah.

"All Hallow's?" Thomas whimpered in fear. "May the Lord protect us. Not that night of all nights!"

"They were right after all," Billy whispered to Simon who looked back quizzically. "You know, back when the hill moved. They said then that this place survived because he was some kind of male witch. A warlock! We should've burnt it down then and taken our chances with being able to find someone to take us and Lady Margaret in."

"Hush!" Sarah hissed at him. "Not in front of her!" She nodded to the weeping Margaret, so Billy pulled Thomas and Simon out onto the staircase where they all sat beneath the big window.

"Nought but trouble this place has been from the start," Thomas said mournfully. "We should've taken more notice of what Amos and Ezra said right back when they put the floor-plates in and after."

"Aye. Poor Sam being murdered – and don't tell me he wasn't 'cos I don't believe he just disappeared – and now this."

"But what can we do?" Simon asked, long ago having given up any pretence of being in authority over the other two men in the face of such strange events.

"We could ask the priest if Margaret and the baby could spend the night at the church," Billy suggested.

"Oh Billy, don't be daft, she hasn't been properly churched yet," Simon protested. "If she can't even go into the church for a service how can the priest give her sanctuary?"

"She don't have to go *in* though, does she?" Billy defended his plan stubbornly. "If that outlaw over on the border got away with claiming sanctuary by getting to the porch, then so can Lady Margaret! What we do is get lots of blankets to keep her and the baby warm and borrow old man Holmes' cart to get them down into the village. Then we sit her in the porch right by the door with Sarah and Maud by her, and we three guard the porch door. It'll be a cold night for us all but it's the safest place."

"Yes it is," Maud's voice came from behind them making them all jump. "And there's more power than just the church in that old church yard. That old yew by the porch is more potent than most folks round here care to remember, that's why it gets things tied on it when the priest ain't lookin'! He done try to keep takin' them off but they gets put back on the side away from the church."

"Are you talking about witchcraft, Maud?" Simon asked disapprovingly.

"Don't be a fool, boy!" Maud retorted, giving him a clip round the ear as she'd done when he was a little lad. "If you'd remembered what your Ma told you, instead of all this stuff the priests chant on about, you'd recall that there's two sorts of what you call witchcraft. The old way is potent, boy, and don't you forget it! Most of what gets handed on from mother to daughter goes unnoticed 'cos it's all about helpin' folks. A poultice for this ailment. A tea for this upset. I ain't never told no man this before, but the rule is, if you do harm with the Craft, it'll come back to you threefold. So no woman with a mite of sense would dream of doing evil with it – it takes a man to be so blind and daft!"

"Well blind and daft or not, he's doin' it and he's got some pretty potent stuff goin' on at the moment," Thomas protested. "I ain't doubtin' you, Maud, but how long does it take for this stuff to start comin' back on him? 'Cos we ain't got much time left and he seems to have the upper hand!"

Maud couldn't answer him that but promised, "It'll all come right, I'll make sure of that." Then astonished them all by going and fetching her capacious heavy shawl and bonnet and declared she was going out.

"Dear Lord, Maud! What are you a thinkin' off!" Thomas exclaimed. "Especially at this time of night!"

"I got people to see and work to do," Maud said mysteriously, although she did accept Thomas' offer of an escort down as far as the hamlet armed with one of the cudgels and a lantern, after she'd made him solemnly promise never to divulge who she went to see.

When they'd gone, Simon went back to keep Sarah company comforting the still distraught Margaret, leaving Billy alone on the stairs. They couldn't afford candles simply to light passageways and so by the light of the waning moon he sat and stared at the mural. Without realising what he was doing he found himself scouring the painting for the picture of Sam's face that he thought he'd seen months ago. The more he looked the more he was convinced that the picture wasn't the same as the last time he'd seen it, and Sam was nowhere to be seen.

"Oh Sammy I do miss you, you grumpy old bugger," Billy said to the picture. "There's evil afoot here and I don't know as I won't be seein' you sooner than later if that wicked bastard Parker does whatever it is he's plannin' on doin'. Keep a place in heaven for me will ye? If that's where you are, and I surely hope it is."

He was just cuffing a tear from his eyes when he heard a soft voice say,

"Did you say Parker?"

Billy jumped and looked around him but there was no-one there. The voice had been muffled as though coming from behind a screen or hanging.

"Who's there?" he asked timidly, truly frightened now.

"Here," the voice said, as Billy turned around frantically trying to see someone. "You're looking straight at me. In the wall!"

Billy felt his heart skip a beat as he turned to the mural and saw a figure step from behind one of the large bushes.

"Oh Lord protect me! Mary, Mother of God, help me!"

"Don't be frightened, I won't harm you," the tall dangerous-looking figure said. "I heard you speaking. Did you say Parker? Is this the same man whom Sam spoke of? The evil man who killed him?"

Billy could only nod in acknowledgement.

"Is he planning something else?"

"Yes," Billy's voice was a hoarse squeak. Then his courage began to return enough to ask, "Can you help?"

"What is he planning to do?"

"He wants to kill Lady Margaret's new-born baby in just under a week's time on All Hallow's Eve."

"Is that Samhain?" the figure asked.

"Might be," Billy said with a nod. "Best one to ask would be old Maud but she's gone to the village to round up some other old women by the sound of it. Said somethin' about the old yew tree in the churchyard, but I don't know what that's all about."

"Then I have a message for you for Maud. Tell her to bring her circle here and to invite us in. Conceal the women in the rooms above and ask them to do what they must here on the stairs where you're standing. Tell them to invite Lord Elfan and Lady Ferylt. Have you the names? It's most important they call them by name! Lord Elfan and Lady Ferylt. If they call us before the evil one begins, we will come to your aid. We won't leave you to face him alone."

With that the figure turned and ran off into the distance in the mural leaving Billy standing rooted to the spot in astonishment.

The following morning, he told the others, and Maud especially, of what had happened. Simon immediately marched him up to the mural and demanded to see the figure, but there was no-one where Billy had seen them the night before. Maud on the other hand said little, but her eyes had begun to gleam and she'd already set off for the village again by the time Simon was marching Billy downstairs, with dire warnings of mentioning such foolishness to Lady Margaret and upsetting her, or giving her false hopes. Out in the garden in the privacy of tending the root vegetables, Billy managed to convince Thomas of what he'd seen, but Simon and Sarah refused to even talk of it, believing that Billy had imagined it all out of his deep desire to help.

Come the morning of the thirty-first Maud went and stood outside the kitchen door and refused to come in out of the biting wind. She wouldn't say why she was there, but within the hour a figure was seen coming across the fields to the manor, and then another from a different direction. As the first came into the courtyard it turned out to be Lizzie Wright, old Nanny's daughter, who now lived near Crow Hill and performed much the same services for the farming community there as her mother did for the hamlet and surrounding families.

"Merry meet," Maud said embracing Lizzie, who responded the same. Without another word Lizzie nodded her greeting to the assembled household, and then walked past them with a smile into the house where they heard her heavy wooden clogs going up the stairs.

"Hope she wiped her feet!" muttered Sarah and getting a glare from Maud. "Well I know who'll have to clear it up if she's traipsed mud off the fields inside," Sarah grumbled, but more softly this time.

The next to arrive was Nanny herself, puffing and blowing from the uphill climb. After the greeting of "merry meet" she paused to catch her breath.

"I bin up all night with the Rogers' daughter," she told Maud with a shake of the head. "Daft girl tried to use some potion she got from the fair in Ross to get rid of a babe got on her at harvest by some travelling man. Her pa's fair stampin' mad. If she weren't so ill she wouldn't sit down for a week."

"All well now?" Maud asked.

"Aye, she'll live, but I weren't easy on her. Could've done without her foolery when we've got more serious work to do this night," she tutted with a shake of the head. And with that she followed her daughter inside and up the stairs.

"Do you mind telling us what's going on?" Simon demanded as three more figures came in sight.

"Yes, I do young Simon," Maud said with great firmness. "You should've listened to what Billy said, and that's all I'm goin' to tell you!"

Simon gave Sarah an exasperated glance and the two of them went inside, but Billy and Thomas were intrigued and stayed. A threesome then appeared up the lane, which turned out to be led by the truly ancient Nanny Ransom who lived in a tiny cottage near Dymock. Too old to make the walk, she was being pushed in a well-cushioned handcart by the man generally known as her son, Bryn, although he was nothing of the sort. He'd been found on her doorstep as a tiny child and had quickly turned out to be very simple-minded. Even now, grown to manhood, he had the mind of a young child, but he had a good life with Nanny Ransom doing the heavy work she could no longer manage and being cared for in return. The third member of their party was unknown to Billy and Thomas, and apparently to Maud too.

"Merry meet," Nanny Ransom wheezed. "This is Rachel. I'm teachin' her the craft to take over from me when the time comes. Emily sends you her love, but has a wicked cough, so we agreed that I should bring Rachel in her place for the girl to get some real experience."

"Does she have the strength for this?" Maud asked.

Nanny Ransom gave a toothy grin. "Oh aye! That's why I picked her! She got turned out of her place in some fine household for lookin' at the master funny when they was stoppin' at Ross on the way to somewhere else. I found her beaten black and blue under a hedge when Bryn took me to market. She's got real talent!"

Indeed, Rachel seemed to have a cast in her left eye, for it was staring off to one side in a disconcerting manner, but other than that she was a striking-looking young woman. It didn't take much imagination to see that she must've caught the eye of her master, who'd then taken his revenge on her when he'd been spurned.

"Merry meet, then, Rachel," Maud said stepping forward to embrace her. "Can you help Nanny up the stairs?"

"Willingly," Rachel spoke for the first time, turning out to have a warm and friendly voice.

"Billy? Thomas? Can you find something for Bryn to do out of sight of the house?" Maud asked them.

Thomas immediately took Bryn by the arm and guided him and the handcart into the stables out of the sight of Parker for whenever he decided to come. For the rest of the day the household tried to keep some semblance of normality going. Poor Margaret was in an awful state, but Maud didn't dare tell her of what they planned because she was so in awe of Parker, they couldn't guarantee she wouldn't tell him in fright. For a little while around sunset they all had a moment of optimism when Parker failed to appear, hoping that it had been a false threat after all. But it didn't last. As soon as true darkness fell the front door of the hall crashed open and there was Parker, clad head to toe in black and with a demonic glint in his eye.

He said nothing but strode to the staircase and up it into Margaret's room. Sarah was comforting her, and was thrown back against the wall before he hauled Margaret to her feet with the baby in her arms. Still without speaking, he dragged her screaming and struggling down the stairs and into the hall, thrusting her onto the cold floor in the corner. Simon tried to rush him, brandishing the heavy poker from the kitchen, but found Parker possessed of unnatural strength and the poker being turned back on him. A heavy blow to the head felled Simon, and before he could come round, Parker had produced rope and trussed him up like a chicken for the spit.

"Where are the other heroes?" Parker finally spoke.

When Simon refused to answer, Parker walked to Margaret and brandished the poker over her head. "I only need the babe for my virgin sacrifice, but she can go too if you're determined to be stupid."

"I'm here," Thomas said before Simon could reply, stepping out from the north wing with a mattock in his hand but dropping it on the floor.

"Where's the other one?" Parker demanded.

"Billy? He's working over for the Dean in Hereford again today and tomorrow," Thomas lied, hoping like mad that the Doctor hadn't been watching them during the day to know the difference. This had been set up between him and Billy, who was currently upstairs listening from the landing with a hand clamped over Sarah's mouth to stop her screaming. If Parker hadn't spotted Billy about the place today then he was unlikely to have seen Maud's friends arrive either.

Billy gave Maud the nod, and the five women began to silently creep down the stairs to the landing beneath the window. With Parker standing in the hall, he couldn't see the staircase unless he turned back around towards the south wing, and by coming in through the door to north wing Thomas had made sure Parker stayed facing the other way. Clearly thinking that Thomas was cowed, Parker told him to sit on the floor with his hands on his head, and Thomas sat down in the doorway where he could see across the room through the hall screen's southern archway to the staircase and keep eye contact with Billy.

By now Sarah was calmer and seemed to have recognised that there was nothing she could do for Simon or Margaret, and so Billy was able to let go of her and slip down the stairs past the five wise-women to where he could keep watch and see Thomas. As the mad Doctor began to pace about the hall placing candles and muttering under his breath, the five women formed a circle on the landing beneath the mural and linked hands. At first Sarah saw and heard nothing, but then the women began to chant very softly. So softly that close as she was Sarah couldn't hear the words, but then a movement caught the corner of her eye and it took all her willpower not to scream again. In the mural figure after figure was lining up. Tall, dark-haired, stern men and women armed with swords and bows and clad in some kind of lightweight mail.

As the five softly called the names 'Lord Elfan and Lady Ferylt', the painting seemed to begin to glow, and suddenly the figures began to step out of the wall and become solid. Warrior after warrior nimbly and silently ran down the stairs to assemble behind the dividing screen from the hall. However, the leading lady and man stopped beside the five women and greeted them.

"Our thanks to you," the tall lady said. "We are in your debt. We've tried to access the portal before but the passage was difficult and we feared losing too many warriors. You've just opened the door properly for us from this side again, for which we are grateful."

"Just save my dear Margaret and her babe," Maud answered, and got a bow in return from the lord.

The two leaders swiftly joined the others below, and at their command the warriors streamed out from either side of the screen to form a circle in the great hall. Moments later two returned carrying Margaret and the child with them, but went straight past the women and through into the mural, where Sarah saw them being led away and sat on the ground where others came to tend to them.

"Safe now," Maud breathed with a sigh of relief, and the circle broke and moved to sit on the upper stairs, all looking quite drained of energy.

"Been a while since we had to do that," agreed Nanny Ransom as she mopped her brow. To her right ancient Nanny Wright seemed in danger of nodding off, propped up by the newel post, while the two younger women seemed only marginally less stunned than Sarah at what they'd done.

Down in the hall, however, there was no time for reflections yet.

"Noooo!" snarled Parker, his lips drawn back over his teeth with feral savagery. "My lord needs his innocent blood! I failed him with the woman! I won't fail him with the child!" Yet even as he spoke his shape seemed to waver and change as he stood over the dark stain which Sam's blood had made in the flagstone floor and had never been successfully removed. Like black oil leaking out of the floor and rising up around him, a second shape began to appear, slowly metamorphosing into something vaguely crow-like, leaving Parker standing temporarily dazed.

"We see you, Feannag," Elfan called out bringing his drawn sword up to point at the crow. "You can't fool us."

"Noooo!" screamed Parker again. "You shall not have him! You shall not have my god!" and launched himself at the nearest warrior.

Parker collided with one of the Elfael, who dwarfed him and clearly expected to be able to contain Parker. But the Doctor was still linked to the summoned Feannag and had more than human strength, so that the warrior found himself fighting for his life. Two more of Elfan's veterans joined in to help and even then, they couldn't easily subdue him. At this point Feannag struck out at Elfan, and suddenly the hall was a battleground. Thomas reached out and grabbed Simon's collar and pulled him back to the safety of the recessed doorway into the north wing, where they cowered in terror. Feannag rose into the air, seeming to expand to encompass the ceiling of the hall, and struck down at its attackers with its vicious beak and claws, whilst battering them all the time with its armoured wings, creating mighty drafts which buffeted the building.

For a heartbeat it seemed as though the Elfael were gaining ground, but then the distant church rang the midnight bell and the very floor of the hall seemed to become porous as figures began to emerge from it. By now Simon was near catatonic with fright and closed his eyes, repeating the Creed over and over again with his hands clasped in prayer. Thomas was also terrified but found himself unable to tear his eyes from the mystical battle being played out in front of him. More Elfael warriors now streamed past Billy to join in the fray, as ghostly dark figures with twisted and distorted bodies rose up out of the ground and began to fight on Feannag's side.

"Kill the familiar!" a voice screamed from behind Billy, and he saw the five wise women hurrying from the kitchen with every knife they could find.

"Take this," Nanny Wright said, thrusting the big carving knife into Billy's hand. "You have more strength than me. Plunge it into the cursed Doctor's black heart!"

"What?" Billy gasped. "What can I do against magic?"

"Iron," Maud said from his other side, even as she spun him back towards the hall. "Iron is the thing for the evil fae!"

"But those other people have swords and they're getting nowhere! They must be made of steel?" Billy protested as he ducked a blade swung by one of the Mearcstapan – for it was they whom Feannag had summoned when the veils between the worlds were thinnest.

"Maybe," Maud said, ducking and dodging blows behind him as they edged around the hall towards Parker. "But maybe it's the hand that delivers it which makes the difference. Or maybe it has to be iron from our world not theirs! Don't quibble lad! Do you want to miss the chance if it will work?"

Having got as close as they could round the edge of the room, the two of them waited for their chance to strike at Parker. Seeing them there, one of the Elfael suddenly redoubled his efforts, not trying to strike Parker himself, but keeping up a battering which began to drive the Doctor back towards Maud and Billy. His fellows saw what he was doing and two more joined in, pressing Parker steadily backwards until, crossing himself more in hope than conviction, Billy stepped forward raising the blade and plunged it as hard as he could into Parker's back.

There was an eldritch scream and Parker staggered, trying to grasp at the carver imbedded in his ribs. With the thick woollen coat the Doctor was wearing, Billy hadn't managed to get the knife in very far – certainly not enough to be fatal – even though Billy was a strong man. But something changed.

"It's loosened the bond!" Ferylt called to her archers. "Loose!"

And with that the Elfael archers let fly their arrows as their male counterparts dropped to the floor out of the way. Billy just managed to drag Maud down in time before the volley, but Parker took on the appearance of a hedgehog in seconds. With a strangled whimper he took one step and then keeled over onto the floor, stone dead. As he fell, Feannag gave an ear-piercing screech and began thrashing about, but slowly his shape began to waver until the Elfaels' blades were passing through a black mist rather than solid form. With a final ululating cry the creature blasted the door open and disappeared into the night to be blown away on the wind. At that point the Elfael turned and began to attack the Mearcstapan with a renewed ferocity, and this time they were winning.

In no time there were no more Mearcstapan left alive, and the Elfael leant on swords and bows for respite from the fight.

"Our thanks to you once again," Elfan said, coming across to where Lizzie and Rachel were helping Maud to her feet.

"You're welcome, my lord," Maud said, as though it was the most normal thing in the world to be carrying on a conversation with a regal figure out of legends in the middle of a hall turned battlefield. "Always glad to help the fae."

"Indeed," croaked Nanny Wright, as she hobbled back into the hall with Nanny Ransom, both clearly exhausted but with big grins on their faces.

"Would either of you two care to come with us?" Ferylt asked, seeking some way of rewarding them. "Your age would sit less heavily on you in our world."

"Oh thank ye kindly, ma'am," Nanny Ransom said cheerily, "But I got this new girl to teach or the folks will be left wanting when I go." She reached out and took Rachel's arm and patted it. "There's more to learn than you thought, my dear, isn't there!"

Rachel could only nod in awe, but Ferylt smiled in understanding. "And what about you?" she asked Nanny Wright.

"Oh I thank you kindly too, but I think there's still a bit of life in the old girl yet, ma'am. And my Lizzie here still needs her Mam to teach her a thing or too yet."

"Oh I do, Mam, I do," Lizzie said from the heart, coming to wrap her arms around her mother in a big hug.

"Excuse me, ma'am," Maud said respectfully stepping forward, "but is there anything you can do for him?" She pointed to the figure of Simon who was still sat on the floor rocking with his head in his hands like a frightened child. "He's a good man, but the Church has a strong hold on his mind. I don't think he'll recover from what he's seen this night on his own."

Ferylt looked on Simon with a sympathetic glance, as Sarah rushed in and began to cradle her husband in her arms, and then to Billy and Thomas who were supporting one another off to one side.

"I can give him some potion of our seer's," she told them. "It should make him believe it was a bad dream and that some unknown other man killed the Doctor. It may make him feverish, and that might help convince him it was all part of an illness and nothing of the real world. What of the rest of you?" She looked first to Sarah, but Sarah stood up and smoothed her crumpled skirts before making a curtsy.

"With all respect ma'am, no thank you. I think one of us should remember the truth of what happened." Then to everyone's surprise she turned to Maud. "If

Lizzie is learning from her Mam, and Rachel is learning from Nanny Ransom, then I want to learn from you."

"Are you sure?" Maud asked in amazement. "Simon won't like it, you know."

"Simon's not going to know," Sarah said firmly, "and what he don't know he won't fret about. But I've seen tonight what harm can come to even God-fearing Christian folk through no fault of their own. Who knows what would have happened to us without you three to open the way for the lord and lady and their folk. Sometimes prayer isn't enough, and there's no point in being so heavenly that you're no earthly use, if you understand me. Sometimes you have to know how to help yourself, and I don't want that knowledge lost."

"I think you've made the right choice," Ferylt said approvingly. "But what about you two men?"

However Billy was swiftest to shake his head. "Oh no! I mean with all respect, ma'am. But no! I've seen wonders here in amongst the nightmares and I don't want to forget. All I ask is, can you tell me what happened to Sam?"

"Sam died the death of a hero saving the life of my lady Ferylt here, and the rest of us and you, if you did but know it," Elfan answered for her. "He attacked the creature you saw here tonight when it was even more powerful and took some of its power away from it. Without Sam tonight we would have had a greater battle with far more Mearcstapan – if we'd even survived beyond Imbolc to get this far."

Billy whistled. "Our Sam a hero! Well I never! I wish he wasn't gone, but I'm glad he went a good way – if there's such a thing."

"There is. There most certainly is," Maud said emphatically, coming to link her arm through his and give it a comforting pat.

"In which case, as long as I've got Billy I can talk about it to, I reckon I can cope too," Thomas said shakily. "Although I don't think I'll be tellin' the priest at Church on Sunday! I don't want to forget in case things aren't as sorted as they seem. ...If you see what I mean."

However, the Elfael were convinced that, without Parker, Feannag would take a long time to recover, if ever. At the very worst it would have to find another host and take the time to build its strength up again.

"This house is its gateway," Elfan told the little cluster of humans gathered before him while Ferylt tended to Simon. "It would take another arriving with as much desire to do evil to set events in motion again. However, I do warn you. For those who have that hole in their soul, this place will draw them like bees to honey. You must be vigilant and drive off any who appear to have an unhealthy interest in the place."

"What of Lady Margaret?" Sarah suddenly thought to ask.

Elfan turned to one of the others who hurried off to inquire, but it was the venerable seer, Seithmath, who came back in front of four others who seemed to be almost carrying Margaret on her own.

"May I offer some advice?" he said cocking his head to one side to listen for where the household were standing.

"Please sir, do," Maud spoke for them all.

"Allow us to keep the child. It's an innocent at the moment, but its father's blood will make it a temptation for the wicked to draw it to the wrong path as it grows."

"But what of Lady Margaret?" Sarah protested. "The poor soul is half mad with grief already! What will she be like if she loses her baby?"

"Maybe no worse than she is now," Seithmath said gently. "You're right. She borders on the edge of insanity as it is. But that also means she's in no fit state to cope with a child right now. Let her believe it died naturally when she recovers. Let her mourn it and let grief take its course. If the gardeners among you can advise us as to where the best spot is, we will bury her wicked husband for you.

"Then when time and nature have taken their course, and it is less clear how he died, you may 'discover' his body and declare her a widow. That way she'll be able to remarry and have other children to ease the loss of this little one. If he stays with her now, even if she is recognised as a widow, who will want her with the child of such a villain at her side? I promise you he'll be given all the love and care he needs with us, and in our world, he can grow up without any taint of his father's clinging to him."

"It's the right thing to do," Maud said gently to Sarah who was shaking her head in protest, the tears flowing for Margaret.

"I think so too," Billy agreed, and Thomas was also nodding his head. "Can your lady make Lady Margaret forget the last few hours and think that the little one only lived for a few days?"

"Yes I can," Seithmath replied, and they saw four of the Elfael carry a now sleeping Simon towards the stairs.

"Best do it then," Nanny Ransom said firmly. "Come on Rachel, I'll show you a good tea to make to calm the nerves of the distressed. And we'd better make sure Bryn is all right too."

Bryn, in fact, had slept through it all out in the stable loft, bringing it home to them how localised the trouble had been. No-one even in the nearest houses were likely to have heard a thing. So the household adjourned upstairs, and once Ferylt and her helpers had taken Margaret back up to her bed and treated her, the Elfael departed back through the portal. With a final salute they walked off into the greensward and the mural settled back to its more normal appearance.

For the household normality took longer. But as Seithmath had predicted, Margaret slowly rallied. After a year had passed Billy and Thomas 'discovered' the body of Doctor Parker and informed the obnoxious Master Bertram, who finally allowed that Margaret should be declared a widow. Another five years passed and then Margaret married the younger son of one of the nearby farmers, who thought himself lucky to have a fine house to come to and treated everyone with kindness. Time passed and the world moved on, and all but a few old folk forgot the events of the night of Samhain in 1575.

Chapter 7

The present day

The next morning, they were just having breakfast when the phone rang. Robbie answered and Drake could only hear his periodic "yes, sir"s, and "I see sir"s from the conversation.

"No, we understand, sir," Robbie concluded. "In fact, I think we might as well take through to next Friday as holiday and make a week of it, don't you? We both have plenty of leave to take. ...Yes, sir. ...Thank you," and put the phone down.

"What?" demanded Drake, aghast. "What are you talking about? Leave? We're in the middle of an investigation!"

"No, *we* aren't! Hobson is, but we're off the case."

"Bollocks to that!" Drake exploded. "No we are *not*! Give me that bloody phone!"

But Robbie stood in front of the phone and, with more authority than Drake had hitherto heard him use, said, "Sit down!"

Drake stopped in his tracks and gave Robbie a startled look, but Robbie didn't give him time to start arguing again. Instead, he gestured Drake back to the stool which he'd just got off beside the kitchen breakfast bar.

"Sit down and listen, will you! This isn't the Met, and like it or not you're a clerical now, not the bloke in charge of the case."

Drake's expression returned to the habitual sneer he'd first arrived with. "I wouldn't have thought you'd have given up just like that. I credited you with a bit more backbone than being the Super's good little puppet."

"Shut up!" Robbie snapped forcefully. "I said listen and I meant it! You're used to working in a big city force and calling the shots at that, but now you've got to learn how to adapt to very different circumstances. So wipe that look off your face and stop being so arsey!"

He got the tea pot and poured himself another mug before coming to stand by Drake. The difference in their height was emphasised by the fact that for once Robbie was on a level with Drake now that he was sat on the tall stool. However, it did mean that for once he could look Drake straight in the eye.

"Now then, for a start the Super's a decent bloke, so don't start running him down to me! He's got the unenviable task of balancing the budget, so that means that he has to reserve the overtime for any major cases which might come up. That overtime does *not* run to paying two old gits in a cold case office to run around the neighbourhood for an oddball case over the county border!" He held up a hand to silence Drake's protest. "I know we're all one big force, but as far as he goes that's someone else's patch and someone else's departmental budget. And you're not the golden boy up here who gets what he wants by stamping his foot. Join the ranks of the ordinary coppers, Drake! We have to live with this every day."

His words seemed to hit home, and Drake visibly wilted so fast that Robbie wondered whether he'd overdone it. But it had to be done or Drake would wreck everything. He softened his tone.

"Now then. We worked through last Saturday, and put in a lot of extra hours in this week which the Super' works out as two and a half more days each. So we've got today – Friday – off for last Saturday, and then Monday through to Wednesday afternoon off for the extra hours – whether we like it or not! But before you start grumbling again just think on this. The Super's been good enough to give us the time right here and now. He could – given what a pain in the arse you've been to other bosses – have made us just work short days to get shot of the hours. That would've been no use to man nor beast, would it? But instead, he's let us take the time as full days and right now, when the investigation is still fresh and with whole days for us to have time to get things done in."

Slowly comprehension dawned on Drake's face. "So he's effectively saying that if we want to carry on in our own time he's not stopping us?"

"Bingo! Now do you get it? We can't do much with the current cases anyway. Carrie's case is still in the hands of the Oxford lads officially, and Hobson has jurisdiction over Helen as far as the force is concerned. But I left a note for the boss the last time we were in the office telling him that the house has some seriously dodgy history.

"Don't you want to know why this stuff keeps happening in this one house? Why we have centuries of disappearances going on in one place? I can't give you back the thrill of the chase you used to have in the Met, but I reckon we could go a goodly way to finding out what the hell is going on at that place in the week we have to ourselves. And you never, know, we might even find something which will have a big impact on Hobson's case."

Mollified, Drake's antagonism melted away, and he even had the good grace to apologise to Robbie for snapping at him.

"Where do we start then?" he asked Robbie.

"Well *you're* going into town and buying a flip chart and some marker pens, and anything else you think we need to set up our own little incident room in the front room. In the meantime, I'm going to drive over and fetch the paperwork from the office."

"Can you do that?" Drake was genuinely surprised that this rural Superintendent would let departmental files on something so sensitive as a child's disappearance out of the building.

"Not the current casework, no of course not," Robbie clarified. "But there's all that stuff we got on the history of Weord School from the record office, and all those copies of parish records and stuff. They're just dust collectors as far as the force is concerned, nothing to do with criminal records at all. So no-one cares what we do with things which are already in the public domain – albeit ever so obscurely. And that's the stuff we need to get to grips with, because I don't think we'll ever get to the bottom of the present until we've got a handle on the past."

By midday Robbie's front room had taken on an altogether more businesslike appearance, and the two of them were standing looking at the flip chart which Drake had set up in the one corner. On the front sheet Robbie had written brief descriptions of all the bodies they knew had emerged from the grounds of Weord so far, and the approximate dates of their deaths.

"They definitely seem to go in phases," Drake observed, thinking of what Carol had said to them earlier. "They seem to cluster together and then go for years without a thing happening – or at least as far as we can tell."

"Well then, let's get back to basics, as far as we can go," Robbie said, going to fetch a small red book off one of his shelves. "This is the 1086 Domesday Book for Herefordshire." He flicked through the index and then forward to the first entry in the ancient survey.

"Ah ha! ...Much Marcle was held by Earl Harold. To you, Mr Non-historian, that's Harold Godwinson who became King Harold and got shot in the eye at the Battle of Hastings." He paused as he quickly read on, then looked up at Drake to relay the next batch of information.

"Back then it was one pretty impressive estate. They have lands gifted to one of the Norman abbeys – no make that two abbeys! So they were doing well! A mill, woodland, connections with the Droitwich salt trade and what looks like iron mining or working. Everything that a medieval estate would need to be not only self-sufficient but turning in a nice little profit. Mmmm ...and after the 1066 Conquest it seems to have stayed in the King's hands for some time too."

Suddenly Robbie gave another "Ah ha!" and dug out one of his sheets of notes which were spread across the big desk. "Now that makes more sense of what you found out on the microfiches at the record office. Even as late as the sixteenth century the Crown must have kept some rights to land in the area, because the Kyrles purchased the estate of what is now Homme House from the Crown."

"That's the big place outside Much Marcle that does all the functions and weddings?" Drake checked.

"That's the one. Rebuilt in 1623, as we found out last week. Now the other really important house in the area is Hellens, which gets its name from its tenant in the mid-1300s – Walter de Helyon. But our place is neither of those."

"Is that unusual?" wondered Drake. "To find no records like that?"

"Not really," Robbie answered. "I'd guess that this first eleventh-century reference we have – to what eventually became a village – means that what we have here is the gradual development of the whole area from one manor – in other words a single estate – into several. I've got a book on how towns come about and it's full of stuff like that. You'd expect to see something like this in almost any part of a county with good farming land like this.

"A lot tends to change after the Black Death in the 1350s. Men who were at the top of the peasant farmers get the opportunity to get land of their own, because the population was so cut down and there was land to spare. I'd guess that this Margaret, 'daughter of Sir Timothy,' whom we find cropping up on the sixteenth century land records, was probably from a family who first got their leg up the social ladder at that time. By the time we get to this record of a building being started in 1574 they'd have had two hundred years to climb the local social ladder. All round the Teme and Wye valleys you see these glorious half-timbered farmhouses which must've been built by gentlemen farmers to show off their new wealth."

"So in itself the appearance of Weord Manor is nothing unusual," Drake summarised.

"No, not at all."

"So it's something to do with what happens next that possibly sets things in motion," mused Drake.

"I want to look at these runes which were carved on the inside of the house," Robbie said tapping at the page he'd written notes on. "Now those really are right out of the ordinary for the time! Downright bloody weird, in fact! Totally out of period and context."

"Why do it then?" Drake puzzled. "I mean if the house is supposed to be keeping up with the Tudor era

Joneses, wouldn't its builder have wanted all the latest fashion?"

"You'd think so, wouldn't you?" agreed Robbie. "All I can tell you is that it's about at this time that people start getting interested in the past all over again. You get these men we call antiquarians, who go around picking up all manner of things they think are important. Over at Hereford they start getting curious about the old Roman camp of Kenchester just up the road, for instance.

"At the time of Henry VIII, you get a chap called John Leland who goes around the whole country cataloguing all things ancient for the king, and his itinerary got published later on and is still in existence. It doesn't help us much because our place, quite aside from not even having been built in Leland's day, was hardly the sort of place he'd have bothered with anyway, because it would've been an everyday house for him. But I can only assume that whoever built Peorth, as it was called then, was one of these antiquarians."

"So in a cock-eyed sort of way he was showing off?"

"Yes, that's a good point. I think you're right. It was showing intellectual status since he couldn't compete in a physical way – with cold, hard cash – by making it fashionably bigger or fancier than his neighbours'. Let's go and see if the place will give up a few of its secrets, shall we?"

The two of them drove out to the manor, which was mercifully quiet with only a bored PC guarding the lane up to it, and the archaeologists, who were still rummaging in the woods on the far side from the house. Letting themselves in Robbie and Drake headed for the old hall, armed with flashlights and notepads. It was like nothing Drake had ever done before, but he had to admit that he was beginning to get curious in a reluctant sort of way.

For a couple of hours Robbie searched the woodwork with a flashlight. As he found each set of runes, he pointed them out to Drake who was given the job of copying them. At first Drake had protested that he hardly knew what he was looking at, but Robbie pointed out to him that he was the better one of them to do the job of tracing the markings since he was less likely to feel obliged to fill in any gaps. If all he saw was a straight line then that was what he'd copy, whereas Robbie would waste time looking for tails or crossbars which might not be there, or could just be the grain of the wood. It took all of the rest of the day, and they went back again the following day, when the weather was brighter, to make sure that they hadn't missed anything.

Having brought a flask and sandwiches this time, they sat on the stairs at midday to take a break and go over what they'd found so far. In the April sunshine the house took on a whole different character, and Robbie used the screwdriver on his penknife to undo the screw holding the window latch shut to be able to fling it open and let the fresh air in. As they sat eating in a patch of sunlight, with a gentle breeze filtering in, and the sounds of birds in the trees and the occasional bee buzzing about, it was hard to believe the house had been the site of so much misery. Even Drake seemed to be warming to the place as he gazed about him with less disdain.

"This could be a lovely family home," he even went so far as to say. "Needs a bit of working doing on it, of course, and a few more mod' con's wouldn't go amiss, but down in the south-east it'd fetch a fortune."

"These old places fetch a fortune up here too," Robbie corrected him. "It's only been the legal wrangling over who owns what from the school that's meant it's still empty and not been sold."

He sat back against the newel post of the turn in the stair and looked again at the notes. "This has really got me stumped," he confessed to Drake. "I brushed up on what Old English I have copies of, and although I would be the first to admit I'm no expert, I have to say that these look like nothing else I've ever seen."

As Robbie continued to puzzle over the markings Drake found himself starting to drowse off. It was so easy to simply relax after the tiring few days they'd had, and although he wouldn't have admitted it for the world, it had made him realise that his heart-attack had taken its toll on his stamina. It was going to take some time before he'd be able to work around the clock as he once had. So he leaned back against the wooden dado panelling and gazed up at the mural, letting his eyes droop. Then suddenly he was awake.

"Did you see that?" he demanded of Robbie.

"See what?"

Drake suddenly realised how daft it would sound to say what he thought he'd seen. "Oh nothing."

Robbie looked at him carefully. "Come on, what was it?"

Drake snorted. "Must have been dreaming, that's all."

"Why?"

"Well I could have sworn I saw something move in those bushes up on that painting."

Robbie stood up and looked carefully at the mural. "Do you know, I thought there was a figure here when I looked before. How odd! ...Well either something even stranger is happening here, or we really do need that holiday the Super' was talking about! Come on, Ric.

Let's go and have a look around the rest of the place. I'm curious to see if there are any other odd markings."

Carefully closing the window again, they went on up to the upper floor and through a newer doorway into the Georgian wing again. However, no matter how hard they looked there was no sign of any other carvings anywhere else in the house, except for the usual kind of schoolchildren's graffiti. The tables and chairs remained set out in the farmhouse incident room, but without the press of people around them, Robbie was able to point out some of its more interesting features to Drake.

"Once upon a time this would've been at the heart of the second phase of the manor," he told him. "The hall would've been where you'd show off to your neighbours. There would probably have been a big dining table, and it would've been separated from this front door hall by a fancy wooden screen instead of divided into two rooms like now."

"Not as big as the other hall," Drake observed.

"No, but much easier to keep warm!"

Robbie opened the front door and stepped out to look up at the surrounding stonework. "It's much simpler, but that was more of the style of the time. I'd say this was definitely the new front."

He led Drake back inside and straight through a back hallway to another door. With a bit of working the bolts came undone and they were able to turn the key which had been left in the lock. With some asthmatic creaking the door opened to let them out into the triangular enclosed courtyard.

"Oh yes," Robbie breathed appreciatively, then began to point out what he'd seen to Drake. "You can see that this door is much plainer than the one back down the hall. I don't think there's any doubt that this was the back door onto what must have been a nice little working farmyard. Probably had chickens scratching about in the dirt and the odd farm cat basking in the sun!"

Then he pointed to the blocked-up doorway into the old hall. "On the other hand, look at that lovely porch. Even you can see that that's high-status stuff. That's what they call it on *Time Team* and in the books – high status! It must've been quite an impressive frontage when it was built, and I was right, that chimney-breast came later because look how it disrupts the line of timbers. You wouldn't build it like that from scratch, it's too ugly for that. I'd guess that the door only got blocked up when the place was turned into a school – it looks very modern brickwork."

"Why do it then?"

"Well there's a door opposite it in the original hall too. It must've been draughty as hell in the winter with two doors for the wind to whistle through. Once the Georgian front went on, I doubt there was any need for two doors into the courtyard. Remembering that the Victorian family were hardly ever here, and would've occupied the new bit anyway, I suppose no-one could be bothered to do anything about it until the house was in use all year round."

"Makes sense."

Curiosity piqued, Robbie then led Drake back through the way they'd come, and round the outside of the stone farmhouse to look at the old manor's rear side. Neither of them had seen this hidden side until now and it came as quite a surprise. Of all the building this seemed to have been the least changed over the years. Always the servants' entrance, its function had never changed, and even as a school must have been where deliveries came to the school's kitchen. The peculiar angle of the wings was clear even to Drake now, but Robbie stood in astonished silence at the sight which greeted them.

"What is it?" Drake prodded.

"Look at it!" Robbie gasped. "Look at the wooden framework! Can you see them?"

Drake squinted at the main building, then realised that Robbie was staring at the two low level ends of the wings, and suddenly he saw them. "Bloody hell! More runes! Right in the fabric of the building!"

"Exactly!" Robbie said excitedly.

"But why here?" Drake wondered. "I mean, you were talking about these houses being showcases. So why put the work which says, 'look at what a smart arse I am' round the back where none of your nobby friends are going to see? It makes no sense!"

Robbie exhaled heavily and scratched his head. "You're absolutely right! And it's a puzzle and no mistake! One reason why they're here I could guess as being because they had to be on a single storey building. Look at the way the cross-bracers on the upper floor on the main range are clearly supporting the whole structure. These runic pieces are too erratic and detached from the main load-bearing timbers to be much help with making the place stable. But why didn't the builder want them displayed on something round the front? That lovely porch would have been an ideal place."

"Knew people would know he was up to no good," Drake muttered sardonically, not expecting Robbie to take his words seriously. But his partner gave a gasp of approval.

"By golly, you've hit the nail on the head, I reckon! Why didn't I think of it? This would have been built in the reign of Elizabeth I. That's not so far from the religious upheaval which followed Henry VIII when England broke from the Roman Catholic Church. Good grief! You wouldn't have wanted as much as a whiff of something arcane going on at that point in time. Far too dangerous!"

"Why do it at all, then?" Drake puzzled. "I mean, these runes can't have been done to show off if that was the case, can they? If they're endangering your life, you'd almost think that they would've been really hidden away – in fact not on the building at all, and certainly not outside."

"Unless it had some ritual purpose? I hate to say this when I've told Hobson that there's nothing cultish going on, but this might mean we have someone here who was trying to create some kind of bizarre ritual."

"Like what?"

"Haven't a clue! But it's the only explanation which makes any sense. Come on, we need to make copies of these too. ...Sod it, I forgot the digital camera!"

"Hang on," Drake muttered, rummaging in his pocket, and pulling out a sleek modern mobile phone. "This thing's got a camera on it." He laughed dryly. "First time I've had one of these fancy ones! My old one died months ago. I was only able to get this one after you rescued me and I saved on paying out this month's rent. Well your good turn is being repaid, Robbie!" He fiddled with it and then held it up to point it at the first set of beams. "No use for trying to copy those runes inside, unfortunately. Not enough light for it to cope with – I tried! But it should be okay outside in bright light like this."

In no time at all Drake had taken shots of the runes and any other bits of the structure which might be even vaguely rune-like. They carried on round the whole of the outside but it was clear that the outside runes were also confined to the oldest part.

"So the families who came after certainly weren't trying to continue some strange tradition," Robbie observed as they got back into the car to head for home. "Maybe they bought the place in complete innocence and it was only later, when strange things started happening that they realised there was something wrong with the place?"

"But that still doesn't explain who was taking all those children, though," Drake replied with exasperation in his voice. "Or why the name stays in an old language no-one had any good reason to know anything about!"

On the way back they stopped at the local chippy and bought cod and chips, which they sat munching in the front room filling the place with the smell of salt and vinegar. Robbie had discovered that Drake had seemingly lived on a diet of takeaways in his last few years down in London, and was now trying to convert him to a healthier eating pattern. So far Robbie had cooked every night, but conceded that he needed to give Drake something familiar every now and then. With a bottle of Badger Ale each as well it felt almost holiday-like to Robbie after a day out of the office, but Drake was clearly feeling chirpy at returning to something he saw as his working routine.

Having downloaded the pictures off Drake's phone onto Robbie's computer they sat and stared at the external runes as they ate, but the more he looked the more confused Robbie became. Once his hands were free, he went and got a couple of books to refer to, yet even they didn't help.

For the rest of the evening, he looked through book after book, until he sat back with a groan as Drake brought him a malt whisky through from the lounge, where he had taken the other files to look at.

"Any luck?"

Robbie shook his head in exasperation. "I thought at first that they'd turn out to be some runic version of the Old English riddles, or one of the psalms, or a prayer or something. But I can't find anything that these carvings look like. There's not a mention of runes as any of those things in my books either. I've even done some Internet searches on inscriptions, but aside from a collection up in Orkney there's nothing else runic which is anything like as extensive as this in Britain. I've got nothing to compare it to, Ric.

"The only bit of Old English poetry which seems to exist with any number of runes is a poem called *The Dream of the Rood*, and what was carved around the hall certainly isn't that! I don't think I'm up to this. It needs someone who's a lot more of an expert than me. I'm almost wondering whether to get in touch with a university and tell someone, because this looks like something completely new."

"Is that possible?" Drake wondered.

"Oh, it's possible," Robbie admitted. "More than possible. There's so little surviving from the Anglo-Saxon period that the vast majority of what must've been written has been lost. So although it's unlikely, yes, there is a chance that something will come to light which is totally new. Usually, it would be some old bit of vellum which got reused on another book, which would turn out to have a piece of Old English written on it. That sort of thing is most likely to turn up in the course of conservation work in a library. It's much, much less likely to happen like this because people alter houses more.

"And of course, you're also left with the question of whether it was copied correctly. After all, this house was built over five centuries after Old English began to change into Middle English – the stuff Chaucer wrote in. So you have to assume that whoever had this done was working from an old piece of writing which he may not have had a clue as to the meaning of. Especially as these things have been *carved*."

He tapped the copy he'd carefully made from Drake's notes. "The issue of copying is something I've kept falling over in all these books I've been scouring – and God knows my collection on this isn't as extensive as it needs to be! I've just reread the introduction to *Beowulf* and it's even an issue with that, because the words apparently don't quite marry up with the date the experts put on the manuscript it was found in."

"Hmmm..." Drake pondered. "You mean a bit like finding some local felon dishing out counterfeit bank notes when you know he hasn't got the brains, or the equipment, to have done the work himself?"

"More like finding him using printing plates which he's copied from someone else, but the flaws give it away that he didn't copy it from an original note himself, or even from the first copy."

"Bloody hell, that complicated?"

"Pretty much. You see, the commissioning antiquarian may have had a glimmer of knowledge of the meaning of runes, or at least have known they were Old English. But you could guarantee that the carpenter who did them didn't. And if he went wrong there's no way he could have put it right even if his boss spotted the mistake. You can't just rub out a carving! And less so again with the structural stuff. This is going to be a long process, Ric. Tomorrow I'm going to have to put a letter to every one of these runes. And then when I've done that I'm going to have to see if each word works as an Old English word..."

"...and then translate it into modern English?"

"You've got it," Robbie yawned. "But there's no way I'm starting that without a decent night's kip!"

In the morning Drake carefully copied each of the external runes out in bold marker onto the flip-chart, and then carefully blue-tacked the sheets up around the room on the bookcases and walls. For the rest of the day, they struggled to put a letter to each twig-like shape, finishing so shattered that Drake went and bought them a takeaway rather than expect Robbie to start cooking. The extent of the problem was hammering in on him, but the next day, as Robbie got down to the even tougher task of making words from them, Drake could do nothing to help other than keep Robbie fuelled with plenty of tea.

"It's gibberish," he finally declared to Drake in frustration by the time he staggered into the kitchen at the end of the afternoon, roused by the smell of Drake concocting what smelled like a curry. "I think the main problem is that the rune for an 'A' doesn't lend itself to a structural role, and 'O' isn't much better. They both have short 'V'-shaped bars which would be near impossible to do in big chunks of wood. I'll give the carpenter his due, he's tried really hard. Unfortunately, though, what he's done is put in the runic 'F' instead, and even in Old English you need vowels for rather a lot of words!"

"Can you make a guess?" Drake asked.

Robbie sighed and went to stand in the doorway, and stretched as he drank in several deep breaths of fresh air to clear his aching head. Then he took the beer Drake proffered, and with a twitch of his head indicated for Drake to follow him back to the front room. He pointed with his glass to a new sheet which he'd pinned up symbolising the work he'd done that day.

"Well, at a guess – and it really is a guess – the northern outside runes say something about a 'grymma gryre'." He pointed to the strange words he'd copied out. "Which roughly translates as 'a fierce, savage or painful'... 'horror or terror'. Might mean a horrible thing which is fierce or savage or painful, or a terrible terror. Take your pick really."

"Could it be a warning?" Drake wondered.

"Well that's how we'd read it," agreed Robbie, "but does that fit with the profile of our builder? If it's a warning why put it on the backdoor? We come back to the question we had before. Shouldn't a warning be somewhere where most people are likely to see it? I could say it was a warning from the builder if we didn't have the record of this bloke commissioning runes on the inside too, but that makes it look as though the runes outside were part of the plan from the start."

Drake thought, then threw in another suggestion. "What if it's an invitation then? For a horrible beastie or whatever it is? Our chappie knows the locals will throw a hissy-fit if they know what he's up to, and so he puts the funny stuff round the back where only the illiterates will go. No-one to spot his dastardly deed back there!"

"That would work," admitted Robbie. "Yes, I could see how that would fit." He took another look at some of the copies of the old documents and the notes he'd made. "In that light it would be more understandable why he commissioned these builders from Cornwall to come all the way up here to build the place. He was keeping all the commissioned work spread as far as possible so that no-one would talk to one another."

"What about the other side? The stuff from the opposite little wing?"

"Oh, that's no better either. I've got two very similar words ...I think! They could mean nightmare, or elf-bright or radiant, or a whole army or host. It's the same problem with the rampant 'F's! I can't tell whether it's meant to mean an elf-bright army or a radiant nightmare! Not that either makes much sense anyway."

"Better get started on those runes on the inside then," Drake said only meaning to tease, but Robbie was too tired to see the humour and insisted he wait until morning.

"It's bloody hard work for me," he told Drake, "I'm only a hobbyist at best, and it's not a job I want to start when I'm already tired. I'd probably only make a mess and have to start again."

However, come the morning he entrusted the kitchen to Drake again to make breakfast and started on the runes as soon as they got up. He plodded on for most of the morning, but by lunchtime Drake realised that Robbie had a splitting headache he was doing his best to disguise. Robbie was vaguely aware of Drake using the phone, but was too engrossed to take much notice until Drake walked back in.

"I've just phoned Williams and asked for another week's leave for both of us. I told him I felt you needed a rest, and that the excitement had been a bit much for me too. And anyway, that there wasn't much point in me coming in to the office on my own in case I made a mess of things without you. So you can put that pen down and come out to *The Bell* for a pint with me."

Robbie looked at him blearily.

"Come on," Drake insisted. "It's a lovely day out there and it's not as though those corpses are going anywhere fast!"

With relief Robbie left the inscriptions and spent the rest of the day going for a walk down by the River

Severn and then having a relaxing pint. Drake was beginning to lead him into bad ways, he thought without much rancour as another pint appeared in front of him. He normally only had a drink on weekends out, but he'd had a drink every night since Drake had moved in! No wonder Drake's heart had given out!

Drake, on the other hand, was beginning to wonder what kind of life his odd rescuer actually led when he was on his own. This was a friendly little pub and only a few minutes' walk from Robbie's house, and yet none of the locals seemed to know him. Back in London Drake could have walked into any one of half a dozen pubs near where he lived and found someone he knew to talk to. And more and more he was coming to the conclusion that, because Robbie was usually so divorced from the normal operations side of the police force, he had no mates amongst his colleagues either. Considering that Robbie was such a congenial person, Drake found it astonishing that he had so few friends.

That in turn made him wonder about why Robbie was allowed to moulder in his tiny office when he was so able. Used to being a team leader for most of his life, Drake had fallen into thinking of Robbie as his team, even if it was a team of only one. And that brought with it the old feelings of protectiveness. Drake had always stood between his men and the superiors he so often thought were both ineffective and incompetent, and not worthy of the efforts the men of the lower ranks made. Which was why he'd taken it upon himself to deal with Williams and not leave it to Robbie. Clearly the Superintendent was more than happy to allow Robbie to use up his personal leave to solve a case which wasn't even on their books in order to gain kudos with other senior figures, while never thinking what the effort would cost Robbie.

It wasn't that Drake didn't want the Helen and Suzanna Fisher cases solved – they'd haunted his life for so long that it would be wonderful to put them behind him after all this time. But he wasn't prepared to use Robbie's talents so gratuitously and with so little regard for his wellbeing. If it took longer to do it without driving Robbie into the ground, then longer was what it would have to take and to hell with Williams, for no-one appreciated the amount of effort Robbie was putting in more than Drake.

This set the pattern for the next three days, with Drake dragging Robbie out for a walk at midday and then a pint in the evening to stop him working into the small hours.

In the midst of this, however, Robbie vaguely registered sounds of someone desperately trying to start a car nearby on the second day.

"What's up?" he asked, poking his head out around the front room door as he heard Drake go out onto the drive.

"The lasses next door have got a flat battery by the sound of it," Drake called back. "Have you got any jump-leads?"

"Somewhere..."

Robbie followed Drake out and rummaged in the boot of the old Honda, while Drake went and talked to the three young female students who rented the next-door house, and who were obviously intending to head out for a picnic, scantily clad in shorts and cropped tops. As he walked over to them Robbie was baffled by the way the three young women were apparently casually flirting with Drake.

As Robbie sat in the Honda keeping the engine running, he watched Drake, leant over the engine of the other car, shirt sleeves rolled up and utterly relaxed despite two of the girls giving him a full view down their low-cut tops as they bent over too. The remaining girl suddenly laughed out loud and playfully smacked Drake's arm, but only in the lightest way. Clearly no real offence had been taken and it was no major reproof. Then they all laughed, leaving Robbie feeling strangely left out.

Between them Drake and Robbie got the girls' little Peugeot started, and then waved them off before returning to the mini incident room.

"How do you do it?" Robbie asked once they were alone again. "If I started chatting up young women like that I'd get my face slapped at the very least."

Drake grinned but shook his head. "You've got it wrong. ...Oh I'm not saying it wasn't a tonic to be bending over that engine with three lovelies giving me an eyeful down those skimpy tops! I wouldn't be human if it wasn't, and I do like women! But I'd never dream of doing anything with lasses that young. And the key thing, Robbie, is that they knew it too. There's no harm in a bit of innuendo if you keep it in check, and you know you're not causing offence.

"But the trick is knowing when to draw the line. Too many blokes I've known just plough on without realising how much they're causing upset. Anyway, I'm old enough to be their dad, and I wouldn't dream of doing anything that wasn't what their dad might do, if you follow me. And I don't mean some perv' of an old man either!

"Anyway, that pretty little dark-haired one needed a bit of cheering up. The others said Mandy's boyfriend just dumped her, so that's why they were going out, to cheer her up. I told her he was a daft bastard with no taste!"

"Was that when I heard the tall one say, 'you're in there', then?"

"Kirsty? Yeah! I told her if I was twenty years younger the lads wouldn't get a look in."

"Which was when she swatted at you?"

"Yeah...! I also said if I tried anything now with someone as fit as her it'd probably kill me, too!"

"Incredible! ...Oh! So that's why they were all laughing?"

"Oh yeah! Nothing dodgy going on, you see."

However, Robbie was too preoccupied by the puzzle he was trying to unravel to pursue the matter with Drake, and by the end of the fourth morning, Robbie thought he'd made significant progress.

"The chap who did this inside work was a really gifted carpenter," he told Drake as he chomped on one of Drake's magnum cheese and pickle butties. "Much clearer than outside, although this chap must've thought he was just doing high quality decoration. Luckily his work wasn't load-bearing."

By the evening Robbie was fairly sure he had the translation, and went for a walk in the garden to clear his head while Drake copied it up onto the flip chart so that they could look at it together. When he returned Drake was staring at the words with a cross between disbelief and disgust.

"What a bloody cockeyed thing to want written on your walls," Drake grunted. "Do you think he actually believed this bollocks? The owner, I mean, not the poor sod copying it."

"Oh, I think there's no doubt about that. You have to remember that this was written in the days when things we have a scientific explanation for were thought of as magical and coming without provocation. They really thought there were such things as witches and wizards, and that they were powerful people to cross. That was part of the Church's hold over people – that it protected them spiritually from attack by the ungodly. It wasn't just swatting up for the afterlife the way people think nowadays. It was something which could affect you right here in the physical world."

"So when it says, 'If by witches or by wizards the sign of the cross is wished to be reversed,' they really believed it?" Drake had read the first bit off the flip chart.

"Witches and wizards, yes. And I think you can take the 'sign of the cross' to mean the Christian Church. You see there was a lot of anger over corrupt priests. Many people thought things would be better once the Church broke from Rome, although not the majority I'll grant you. But within a few years there were people making a tidy penny out of the gullibility of others all over again, on top of what they could legally get – a bit like our modern Internet scams that go on! To some a return to the really old ways, without any priests to claim a tenth of everything and more, must've looked quite attractive – if rather dangerous to voice."

In silence they sat and read the whole inscription over and again.

> *If by witches or by wizards the sign of the cross is wished to be reversed, summon the enchanted ones on the old holy days. I, the rune-master, have hidden powerful runes here. A charm of victory I intone. May the sorcery spread throughout the land. I know his/its(?) power. The fiery family gave light to people, which shines in hell so that none of them will receive burial. It will consume you like burning coal within the nearby hill. The crow .... The wild ones who fled to the woods will return to fight once more. Trust to them and summon them by name.*

"It's a pity that the bit about the crow is missing," Drake sighed.

Robbie shrugged in resignation at what couldn't be changed. "I think that once upon a time that old great hall would also have had a screen, separating the hall from the stairs, because the doorway between the stair room and the hall is a later addition again. I'd guess the inscription ran all the way round and on to that bit by the stairs. I've a nasty feeling we could be missing a good third of the original, so the crow bit is only a small part of what we've lost forever. The first bit sounds like a summoning, but what the crow had to do with it we'll never know, although it may have been vital to what was expected to happen."

He sighed and rubbed his stiff neck as he grimaced in frustration. "All that work and we're still no closer to getting clarification over what was going on there. I really thought it would tell us something useful, damn it!"

His crestfallen expression elicited sympathy from Drake, who had been more impressed than he would ever have expected at the amount of effort Robbie had put into the problem. In a desperate attempt to cheer his friend up he produced his own results, not expecting them to be anything like so impressive.

"Well one bit of the puzzle I think we can put in now is who this builder was," Drake said with a mocking triumphant flourish. Robbie had been so engrossed in the translation that he hadn't really taken in what Drake was doing over the days with the rest of the papers.

"I had another look at the copies from the records in between making you endless mugs of tea, and I reckon the builder bloke we're looking for is this Doctor Parker. There's a marriage recorded late in 1574

– at Christmas actually – between him and our Margaret, which would be right for the manor. He must've been an outsider because he doesn't appear anywhere earlier, or later for that matter. God knows what happened to him because not many years later our Margaret gets married again, this time to local farmer Matthew Bury, and they have two daughters and a son, Roger.

"Roger marries a local woman called Patience in 1598 and stays local, eventually seeming to move into the manor when Matthew and Margaret are dead – Roger's youngest son is born in 1616 at which point the family is still recorded at the farm cottage, so it's after that. Now it's this Roger who builds the stone farmhouse in the 1620s. So clearly this branch of the family has no interest in runes and things because we don't get anything carved on or built into the new extension.

"Roger's older sister marries but doesn't have much luck. Husband number one dies in what I would guess is some king of farming accident because it happens right about harvest time. She remarries quite quickly but then she and her new husband get smallpox, he dies but she lives. She must've only been in her mid-twenties but she must've been badly scarred, because that seems to be the end of marriage proposals.

"The next thing we hear of her is her death alone years later – but in the farm cottage Roger vacated, not the big house – so there isn't a hint of her following some strange family tradition in the house either. The younger sister marries too, but then must've moved some distance away because she disappears from the records we saw. So I don't think we can pin the runes on any of the Burys, which is why my money is on the doctor. Mind you the records are a bit disjointed."

"Oh, consider yourself lucky we have that! Believe me, you've worked wonders to get this far," Robbie praised him, surprising Drake. "Many places lost everything in the Civil War. Most people trying to trace family trees can only get back to the very late seventeenth century with any real degree of certainty. Before that, like you, they have to make a few leaps of faith that odd records relate to one person and not three or four who just happen to have similar names.

"But well done for getting that. Did the parish records help?" Drake nodded. "I'd agree that this doctor sounds like the best candidate. ...Hang on. Does that correspond with the bills for the manor?"

They looked at the ancient inventories which had also been copied with Robbie's digital camera and were now on the computer too.

"Could be the name Parker," Drake said hopefully, enlarging the image on the screen, and Robbie agreed,

"It's as close as I suspect we'll ever get. Unfortunately, that doesn't help us much with what's going on, though, does it? It's great that we know it all begins in 1575ish with Parker, but, as we can't say what he was a doctor of, the trail rather grinds to a halt."

"Other than the fact that Margaret's family were doing rather well for themselves up until that point. I found her father, Sir Timothy, because he dies – rather too fortuitously – in May 1575!"

"Does he now!"

"Mmmm! And it gets better. The estate goes to a distant cousin, but within a few years there's a court record – in those Rolls things you got copies of – of debts needing to be paid. Then low and behold in 1583 Sir Timothy's old house goes up in flames and the new master with it! The original estate, such as it was by then, was divided up between his debtors, so it's not surprising that that one eluded us. So all that's left is Peorth Manor and nothing of the estate which it was once part of."

"Good grief! You're turning into a regular local historian!" Robbie complimented Drake, who felt well pleased at having made his own contribution to the case.

Together they rechecked the records for the seventeenth century, but things were so sparse that they could make no headway. However, the one thing that they could say was that by 1700 the house was in the hands of a totally new family. An earlier but undated bill of sale recorded the purchase of Weorth, as it was now called, by someone called Phelan from the Edwards family, making it clear that the original family had finally disappeared from view.

"I wonder what happened to them?" Robbie said thoughtfully.

Drake shrugged. "Would've thought there were plenty of disasters waiting in that world. Smallpox? Pestilence, famine, plague, war? It's like the bloody four horsemen of the apocalypse were set to ride through! Take your pick! Which one do you fancy?"

"War!" Robbie said with sudden certainty.

Drake quirked an eyebrow with sardonic humour. "Okay, oh mighty Watson-type person? And how do you know that with such authority?"

"Because of what Carol said to us, don't you remember? They found eight bodies of soldiers right there in the grounds of the house! No major battle sites round there at all. But I did check on my local history after Carol told us that, and guess what? The Scottish army of the Covenantors got themselves an evil name here in the west because of the damage they did marching through. We've got records of them around

Worcester and then moving westwards, living off the land and causing mayhem until they got to Hereford.

"That was in 1645. The local men were so worried by the constant foraging they formed an armed association. Like a kind of militia, specifically to defend their homes against all-comers, no matter which side they were on. Now eight men isn't much for a company on the move fighting battles, but it would be about right for a foraging party who ran into something they didn't expect!"

Drake grinned. "Now we're getting somewhere! So you're saying there isn't much left to argue over after the war, or maybe not many of the family still living there, and so maybe it gets rented out and eventually sold on?"

"Pretty much," Robbie agreed. Then groaned and said, "Of course you realise what we've also got here?" Drake looked suspiciously back at him. "Well you said the marriage takes place at Yule 1574. The woodwork for the house is commissioned at the previous Beltane, and this carpenter chap is hired to start the runes at Samhain. The father of our bride Margaret dies just about the following Beltane in 1575. And our assumed Covenantors turn up at around Lughnasadh in 1645. We're back to perishing pagan Sabbats again!"

Chapter 8

The Year of Our Lord 1645

Anne Holbrook stood in the yard of Peorth Manor, scattering feed for the chickens who happily scratched on the flagstones, and wished her life was as uncomplicated as theirs. The last of the grain gone, she nonetheless refrained from going back inside just yet. It was far more pleasant to stand out here in the summer sun and let the world go by without her than return to the conflicts inside. The whole world's gone mad, she thought, and then wiped a tear away at the memory of the husband she would now never see again. It might sound odd to some, but her arranged marriage to George had been very happy until their family had been torn apart by the war which currently raged across the length and breadth of England.

It seemed no time at all since she'd been a little girl coming here to this house to visit her grandmother Margaret, but Margaret had been dead over twenty years now. Yet Anne still missed her and her faithful old servant Sarah dreadfully. The two old ladies had had more time for Anne than ever her own mother had, often sitting her between them and telling her tales of days gone by. Or in Sarah's case remedies and cures which had been handed down over the generations – which was always frowned upon by her own inappropriately named mother, Patience. The trouble was that Patience was very distantly related to the Sandys of Ombersley, and as such, for some reason always thought that being forced to marry Roger Bury of Peorth, a mere farmer's son, was somewhat less than she'd deserved.

In reality Roger had been very much a gentleman farmer, having built on the prosperity his father had created. But for Patience that counted for less than having a recognised name in county society, and the hint of an ancient scandal in his mother Margaret's past was almost more than she could tolerate. As Roger's wife she wasn't of a station to socialise with the Kyrle and Helyon families of the two great local mansions, and that rankled beyond measure. It had only been her father's need for the Bury's connections which had forced her to marry.

As the Bury's only son Roger had inherited everything, but to Patience's fury he'd refused to turn his mother out into a cottage when his father died, and she'd been forced to wait years until Margaret's death to get possession of the manor house. Once she had, though, the building of the new wing had begun almost immediately and now the warm gold-coloured stone farmhouse stood at right angles to the old timber Tudor house, forming the yard which Anne now stood in. Even then Patience had not been happy, for Roger's widowed oldest sister had taken over their previous smaller house since Roger felt obliged to see to her welfare. Anne could never understand her mother's fury over that, for the younger of her brothers had only been four when they'd moved, and therefore was hardly in need of a living of his own yet.

Things were all very different now, though. The older of Anne's brothers had died early in the war at the Battle of Edgehill in October 1642 fighting for the Royalist cause. His widow, Lucy, with her youngest child Emily, had been sent to Peorth to endure

Patience's sharp tongue with no defence. In their turn Lucy's sons – barely into their teens – now fought with Prince Rupert, but who knew where at the moment. Anne's younger brother was in the army, but hadn't been heard of since the Battle of Naseby a month ago in June. Moreover, he'd shown himself to be remarkably resistant to his mother's pressure on him to marry and produce an heir, and so the manor's future once more looked uncertain.

Anne herself had never been in her mother's good books. As the oldest child, Patience had believed Anne should have been a boy, therefore limiting the number of times she would have to endure childbirth. Henrietta had followed Anne, and then Maria had been born before the two boys, to add to Patience's ire. It was hardly surprising, then, that the girls had all been married off early.

Anne's George had been a successful glover and merchant in Worcester, and they'd enjoyed a happy family life with the sunny-tempered George being unworried by the three daughters they too had had, instead of the sons Patience had kept reminding them Anne should have born. Yet even Patience had been unable to find fault with George a few years later, when Maria had died in childbirth and her feckless husband had brought their two small daughters to Anne and George before promptly disappearing off to sea. With never a word of complaint George had added the two girls to his own family. Agnes and Milly now thought of him and Anne as their parents, and would never have remembered otherwise without Patience's constant reminders of their father's irresponsibility.

Once her grandmother had died Anne had rarely come back to Peorth, choosing to avoid her mother as much as possible, but the war had changed all that.

When Worcester had been besieged it had become clear that the city was no place for a household of women, and so when George subsequently went off to fight, he'd begged Patience to take them in. Typically, Patience had assumed that George was fighting for King Charles, and the truth that George fought with Cromwell was only revealed when the fiery Milly let it slip in a furious verbal assault after Patience had cursed all Parliamentarians. For one awful night Anne had feared her mother would turn all of them out. But for once her sister Henrietta had sided with her, and Lucy had found the courage from somewhere to face up to Patience too, and so they'd stayed.

It didn't make for a comfortable household, though. Patience and Henrietta, plus Henrietta's shrewish youngest daughter Euphemia, were all vocal Royalists, with Lucy and Emily silently complicit. Along with Henrietta's younger, crippled son, Charles, and her pregnant daughter-in-law Catherine, they occupied the new wing of the manor, mourning the loss of the men on their side. Anne, plus her oldest daughter Hope, with her own two small children, Matthew and Georgie, along with Milly and Agnes – who was also pregnant and near her time – had taken over the old manor and formed a small Parliamentarian household of their own, mourning the loss of George and his brothers at Marston Moor. But even then, it was never peaceful. Ten women ranging from seventeen to seventy living under the same roof with little chance to get away from one another was a recipe for disaster; and even within the same political groups there was always someone not speaking to someone else over some minor slight.

Nor did it help that Anne was worried sick about her other daughters – the middle one living in Evesham, which had been taken by Massey from King Charles in a ferocious fight two months ago in May, and the youngest had been on the receiving end of a brutal attack by drunken soldiers when Prince Rupert sacked Birmingham in the April of 1643. Agnes and Milly made little attempt to conceal their contempt for the soldiers who'd so vilely assaulted their beloved older sister, and it had come to hair-pulling, scratching and blows between Milly and Euphemia on two occasions already.

All of which meant that somehow it was usually Anne who got caught in the middle, being forced to play peacemaker even when she didn't feel like it. So when she could find chores to do out of doors she seized them with relish. Today Milly had been dispatched to ride into the village to buy certain essential supplies. Henrietta and Euphemia were happily occupied haggling with the journeyman who'd come to purchase the fine lace weavings they'd made. Meanwhile Lucy was tying up herbs to dry in the brew-house, leaving Catherine and Agnes to sit in companionable silence stitching baby clothes. And Hope had taken Matthew, Charles, and Georgie to have riding lessons on the old pony down in the field so that Patience could be left to snooze on from her afternoon nap, thus giving everyone some breathing space.

Anne had just settled contentedly on the bench and was leaning her back against the warm bricks enjoying the calm when she heard the pounding of hooves. Before she could get up, Milly flew into sight on the only horse they possessed and leapt off.

"Mother! Mother!" she screamed, clearly in a state of extreme fright.

"Whatever is it?" Anne wondered even as she clasped the young girl to her, and the two ancient male servants came hurrying out of the barn to see what the commotion was.

"There are soldiers heading our way!" sobbed Milly.

"Which ones?" Anne demanded "Which army is coming, child? Which one?"

Neither was good news, but if it was the Parliamentarians, Anne would do her best to shield all of her family, which was more than she could guarantee Patience would do if they were Royalists. But Milly's reply froze her bones to the marrow.

"It's the Scots, Mother! It's the Covenantors who're coming!"

"Dear Lord preserve us!" Anne gasped. Of all the armies this was the worst. The Scottish army's reputation had preceded them for looting and pillaging, and leaving a trail of broken homes in their wake. "How many, Milly? How many are coming?"

But Milly could only shake her head in horror and sob. "So many, Mother, so many. ...I saw them down in the valley from off the ridge, and they were chasing two girls across a field like a pack after foxes. ...They pulled them down, Mother! I saw them go under all these men! ...I think it was Susan and Mary from the farm by the river! ...Oh, Mother, it was horrible!"

"Shush, my love, there, there," Anne soothed her even as she hurried her inside. Once in, she pushed Milly into Agnes' startled arms as she told them the news. "Quick! Get some food made up into bundles. As much as you can! And water. Put it in the hiding places! I'm going to fetch Hope and the children from the meadow. Catherine? Can you see if the journeyman is still with your mother-in-law and Euphemia? If he is, don't say anything – I don't want him thinking we're easy pickings and telling someone to save his own skin – but if he's gone tell them and Lucy we're all in great danger."

And with that she hoisted up her skirts and ran out of the door. Mercifully, Hope was already leading the children back with Charles on the pony, and so carrying a child each, Hope and Anne ran back to the house. For once even Henrietta had no time for Patience's I-told-you-soes, and they left the old woman muttering darkly to herself as they hurried to prepare for the coming storm.

"What are we going to do?" Henrietta asked Anne as they bundled up some of the children's clothes.

"We have to hide the young ones," Anne replied. "You and I might take a beating, but they're unlikely to rape us as readily as they will Milly, Emily and Euphemia," then shivered at the thought as she added, "and their condition may not save Agnes or Catherine. And we must hide Charles."

"Why him? My boy's done nothing wrong!"

"Because he's crippled and those religious fanatics will see him as marked by the devil!" Anne shocked her sister by saying. "Even their own side fear these men! They're filled with a fervour and hate of anything that they see in their warped way as being Catholic and therefore ungodly. They'd go further than any other group towards changing the Church and woe betide anyone foolish enough to get in their way. This is the worst possible fate to befall us!" Then she looked at her sister and stepped closer to hug her. "Oh Henrietta! What has this war done to us? I love you, you know that don't you? We might have our differences but I would be heartbroken if anything happened to you."

"I know," Henrietta choked through tears of her own. "I'm so sorry Anne. So sorry for all the dreadful things I've said. I've never told you this before, but I envied you George. I wouldn't be at all sorry if my Edward never came back from the war. He's a hard man and hard to live with. He told me outright when Maria died that he wouldn't have what he called her bastards under his roof. And then I looked round and there was your George hugging them and playing with them, with never a word about two more mouths to feed – and I know you had less money to live on than us. I'm so sorry he's gone, Anne. When this is all over – if we all survive – I promise I'll help you get your home back, I promise!"

For a moment they held one another close until Euphemia came in and gave a startled and rather angry gasp.

"What are you...!"

"...Not a word, my girl!" her mother cut her off. "There's no time for petty squabbles now. We're all in real danger. Never mind what your grandmother says from now on! If I'm not about you do as your Aunt Anne tells you, is that clear?"

Too stunned to argue, Euphemia nodded, and the word was passed around the household, although no-one bothered trying to tell Patience since they knew it would be a waste of time. Within a couple of hours, they'd cleared out the cupboard which lay under the staircase in the old hall, and had put cushions, blankets, and emergency supplies in it for the three boys. Some dusty old brooms and lumber were left just inside the door in case someone got curious, but there was room for the three youngsters to slip in and hide at the lower end where it turned a right-angle under the lower flight.

It was more of a problem deciding where to put the girls. In the end they decided that Catherine and Agnes would have to stay with the older women since they were too bulky to squeeze into hiding places and too pregnant to hope to run anywhere. Euphemia would take Emily and hide in the roof space on the first floor of the north wing of the old manor, while Hope and Milly would do the same in the south. Anne was reluctant to put anyone in the main roof in case the soldiers decided to burn the place down and they became trapped by fire. At least the two wings gave access onto the single storey roofs, which would give the girls an escape route if fire was a threat.

After that it was simply a case of waiting. Night came with no sign of trouble, but with the dawn they heard the sound of the soldiers' approach long before they came into view. The boys were hurried to their den and the girls to the lofts leaving Anne, Henrietta, and Lucy to comfort the two pregnant girls, while Patience stamped about brandishing her walking stick and threatening violence to any man who tried to force himself on her. Within the hour the front door was smashed open and a grim-faced officer barged his way in with a bunch of thugs at his heels.

"A hoose full 'a wumen!" he declared with suspicion. "Wur are yer men?"

"Off fighting with General Waller," Anne replied quickly, before anyone else could say anything. She'd picked Waller because the Parliamentarian general had famously been active around Hereford and then Worcester less than a year ago. If these ruffians thought they were in a Parliamentarian household, and with the men not that far afield, they might think twice about committing the worst excesses.

"Waller, eh?" the leader sniffed, clearly not that impressed with an officer less radical than his own.

He almost seemed to believe her, though, and seemed unwilling to push his luck too hard in case the men were nearby. He was turning to gesture his men outside when Patience chose her moment to put in an appearance. Using language Anne would never have believed Patience had ever heard, let alone knew how to use, the old lady flew at the leader brandishing her blackthorn walking stick like a cudgel. In that moment the mood changed and Anne saw disaster overtaking them.

"A witch!" one of the men called out, and who could blame him? Dressed from head to toe in the black widow's weeds she'd refused to ever leave off, face a mask of hatred, and gibbering no doubt incomprehensibly to the Scots, Patience fulfilled every one of their preconceptions. The cry was taken up with far too much relish and the old lady was seized and dragged towards the door.

"A burning! A burning!" was the next cry, and that was the end of trying to save the family.

It was too much for Henrietta, who might never have loved her acerbic mother much, but nonetheless held many of the same views. With a furious scream, Anne's sister launched herself at the men just as some of them turned back towards them, evidently thinking that where there was one witch there was sure to be more. As they grabbed hold of Henrietta, who managed to claw the eyes of one of them before her hands were pinned, Lucy began to step forward almost as if in a dream, while Catherine seized a large vase off the mantle-shelf and hurled the stoneware with all her might at the head of an approaching sergeant. Now noticing the pretty young girl, several more men turned her way, giving Anne what she feared would be her only chance. She seized Agnes' hand and dragged her backwards towards the little servant's door to the left of the fireplace, opposite from the door leading out into the hall where the main scuffles were taking place. Even then one of the men spotted them and was heading their way when the small door crashed open in their faces and Euphemia charged through it with a pitchfork in her hands. Her momentum and advantage of surprise carried her forward and she skewered the man on the tines of the fork, his scream of pain alerting others.

Knowing that nothing she did would save the others now, Anne thrust Agnes through the door and slammed it shut, sure that no-one would hear the sound above the din. For once she had cause to thank Patience's pretensions of grandeur, for she'd ensured that the doors to the old house opened into it and not into the new wing to spoil the lines of the rooms. On the wall to the right of the door there was a big old oak chest, and Anne now ran to the other side of it and began shoving it towards the door.

Suddenly she had help as Nancy, the cook, came running through from the kitchens brandishing a rolling pin and saw what she was trying to do. Mercifully the floors in the old house were well polished oak and so the chest moved more easily than it might have on the carpets of the new wing. It was also lucky that the door was in the corner of the room, so that once the chest was against it anyone pushing at the door would only be imbedding the chest harder into the corner of the room.

Another door into the new wing lay at the other end of the same wall, in what had once been the north parlour of the old house, but luckily it led into the room at the back of the new wing behind the one they'd just fled from. Fumbling with the housekeeper's keys at her belt, Anne found the key to that door and swiftly locked it. It wouldn't hold forever, but that door had always tended to stick because Patience had skimped on the quality of wood for it, and with the solid iron lock turned it would certainly hold back the evil tide for a while.

"What about Harry and Walter?" Anne asked

Nancy, trying to brush away the tears that wouldn't stop.

However Nancy had no idea of what had happened to the two old serving-men and they could only assume the worst. With Nancy helping her, Anne half carried Agnes at the run into the old great hall and made for the huge chimney in the south-west corner. When Matthew Bury (after whom Hope's son was named) had married Margaret, his first alteration to the house had been to put an appropriately sized fireplace into the bleak hall. Less bothered by pretensions than the house's builder, he hadn't worried in the least that putting a huge brick chimney in next to the front door would spoil the lines of the house.

Matthew's mother had been a Catholic in the days when, as now, it was dangerous to be one. Ever the practical and cautious man he'd had two hiding places built into the new brickwork, just in case they might need to hide someone again, and Anne now blessed his foresight. Clearly Agnes couldn't run far in her state, and thank heavens it was summer and the fire not lit, for the first hidey-hole was reached by going up steps in the brickwork from the hearth. Matthew's builder had cleverly made it look like decoration by putting the same pattern of protruding bricks on both sides, but only the left-hand side went up to a concealed chamber.

With both of them pushing her, Anne and Nancy got Agnes up and heard her call back,

"I'm in!"

"Close the trapdoor!" Anne hissed urgently, again thanking her own cautious nature which had had Walter up there not four weeks ago easing the hinges and bolts, and then covering the oil and wood with soot again to make them invisible once the trap door was lowered back down. Agnes stood on a brick ledge and was then able to lower the trapdoor back down, giving her a space the depth of the large chimney breast and if anything, a little wider where she could sit down. A few sections of mortar had been left out of the external wall of the hiding place to let air and a tiny amount of light in, so there was no danger of Agnes suffocating.

As soon as she was safe, Anne turned Nancy towards the stairs. They were the only way up to the upper floor of the old house, but on that floor, there was access to another hidey-hole in the chimney breast from one of the bedrooms. As the hall's new chimney had covered the original window, there was a new little window alcove which sat on the brickwork of the lower chimney. The wood which lined the alcove's walls had a moveable panel and that was where Anne was now heading. It would be a squeeze for her and Nancy, and they would have to remain standing with no room to turn, but at least there was a gap the size of a finger in the floor going down into the ceiling of the hole where Agnes now hid. The three of them would be in contact, if ever so quietly, and Agnes wouldn't feel abandoned.

Yet even now fate took a turn for the worse. As Anne and Nancy got to the bottom of the stairs, and Anne urgently hissed to the three hidden boys to stay hidden no matter what, Nancy tugged at her sleeve and pointed upwards. There at the top of the stairs were Hope and Milly frantically trying to drag a catatonic Emily back with them. As Anne and Nancy rushed up to them Hope whispered at them,

"We heard Euphemia go screaming down! Milly crept out and saw Emily just standing on the middle landing. We can't get any sense out of her! She just cries or keeps saying the paintings talked at her!"

Anne felt like she'd had the wind taken out of her. All of a sudden, the memories rushed back of things

Grandmother Margaret and Sarah had told her. Of why the painting on the stairs should never be covered and that if danger truly threatened the house she should go to the landing beneath the big window and invite someone to come and help. At the time it had seemed like fairy stories to a little girl, but with hindsight Anne realised how insistent they'd been that she remember their words. However, just now there was no time.

"You two get back in the roof!" Anne said firmly. "We'll deal with Emily!"

Without regret Anne slapped Emily hard across the face. It might seem brutal but it did the trick in jolting Emily out of her frozen state. As Hope and Milly ran to the right and shinned up onto the heavy old washstand to climb into the roof hatch, Anne and Nancy dragged Emily left into the corridor which connected the bedrooms and into the first one.

"We'll have to use the north roof now," Anne told Nancy. "We'll never get three of us into this one and she's going to collapse the moment we let go of her."

"Will she scream?" wondered Nancy.

Anne looked at Emily's blank eyes and shook her head. "I think if she was going to start screaming she'd be doing it by now." And with that they pushed the girl into the upper chimney hiding place and threw a bag of food in after her. Calling down to Agnes, Anne told her that Emily was now above her and not to worry if she didn't answer, then closed the door. Both girls now had food, water and air and were safe as long as they stayed quiet.

Running into the north wing Anne and Nancy suddenly realised that a red glow was flickering through the windows.

"What's that?" Nancy asked, and before Anne could stop her, she had stepped to the window.

Grabbing Nancy's apron strings Anne hauled her back out of sight, then saw how ashen Nancy's face had gone. Fearing the worst Anne slid along the wall and peeked out through the side of the window. There, on what had once been the garden, one huge bonfire had already been lit and another was being prepared. She felt her stomach lurch and ran to the other window and vomited out of it. The broken bodies of Lucy, Euphemia, and Catherine lay spread-eagled on what remained of the lawn, men still clearly taking their turn at the younger women. That no doubt accounted for Emily's shocked state if she had seen the raping taking place.

But what left Anne shaking like a leaf was the glimpse she'd caught of the stake in the middle of the bonfire to which two very female shapes were tied. She hadn't needed more than that glance to know the fate of Patience and Henrietta, and her heart felt as if it had been torn in two. It was Nancy who took charge now, pulling and pushing Anne into the loft space to hide among the family's unwanted belongings, and then hugging Anne tight as they hid in the darkness waiting for even worse to happen.

For what felt like an eternity they huddled together, straining their ears for every sound. As Anne expected, the soldiers eventually found their way upstairs, and they had to endure the terror of waiting to see if their escape route was spotted. Their luck held in that Anne had forgotten to close the window, which looked out into the courtyard, after she'd been sick. It wasn't a long drop down to the ground, because either Harry or Walter had abandoned the gardener's handcart beneath it. The soldiers therefore assumed that the women had left the house that way, hidden from their sight by the strangely shaped wings of the old manor. Instead, they took their revenge on the home of their escaped prey by dragging the mattresses off for their own use, and the two women heard one of the men urinating in the room.

"Pigs!" Anne heard Nancy whisper ever so softly, but with great venom.

Having given the soldiers time to get back downstairs Anne then risked working at a slightly loose tile on the roof until they could see a glimmer of light by which they would be able to tell when night had fallen. When the dreadful day eventually dragged to a close and the house fell silent, the two women dared to have a hushed conversation. Their first thought was for the others, but both agreed with relief that they hadn't heard anything which would make them believe that anyone else had been found.

"What are we going to do?" Nancy asked. "Do we risk making a run for it?"

"How can we?" Anne whispered back. "Agnes can hardly be got out, for I'm sure the men must be in the great hall, and that means we can't get to the boys either. I could never leave without them, and I doubt Hope would either. We'll just have to sit tight and hope that those monsters move on tomorrow. It's not as though we have much for them to plunder."

For a while they settled back into silence until Nancy asked,

"What day is it?"

"What?"

"The date I mean."

"It's the last day of July," a puzzled Anne told her.

"Isn't that the eve of the old feast of Lughnasadh?"

"I believe so. Why?"

Nancy sighed. "Just my mind playing tricks on me. I was remembering my grandma Rachel telling me that the first of August was the feast of some old god of fire, or something. It just seemed too horribly true after what's happened today, that's all. It was hearing those monsters singing their hymns at the end of the day after they'd committed such evil that set my mind jangling."

For a moment Anne was too stunned to speak as more of what Margaret and Sarah had told her seeped back into her consciousness.

"Tonight!" she whispered back urgently. "We must do it tonight!"

"What?"

"Didn't old Rachel tell you anything about calling for help here in the manor if we were ever in great danger?"

"Dear Lord above!" Nancy gasped as Anne's words jogged her own memory. "But can we do it? I mean they were ...well, they were witches, weren't they. And I thought Grandma Rachel said something about needing five women. Something about the number five being sacred to the fairies?"

"Well we can sneak out and see if Hope and Milly are all right. That would give four of us of direct descent from Margaret and Rachel. I'm afraid that might have to do. Agnes would help but we can't get to her, and Emily's too fragile. She'd be more of a hindrance than a help. We'll be taking a big risk as it is, because we've got to get to the turn in the stairs, and that's going to take us horribly close to the soldiers."

"I don't think we have much choice but to risk it," Nancy admitted. "If it was just grownups hiding, we could hold on for a bit longer. But those boys are likely to start getting fidgety, and Mistress Milly isn't exactly a patient soul."

"Better do the best we can, then," Anne agreed and they edged to the ceiling hatch.

When they slithered down into the room, the destruction almost made them turn back. It was as though a pack of wild animals had found their way inside, and the stench from defecation was already beginning to rise. With their hearts in their mouths, they crept into the corridor. At each of the next two doors they listened carefully, but there seemed to be no sounds from inside. At the door to the room where Emily was hidden, they paused and looked at one another. Should they go and see if she was all right or not?

Both paused and then shook their heads at the same time, clearly thinking the same – that if they showed their faces, Emily might start crying and talking at them without thought for who could hear. Better to leave her where she was for now. Creeping onwards to the top of the stairs they paused and listened. Now they could hear the sounds of men snoring and one of them muttering in his sleep. Whatever he was saying sounded like a chant of some sort but in very old-fashioned English, which was why they were sure he wasn't talking to someone else.

However, looking down the stairwell they could see that the old mural was beginning to shimmer in an odd way in the moonlight.

"You were right," Anne mouthed silently to Nancy, who nodded.

"You go and get the girls and I'll stand guard," she mouthed back.

With a returned nod, Anne crept on into the south wing, and after some muted rustling returned with Hope and Milly, both of whom looked terrified but not ready to panic just yet. Together the foursome began the descent down the upper flight of stairs, silent and fearful as mice, hugging the wall until they reached the midway window. Anne gestured them to hold hands in a circle, and then with as much courage as she could summon risked speaking aloud, even if it was little above a whisper.

"Lord and Lady, help us please in our hour of need. Help us please! We're inviting you in. Help us or we all may die at the hands of these wicked men. Come to us here, please!"

From below there came a sound of movement, and they cowered back in terror only to see the small, white face of Matthew looking up at them.

"Mother?"

His little voice was hardly loud, but it seemed to echo in the darkness, and almost instantly they heard a heavy movement from behind the wooden panel which separated the stairwell from the great hall.

"Well, well, what have we caught! A little royal chicken!" a nasty voice said in the darkness, and they saw the bulky form of a soldier rising to his feet.

Yet before any of the women could respond another voice spoke, but this time with a strange lilt and great authority.

"Leave the child!"

"Who says?" the soldier sneered, coming into a pool of moonlight beside Matthew and leering up, clearly expecting to see another of the family. The women barely registered the shock which swept across his face before they felt someone move past them, and they saw a tall, lithe, mailed figure with braided dark hair carrying a sword.

"Who're you?" the soldier demanded fearfully, then took a deep breath, clearly going to call for help. The words never got out, for there was a thrumming noise and then an arrow appeared in his throat.

"Vermin!" Again from behind them, a disgusted female voice spoke.

The women turned to see an equally dark and elegant woman lowering a longbow, but stringing another arrow in readiness.

"Who are you?" Milly's tremulous voice repeated the question.

"I am Ferylt, Lady of the Elfael, and this is my lord, Elfan." The lady stepped to one side, and twenty or more tall and rather dangerous looking figures walked silently past her and her lord down to the floor.

Elfan himself gently passed Matthew and then Georgie up to others of his company, before lifting little Charles up and carrying the crippled boy upstairs to the landing when his cramped limbs wouldn't work. Another of their people took Charles off him and took him into the mural along with the other two boys.

"They'll be safer there," Ferylt told the frightened women.

"Milly, go with them," Anne ordered.

Milly looked set to protest but Anne forestalled her by saying, "they need an older one of us with them so they won't be frightened. Take care of your little nephews!" Then she realised she hadn't asked this strange woman if that was permitted, but saw that Ferylt was smiling her assent.

Elfan was already going back downstairs as he said, "Leave this to us now. There are things at work here which you know nothing of."

"Is this to do with what happened to Grandmother Margaret?" Anne asked.

He nodded gravely. "Yes. The evil one we repelled then has been gaining in strength again over the years. We made a great mistake back then. We should have washed the blood of the fallen out of the house there and then. Instead, we left the blood of those whom the evil one summoned to fight with him, and that meant he never lost his grip on the house. It pervades it, and these men were ripe for his picking.

"They must have been drawn to this house like flies to a midden! Fennag's influence will be stronger at the time of the old feast days, and although he could not manifest himself yet he could have lured the wicked this way. But blood has now been shed here again and on a potent night, and that has loosened the boundaries and fed his power even more. Enough to invade one of the weaker-minded men as he sleeps and get him to chant the spell he needs."

With no time for further explanation, he hurried to the head of his people, for there were sounds of the soldiers stirring and calling out to one another. Like a spark triggering a cannon's fire, the house suddenly erupted once more into violence.

The four women stayed huddled together on the landing, too scared to move. Elfan led his men into the dark hall and for the first exchange of blades the Elfael had a clear advantage with their sharper sight in the dark. However, the tide changed the first time one of the Covenantors fired a pistol. The Elfael had no experience of firearms, and the explosive percussion and the sight of one of their number falling when no blade had touched him was stunning. For a moment they froze and, in that instant, the Covenantors saw that they had an opponent they might yet defeat. The Scots were hardened soldiers to a man and had no scruples about fighting dirty, turning on the Elfael with a savage fury and slaughtering three before they had a chance to recover.

However, as several Elfael were forced backwards through the screen archway into the stair-hall, they came into range of Ferylt and her archers who lined the stairs. Those Covenantors were instantly slain with multiple arrow wounds, and Elfan saw a way to reverse his misfortunes. Calling out in his own language, he ordered certain of the warriors by name to fall back as they came close to the heavy oak screen which divided the main hall from the stairs. Twice more they managed to lure the soldiers into the waiting fire of Ferylt's archers, and soon eight Covenantors lay dead at the foot of the stairs covered with arrows. Yet their leader finally realised what had happened and bellowed an order to his men to avoid the stairs.

The Covenantors now fell back and relied on their firearms, and Elfael might well then have been defeated had it not been for the appearance of Feannag. It had taken possession of a soldier sleeping on the floor in the middle of where Parker had drawn the original charm, choosing him out of the others around him by the blood of Patience, Lucy and Catherine which stained his clothes. The front of his breeches was still stiff with the blood from where he'd raped the haemorrhaging Catherine, and the blood of her unborn child had only served to strengthen the evil bond.

As he had slept the otherworldly monster had attached itself to him and now chose to use him as its gateway into the world. Yet the act now backfired on the beast. The religiously fanatical Covenantors saw the black crow-shape of Feannag appearing out of their somnambulant fellow and assumed that it was the doing of the witches they'd lately burned at the stake. With cries of horror, they turned their pistols onto him, and began chanting prayers as they retreated back towards the new wing.

The iron pistol balls killed the soldier and broke the bond between Feannag and its host. As Elfan and his warriors attacked the Covenantors with renewed ferocity, having realised that these dire new weapons nonetheless took time to reload, Ferylt's archers stepped into the hall and began firing at Feannag. The scale-feathered, hooded crow was pressed back until it finally came to the great fireplace. Yet something changed even as its scaled wings were impaled on the brickwork by the Elfael's arrows. Instead of dissipating into the air as it had before, it gave what sounded awfully like a triumphant caw and appeared to meld into the brickwork leaving only a black stain on the surface.

"What happened?" one of the archers cried out in dismay.

Ferylt didn't answer but instead edged towards the fireplace, arrow nocked in the bow and every sense alert. The others followed her, fanned out and prepared for Feannag to appear at any second.

"What's wrong?" demanded Elfan as he and the warriors reappeared, having seen the last of the Covenantors running down the hill as fast as their legs could carry them.

"Feannag," Ferylt answered not letting her eyes off the chimney breast for a moment. "It seemed to melt into this wall."

Elfan strode to her side and the Elfael leaders examined the chimney breast.

"Sweet Goddess!" Ferylt suddenly exclaimed. "There's blood dripping from above in this cavity!"

"Noooo!" Anne's scream came from behind them, the four women having ventured into the hall as the sound of fighting had stopped. "Agnes!" she screamed. "Oh dear Lord, no! Agnes! Oh my darling girl! Agnes!"

The Elfael stepped back as she and Nancy ran to the fireplace and into the grate and began pushing on the trapdoor into the hiding place.

"Here Mother!" Hope's voice came from behind them holding out a lighted candle in a holder.

Bringing the candle in to light the darkness of the chimney, the three of them could see that there was a slow but regular drip of blood coming through the wooden floor, yet there was no sign of any pistol having been fired at the wood or of any attack with a blade.

"Upstairs!" the distraught Anne cried, and turned on her heels to race up the stairs and into the bedroom where they had hidden Emily. The hidey-hole's panel stood ajar and to their increasing distress there was no sign of Emily. Anne fell to her knees and pressed her face to the floor of the compartment, almost burning her hair as she held the candle down to light the chamber beneath. With a howl of grief, she fell back and began a heart-wrenching keening. Milly threw her arms around her mother's neck and began hugging her for all she was worth, while Hope looked to Nancy. The cook only had to look at Hope's face to know that she didn't dare look to see what had finally broken her mother, and so she stepped forward on shaking legs to retrieve the candle and go to the hole. However Ferylt took pity on her and stepped into her path.

"Let me," she said gently and knelt down on the floor. With her keener eyesight she needed no candle, but that made the sight no easy to behold. Through the gap in the floor, she could make out the spread legs of a woman and a new-born babe with its umbilical cord wrapped tight around its neck, and a huge puddle of blood. "Sweet Goddess protect them both!" she sighed, standing up and turning back to Hope and Nancy. "One of your family?"

"My sister," Hope replied, tears already streaming down her face. "She's dead isn't she."

"I'm so sorry," Ferylt said coming to embrace the young woman as she too began to collapse.

As Nancy caught Hope from the other side, she looked up at the taller Elfael lady. "Poor mistress Agnes was only a month off her time. She shouldn't have had all this strain. Her husband might be dead already and she lost her father only a month ago."

Even the stern Lord Elfan looked shocked as he realised that Agnes must've started giving birth in the confinement of the hiding place, and died because there was no-one there to help her. Then another thought hit him.

"That's what drew Feannag! The blood of a new-born! That's why it bonded with this place. It got its innocent sacrifice after all! The blood is in the wood and stone and now it has a permanent foothold, a door way it can use at will!"

"We must get you out of here," Ferylt told them anxiously, but Milly stepped in front of her, white as a sheet but still resolute.

"There was another girl hidden up here. My cousin Emily. She's missing."

"Spread out! Find her!" Elfan ordered instantly.

The warriors and archers paired up and ran out of the room as their leaders guided the grieving family down onto the stairs.

"We'll never be able to get her out," sobbed Hope. "Her weight is on the trapdoor. We'd need to demolish the chimney breast to get her out to bury her. Oh God! Oh sweet Mother of God! She'll not be buried on holy ground! What will happen to her soul? Her babe not christened! They'll rot in the fires of hell without their sins absolved! Oh Agnes!" The last was a hysterical howl echoed by Anne, and Ferylt began to look seriously worried.

"Your sister is in the Summerland, child," she said, bemused but trying to find some way to offer comfort. "And her little one with her. No harm will come to them there! What sort of faith do you have that would condemn innocent souls to this wicked place you speak of?"

"Mistress Anne's husband, their father, was of the Puritan turn of mind," Nancy tried to explain through her own tears. "They can be a mite severe. It isn't a path I'd choose to walk, and luckily our vicar's a bit more compassionate about the rights and wrongs of things. If he's still alive I think he might be persuaded to come up here and say what words he can when the danger's gone."

At that point one of the Elfael came to the bottom of the stairs and gestured to Elfan. He turned to the family, about to say that Emily had been found, when something in the warrior's face made him pause. Luckily Nancy had seen it too.

"Will you look after my mistress and the young ladies if I go with your lord?" she asked Ferylt, who caught on immediately and wrapped an arm around Milly too.

With Elfan offering her an arm to lean on they followed the Elfael warrior outside and round to the other side of the chimney in the yard. Without a word he pointed upwards and Nancy had to fight to choke back the scream which rose in her throat. It must've all been too much for Emily.

Maybe she'd heard Agnes' death throes and that had tipped her over the edge, but she'd climbed out of the window and up onto its tiled roof. Sitting up there straddling the chimney pot she'd used the knife they'd put in the food bag to slit her wrists. The knife lay on the yard floor undisturbed, so there was little chance of any of the soldiers having been directly involved. Instead, she was draped like a sad, lifeless doll staring up at the sky with her blood drenching the chimney bricks.

"That's what truly did it for Feannag," Elfan breathed. "Not two deaths but three! A triad! And with one of those a new-born, and on a potent Sabbat as well. What dire misfortune!"

"Can you get her down please?" Nancy pleaded as she clung to Elfan on shaking legs.

"Of course," the nearby warrior said sympathetically, and gestured to two of his companions whom Nancy now spotted already in the window. With nimble grace they slipped out and onto the roof, lowering Emily with great care into the arms of others who came to the window to receive her.

"Where would you like her buried?" Elfan asked as he supported the shaking Nancy back into the house.

"I'd say the churchyard," Nancy gulped through the flood of tears, "but one look at her and the priest will know she took her own life and won't allow it."

"What a strange world you live in," Elfan mused, unable to reconcile such a judgmental stance in the face of family grief. As they rejoined the others inside, he asked, "What will you do now?"

None of the women seemed capable of answering, too stunned to think beyond their bereavement.

"I think it would be dangerous for you to remain in the house," Ferylt said, having been joined at the portal by Seithmath.

"Yes, very much so," he agreed. "Do you have anyone whom you could stay with away from here?"

"I do," Nancy replied from behind her handkerchief, "but the family all came here because their own homes were already too dangerous for them to stay in."

Drawing her to one side Seithmath asked, "Are there any more of them left?"

Nancy struggled to order her thoughts.

"It's hard to say. Mistress Anne didn't want to say much in front of the girls after their father died last year, but we haven't heard anything from Mistress Hope's husband in a long time. So although we haven't had a direct report of his death like we did for Master George, I think we all suspect he's gone. Mistress Agnes' husband might still be alive, as might Mistress Lucy's two sons and Mistress Henrietta's oldest. But where they are is anybody's guess, and it might be years before they get back here. Poor Mistress Anne's middle daughter is missing and the youngest lost her mind. She's lost everyone except Mistress Hope here and her boys, and Mistress Milly over there. Mistress Anne's sister – that's Mistress Henrietta – had two daughters over Bristol way, but they never came back here once they were married, and the news hasn't been good from down there. Dear Lord preserve us all! All those souls gone in so short a time!"

Elfan looked down on her with kindness and sympathy. "And what of you?"

"I've got a brother who farms in an out of the way spot down by King's Caple. I doubt the war has gone near him 'cos there's no river crossing by that bend in the Wye. And my sister's safe on the other side of the river to him near Sellack, married to a shepherd."

Elfan seemed to come to a decision. "Can we ask you to go there in the morning? I will stay here with you for as long as the portal remains open, which should be until first light. Once day comes, you'll be safe from Feannag until tomorrow night, but you must be out of here by then."

"But what of Mistress Anne and the girls and their boys? I could never leave them!"

"They will come back with us. I cannot leave them unprotected in the face of such danger. I'm sorry, you will never see them again, but please take my word on this, they will be safe with us. The children will grow up away from fear and danger and the young boys' mother, her sister, and the one you call Anne will have time to heal and grieve. We will take the body of the young one who took her own life and lay her in the sanctuary in our world.

"I can do nothing for the one with the babe, but without the third body, maybe Feannag will be weakened just a little. If any of the family return you must tell them to rip that chimney down! Spread the bricks as far afield as they can! We will continue to watch as best we can. All I can hope is that if the barriers between our worlds have been weakened by Feannag we also may now be able to pass through another time without being invited – but there is no certainty in that."

Nancy stood for a long time without speaking but in the end could see that Elfan's plan was the only way the tattered remnants of the family could stay together for certain. Anne and the girls were too distraught to really understand what was happening anymore, but Elfan and Ferylt remained comforting Nancy while they were led away into the sanctuary of the Otherworld. True to his word Elfan remained to the very last moment by Nancy's side and Ferylt was only on the other side of the portal.

As light tinged the eastern sky the two of them wished her well, and stood where they could see from the mural out of the stair window. In the grey light of dawn, they saw Nancy's still sobbing figure leave the yard and head out onto the little country lane, safely out of the house at last.

The bodies of the soldiers had been buried in a mass grave to the north of the house, but Harry and Walter, who'd been found hung in the stables, were buried with reverence by the spring. The remains of the five women who'd been burned had been reverently gathered up and taken through the portal to be buried with Emily, where their grave would never be desecrated. With all doors barred from the inside, except the one locked by Nancy on her way out, the house settled into an empty, eerie, expectant silence.

Chapter 9

The present day

The following morning, at Drake's own request, Robbie checked over his interpretation of the sources for the previous days' work, since Drake was the first to admit that such historical delvings were new ground for him. Robbie was a good teacher, and quick to give encouragement and praise, so that to his great surprise Drake had found himself enjoying the challenge. He was even more pleased with himself when Robbie said he could find no fault with the work. However, Robbie did find something which Drake had missed simply because it had meant nothing to him.

"They had priests' holes built!" Robbie exclaimed suddenly, looking up from the building accounts.

"What are priests' holes?" demanded Drake.

"Places you built to hide people, essentially. There were times when it was really dangerous to be a Catholic in this country. Some families were very devoutly attached to the faith in spite of that, and had their own Catholic priest to attend to them and their close servants. There are some big houses which are riddled with the things – Harvington Hall up the road being a famous one. But what they all have in common is that these chambers were small and were built into things like the thickness of a wall, or stairwells, or between floors. Places where they weren't obvious.

"Normally you wouldn't get them being made known, but your farmer, Matthew Bury, seems to have had these built more as a precaution against bad times to come, rather than in time of need. That's why they're openly billed for by this chap who put in the big chimney... "One chimney to be bylt on the halle, and two hyden chambyres withyn yt." A good job he picked that particular bloke who went on to do the whole farmhouse for his son, so that all the documents were bundled together, or this one small record might not have survived. Mere chance, but we've got it!"

"Can we go and find it?" asked Drake just as the phone rang.

Robbie picked it up, then said, "Oh hello, Carol!"

"I've just called your office and they told me you were officially on leave. Williams balancing the budget again?"

"No fooling you! Yes, he is, but he's being decent about it."

"Well I thought you'd be interested in this, and as it's not to do with the modern cases I didn't see any reason not to tell you. The thing is, the archaeologists decided that they'd take a look round the rest of the garden. Up at the back of the whole complex they found a lovely little spring. I guess that once upon a time it would've been the water source for the house, but over the years it's been turned into more of a decorative garden feature. Around the spout area there's the usual Victorian grotto paraphernalia, but above it there's this nice little natural terrace. It's been overshadowed by the trees from the arboretum for donkey's years, so not much undergrowth, which is why the archaeologists thought they could see bumps in the ground. They got their trowels back out and guess what?"

"More bodies?"

In the background Drake groaned, but was waved to silence by Robbie as he tried to listen to Carol.

"Yes! But not buried like the others! Sylvia's quite excited and she's heading down there straight away and asked me to join her. Apparently the eight soldiers looked like they'd been just dumped in the ground. No ritual or care taken over them at all. But these! They've been carefully laid out like medieval knights on one of those tombs you see in churches, except that they have Civil War swords laid on their chests, like they're a symbol of respect or something. Do you want to come down and have a look?"

"You bet! And we might have something for you too!"

No sooner had Robbie put the phone down than he was heading for the hall and his coat. "Come on!"

"What's happened?" Drake wanted to know as he saw Robbie grab a large DIY-type measuring tape on the way out.

"They've got two more old burials of the Civil War, but they're different to the others! Carol's just given us the heads-up!"

"Way to go, Carol!"

Robbie got to the manor in record time, parking by the side of the coroner's wagon on the forecourt of the Georgian house. Taking the short cut around the side, the two of them made the short uphill climb to join Carol and Sylvia, and a rather muddy but enthusiastic young man who was introduced as Mike.

"Have a look at this," Mike said, leading them to the side of a steadily enlarging trench.

In the muddy soil a skeleton was emerging, boney fingers still clutching the sword.

"The curious thing is, he's old," Sylvia told them. She was a silver-blond, svelte lady in her late fifties, who looked more like a business woman than one of the diggers. "And I do mean old! Look at the state of those teeth! And that's severe arthritis in those twisted hands and probably more in the hips and knees. It's really bad. This poor old stick would've been hard pressed to walk far, let alone fight. So why would someone bury him with a sword he could never have used?"

"And the other old chap was in an even worse state," Mike added. "He's not lying quite flat because he had dreadful curvature of the spine, yet he's got a sword too!"

"Are they definitely Civil War?" wondered Robbie. "I mean they're not later burials where they're resting on laurels gained in their youth, or even buried with their father's swords?"

Mike's grin got even bigger. "Well Sylvia will do her stuff on them in the lab, of course, but we found two new-looking pennies without any signs of wear on each of their eyes. They each had coins in what must've been their pockets too, and guess what? Nothing beyond 1645! We're thinking that it must be to do with the war because they've been buried up here and not in the churchyard. In peacetime the local vicar would've been keeping close tabs on who'd died and when, because the church got money from the locals when they conducted burials – and you know what the Church of England is like for keeping its hand on the communal purse! So there's not much chance someone could've managed even one illicit burial, let alone two, in a small community like this.

"When we've dug around graveyards in medieval cities you sometimes get the skeletons of infants turning up, because folk wanted them on sacred ground. You see, if they died before they could be baptised, the priests wouldn't have them in the churchyard, so the families would often creep in at night and bury them in secret right up by the walls. But remember, old men like these two would've been around for a long time and folks would notice their absence. That's the big difference between them and the large numbers of kids who died at, or shortly after, birth. Their going would've been missed, and that's what makes us pretty positive these must've happened when the place was in uproar during the worst of the fighting."

"So you've got two very different styles of burial going on at the same time," Robbie agreed. "Interesting."

Before they could get into the problems of that, Sylvia was called to the second burial, whose excavation was further on and the skeleton ready to be lifted.

"Look at his neck, Sylvia!" said a girl with dyed flame-red dreadlocks and a Nirvana vest-top. "Those vertebrae!"

For a moment the skeleton disappeared behind the clustered team and then Sylvia stood up to tell Carol, Robbie, and Drake, "It seems fairly likely he was hung!"

"As in lynched?" checked Drake in his surprise, and got an emphatic nod. "So he died a violent death, and not one we expected either. Why on earth would someone hang a poor old sod like that? He couldn't have been any threat to anyone in his state! And then go to all the trouble of laying him out so neatly? But I guess that also kind of rules out the idea that he died in his dotage reliving old battles, doesn't it?"

"Certainly does," Carol agreed. "My only other guess might be that it was suicide. That was still illegal in those days and again, like the babies Mike just told you about, it would've excluded him from being buried on sacred ground."

Robbie was shaking his head even before she had finished. "No, I don't think so. You could say that if he was up here on his own. But what about our other old chap next to him? Are we really saying that they had some kind of suicide pact to go together? No, sorry Carol, but that just doesn't ring true to me, does it with you Sylvia?"

The svelte forensic archaeologist shook her head. "No, it doesn't. And of course, we have to acknowledge that there might be others up here we've yet to spot. We're going to get the geo-phys' team in here. It's a small area, so it won't take long and it's the right kind of terrain for their ground penetrating radar to work. That way we can tell if there's anybody else up here."

"Jesus! You don't think you've got another whole burial ground going on up here as well, do you?" Drake asked, aghast. "Poor old Hobson will be down there with them if you give him that kind of shock!"

"Well hopefully we haven't, but it's best to double check," Mike told him apologetically.

Leaving Sylvia to raise the two sets of bones with Carol helping, Robbie and Drake wandered down to the house with Mike, who was terribly interested in the prospect of finding a priest's hole. With his help they measured the oldest main chimney breast, collectively deciding that the wooden panels in the two relevant bedrooms warranted closer inspection. The room to the left of the chimney breast didn't appear to have enough brickwork to accommodate any spare space on closer inspection, but the one to the right appeared to have a lot to spare to the right of the small bedroom grate. Mike and Robbie carefully probed the panelling, and then Mike pressed a tiny carved Tudor rose and they heard a catch pop. Drake had been down to the car to get a crowbar and a hammer out of the boot, in case the wood needed some encouragement to give up its secret, and just got back in time for the revelation.

"Voilà!" Mike proclaimed cheerily, then went very white. "Oh fuck!"

Drake shouldered him brusquely aside even as Robbie's face fell in appalled shock, and said sternly, "Go and get Carol! Now!"

Mike disappeared at the run, suddenly thankful to get out of the room, and Robbie and Drake were left standing shoulder to shoulder looking into the grisly sight.

"Oh fuck!" Drake echoed as he saw what Mike had seen, but with far more worldly weary cynicism.

"Poor little buggers!" Robbie sighed.

In the confines of the tiny space were stacked the remains of several people, or to be more precise, children. The remains of a school uniform on the top body gave it the appearance of a dropped rag-doll, although she – for it undoubtedly was a she – had been there for some time.

"Do you reckon all these are from the same time as Suzanna disappeared?" wondered Robbie softly as he crouched down to try and distinguish which limbs belonged to which body, and how many there might be in the cramped space.

"Bloody hell, I hope not!" Drake wished fervently. "That would mean we missed other girls! I didn't think the blokes down here were that incompetent, even back then! ...Christ! How many are there in this tangle?"

Then Carol arrived with Sylvia hot on her heels and the two detectives stepped aside to give the experts some room. Pulling on fresh latex gloves, Carol bent down, and with great care began to examine what she could see lying below the top body. Sylvia peered over her shoulder, her silver-blond hair blending with Carol's brown and grey as they whispered in consultation.

"At least four?" Sylvia said as they straightened.

"At the very least," Carol said wearily. "Damn it, Robbie, I thought you were my friend! I'll be doing overtime for another week now!"

"Sorry," Robbie said so dejectedly that she stepped up to him and embraced him, although still keeping the gloves clear of him.

"No, I'm sorry, I forgot," she said. "Would you break the news to poor old Hobson? He's going to love this after everything else."

Robbie nodded and led Drake away to make the phone call, leaving the two women staring at the remains.

"What was that about?" Sylvia asked. "Forgot what?"

"Robbie and I met when I'd just started the job. I had the horrible task of doing the post-mortems on his wife and two children."

"Good God!" Sylvia gasped.

"Yes. ...It wasn't much consolation to be able to tell him that they wouldn't have felt a thing when the milk tanker which went through his house crushed them. He's a copper. He's seen too much to be fooled by platitudes. Dead kids really get to him more than most, though, as you can imagine.

"That's why he's glad to keep to the paperwork normally. Over the years we keep running into one another, and I've come to realise that he was the real thing, the total family man. He must've adored his kids and been a wonderful dad. ...Jesus! This job's a bitch sometimes! Why in God's name did it have to be Robbie who found this?"

Sylvia put a consoling arm around Carol's shoulders. "Never mind hon, I'll give you a proper hug when we get home. Why ever didn't you tell me before?"

"Well since I re-met Robbie up here it's all been very straightforward and friendly. I wouldn't go as far to say he's forgotten, but he has moved on, and he never took his grief out on me even in the beginning. Years ago he met me out one time with my previous partner down in Wales, but he's never pressured me or made any comment. ...Or made a pass at me in that macho way some male colleagues do, thinking they'll 'convert' you back to the straight side – not that I think he dates anyway.

"And he's the kind of person I could always ring up for information from files without him making it sound like I was asking him to repaint the Forth Bridge. Some of the coppers grumble like hell if you ask them to touch the old records. Not Robbie. He always asked if it was enough, and did I need any more information, or more copies?

"I honestly like working with him, Sylv'. And I've often asked for him out of choice, even when he wasn't involved in a case, because I've known he'd get me all the details not just the first thing that came to hand. He gets involved in local history groups too, so he knows how important a paper trail can be at times. He's one of the few in this job I'd call a friend."

"Hey, your mate, my mate! Not another testosterone-fuelled misogynist, then. I tell you what, I'll try to get him access to some nice sanitised historical stuff when this is over to make it up to him," Sylvia promised.

However, for the time being the bodies were a higher priority. Within the hour a mournful looking Hobson drove up with more of his team and others of Carol's, and they spent the rest of the day sorting out the grisly remains.

Somehow Robbie and Drake found it impossible to walk away until they knew the worst, and it was Drake who eventually suggested they try and find the other priest's hole.

"Better get it over and done with in one go," he said, getting up and squaring his shoulders. They'd retreated to the stairs of the old manor to get out of the forensic team's way, but had talked the probabilities over and over until they were going in circles. "In Hobson's boots I'd be even more pissed off I got this lot sorted, and then had to come back for yet more. I don't think he loves us as it is."

He'd watched Robbie's face after they'd found the children, and it had made him realise that the kindly detective was made of very different stuff to him. For himself he found it appalling that anyone could behave like that to another human being. But years in inner city stations had hardened him more than he'd realised until now. There was little that people could do to one another which would really shock him anymore. Instead, it just depressed him each time he came upon a new variation that some sick bastard had thought up on an old theme.

The one thing which could rattle him sometimes was the scale of things, as here, but nothing like what this was doing to Robbie. The man had been good enough to rescue him when he'd truly needed it, and Drake thought it was about time he repaid the compliment. He couldn't make the horror upstairs go away, but he could give Robbie something else to occupy his mind.

In the spirit of which, he kept Robbie busy making measurements in the room downstairs and checking brickwork. Finally they agreed that there was no external panel, as in the room above, which left only one place it could be.

"It has to be up inside the chimney," Robbie concluded, at least having a bit more colour in his face now, even if he was hardly his normal cheerful self.

They brought the flashlights from the car and began investigating the inside of the chimney. Being a good six-foot-two Drake had to struggle to duck under the mantle, but once inside he managed to straighten up and could see further up than Robbie.

"Nothing on the right. The decorative brickwork runs out and there's just..." there was a thump as he hit something with the crowbar, "...just bricks curving inwards."

With some grunting and struggling he wriggled around to the other side of the grate. Robbie had loaned him an old waterproof he kept in the car for emergencies, which was a good thing because it was getting covered in soot.

"Phaa!" Drake spat out soot as his face got another showering. "Jesus! Couldn't they have afforded a chimney-sweep once in a while? Tight bastards! ...Ah ha! ...This could be more like it! Those decorative bricks are actually sticking out more rather than less."

"Could they be used as steps?" Robbie quizzed him, trying to squint up from the corner of the hearth.

"For a short-arse like you, yes!" Drake quipped. "Someone like me would be struggling."

"Hey, short-arses ruled in the Middle Ages!" responded Robbie with more of his normal humour. "I would've been considered a fine figure of a man back then!"

"Well you vertically-challenged folk would've been all right up here! You could've your own little kingdom away from it all."

"I said I was short, not one of the bloody Borrowers!" Robbie protested, trying to keep clear of the little puffs of soot Drake was dislodging, since Drake had the only protective coat.

Drake gave something else a good thump and to their surprise Carol's voice floated down from up above,

"What the hell are you two up to down there?"

"Trying to find the other priest's hole," Drake called back.

"Shit! You mean there's another one?" Hobson's weary voice called back.

"...'Fraid so," Robbie joined in the conversation. "But it's interesting that we can hear you through the fireplace but not the room's floor. Since Drake's thumped some of the soot out of the way you're getting clearer all the time. Have you reached the floor yet?"

"I can see it in places," Carol called back.

"Well can you get something and give it a thump?" Robbie asked.

There was a scuffling up above and then a grunt and a thump.

"Got it!" Drake called up to her. "You must be to the right and a bit back from me." He scraped at the area above his head. "Hang on, I've got wood not brick here. What's your floor made of?"

"Wood too," Carol replied. "But I don't think you're so close that it's just one layer of wood between us. From this end there's a bit of an echo – like there's a space in between us. Must be your hole."

Drake scraped some more and then asked Robbie for the hammer which had a claw on it. Wedging it in a small crack he'd found, Drake hauled on it hard and there was a creak, a groan, and then a rumble and thump.

"God Almighty! What was that?" Carol demanded, her voice suddenly less distant. "Are you two demolishing the place?" But all she could hear was Robbie's hoots of helpless laughter, and Drake coughing and sneezing.

Running downstairs, she was greeted with the sight of Drake's legs in the hearth doing a macabre dance as he struggled with a set of bones which seemed to be fighting him even as they fell separately into the grate.

"Fucking help me you bleeding Welsh midget!" he yelled to Robbie.

Struggling to contain their mirth, Carol and Robbie helped Drake out of the fireplace, and while Robbie dusted Drake off, Carol took a look at what he'd found.

"It's all right, Hobson," she called back upstairs from within the chimney. "These remains are much older. Come on down, Sylv', these are in your territory."

With Drake now smothered from head to toe in soot the only thing Robbie could do was to take him home for a shower. However, Carol promised that she'd ring him as soon as she had the full body count.

On the way back, even Drake was able to see the funny side of what had happened, and by the time they got back to Worcester they were both giggling like schoolboys. It didn't stop him making straight for the bathroom once they got in, though, and he seemed to spend an eternity under the shower scrubbing the soot of ages out of his skin and hair. After Drake's ordeal Robbie felt obliged to make him a good dinner, and he'd got sirloin steaks defrosted and in the oven by the time Carol rang. Drake had emerged from the bathroom, very pink but clean, and so Robbie put the phone on speaker so that they could both hear what she had to say.

"This is just the preliminary findings, you understand," she began, "but this is what we've found. The top body was a girl from the school going by the uniform, as was the next one down – possibly deposited at the same time. They could be the sisters you reported going missing after Suzanna, and as we have their father Albert, it won't be hard to run DNA tests and check that. So they could be Emily and Julia Walters. They could be complete strangers, of course, but the fact that you've established that two girls of the right ages went missing, and at about the right time, means it doesn't seem overly optimistic to think we might have already identified them.

"Now since you're not officially on the case I haven't told you this if anyone asks, but Hobson's team have found more on the father! They started digging into Albert Walters' past, and it turned out that he was initially *fostered* and then *adopted* by the Walters family. So whoever the Walters family were in general, is rather by-the-by as far as this investigation is concerned. They checked them out of course, but as a family they come up squeaky clean.

"Which is more than can be said for their adopted son. Checking Albert's recorded appearances, Hobson's folks found him working in this area for a while but nothing to tie him to the school, but he does seem to have made his money from some very dodgy dealing. In fact, they can't quite figure out where it all came from, and Hobson's starting to wonder whether he blackmailed someone, because one minute he's as poor as a church mouse and the next he's loaded.

"He was also quite old to have two young teenage daughters, and Hobson's team dug deeper and have found that he was married before. The worrying thing is that now they can't find any trace of his ex and their daughter either, not to mention Emily or Julia's mum – the second Mrs Walters – who's also strangely absent from records. The grounds the first Mrs Walters gave for divorcing him were mental and physical cruelty, and she'd told neighbours that to protect her girl, she was moving far away from the area as soon as the divorce came through. The divorce appeared and she went, which is why no-one picked it up that she never arrived anywhere." Carol sighed. "But the third body is the right age and sex for it to be the oldest and third missing daughter."

"Shit!" Robbie swore. "Well at least he didn't get away scot-free."

"Oh, it gets better," Carol carried on. "Thanks to you two giving them that old background stuff, some more of the information has fallen into place. As I said, Walters was the name of the family who adopted him and whose name he took on. Now get this! His natural parents were named Claypotts!"

"Claypotts?" Robbie gasped. "As in Sidney Claypotts, the pervert who was the third male body you dug up and the school's odd-job man? The one whom we thought might have something to do with the two boys who went missing during the war? ...No, hang on, Sidney can't be implicated in this tangle if it relates to Suzanna Fisher's time at the school."

"Christ, not our Sidney's son surely?" Drake protested.

"Unlikely! Remember we found out that this deceased Albert was born in 1942," Robbie said before Carol could respond. "And don't forget we also found that murderous Sidney died early on in the War in December 1940, because his successor started at the school early in the next term. As we dug up his body here, it's unlikely he went anywhere else and then came back. So no, not a son... Not with a minimum of eighteen months difference between Sidney's death and Albert's birth. He'd have to have been one hell of a ghost to pull that one off! Maybe a nephew of his?"

"A nephew!" Carol confirmed. "Well spotted Robbie! Sidney's younger brother, Henry, was his dad. The thing is, Albert was taken off Henry and his downtrodden wisp of a wife because of abuse – which in itself is a clue to how bad it must've been, because it's rare to find that sort of thing going on back then – separating families, that is. It tended to be hushed up in upper circles of society, and accepted with weary resignation down amongst the poor.

"To have made someone sit up and take notice it must've been something pretty spectacular by our modern standards. Which probably means Albert was pretty messed up psychologically right from when he was a little kid. He might have been less bad than mad, if you follow me."

Drake sighed. "Oh Lord, I've had a couple of cracking cases like that in the past. So you mean in his warped and twisted way he might've been one of those sad sods who thought he was protecting his girls by killing them before some bloke raped them, or something equally bizarre? That kind of thing? Not exactly cold-blooded killings, because he was too out of this world to realise that what he was doing was just as bad as the nightmare going on in his head?"

It was an unexpected show of insight from Drake, reminding Robbie and Carol that there was more to him than the tough-nut facade. Of course, Robbie mentally chastised himself, Drake would've run some pretty complex cases in his time. If he wasn't up to speed on the archive side of policing, it was because he'd spent far more time at the cutting edge of things. No wonder he was struggling to find something to catch his interest in the normal run of things out here in the counties. Robbie vowed to find some more challenging cases out of the vaults when they got back to the office, but for now had to focus on Carol, who had more to tell them.

"Now because Hobson already knew Sidney had ended up here, and didn't like the coincidence of another member of the family turning up, he dug a bit deeper into the Claypotts family past, and lo-and-behold they came from this area. Following your lead, Hobson sent someone to check the census in the Record Office again and bingo! Guess what? Mr Claypotts senior – that's Sidney and Henry's dad and therefore Albert's granddad – was the gardener at Weord in the 1920s.

"They had to move out of the tied cottage they lived in on the estate when the family sold the house to become a school. It forced them to move to Birmingham, where they ended up in a real slum right in the old city centre that's since been demolished, and then they moved up to Liverpool to some place not much better. But Sidney and Henry were both born and first went to school themselves down here, and may even have come into the big house if their mum did some housework for the big family."

"Damn, that's why Claypotts sounded familiar," Drake groaned. "I must've seen it while I was trawling the census records while Robbie was doing the older stuff. I just saw so many names, it didn't connect where I'd seen it when we got to the more modern stuff about the school, and Sidney came up."

"Well at least it's all starting to make a bit more sense now," Robbie consoled him. "What about any others? Back at the house you said there were at least four bodies."

"Turned out to be six actually. Two more little boys possibly from the War period by the remains of the shoes and clothing, and then beneath them another little boy. I did wonder whether Sidney and Henry learned their nasty ways from their dad given that both of them turned out bad.

"Unfortunately, it then occurred to me that the gardener would hardly be likely to have access to the rooms upstairs, so neither of them would be likely to know about the priest's holes. That means that, while we can lay the deaths of the boys we found in the garden beside Sidney at his door, it's not that easy to make a case for him or his brother Henry coming along and killing the three boys we've just found. I mean, why would either of them have left the children's bodies upstairs – where they should've assumed the smell of decomposition would alert someone – when they could bury them outside in the wood?"

"I doubt any of the Claypotts clan would've got further than the kitchen door," Robbie confirmed. "Even Sidney was more of the school grounds-man rather than an indoor handyman. Oh ...Hang on a minute."

Drake had gone back to the photocopies which had come with them from Robbie's office while Carol was speaking, and was now gesturing frantically at Robbie. He hurried over and spoke to Carol.

"You need to let Hobson know this! I've just looked at the information again while we were speaking. Remember we said that the merry widow from the 1920s with the missing kids married the local bad lad, Gregory Smith? Well Gregory would've been born about the same time as Claypotts senior – Sidney and Henry's dad again. The village school was only tiny so it seems more than likely they went to school together.

"If *Smith* was the local kiddie-fiddler it might well have been *him* – not their dad – who started the two Claypotts brothers on the downward slope. He may have had some kind of hold over the young boys, but equally it might be worth finding out what happened to Smith's son by the merry widow. The one the family stepped in and took away after Smith vanished. If the son's done well he might be the person Albert Walters – or Albert Claypotts to be more precise – blackmailed. Threatened to bring it out that young Smith's dad was a paedophile and cause a stir, something like that. That little boy's name was Theodore, Theodore Smith."

"And the gap makes sense," Robbie added. "If you have a boy from the 1920s, then do you think that maybe Gregory Smith made an opportunist killing and hid the boy there? That would make the oldest body, chronologically, which you've just taken to the morgue one of the missing kids from the 1920s. Don't forget we have three boys from the 1920s family missing aside from the one whose death caused all the stir back then. I wonder if Smith did for another of them? But maybe the request for an exhumation of the oldest stopped him in his tracks and he had to leave the body hidden in the priest's hole instead of wherever he was planning to plant it – possibly to look like another 'accident'?

"If it took some time for people to move in to the new school, then the smell might well have already dissipated. I shudder to think what happened to the other two, but it doesn't look hopeful. Could all three be your newest inhabitants of the morgue? Are you sure two are from the Second World War period and not the 1920s too?"

"Sorry Robbie, there's no doubt. It's the clothing which clinches the dates, but the lowest child in that unholy mess could be one of your 1920s family, I'll agree."

Drake could see the wheels turning in Robbie's mind as the little detective carried on working out his thoughts with Carol. "Hmm... Alternatively, then, you could have a gap when the place is a school, until the arrival back in the area of a now grown-up and very nasty Sid in the Second World War! If as Drake's suggested, it was our first twentieth century bad-guy, Gregory Smith, who was into harming Sidney and Henry, then it makes it more likely that Sidney would've known about the hiding place from his childhood.

"Maybe Smith had even threatened Sidney with being incarcerated in there. Used it as some kind of nasty game with his victims before he had to hide a body there. So when Sidney comes back and can't resist the temptation to start his nasty ways again, he lures two kids to their death, then remembers the old hiding place. But then realises that the smell's going to start causing comment..."

"...Or simply finds that it's not so easy to bury them in the garden and is forced to use the indoor hiding place?" interrupted Drake. "Don't forget that if Sid was just the grounds-man he would've had to find excuses to get into the house, or find a time when no-one was around. Personally, I'd be looking at it from the stance that he'd tried to bury them outside and something went wrong. Maybe someone in the place had a dog which was always round the places he dug. Something which was drawing too much attention to outside.

"Or maybe, by planting the later bodies from his killing spree indoors, he was hoping to deflect attention away from himself? Let's face it, even the teachers weren't exactly a saintly lot at that school. Perhaps he knew one of them had form and thought he could shift the blame that way? Who knows. But what I would say is that all my instincts say that he used the indoors site as a last resort, rather than the bodies going in there first with the intent of moving them, because that fits with Claypotts much better."

"Oh, I'll pass that on! That's good, more loose ends getting tied up," Carol said with satisfaction. "Well at least if you found more bodies for us you've shortened the inquiry time substantially. Don't suppose you can shed any light on who the two later little boys are?"

"Not without you giving us something like a date to work on," Robbie said sadly. "There's still the missing gypsy child we told you about, of course, but beyond that it's a nightmare. Remember child mortality was far higher then than now. And you're talking about the end of the Depression in effect. Lots of families moved about desperately trying to find work. You'd have had families from the Welsh mines coming here for work, and families from here going to the cities for the same reason. Too many to choose from. That's why the records are a right tangle for that period. Families appear and are gone again by the next time anyone's taking note. It's near impossible to say which of these itinerant families was in the area at the time Sid was plying his miserable trade."

After a few further exchanges Carol rang off and Robbie and Drake were left to eat the roast dinner, which Drake attacked with gusto.

"I love it when you get to this stage and all the nasty coincidences turn out to be properly connected," he said as he dolloped more mustard onto the side of his plate. "God this beef is good! I haven't had meat like this in years!"

"Handpicked while on the hoof by our local butcher," Robbie replied with satisfaction, glad that

Drake wasn't sliding into depression at being close to going back to the cold cases just yet. He too was enjoying feeling that at least he'd done something practical to help in this case for once. Too often he found himself wishing that he could've stepped in when he saw gaps in other people's work when he reviewed files, although for most of them it was far too late by the time they crossed Robbie's desk.

"What next, then?" Drake asked, swirling his celebratory glass of Rioja with satisfaction.

Robbie took a deep breath. He had no desire to burst the bubble of Drake's good mood but one element was bothering him. "Well I don't know about you, ...but I can't help wondering about the modern bodies. ...I mean, ...if your Suzanna Fisher was killed by Albert Walters (née Claypotts) along with Walters' own daughters, that's quite one thing, isn't it. Some vigilante or outraged local took it into their heads to polish him off and dump him in the woods for his sins.

"But in that case who on earth killed Suzanna's sister Helen? We're back to your old nightmare case again. I suppose Albert might've been killed *after* he attacked Helen. Carol hasn't said exactly when he died. Or maybe whoever killed Albert had seen through him when he was there masquerading as a concerned parent, and in fact it was his assault on Helen which brought down this mystery person's retribution on him.

"But more than that, it keeps niggling at me that now, all these years on again, Carrie Lewis should die in the same spot. Did her stepfather take her there? And if so, why? That bloody house must've drawn Timothy Wiggins like a magnet, Ric, but why?

"How did he know about it? It's hardly going to be common knowledge for a scallywag from the south-east, is it? Not tucked up here in the back of beyond.

Would any of your former felons you banged up in London have a clue where this was? It's hardly on the tourist route even for locals, and he didn't seem the type to have an abiding passion for 'Georgian restorations of old farmhouses in the Welsh borders'!"

Drake gave his Rioja another thoughtful swirl. "Can you call Carol back and ask her about Albert's time of death?" he wondered.

Robbie paused for a moment, but then remembered his vow to listen to Drake's experience and picked up the phone, hitting the last caller number without saying a word. With their phone again on speaker they both heard Carol answer on the hands-free in her car. When Robbie explained why they wanted to know she was quick to see the point. Telling them to hold, they heard her pull the car over and stop and then rummage amongst paper in the briefcase, which must've been on the passenger seat beside her.

"Ah, here we are," she said after a short silence. "Albert Walters. Well given the difference in the way they were buried – him outside and his probable daughters in that priest's hole – it does make comparisons a bit harder. When did you say Walters supposedly left the school with his daughters?"

"Suzanna disappeared in late October 1990, so he *disappeared* in that December with daughters Emily and Julia, and Helen vanished in February 1992," Drake said without even having to consult his notes.

"Ah! In that case, the fact that Walters had in his pocket a 1991 pound coin, and two '91 ten-pence pieces, makes it unlikely that he died at the same time as his daughters. You could be right in thinking that he was still loitering in the area and spotted Helen."

"Wouldn't he have stood out?" wondered Drake, but Robbie and Carol both came up with the same response nearly together.

"Not with so many travellers passing through the county," Carol said as Robbie added,

"It may be that he hooked up with travellers and spent the summer away from there, only coming back when the weather turned and jobs like fruit picking dried up. Jobs where he could earn a wage without anyone taking too much notice. I know Hobson reckons he's a blackmailer, but if, as you say, he was a bit mentally unstable then money might have run through his fingers like water. On the other hand, he might have killed Emily and Julia and wanted to get away from the scene of the crime for a while. Or maybe he took the chance to move about so that whoever he was blackmailing couldn't set the police onto him so easily."

"I tell you what," Carol volunteered, "I'll ask Hobson about this, as if it's my own curiosity. I'm sure he said they'd got Walters' bank details. It'd be interesting to know whether he tapped into that money he supposedly had squirreled away during the summer of '91. It might even throw up an answer as to where he got to if there are cash machine records or credit card transactions."

They both thanked her profusely then settled back to contemplate the case again. Drake agreed that the coincidence of Carrie Lewis just turning up dead at Weord School was now too much for them to believe in the light of the house's history. However, neither of them could think of a plausible connection and they called it a night.

Come the morning they were surprised by the speed with which Carol got back to them.

"It seems as though the same thought occurred to Hobson," she told them in a hurried phone conference from her office, where they could hear her occasionally typing something into the computer even as she spoke. "He's convinced that Albert Walters did for Helen as well as his own daughters, and that he can also build a case for him killing Suzanna even if we haven't found her body yet.

"And your clue worked out! They've run Theodore Smith through the computer and he died in 1988. Hobson's getting access to his bank records even as we speak, but it looks like your guess about the connection might've been right on the mark, because his death was recorded at some important sounding house in Wokingham – not the address of a pauper! And he was on several company boards. At first glance he certainly looks the sort who could've stumped up money regularly to a blackmailer. It must've taken some time for Albert to track him down, because Hobson says Albert only came into his money around 1982 – just in time to be able to send his girls to private school."

Robbie interrupted her. "Hang on, you'd better tell Hobson, then, that Emily and Julia Walters were only registered at Weord School for two years before their disappearance. The records say – if I can read this bloody awful photocopy right – that they came from a school called Hadley Grange. Hobson might want to see if there were any complaints about peeping toms or girls going missing from there too."

"Absolutely," Drake agreed. "If Walters was into abusing and maybe abducting girls it's unlikely that he suddenly started from out of nowhere..."

"Oh fuck!" Carol's voice interrupted him unexpectedly. "Oh hell! Shit, shit, *shit*!"

"What?" Drake and Robbie chorused wondering what on earth had triggered her outburst.

"You said about Carrie Lewis? I think I've just found the connection!"

"What is it?" they demanded in unison again.

"Who!" Carol corrected them. "It's Theodore Smith! I've just been looking again at the records I've got for Carrie's stepfather because I'm typing up that report. Said Timothy Wiggins ran away from *his* foster home repeatedly, it says here, claiming that his foster-father was sodomising him and interfering with him. Because he was such a bundle of trouble no-one took the accusations seriously, especially when the social worker assigned to him wrote that he was lucky to have been given the chance to go to such pillars of the community as Mr *Theodore Smith* and his wife!"

"Fucking hell!" Drake gasped. "Truly his father's son, eh? Gregory Smith sets the Claypotts boys on the downward path, and then low and behold his son does the same to Wiggins. Christ! No wonder the coincidence seemed a bit too close for comfort."

"When was this going on?" Robbie wanted to know.

"The report on Timothy has him going into a children's home in 1986 aged fifteen and already with form." They heard her gasp and pause. "God this so fits in! He must have left Smith in '85 and alleged the abuse had been going on for years."

"So let's get this straight," Drake said, frantically scribbling notes on a pad as he spoke. "You're saying that Albert Walters starts blackmailing Theodore Smith sometime in 1982 because he gets the dosh to fork out expensive school fees for his girls. At this time Theodore is not only the son of the very dodgy Gregory who probably knocked off his step-sons in the 1920s, he's also got his own nasty little set-up going on with this lad Timothy Wiggins whom he's fostering, who finally gets out in '85. So it's a fair bet that if Walters is getting close enough to Theodore to blackmail him over the old stuff, then he's also spotted the current goings on!"

Drake steepled his fingers and stared off into the distance for a second before wondering aloud,

"Hang on, did Walters first blackmail Theodore over his father's past? Or was it his own indiscretions? ...I mean, ...I was speculating on the basis that it was all to do with Gregory Smith. ...But if Albert tracked down Theodore, and then saw him doing the same awful things to other lads as he'd had done to him as a child, then his motivation could've been very different, couldn't it? ...We shouldn't forget that Albert was an abused child himself.

"His motives for tracking down Theodore might initially have been nothing more than to get him to pay up. Perhaps because Albert blamed Gregory Smith for putting his own dad, Henry, on the path to abusing Albert himself. And at that stage Albert could've had quite a detached view of the Smiths. It would explain why at this point he was apparently the doting father to his own kids. But if somewhere along the line he witnessed Theodore doing something dreadful to young Timothy Wiggins, then that might have been what tipped the balance of his mind. Because five years down the line he's sufficiently unstable to kill his daughters, and something must have been the trigger point for the change."

"I'd say it might very possibly be both," Robbie agreed. "Walters tracked Smith down as a potential easy mark – given his social standing and him presumably not wanting any past scandal coming up and ruining the family name. Theodore Smith was hardly inconspicuous within society. He'd have been easy enough to find. But

I reckon Albert may well have seen what a chip off the old block Theodore was even if the abuse was different in detail to what he'd suffered. What if Albert approached Wiggins and offered to help him? Offered him a way to make Smith pay for both their suffering? That might be another way this strange set of connections were made."

"And another nasty thought occurs to me," Drake added. "You know when we were talking about missing kids in the War? Well you said one of them was a gypsy kid called Smith?"

"Yes," Carol was heard clicking the computer mouse, then, "William, William Smith."

"Well Smith is a common gypsy name. That makes me wonder whether our 1920s paedophile Gregory was some relative of young William's? If Gregory was a gypsy too, it would also explain some of the local outrage at the merry widow marrying him. After all it was hardly going to be acceptable in polite society to have a traveller sitting at the dinner table next to you. Hobson might want to look for a connection, because Sidney Claypotts might've been taking revenge on the next generation of Smiths for what Gregory did to him as a little lad.

"Do you see what I mean? Assume the 1920's boy from the fireplace is Gregory Smith's victim – establishing his form as a serial killer of his stepchildren if nothing else – along with the kid we have the old autopsy on for falling from the top floor. Now then, if one of the Second World War boys you have in the morgue is William *Smith*, maybe he died because twenty years later Sidney Claypotts – now back at the school – was getting back at the Smith family for what they did to him all those years ago when he himself was a child!

"...Do you follow me? Because all my instincts say that Sidney was just a nasty perv' up until he came back to his old stamping ground. An ugly and twisted molester, to be sure, but not a killer. Something tipped *him* over the edge when he came back to the old place in the same way that something tipped Albert over."

"Right," Carol declared. "I'm going to ring off and get on the phone to Hobson with all this. God, the brass are going to love you two for this! How many cases solved?"

"Hardly solved," Robbie demurred, but didn't detain her further.

They carried on sifting through the records they had in the hope that something might surface as to who was the killer of Wiggins, now that they'd connected him to the place. Both were desperate to find out what had brought Theodore Smith's victim back to his abuser's ancestral home, and had vague hopes that if they could discover that, then they might also find his killer. They were horribly aware that although most of the bodies they had discovered were very old cases indeed, whoever had killed Timothy Wiggins only weeks ago was very much in the here and now. Never mind that it might have been as a result of seeing him kill little Carrie. Most normal people would have called the police, not acted like a vigilante.

They were so engrossed that they lost track of time, and were surprised by a ring of the doorbell to find Superintendent Williams on Robbie's doorstep just after six o'clock that night. As Robbie went to the door Drake made himself scarce in the front room, dreading what might have prompted such a visit.

"Evening, sir," Robbie greeted him cordially, but fearing that somehow they had overstepped the mark in their unofficial investigation. "To what do we owe the honour? It's not like you to make house calls."

"No," Williams agreed, then caught sight of Drake through the front window. "What's he doing here?" he asked softly, somewhat surprised.

"I seem to have acquired a lodger," Robbie said turning from the window so that Drake wouldn't inadvertently read his lips. Williams' eyebrows raised quizzically, forcing Robbie to explain. "Well you did say to take care of him."

"I wasn't quite thinking of it in quite these terms," Williams remonstrated.

"No, I know you weren't, sir. But it wouldn't have done to have him dying of pneumonia on us, would it? A headline of 'decorated officer dies in Worcester doss-house' would've been as bad as the others you spoke of."

"Good God!" Williams exclaimed softly. "As bad as that? Why? How?"

"Three messy divorces and a lot of alimony is the short answer. He hasn't got two brass ha'pennies to rub together after all that lot goes out each month. That bedsit's rising damp had risen as far as it could go and was running back down the walls on the inside! I couldn't leave him there, could I?"

Williams gave him a wan smile. "No, I don't suppose *you* could, although there are others who've served with him who no doubt would!" By now Robbie was leading Williams in through the front door and the conversation changed. "Well as I have you both here," he said as Robbie gestured Drake to follow them into the lounge, "can I say how pleased I am at what you've done to help Hobson. I'm sorry it couldn't be done officially, but I'm already overspent on the piss-poor budget they expect me to keep to."

"But that's not what you're here for, is it?" Robbie probed.

"No. The information you passed on through Dr Whitmore has tied up the succession of crimes, no doubt about it. The Smiths who lived in the village were gypsies who'd settled, but the rest of the family did come through a couple of times a year and stayed to see the others. Hobson's team have still got some way to go sorting out the details, but it certainly seems like Sidney Claypotts was motivated by revenge against the Smiths for whatever it was that Gregory did to him. We'll never be able to prove it conclusively, of course, but it will do to tie the case up.

"Unfortunately, Theodore Smith and his wife had no children of their own, so we don't have any living Smiths we can compare the little boy's DNA to – which would have helped no end. Theodore was cremated, so that the end of that link. Can't do an exhumation to check, unfortunately. Mind you, we're also trying to find out if Theodore Smith actually ever had any contact with his father's family, given that he was taken in by his mother's when she was committed, but you two might have more luck there."

He cleared his throat and folded his hands in his lap – actions which set Drake's nerves instantly on edge. He'd never liked or trusted Williams, and now he was alert to what he might be expecting Robbie to do off the record, or at least out of hours when he could get something for free and not have to budget for it. Drake was all ready to put his foot down if he got the feeling Robbie was being used.

After all, Williams had set the tone by coming out here. Any insubordination would be his word against theirs, and Drake knew from past experience that other senior officers would take a dim view of Williams putting himself in such a position in the first place. He therefore braced himself for a head-to-head confrontation, as the Super' began again.

"What everyone's wondering now is whether Albert Walters, a.k.a. Claypotts, ever met young Carrie Lewis' stepfather, Timothy Wiggins, face to face? Did he tell him about Weord House? Or did Wiggins stumble on the fact that Walters was blackmailing Smith and find out for himself about the family home? We're double-checking Wiggins' details, because the way this family feud keeps swinging to and fro, we don't want to find out later that Wiggins was in some way related to the Claypotts, and that was why Theodore Smith latched on to him and abused him. It might be farfetched but better to check now."

"No, quite!" Robbie murmured, feeling it better not to tell his superior that they were one step ahead of him in thinking about those questions.

"But you didn't come all the way here just to bring us up to date, did you sir?" the very suspicious Drake questioned.

"No, I didn't. I was wondering if you have any way of working out where the two Mrs Walters might be from your old discoveries? Hobson's team's checked for death certificates and there isn't a hint of them anywhere. Muriel Walters, née Rathbone, who seems to have had to marry Walters in a hurry in 1964 – given that daughter Rita appears five months later – is well documented up until her divorce, and only disappears afterwards in 1978. Dr Whitmore has been able to say that although she hasn't yet got to the post-mortem of the girl we think is Rita, at the moment there's nothing against the theory of her having been killed in '78."

"Hang on," Robbie interrupted. "The two other daughters, Julia and Emily? By their ages they must've been born in '76 and '77! So if Albert doesn't divorce this Muriel lady until 1978, was Albert a bigamist to add to his sins?"

"You're on the right track," Williams acknowledged. "The problem Hobson's team are having is that there's no marriage certificate for the second '*Mrs*' Walters. The crafty bugger used his old marriage certificate for Muriel to satisfy the school's requirements when he registered Emily and Julia. So all we can guess at is that maybe wife number two had the same name as Muriel's second name, Elizabeth, because Emily and Julia are recorded as being the daughters of an Elizabeth Muriel Walters. As if he conveniently swapped the names around.

"Either that or the second 'wife' was as gullible as hell or scared stiff of him already. No maiden name or anything we could trace her by. More likely she never married him at all, of course!" Williams sniffed in disapproval of unmarried mothers and failed to notice Drake's deepening scowl at his pomposity. "The thing is, the first wife Muriel and daughter Rita lived in Worthing, where we have Albert on the census too in the early '70s. That's not in doubt. Meanwhile Julia and Emily's births are recorded in Liverpool, with again an Elizabeth Walters as their mother, and the only address is for a rented flat in a red-light area which got demolished in 1980, according to Liverpool council. Walters must've been travelling about a lot to keep his two families going at the same time."

"And Muriel cited cruelty not infidelity for her divorce," Robbie observed, too wrapped up in the puzzle to notice Drake's rising exasperation. "Maybe she knew nothing of his other woman and children."

"Or she did and didn't want to lose her daughter," was Drake's thought, thrown in redolent with cynicism which Williams totally misinterpreted as a comment of the woman. "By citing cruelty, she had much better grounds for denying him access. If he could produce another woman testifying what an upstanding chap he was, he could've reasonably asked for Rita to spend time with him if infidelity was the only reason."

"Good point, Drake," Williams agreed condescendingly. "So what I also wanted to know was, have you come across *anything* which would give us more of an identity for the second Mrs Walters? School records? Appearances at school fetes in the local newspaper? I know we've no body for either of them, but without even a definite name for these women we can't rule out that they're still alive somewhere.

"I don't want to issue a press release saying what we've found, and then have some woman appear out of nowhere saying it's all rubbish because she's been alive and well and living in Newcastle with her daughter for the last ten years. After all, we've only identified Julia and Emily by the fact that their DNA fits with their father. Terrifying though it sounds, there could be other daughters he bumped off meaning that it isn't Rita or Julia or Emily in there at all."

Robbie went and retrieved the school file from the front room, while Drake volunteered to make coffee to get himself out of the room and stop him from speaking his mind. But a second perusal brought nothing to light on the missing women. The second Mrs Walters never seemed to have set foot in the school, and the only note Robbie and Drake had found simply described her as an invalid and all correspondence to go via Walters himself. For all they could tell the poor woman could've been dead for years before then.

"I hate to say it," Robbie sighed, "but I doubt you'll find either of the wives from anything this investigation will throw up. I reckon they'll appear as some chance discovery. All we've done is make sure their children's DNA is on record so that they'll be identifiable when the time comes."

"Ah well, it would've been a feather in our caps if we could've solved those too," was Williams' regret, which Robbie read as a means to get the desperately needed funding it might have brought into the team. Nothing attracted financing like success. "I know they're old cases, but it does look good when you can wrap all the ends up and show that we were still on the case after all this time. I really wanted to include that in the press release I'm making tomorrow."

After a couple of pleasantries Williams left, leaving Robbie and Drake to their own devices.

"Well that was a short-lived investigation," Drake said bitterly. Robbie was puzzled as to why for some reason Williams' visit seemed to have burst the bubble of contentment he'd had earlier. "Nothing left for us to do. Hobson will get his moment of glory and we go back to the filing. God!" he spat furiously. "Does that bloody man think of nothing but his bleeding funding? That's all he wanted, you know! Us to work on our own time to tie up more cases so he looks good! Miserable tosser!"

"Fancy another cuppa?" Robbie asked, hoping to placate Drake from this new burst of cynicism, but Drake shook his head and clumped off upstairs to bed in a haze of gloom. Robbie went into the kitchen and put the kettle on, and as he was waiting for it to boil wondered what he was going to do about Drake. Clearly the former high-flying detective had revelled in being back in the game, even in a back-up role, and Robbie could foresee him sliding back into depression if he wasn't given something to take his mind off the lack of excitement. Drake obviously needed something to battle against, a challenge to take on. It was in his basic personality and at his age he was hardly likely to change, but at the same time Robbie had seen him on several occasions rubbing his chest in discomfort when he thought no-one was looking. Too much excitement was going to be the end of Drake if he wasn't careful.

Taking his tea and a couple of jammy dodger biscuits through to the front room, Robbie sat down at the desk and prayed for inspiration. His head was telling him that Ric Drake was an adult and could sort his own life out. Drake's heart-attack was as much self-inflicted as anything, and he would have to come to terms with the results of it for himself. But Robbie's kindly nature dreaded the thought of standing at Ric's funeral, at some time in the not-too-distant future and possibly as the only mourner, with the knowledge swirling around in his mind that there was something he could've done to help.

He knew that when Williams had seen Drake at the house his first thoughts had all been of adverse publicity over gay policemen. It had been written all over the Superintendent's face – even though Robbie thought they were more like some latter-day *Odd Couple*. And since there was nothing, and never would be anything, between them in the way Williams had thought, Ric was hardly his responsibility. But as a friend, Robbie couldn't help but care about what happened to his cantankerous tenant – that was in his nature just as irrevocable as Drake' thirst for action.

They had cleared up most of the modern murder mystery, and what was left would be wrangled over between the Oxford men who had Carrie's case, and Hobson who had the Wiggins case – and even that was uncertain if the Oxford case leader was the more senior of the two. Even Williams might not be able to prevent the closure of the combined cases going to Oxford when the modern-day murderer got caught. It certainly wouldn't be coming his and Drake's way, that was for certain!

He sighed and began thumbing through the files, and there in front of him was the answer. There was a far older puzzle still there waiting to be answered, and one that might take much longer to resolve. Long enough maybe for Drake to become accustomed to his fate. Tomorrow, Robbie resolved, they would begin looking at the fate of the older residents, and they could start with that bill of sale for the house from 1678.

Chapter 10

October, The Year of Our Lord 1666

Deb sat with her back to the wall – in the same spot, had she known it, where Anne used to find refuge fifteen years before – with a saucepan on her lap, shelling the last of the late fresh peas into it for the family's evening meal. It always sent a shiver down her spine to look up to the chimney on her right, even on a warm autumn day like this. Her Aunt Nancy had told her about the girl who had ended her life up there, and some days she even carried on a kind of conversation with the imagined ghost of the girl when she was out here.

It was a strange old house which somehow prompted strange behaviour, and Deb would never have pretended that she was comfortable living here. There was too much history pressing in on the place. On the other hand, for a young woman like her it was a real opportunity to work as cook, unsupervised, for a well-to-do family. Her Aunt Nancy should have been the one doing this job, but Nancy had understandably said that she would never willingly set foot in the house again.

When the war had finally ended the house had had a succession of short-term tenants, none of whom could seem to settle in the place. Then the Restoration had come six years ago, and Nancy had gone to the law courts to testify to the tragedy which had befallen the Bury family at the hands of the Covenantors. It was judged that the estate should be passed back to the family, along with other scattered properties, but the family was now in a sad state.

Lucy's two sons had perished and so the male line of the family had failed. Anne and George's youngest daughter still survived, but like Nancy had declared that nothing would persuade her to even visit the house, let alone take possession of it. Instead, she and her husband had settled for the reparations made for the loss of the family home in Worcester. Therefore the only connected male left was the son of Anne and George's middle daughter, and with there being no way of reclaiming his family home in Evesham, he had finally been declared the rightful owner of the manor.

In expectation of the family moving back, Nancy had gone so far as to move herself back to the neighbourhood to share Deb's cottage, for she'd not forgotten the message she was desperate to pass on, but Master Samuel had not appeared. Instead, he seemed content to give a young farmer and his wife a cottage in return for managing the lands attached to the manor, the house itself standing empty. Then the rumours had reached them that Master Samuel Edwards was living the high life in London, and not likely to ever be seen in the area. Nancy had been torn between relief and frustration. Relieved that no others would be living in the haunted house, but frustrated that she might never be able to see to the proper burial of the remains of Agnes and her child, still incarcerated in the priest's hole.

With a shortage of young men returning home for marrying after the war, Deb had found herself needing to earn her own living instead of having a husband to rely upon, once her parents' family had expanded so much that she needed to move out of the family home. She'd found a tiny cottage, and begun cooking the things other householders had little time to do for themselves. With fewer men than in the past around to work the land, many women shared that burden, leaving them less time in the kitchen.

She'd done well enough that she'd been glad to have Nancy arrive to share in the baking, and the making of preserves and craft items which she took to market. Most of the time Nancy was good company, so Deb found it hard to dismiss her when her talk of what went on during the war seemed to verge on the fanciful. However, for four years it had seemed as though the events would remain as just stories from the past.

Then on one fateful day in April 1665 the young farmer, Robert, had hurried down to the cottage with news. He needed to find women to work in the house, and in a hurry. Would Nancy come with him? Nancy had sadly but firmly declined, and Robert – knowing about the way the women of the manor had been wiped out before her very eyes – had understood.

But he was in a predicament. Apparently Master Samuel had a wife and two children, and moreover they were coming here with all haste. The plague had come to London and Master Samuel's wife Katherine, with their children and her cousin Jemima, were making their escape to the country. Someone would be needed to do the domestic work for them, and while Robert's wife Betty was willing to do her best about the house, cooking had never been one of her strong points. Certainly not up to the standards of the upper classes, and Mistress Katherine was apparently from a very good family. So with great reluctance Deb had come up the hill to the house, while Nancy stayed in the cottage and tried to keep up with the brisk trade for produce which they'd built up.

Mercifully Katherine had turned out to be an easy mistress to serve, and her cousin Jemima was clearly a poor relation, who'd taken on the role of governess to the children as her own way out of a congested family home. Both women seemed nothing but relieved to be free of London, and Deb soon got the impression that they were glad to have got away from Samuel too. Samuel may have done well for himself in snaring Katherine, but he'd proved a wastrel of a husband, spending her allowance more on the gambling houses and theatres than on keeping his wife and family in the necessities of life. He also appeared not to have noticed that they'd left, for not a single letter came after them.

The summer moved to its zenith and the plague followed it to new heights, so that there was no question of the family returning to the capital now. Instead the family settled into a pleasant domestic routine. In the lush and fertile valleys of this side of the River Wye there were now many fine houses, but Weorth – as it had been renamed by one of its tenants in an effort to dissociate it from the dreadful massacre at Peorth – was no longer amongst them. Rather it had slipped backwards into modest obscurity, thus saving Katherine from the unwanted attentions of local society. Deb even found herself quite enjoying the role of cook and senior house person, for Betty went home every afternoon to tend to her own family, and so Deb was the only one left with the family for most of the days and evenings.

It had been easy to get them to take up Nancy's suggestion that they live solely in the stone farmhouse and leave the Tudor house closed up. With three women and two little boys they hardly needed much room. The hall to the right of the front door scrubbed up nicely into an old-fashioned but comfortable family room; while what had once been a dining room behind it now had a range installed and became Deb's kitchen. The other two downstairs rooms on the opposite side of the hall and stairs were made into a nice parlour for Katherine at the front, and the dining table and chairs went into the smaller back one.

Upstairs there was plenty of room for Deb to have one of the first-floor rooms as her own without having to use the attic rooms. Instead, one of those became a nursery for the two boys, Orlando and Elias, where they could play without disturbing their mother too much on the wetter days. Having had a tribe of younger brothers and male cousins, Deb found that often she coped much better with the energetic youngsters than the other two women, and she frequently took the mending and other such tasks upstairs with her and watched over them to give Jemima some respite.

For over a year they lived quietly, Deb even taking it upon herself to arrange for schooling for Orlando with the local parson, and taking Elias with her into the village to Nancy on those days, where he enjoyed himself hugely. The plague had continued in London, sometimes almost disappearing only to come back again, and with no news of Samuel it was tentatively discussed as to whether he was even still alive. However, the proof of that came when the man himself appeared on their doorstep in early September 1666 with news that a great fire had swept through the capital. The town house which the family had had was no more, and Master Samuel had come to the only home he had left. Deb had never seen Katherine go so pale as when she greeted her husband. It almost made her wonder whether Samuel had beaten her in the past.

The reunion was made even more awkward because the boys had no real memory of their father, for he had taken so little notice of them and been at home so rarely as to be a virtual stranger. Moreover his deeply scarred, and now partially masked, face frightened them so much that they refused to go near him. Deb wondered at the mask, but knew so little of society that she could make no sense of it. Luckily, he seemed not to be inclined to play the affectionate father, and the boys and Jemima often took refuge in the kitchen with Deb where they all felt more comfortable.

However, after a couple of days, Katherine had come in to them on one of the days when the boys were in the village. Closing the door, she'd softly confided in the other two women that her husband wasn't the man he'd once been. Master Samuel had the pox and it was advancing at a rate! That explained his wrecked face which frightened the boys so much. His nose was already eaten away by the disease, hence the mask, and he was already in substantial pain and passing blood. Marital relations would clearly not be being resumed, and to Katherine's clearly intense relief he was only too happy to sleep apart from her.

"I fear he may not be long for this world," she confided to them in a hushed whisper, although her voice carried only thankfulness. "I believe I may have avoided the contagion, for he appears to think that he caught it after Elias was born and he hasn't ...well we haven't ...you know, ...since then."

Deb had to smother a grin at Katherine's unwillingness to speak of the practicalities of marriage. Having been brought up on a farm Deb had no such inhibitions, but Katherine was continuing.

"I'm afraid to have to tell you that the only money we have left is what this farmland earns. He tells me that he's run up gambling debts. So much so that my allowance from my father's estate is already spoken for

for many years to come." Her composure slipped and Deb could see her lip beginning to quiver and her eyes to fill.

"Oh, don't you worry!" she said quickly. "It isn't as bad as all that!"

"But it is!" Katherine insisted. "We have no money at all! I can't pay you! Either of you! And how shall we pay for food for the boys? ...Oh Lord, what will become of us?"

Deb clasped her warmly by both arms, completely forgetting their respective roles and only seeing the other young woman's distress.

"No! Listen to me! When Master Samuel got the estate back six years ago it was in a mess. But the old master before the war was a canny soul. This land was well kept, even if over the years it's lost some of the fields to other farms. It took no time for a good farmer like Robert to get it back into use. For the last three years it's been making a good living!

"Master Samuel never answered none of his letters in the early days, so Robert stopped writing. Instead, he's been putting the money away against the day when he gets asked for it! The farm can easily support you and your family.

"...But take a bit of advice if you will, Mistress. Don't say nought of this to the Master. I've seen men who have to gamble. Even out here in the country we have such men. If you tell him there's money, he'll have it off you one way or the other. He'll tell you there's some grand scheme that's sure to pay off and that it'll settle all your problems. Except it won't! The money'll disappear, and you really will be broke."

"Deb is right," Jemima hissed urgently at Katherine. "Listen to her! Not a word to him!"

"Not a word," Katherine repeated doubtfully.

"When I said it would keep you and the family, I meant it," Deb felt she had to explain. "But it'd be a drop in the ocean against the kind of debts he must've run up in London. Out here, away from society and the need to spend money on all manner of fancy things, you can live well, but it won't get you back into London society.

"You can have a roof over the heads of you and your boys, and food to put inside them. We can clothe them fit for country life and do it well, but not for the city and not to give them city schooling either. They must become either minor country gentlemen or city paupers. The first is possible if you say nothing, but the other is certain if you let your husband have one whiff of any money."

With relief she saw the practicalities strike home with Katherine.

"You're right," she said with almost an air of relief. "I've already told him we have nothing. So I can carry on with that, because in his eyes what we have really is nothing. He thinks in sums of hundreds of pounds, the pence never cross his mind."

"Well there you go then," Deb said with a reassuring pat on the arm. "Just keep thinking of the boys and you'll be able to put on a brave face."

It certainly seemed to work since there was no request for the money put to Robert. However, Samuel's presence nonetheless put a strain on the household. He insisted on unlocking the doors into the old house and seem to spend melancholic afternoons wandering the rooms, the cane he now needed to walk with making an unnerving tapping up and down the wooden floors until everyone was fit to scream.

Then they found Elias sobbing his heart out in a corner one evening long after he had been sent to bed.

His mother and Jemima could get no sense out of him as to what had scared him, but he clung to Deb as though he was drowning. Cuddling the distraught five-year-old, Deb took him to her room and let him share her bed for the night, although it was broken several times by his nightmares. The next day he refused to leave Deb's side, or the day after, and it was only when Samuel was seen walking in the far upstairs of the old house that it came out that he'd suffered some unpleasant attentions from his father.

As his wobbly little voice told how his father had come into the bedroom while Orlando was showing off his reading to Katherine downstairs Deb felt her heart sink. Yet at least she was already guessing at what had happened. For Katherine and Jemima, the shock became physical, and as Deb cuddled Elias once more, she heard Katherine's painful retching outside the kitchen door, and Jemima's incoherent sobbing even as she held Katherine.

"Will he catch it? Will he catch the pox?" Katherine sobbed to Deb that night, as the women held a whispered conference in one corner of the parlour as the boys slept on the sofa opposite.

"No, I don't think so. What the Master did is disgusting and has badly frightened Elias, but the ...ehmm ...physical contact was ...err ...minimal so I don't think he's in bodily danger." It was hard phrasing things like that delicately for Katherine, and what Deb didn't want to say was that she was hardly the person to ask. Out here the pox wasn't exactly one of the regular disease the wise women had to deal with. For one thing there were too few whores, and most men were too busy working on the land to have time to go off pursuing random women. She resolved to ask Nancy the next time she saw her, but realised that Nancy might be none the wiser either. Then Katherine's next words brought her thoughts up sharply.

"I can't believe he's sunk so low," Katherine was whispering to Jemima. "Oh, he's a rake. I found that out within days of our marriage. And I never entertained any dreams that he would ever be faithful to me. If I imagined anything, it was that he would end up becoming one of those old men who are a social embarrassment. You know, one of those whom you couldn't go visiting with because he'd have his hand up the maid's skirt, or be found in the servant's beds in the night. I thought he'd sink to that when his looks went and he couldn't get what he wanted from young ladies. I never, never thought him a ...a ...a sodomite!" The last word was choked out and she dissolved into tears again, but it made Deb think of things Nancy had said in the past.

It took every ounce of courage she possessed, but she took a taper from the fire and lit a candle in a lantern, then left Katherine and Jemima in the kitchen to venture into the old house. The flickering shadows had her jumping every few steps, but something deep inside her knew that she had to take a look at the fireplace in the old great hall. That was where Nancy had said that an evil presence dwelt waiting for the weak and wicked-minded to come within its grasp, and if anyone was weak and easily led it was Samuel. In her soft house-slippers her footsteps made hardly any sound as she crept into the old north parlour, where there were still scratches in the plaster from all those years ago when the chest which had been wedged against it had dug into the wall.

As she reached the door into the hall she could hear muffled sounds, and for a moment her courage nearly failed her. She had to stop and lean against the doorjamb and take several deep breaths before she could go on, and even then, her knees seemed to be developing an independent tremor of their own. Shielding the lantern's flame so that it wouldn't immediately light up the hall, she peeped round the door, then crept out into the recessed doorway. From her hidden viewing point, she was able to see Samuel standing before the fireplace. He appeared to be crying in what sounded like pain, yet at the same time she could see his hand moving rhythmically at his groin.

Quite what happened with him next she couldn't see and didn't want to, but he gave a howl of agony and fell to his knees in the grate where he stayed sobbing. Deb was about to turn and go, thoroughly revolted, when she froze in her tracks. Above Samuel something strange was happening to the brickwork of the fireplace. A dark shape was becoming more distinct and seemed almost to be trying to break free of the bricks, and she could have sworn that she heard a faint, sibilant voice say,

"Not enough! More, I need more! You must give me more!"

That was enough for Deb, though, and she fled not caring whether Samuel heard or not. Luckily Katherine and Jemima had already gone to bed and taken the boys with them, and she was able to retreat to her own room, although she got no sleep that night. She wedged a small chair under the doorknob, but even so her heart began to pound when she heard Samuel's unsteady footsteps coming upstairs over an hour later. He seemed to stagger, and for an awful second she thought he was coming her way, but then he seemed to steady himself and she heard him going to his own room on the opposite side.

The next morning, she made her excuses straight after breakfast, and fled down to the village and Nancy as fast as she could. She felt dreadful bringing such dire news to her aunt after all she'd suffered already in that house, but Nancy was the only one left who might know what needed doing. She found her brooming out the yard and one look at Deb's face was enough.

"It's happened, hasn't it?" Nancy said before Deb could even get the breath to speak. Deb nodded, and Nancy retreated to the cottage and sat down heavily on the kitchen chair. "I feared as much."

"How did you guess? Why now?" Deb wheezed, leaning her hands on her knees as she bent over trying to suck more air into her lungs after running nearly all the way.

"That man," Nancy said with little preamble. "Robert came by and said he'd turned up. He wanted my advice over whether he should tell him about the profit from the farm. When Robert said that Samuel had almost boasted about his 'gentleman's expenses' and how they would need more money if he was to recoup his losses, we both realised he was a gambler.

"That night I had a dream. Like always, it was about that time, but this time it was more about the fae folk and I was talking to the lord and lady. I didn't remember all of it when I woke up, but I did recall them saying way back that the house would draw the weak-minded for its evil purpose. Well that Samuel is surely weak-minded! Then the village children came past all full of giggles and excitement about the coming All Hallow's Eve, and I felt sick."

"All Hallow's? Oh, God preserve us! Oh, dear Lord! I'd totally forgotten in all of this. That's tonight!"

Nancy sighed wearily. "It is. The most potent of the old Sabbats. Too much coincidence, Deb, too much.

I've felt like I've been waiting for a thunder storm to break for the last three days, so come on, tell me what's happened."

Sinking into her old chair, Deb let all the tale come rushing out of her. It felt such a relief to be able to tell someone of what she'd seen the previous night, especially now that she didn't have to prepare Nancy for the worst. Nancy looked suitably revolted but was also obviously thinking hard.

"That all makes a miserable sort of sense," she mused when Deb had finished. "I think it's no coincidence that Katherine says he's never shown any tendency to go after boys of any sort, let alone children, before now. It makes me think that that is the evil creature's doing. It's not because they're boys. It's because it's identified the children as potential easy victims – and remembering the past, maybe more importantly, as innocent victims – and is sending Samuel, who's too sick and far too morally weak to resist it, after them. I fear it's priming him to make sacrifices of them. It may be a Beast of Battle according to the fae folk, but it needs that virgin blood to make the jump between worlds."

"But what are we going to do?" Deb asked her. "Can you remember how to call on these fae folk or whatever they are? And will they come after all this time?"

Nancy admitted that there was no guarantee, but felt hopeful because they'd come after an even longer gap between her and Anne's hour of need, and that of their grandmothers'. Picking up a thick shawl against the chill which would come later in the evening, Nancy shut up the cottage and followed Deb back up the hill. At the sight of the old manor, she had to stop for several minutes to fight back the tears. Deb almost wondered whether she might turn back, but then the two boys saw them and came running out to meet them. Once she'd seen how Elias clung to Deb, Nancy seemed to find an inner strength, and she walked on with a resolute step holding Orlando's hand firmly in hers.

Samuel had apparently not come down from his bedroom yet, and according to Katherine seemed very sick and unlikely to get up at all that day. Urging the boys to go and play in the old stable, Nancy summoned Katherine and Jemima to follow her and Deb into the old hall. For the first time Deb thought Nancy looked every one of her fifty years as she walked across the hall floor, hugging herself as though she felt a chill that touched none of the others. At the fireplace she stopped and looked down.

"Ah," she sighed sadly, then turned back to the other three. "His illness means that he's passing blood and it's blood that's on the hearth."

"Is that significant?" Jemima asked in a timid voice, still reeling from what Deb had been telling her and Katherine as they'd followed Nancy.

"Very," Nancy replied. "The last time the creature fed on the blood from ...from ..." her voice faltered and she struggled to speak through her grief.

"It was the blood of Miss Agnes, and her new born baby, and that from Miss Emily, which quickened the beast the last time." Deb supplied for her.

"Oh! Dear Lord!" Katherine gasped in horror.

"We have to try to get Ag... Agnes out," Nancy stuttered, struggling with the grief which threatened to overwhelm her all over again.

To Deb's surprise it was the timid Jemima who stepped into the hearth with her, and following Nancy's instructions tried to locate the secret trapdoor.

Eventually, covered with soot, they managed to find the edges of the door but there was no question of moving it. Katherine went back to Deb's kitchen to fetch the poker from there to try to give some leverage but it was no use.

"Her blood must've rusted the hinges and the bolt," Deb said sadly, as they retreated to the yard and the water pump to wash away the soot. "And of course, the various tenants all had roaring fires in there in the winter. It must be near baked shut."

"Well we can wash his blood off," Jemima said with surprising and resolute firmness, and went to start heating water. With buckets of boiling water, much soap, and stiff brooms, she and Deb scrubbed the fireplace until they got down to the original golden stone, and even the soot from years of fires was gone. In the meantime, Katherine went to check on the boys and then get them all some food, her role as mistress of the house disappearing in her need to do something to protect her children. The boys thought it great fun to eat crusty bread and cheese, with crisp autumn apples, sat on the stairs of the old hall with Nancy and the others, and afterwards seemed to regain some of their old sense of fun.

Leaving them to return to the stables where they were playing soldiers in their innocence as to what soldiers had done not yards away from there, the women returned to the old house. The staircase was cleaned down and having managed to find a couple of feather dusters, Katherine and Deb, as the two tallest, did their best to sweep years of cobwebs off the old mural. It was surprising how well the paintings cleaned up and the years seemed to have done little to dim the colours of the paints. However, the painting showed no signs of exhibiting the strange qualities which Nancy had described from the past. On the other hand, it felt good to be getting involved in the simple domestic task of getting everything clean and it was only the fading autumn light which made them realise how the time had flown.

"The boys must be having fun," Jemima observed. "Normally they'd be in asking for food again by now." Then the weight of her words hit them all and without a word the four of them ran from the hall out of the old back door and round the north wing towards the stables. Inside there was no sign of either boy.

"Oh my babies!" howled Katherine and poor Nancy couldn't have gone any paler as she feared history was going to repeat itself. Leaving Nancy to console Katherine, Deb and Jemima hurried off to search. Without needing to say why, both of them immediately headed inside and up to Samuel's room. There on the bed lay Orlando. The little boy seemed unhurt, but he was sleeping unnaturally deeply and nothing they did could wake him.

"Opium!" Jemima suddenly said, pouncing on a small bottle on the dresser. "Samuel said only the other day that he was taking it for the pain! He must've given Orlando a dose."

"Will he wake up?" Deb asked worriedly. "Opium's something I know nothing about."

"I think so," Jemima said with more hope than conviction, then helped Deb lift the seven-year-old up to carry him downstairs. They were just in time to meet the other two coming in from the garden, so Katherine and Nancy took Orlando into the kitchen while Deb and Jemima carried on searching. By now they needed candles, and yet even with the extra light there was no sign of Samuel or Elias.

"He must be avoiding us," Deb growled in fury as they rejoined Katherine and Nancy in the kitchen. "I keep feeling that as we go in one door he's going out of the next room."

"I hate to say this but I think the one place we know he'll be is in the old hall at midnight," Nancy said with great sorrow.

"Then we should get to the stairs well before then," Deb suggested.

"I'll stay here with Orlando," Katherine said. "I'm not leaving my son alone."

"No," Nancy told her firmly. "We must take Orlando with us. We need you on the stairs too, and he'll be in the safest place if the fae come through."

"And if they don't?" Jemima said, voicing all their fears.

"Then I doubt that anywhere is safe," was Nancy's worrying reply. "If we had Elias, I'd say we should leave the house tonight, but now we can't."

Katherine still looked dubious, but Deb felt sure that Katherine's reluctance was largely due to worry over partaking in something which would be regarded as witchcraft by their neighbours. Her fear was understandable, for only three years beforehand a local woman called Mary Hodges had been informed against on suspicion of being a witch. Mary had been taken away for examination into her 'practices' by the Church and had never returned – although no-one knew whether that was due to her being found guilty, or her reluctance to ever set foot again in a village, where she knew every hand would have to be seen to be against her in public, even if they weren't in private.

Even so, Mary had not been forgotten. Only last winter when the local gentry had ridden out to hunt, a hare had three times led the foxhounds off the scent.

And in the village Katherine and Jemima had been regaled with tales of how witches such as Mary could turn into hares to draw the hunt from the right path – and of what would be done to them if the likes of Mary were caught.

Deb leant close to Katherine and whispered gently,

"Who's going to tell what we've done? We're all in this together, aren't we? And who else can we go to for help who would believe us against Samuel? It's trust in the Craft, or leave Elias, run away, and risk a possessed Samuel following you and finding you again later when there's no Nancy to help."

Katherine bit her lip and looked at Deb through tear-filled eyes, but nodded her understanding.

Fetching plenty of blankets to wrap around Orlando's still sleeping form, the four of them processed through into the great hall, each holding a lit candle and with spares tucked into their aprons. The hall was deserted, but seemed far colder than the rest of the house and filled with an unnaturally heavy atmosphere. They went through the arch of the screen into the stairwell and started up the stairs. Suddenly Nancy, in the lead, let out a sigh of relief.

"What?" Deb asked from the rear, but in reply Nancy pointed up to the painting up above them.

In contrast to the lifeless mural of this afternoon, the whole picture seemed to be lit with its own moonlight from within. Reaching the halfway landing under the window, Jemima made a bed of blankets and Katherine put Orlando down, then turned to Nancy and Deb who were staring at the mural with smiles on their faces. Jemima and Katherine gasped in astonishment. Where there had only been foliage a few moments ago, there were now several figures looking down on them.

"Hello Nancy," a tall, serious looking man said in an unfamiliar accent.

"My lord!" Nancy said with undisguised relief. "Oh, am I glad to see you! ...To see you all again! ...I was worried stiff we'd have to try to perform some ritual to get you to hear us. How did you know?"

"We've felt Feannag growing in strength again," he replied. "It seemed inevitable that he would emerge soon at one of the Sabbats. It was merely a question of which one. And its bond with the house has had one good effect in that it's opened the way for us more easily too."

"Who are you?" Katherine asked totally overawed.

"We are the Elfael. Talking to Anne and Hope, we've worked out that the last time we walked in your world – the one we originally came from just as they did – was almost exactly a thousand years ago. We lived in this area when it was the borderland between our native people and the in-comers – the ones you now call the Anglo-Saxons."

"Anne and Hope? Are they still with you?" Nancy interrupted, almost fearful of the answer.

"Yes, I'm still here," Anne's voice said cheerfully and she appeared from behind Elfan.

"Oh Anne!" Nancy sobbed, full of mixed emotion at seeing her old friend after all the years.

The years seemed not to have touched Anne at all, but she drew a tall youth forward with a big smile on her face. "Do you know who this is?" Nancy shook her head in confusion. "This is Charles!"

Nancy gasped in astonishment. "But he's whole! He's not crippled anymore!"

"No, I'm not, thanks to Seithmath and the strange creatures whom he talks to sometimes," Charles himself replied. "Hello Nancy. Do you still make those lovely cinnamon cakes?"

That was too much for Nancy and she broke down in sobs of relief. Something in the back of her mind had begun to wonder whether she'd created a happy ending for Anne, and the remainder of the family, because she couldn't cope with any more grief at the time. To see her dear friend and mistress looking hale and hearty, and comforted from her extreme grief, was more than she could have hoped for. But to see first Charles, then Matthew and Georgie grown to strong teenagers, untainted by the horrors of their childhood, was a relief of almost religious intensity. For Deb, seeing Nancy's reaction only brought it home to her how much her aunt had suffered over the years, and she wished she'd been more willing to listen to the outpouring of grief.

Yet Katherine brought them sharply back to the present as she asked,

"Can you save *my* baby? Can you save my Elias from whatever his father's going to do with him?"

"We shall do our very best," Lady Ferylt said with conviction. "This will be somewhat different from the last time we fought Feannag, for we have no idea of how it will behave now that it's bonded with the house rather than a person."

"But it's my husband Samuel who has Elias," Katherine sobbed. "He's just a man, even if he is behaving like a monster. Can't you stop him?"

Ferylt stepped up to her and laid a comforting hand on her shaking shoulders. "To your eyes he may still be a man, but to do what he's done there must be a serious bond with Feannag, and that makes him something different – more dangerous. We might kill him only for Feannag to transfer its control to the child, and would you want us to kill your son in order to stop Feannag?" Katherine let out a howl of horror.

"No, of course you wouldn't," Ferylt said gently, drawing the sobbing Katherine into her arms. "So you see it isn't as simple as it first seemed, is it? Each time we've fought Feannag we've sought to finish this nightmare once and for all. If all we do is kill its familiar, then we've learned by bitter experience that, sooner or later, it'll regain its strength and start more battles for it to feed off."

"It's a carrion eater," Elfan said bitterly. "Not just of flesh but of souls too. It's a Beast of Battle in every way. The more who die in fighting it the more they feed it. It can even drain some meagre dregs out of the souls of the Mearcstapan – the monstrous folk it calls to fight alongside it – but alone they aren't enough. It needs human souls, and for human blood to run, and the trouble is we're not replacing those warriors of ours who've fallen in the fight against it anything like fast enough.

Our growth has been slowed immensely on this side of the veil, and we have few children. So each time there are a few less of us to fight. If we can do no better than we have so far, it'll eventually win, because although it'll take it several more of these battles there'll come a point when there are none of us left to fight. And then what will happen to your world?"

"That's a chilling thought!" Nancy gasped in dismay.

"It is," Anne agreed, tentatively steeping through the portal – not sure of what the consequences of returning would be. When nothing dire happened, she threw her arms around Nancy and hugged her tight. "But we're a long way off losing yet! Oh Nancy, it *is* good to see you again! How many years has it been?"

"Twenty this year," Nancy said tearfully, hugging Anne back.

"Twenty! No! Surely not! Barely half that have passed for us!"

Nancy wiped her eyes and managed a rueful laugh. "These grey hairs didn't come overnight, Anne! And this is little Deb who used to play with Mistress Milly."

"Deb?" a voice from the mural said in astonishment. "Heavens above! Is that really you, Deb?"

From the mural an unchanged Milly ran out to clasp hands with Deb who now seemed far too old to have shared a childhood with her.

"It's good to see you too, Milly," Deb said, but with less of the youthful enthusiasm, "but I'm afraid we have things to do before we can catch up on lost time."

Milly's mouth formed a soundless "Oh!" and she stepped back to look up at Elfan with the others.

"What do you think we should do?" Deb asked the stern warrior lord. "It's only a few hours to midnight. Do we wait for the dreadful hour to come and see what happens, or is there something we can do before then?"

Lady Ferylt, who was still holding Katherine, made the first suggestion. "I think we should take this little boy through into our world, if only temporarily. He'll be much safer there."

"Yes," Deb agreed swiftly, "and take Katherine with him." As Katherine made to protest, Deb gripped her arm and looked firmly into her eyes. "You can't fight this thing, Katherine, so leave rescuing Elias to those who can. You go with Orlando in case he wakes up. What would he think if he woke up in that different world surrounded by strangers?"

Reluctantly Katherine nodded, and allowed herself to be led away by Milly at Orlando's side.

"Well done, Deb," Nancy sighed with relief. "She's in no state to cope with what I fear is to come, and she might just get in the way at the crucial moment." She turned to Elfan. "Should we try to kill Samuel like you did the Covenanter who summoned this Feannag the last time?"

"Not at first," Elfan replied in a voice weighted with worry. "Seithmath says that we should try to draw Feannag out of the house. To put some distance between it and the place it's inhabited over the last years. If we can do that, he'll attempt to cleanse the stones with some preparation he's been working on for years. The big difficulty is that Seithmath apparently needs to be at a distance back in our world when whatever the potion does begins to work or he'll be affected too."

"Then tell us what to do!" Deb volunteered eagerly. "You concentrate on fighting that monster and let Nancy and me do the things Seithmath wants done."

"And me!" Jemima's voice piped up. "I'm in this with you too, don't forget."

"I hadn't forgotten you," Deb said warmly. "Far from it! I was going to say that you should focus on Elias as and when he appears. He's going to need someone he knows too, if he's conscious."

"Then stay by me," Ferylt joined in. "My archers and I will do all we can to get you to the other child."

However, before they could plan any further an urgent whisper came from one of the warriors who had been watching the upstairs.

"Sire! Someone is moving in one of the rooms up here!"

Elfan looked to the three women in query.

"It has to be him, Samuel," Nancy said. "There's no-one else in the house." Then she looked at Anne and they seemed to be thinking the same thing. "Oh God! Why didn't I think of that before! He's been in the priest's hole! The upper one! That's why we couldn't find him."

"The one place where we wouldn't look because of the memories!" Deb groaned. "We only ever stuck our heads around the door because with no furniture in that room anymore we didn't think we needed to do any more, and I for one wouldn't willingly go in there."

They were about to follow Elfan and five of his veterans up the stairs, when they saw the soldier at the top of the stairs backing away from the landing and raising his hands up away from his sword. By the wavering light of the candles, they saw Samuel emerge by the balustrade, which he staggered and leant against as he sidled forward. Weak and drained, he nonetheless had Elias' inert form clasped to his body with one arm, while the other held a knife to the boy's throat.

"Back!" he snarled. "Get back or I slit his throat!"

Elfan gestured his warriors to give the man room to manoeuvre, but stepped forward up another stair himself. "Why would you do that? You need him for your sacrifice to summon the Beast of Battle, don't you? You won't waste him before the right time."

But Samuel gave a maniacal laugh. "Ah! Think you're so clever, don't you! But you're wrong! I can cut him without killing him. I can cut him, and cut him, and cut him again! I can give him pain like I have! He's of my flesh – so let him feel what it's like to have my flesh! My pain! ...Death? Death is nothing compared to this living hell!"

By now he was at the top of the stairs and those below could see the patch of blood on his britches covering the whole of his groin. The disease had clearly done its worst and Samuel was already looking death in the face. The women all exchanged worried glances. Clearly there was no point any more in trying to appeal to Samuel on the basis of saving his life, since there was precious little of that left worth saving. Elfan seemed to have thought much the same and was just turning to gesture to his men when one of those below called out in horror.

Samuel gave a demented giggle, bloodstained spittle bubbling from his disease ravaged lips. "Fools! You're too late! Too late with your precious schemes and plans! This time my master wins! He knows all! He saw what you would do and he's beaten you!"

He stumbled to the stairs and began tottering down them, but hardly any of the Elfael were looking at him now for most of them were running down the stairs. From in the hall a sinister rustling could now be heard, and then there was a clash of arms before one of the Elfael came flying back through the screen to hit the wall at the back.

"He's summoned the Mearcstapan first!" Ferylt gasped in realisation, and spun to gesture at those appearing at the portal. Within seconds the stairs held as many warriors as there was standing room for and there were more to come. This sudden influx posed a problem for Samuel for there was now no room to get down the stairs even though no-one was threatening him anymore. For a moment he stood transfixed with rage, but unsure as to what to do since threatening Elias was going to have little effect.

Then Deb broke the stalemate. "Make way for him!" she hissed tugging the sleeve of the rearmost warrior. "Let him come down the stairs. You come upwards. Quick follow me! Single file, go past him! There's another way down to the hall!"

Elfan's senior man looked blank until Anne translated for him, but then quickly issued orders. The Elfael flattened themselves against the wall and made it appear that they were giving way to Samuel by the only way possible, which was to go upwards. Deb had already made it past Samuel on the wide stairs, and as soon as the first of the Elfael had passed him and reached her, she set off down the landing.

Hurrying to the end, she turned into the north wing bedroom and flung open the window onto the single storey roof. Pausing only to make sure the men were following her, she hitched her skirts up, swung her legs over the sill and let herself down onto the tiles below. Thankfully it hadn't rained in days and so the slates were dry and she kept to her feet. At the gutter she sat down and turned to lower herself to the ground, but the men were not so cautious and two warriors had simply leapt and rolled to come up on the ground on their feet, blades already drawing and checking for signs of the foe. Another caught Deb as she let go of the gutter and even in the midst of this horror she felt a flush of pleasure at the close contact – such a long time since she'd been that close to a man!

However, there was no time to revel in the moment, and she was running to the front of the men, guiding them around to the front of the farmhouse and opening the front door. Candles still burned on the mantelpiece of the kitchen, and she grabbed one as she opened the door into the old house. The lone flame gave barely enough light for the warriors, but they needed no guiding, for from beyond the door in the hall they could hear the desperate fight their friends were putting up against the Mearcstapan. She was left holding the kitchen door open as the warriors assembled in the old parlour beyond by the hall door, then on a signal they streamed into the hall to attack the Mearcstapan's rear.

The element of surprise was enough to halt the way the battle was going, and the Elfael began to regain some ground. But Deb hadn't finished. Grabbing the key to the old front door of the timbered hall, from off the hook where it hung by her cooking range, she led more warriors out of the farmhouse's back door into the yard, and unlocked the hall door from the outside to allow the Elfael to attack on a third front. The door was barely open when a wild gangling figure staggered out with a feral yowl, hacking at three of the Elfael who pursued it out of the door. Deb gave an involuntary scream of horror as its ghastly face turned her way, and fevered eyes like marsh-lights poured their sickly green gaze on her. Then one of the eyes went out as it sprouted an arrow, and looking up Deb saw that Anne had followed her, but only far enough to lead Ferylt's archers to the upstairs windows. The Elfael drove several more of the gruesome figures outside into the firing range of the archers, and others of the Mearcstapan followed of their own accord on hearing the screams of agony of their companions.

Deb retreated into the farmhouse out of the way of the running battle which had spilled out into the farmyard, taking a moment to steady her breathing in the relative calm of her kitchen. Then she remembered that she was supposed to be helping Nancy to do what the strange seer Seithmath had arranged. Seeing a bottle of blackberry wine on the table, for the first time in her life she grabbed the bottle and took a long swig from it without bothering with a glass. As the wine warmed her inside, she squared her shoulders and went back through the small parlour, and then crept up to the hall door.

Against her expectations, the hall was relatively calm in that there were only Elfael prowling about with weapons drawn, staring into every shadow in case another Mearcstapan appeared. Across the length of the hall, she could see Nancy talking with Anne and a tall figure with a staff whom she guessed to be Seithmath. She saw Nancy nod and then Seithmath put his hand on a lad's shoulder and being led away. Screwing up her courage, she stepped carefully out into the hall to allow the warriors to see her and then dashed across to Nancy.

"What do we have to do?" she asked her aunt.

Nancy held up a large glass phial which contained a thick greenish liquid. "On the stroke of midnight, we have to throw this against the fireplace as high as we can, so that it smashes and the liquid runs down over the spot where that thing took up residence."

Then Deb looked around her. "Where are Samuel and Elias?"

"We don't know," Jemima said with a tremble in her voice. "By the time the fighting cleared enough for us to be able to see anything he was gone. Even Lady Ferylt hasn't seen him."

"God rot the man!" cursed Deb.

"I think he's done that already," Jemima managed with weak humour, which raise a faint smile from all of them.

"What do we do then?" Deb asked, but Nancy was looking back to where Anne was standing by the bottom of the stairs gesturing to them with Ferylt by her side. "What's she trying to say?"

Nancy gave a grimace. "Reminding me that there was another hiding place which we used. Under the stairs! It's the obvious place for them to go. They must've got down to the bottom steps and Samuel realised that he could get no further. Lord Elfan was right, Samuel needs Elias alive, or rather that Feannag thing does. I bet it was planning on having the three lives of Samuel, Elias, and Orlando, but even two would be better than none."

The three of them crept over to the archway between the hall and the stairwell, and Anne and Ferylt joined them.

"How do we get him out without endangering Elias?" Deb asked Ferylt.

The warrior lady shook her head. "I don't think we dare try to force him to come out, and to go in after him would only place the child in peril. We must keep Elias alive, not only for the child's own sake, but because of the danger of spilling innocent blood in here on this night, and all that that might result in. Samuel knows it, and might very well let Elias die bit by bit if it serves his master's purpose and goes against us. We must capture them when this man Samuel comes out of his own accord instead – and also, if he is dying then he must do it outside, away from here."

"The hay net in the old stables!" Deb gasped. "That'll do it! We can drop it off the stairs onto him and let him tie himself in knots trying to get untangled."

"Good thinking!" Nancy said, "you go and get it while we keep watch."

Deb raced out of the back door of the hall and into the stables, hauling the net out of a manger and towards the house when a voice behind her said with evil glee,

"Now where are you taking that, my pretty?"

Cursing under her breath Deb realised that they'd guessed wrongly. Samuel had left by the back door in the confusion and was here with her, not under the stairs. In desperation, Deb spun and flung the net with all her might. Whatever Samuel had expected it clearly wasn't that, because he staggered back and fell over as the heavy rope net landed on top of him. Screaming for Nancy and Jemima, Deb launched herself at him, and managed to knock him back to the ground even as he began to struggle to his feet.

"Filthy bitch!" he screamed, lashing out with his knife, which caught in Deb's sleeve but only scratched the flesh, although it still unbalanced her enough for him to get room to start to rise.

That finished it for Deb. What little self-control she'd had left evaporated, and memories of all the hours of roughhousing with her brothers in the barn as a child surged up inside her. No city lady, Deb had spent her life working hard, and when she brought her fist back it carried solid country muscle behind it.

"Bastard!" she screamed as her fist took him straight in the gut. As he folded forward, she came to her knees and lashed out again, this time hitting him on the side of the head. He fell backwards and Deb scrambled on top of him, straddling his chest as she grabbed a handful of hair and smacked his head hard back down onto the flagstones.

"What have you done with Elias? What have you done with him?" she screamed slamming his head back again.

"Stop it, Deb! Stop it!"

She felt someone grab her fist as she brought her arm back to hit him again. Someone else grabbed her other arm and together they hauled her to her feet. As the red mist of rage passed, Deb realised that Anne struggled to hold her by one arm and Jemima by the other, as Nancy knelt down beside Samuel. She looked up and shook her head.

"He's dead."

"Oh Lord help me!" Deb gulped as the reality sunk

in, quashing her fury faster than anything else could have done.

"Don't fret, love," Nancy said rising to hug her niece. "He was so far gone the first blow was enough." She turned and gestured to the body where they could now see a puddle of blood forming around it. "He must've been bleeding inside already. He might not even have made it to midnight."

In the clear light of the night Deb suddenly shivered. "How close is it to midnight now?"

"It can't be far off," Jemima said with a sob. "Oh where is Elias?"

"Well Samuel must've been in the stable," Deb told them. "He was right behind me when I got through the door."

Together the four women ran to the stable door and began searching. In the farthest stall they found Elias' small form folded up like a rag doll. His pulse was so faint as to be barely detectable and Jemima said what they all feared.

"Samuel must have given him opium too, but he's given him too much!"

Between them they carried the little boy out into the yard and away from the house. In what was left of the garden they laid him on the bench of the small rose bower, devoid of foliage this late in the year.

"I'll stay with him," Jemima volunteered.

"Are you sure?" Deb asked.

"Yes. Now that Samuel is dead I'm not so frightened."

"You'll have a guard," a voice came from behind them, and they saw that Ferylt had come to find them with several of her female archers. At a gesture from their leader, four of the women took up station at each corner of the bower facing outwards with bows at the ready. "I'm sorry but if you're to do as Seithmath wants, then you have to come back now," she said to the others. And so, with reassurances that they would return before long, the three women hurried back into the hall in Ferylt's wake.

Inside there was an unnatural calm. Elfan stood in the hall with several of his warriors, all with drawn swords and many with long, wicked-looking spears hefted in muscular arms ready to be thrown at the first sign of trouble. The air crackled as though their very own thunder storm was brewing beneath the wooden ceiling, and Deb felt like she was fighting for air.

"Samuel's dead," Nancy declared without a hint of remorse in her voice.

"Better outside than in," Elfan grimaced, "although it would have been better if he could've waited for another day. Tainted blood so close to the house is less than good at this hour."

Carrying on the autumn air the sound of a church clock striking midnight began to drift up to them. From the brickwork of the fireplace a shape started to emerge. At first it looked like an enormous heraldic crest in bird form had been painted in black upon the surface, but slowly it began to acquire a three-dimensional form. Elfan's warriors regrouped in a semicircle, all facing inwards to the hearth, while Ferylt's archers found lines of sight on the same spot between them. Huddled in the recessed doorway to the north parlour, where ninety years ago Simon and Thomas had found refuge, Deb, Anne, and Nancy fought down the rising panic inside as the apparition took form.

The moment it was fully formed and free of the brickwork, the beast threw back its head, let out a spine-chilling screech and flexed its wings. The crow's head came back down and the savage eyes swept across the assembled host. As its beak struck downwards at the nearest warrior, he did the unexpected and dived towards the crow and under its feet out of the way, pausing only to slash at its underneath on the way. Feannag gave a caw of rage and pain and beat its wings to rise to the ceiling, but by now the Elfael were working to their battle plan and the crow had no easy targets.

Instead, it plunged and struck out with ever increasing fury, always missing by the closest margin but getting attacked in turn. Deb saw Elfan give a nod to someone on the other side of the room and suddenly the door was flung open and the Elfael streamed out into the yard. Enraged beyond measure, Feannag folded its wings and plunged through the door frame after them, revenge consuming its mind above all else.

As its last tail feather cleared the doorjamb, the door was slammed shut by a hidden archer who immediately turned to the nearest window and joined her fellow archers in firing at Feannag outside. The three women needed no further encouragement and ran out into the hall, to be joined by Milly and Hope who had been waiting hidden on the stairs for the moment to come.

"I know we now know that the Elfael aren't fairies," Hope said with an attempt at a brave grin, "but just in case Great-grandma was right about the number five being potent we thought we'd better make the numbers up!"

"Good lass!" Nancy praised her. "Can't hurt, can it?"

Standing together Nancy handed Deb the phial. "Go on, you do it! You've probably got the strongest throwing arm of all of us."

Together Anne, Hope, and Milly began chanting something in a totally foreign tongue which they seemed to have learned by rote, rather than having any understanding of what they were saying. As they held hands behind her, Deb stepped forward with Nancy by her side, weighed the phial in her hand and then launched it right up to the highest spot of where she had seen Feannag emerge from. The glass bottle exploded wetly as the three finished chanting, and there was a pregnant pause which barely lasted a second before the most unholy shriek came from outside. Suddenly a window exploded inwards as Feannag's beak struck in at them. Unable to get its head through the opening due to the central stone pillar, it drew back and began battering at the outside with ever rising urgency.

Luckily the Elfael archer who had shut the door had also turned the key in the lock. The old oak door now shivered under a ferocious battering of the unworldly beak, as Feannag turned its attentions to the larger way back into the hall. But Milly was suddenly pulling on Anne's sleeve and pointing.

"Look Mother! Look at the fireplace!"

A foul black, viscous liquid was oozing out of the brickwork and puddling onto the hearth.

"The buckets!" Nancy cried. "Get the buckets and brooms! We mustn't let it have time to sink into the hearth!"

Dashing back to the kitchen the women grabbed the buckets they'd left abandoned during the frantic search for the missing boys. The water tank beside the range had been refilled in anticipation of more cleaning and was now simmering nicely. Drawing off as much as they could into pails, they grabbed brooms and yet more soap and headed back into the hall. Already the hearth seemed to be absorbing some of the gelatinous substance and Deb hefted her bucket in her hands and sloshed scalding hot water straight onto it without pausing to add soap. Like women possessed, Hope and Nancy shot forward with brooms and began scrubbing with all their might. As their arms tired, Milly and Anne took over, while Deb kept a steady trickle of hot water flowing over the hearth. Clutching the large brick of soap, Deb would also bend down and rub it hard over any exposed part of the hearth where the stain seemed to be sticking.

They were so engrossed in their task that they only realised that it had gone quiet outside when the front door opened. Jumping at the feel of the cold night air rushing in, they were relieved to see the Elfael warriors coming back in. However, they quickly turned the brooms to sweeping the huge puddle of dirty water outside before it settled in the flagstones of the hall floor. As they broomed past the last of the returning warriors Anne was worried to observe how many of them were wounded. Many were leaning on the shoulders of comrades or having to be carried, and too many of those slung over makeshift stretchers from spears appeared to be dead. When they were able to stop, they noticed Elfan watching them, but cradling his right arm in his left and looking very pale.

"My lord, are you all right?" Nancy asked full of concern.

"I've had worse," he replied with an attempt at humour, but was clearly in some serious pain. "Feannag was weakened by what you did. Under our onslaught it was weakened further until its shape broke its bonds. It's been blown on the wind! I doubt it will be able to form its shape again for many years if ever."

"You should go back and let Seithmath deal with your wound," Ferylt told him anxiously. "I'll deal with things here." And for once he didn't argue, which was worrying in itself.

When he'd been led away the women turned to Ferylt.

"Have we done enough this time?" was Hope's first question.

"I think so," Ferylt replied, "although only time will tell." One of the younger Elfael ran up to her and delivered a hurried message before running back, but Ferylt's face broke into a smile. "Seithmath says that we've succeeded in breaking Feannag's bond with the house. It will no longer be able to actually inhabit the place."

"Is that sufficient, though?" Nancy asked. "And what about your bond with it? Will you be able to come and go as easily again now?"

Ferylt gave her a worried look and immediately turned for the garden. "You are right to ask that, Nancy. Which reminds me – I have no wish to be separated from my husband by a closed portal! We should fetch my archers from the garden, and your friend and the little boy, and stay close to the portal in case it closes quickly."

Hurrying out into the garden they could see the four archers staying where they had been posted, but in the quiet of the night they could hear someone crying. As they came up on the bower, they saw Jemima with her head in her hands weeping, and Elias' little body laid out on the floor with his hands crossed on his chest.

"Oh no!" Deb gasped in horror.

"He just stopped breathing," Jemima sobbed. "His breaths got fewer and shallower until they didn't come again."

"Poor Katherine," was Anne's instant reaction, and they all knew she was remembering her own lost children and how that had felt as a mother.

"We'll bury him up with Harry and Walter," Hope said. "It's only fitting."

"What will the priest say, though?" Nancy wondered. She'd refused to attend the local church except on those occasions when she could remain in safe anonymity at the back, her faith having disappeared long ago, so she could never remember the priest's name.

"We could say Samuel took him away," Deb suggested as they began the sad journey back to the house.

However, Katherine would have none of it. Elias would be buried with proper ceremony in the church, and no-one had the heart to argue with her. Samuel too would be fetched by the village undertaker, and Ferylt admitted that it might be better if his body was buried far from the house given the bond he'd had with Feannag. Burning him would've been better, but there was no time if Nancy's guess that the portal would close quicker this time seemed likely to be correct. For the others it was also a time for decisions. Anne and her daughters were willingly going back with the Elfael for that was their home now, but this time Nancy had elected to go with them.

"I'm sorry, Deb," she apologised, "but I can't go through all this again."

"No, I understand now," Deb said with feeling. "I really do. I just wish I'd been able to help more all the years you were suffering. Don't worry. We'll cope."

With Jemima supporting a grieving Katherine at the bottom of the stairs, and Orlando clinging to their skirts in a daze, it was left to Deb to say farewell to the others at the mural.

"I'll be watching for you come Yule!" she called as the mural's vibrant force faded and returned to its original state.

"Is that it?" Jemima asked her a week later as they shared a much-needed glass of raspberry wine following Elias' funeral. Katherine was resting upstairs and Orlando with her. He was still not quite his old self and Deb and Jemima wondered whether he ever would be. He missed his brother dreadfully, and was terribly wary of men now. However, the state of Samuel had meant that few questions were asked about how he'd died, and it had been easy to point to the opium bottle and explain Elias' death as childish curiosity over its contents.

However, if the village was scandalised over Samuel, it was also sympathetic to Katherine's plight, and no-one questioned why the manor was once again to be let and why she was moving to a cottage beside Deb's. The family's belongings had taken little time to pack, and after this day they would be relocated away from the horrible memories. Standing in the old hall that evening neither Deb or Jemima could feel anything of Feannag, and hoped that this was the last the family would ever see of it. But each harboured a suspicion that even though they'd weakened its grip, the death of Samuel, coupled with the wash-away from the hearth, might still have left a residue which would have results in the future which no-one yet could foresee.

"We must watch this place, you and I," Deb said to Jemima. "Especially at the time of the Sabbats, and not only for that beast Feannag. Nancy and Anne may have news for us or things they might need us to act upon. It's up to us to protect the place now."

Chapter 11

The present day

Come the morning Robbie chivvied Drake up and out of the house to go back and look at the school. The worst thing now for Drake, Robbie reasoned, was to sit at home without a clear direction to go in, and their leave still had to the end of the week to run yet. By getting Drake back out to the site, he hoped to revive enough interest to get him enthused about some historical detection.

As they sailed along the country roads, the old Honda reverberated to the sound of Roxy Music belting out music from the *Flesh and Blood* c.d., for Robbie had given Drake completely free range with the choice of music this time as another incentive. Whereas Robbie's musical taste was wide ranging, and covered everything from Bach to heavy metal, taking substantial detours into the blues, folk, and pop on the way, Drake's clearly reflected the time when he'd been happiest. Or at least if not happy, then at least when he'd felt the future was more promising.

As Bryan Ferry worked his way through *The Midnight Hour*, *Oh Yeah,* and then *Same Old Scene*, Drake was leaning back in the seat, eyes closed and softly singing along. Sneaking a sideways glance, Robbie could almost see a younger Drake who'd lived life in the fast lane in London, leading a double life trawling the capital's underworld and wreaking mayhem with the criminal fraternity by day, even as he danced the night away off duty.

And he must've cut quite a figure too, Robbie thought, visualising Drake in the emergent New Romantic club-land of the capital. Maybe he was stretching his fantasising of Drake's life a bit too far, he forced himself to admit, but one thing was for sure, it had surely been nothing remotely like his own younger years.

It made him realise with a jolt that he himself had easily slid into middle age because, disconcertingly, there'd been very little to miss or lose. If it had made getting older easier, it nonetheless made him uncomfortable to realise that he'd been in grave danger of letting the whole of his life slip away with as little effort. Drake may have lived life fast and furiously, but at least he had something more than a couple of years' worth of memories to look back on.

The younger Drake had probably had the money to afford the clothes, his pick of women, and the looks to carry both of them off with ease. Robbie couldn't imagine how that must've felt – it was too alien to his own life – but this revelation did give him a greater sympathy for the man sitting in the passenger seat. It wasn't just the job which Drake was mourning, it was the whole of his lost youth. A complete lifestyle!

As Ferry sang, 'it's still the same old movie ..that's haunting me, ...trying to revive the same old scene,' Robbie thought there could be no better comment on his new partner in crime. What Drake wanted above all else was to be back in that 'same old scene' which he'd loved so much. And that was the one thing Robbie couldn't possibly give him back.

What the hell am I going to do with him? Robbie thought to himself, as they stopped at the traffic lights at a major cross-road, and drew some odd looks from a bunch of local teenage lads lounging on the corner by the petrol station. Then he hoped like mad that Drake wouldn't open his eyes at this point, because the last thing they needed at the moment was for him to see a bunch of smart-arse youngsters laughing at two sad old gits in a knackered grey saloon, playing music which might as well have come from the Ark for all the street cred' it had. Then Robbie's elderly c.d. player creakily made the change and the band changed to the Psychedelic Furs, which mercifully appeared to sound less dated to the hoodied youngster, since the smirks faded and they even seemed to be trying to listen. With a little grin to himself, Robbie managed a fast take-off from the lights, even if it was with a small puff of blue smoke from the exhaust – still some life in the oldies yet!

"Cocky little shits," a voice drawled with a dry laugh from beside him.

"I didn't think you'd noticed."

Drake wriggled more upright in his seat and managed a crooked smile. "Oh, I noticed! The minute you pulled up at the lights! Old habits die hard. Always a dangerous spot for coppers are traffic lights in the rough areas. Too easy a target when you're standing still, even if the doors are locked. Anyway, what was that touch of *The Sweeney* when you pulled away?" he teased. "Not quite your usual style of driving. You normally nurse this thing along like the wheels are going to come off any minute."

"You're obviously having a bad influence on me!"

Drake snorted, "You sure about that?" Then laughed. "Bloody hell, we're a sad pair aren't we!" But Robbie was relieved to hear nothing more than his normal sardonic humour in his voice. The black mood of last night seemed to be fading. "So what are we going to do when we get to Weord, anyway?"

"We're going to try to get a feel of the lie of the land. I've been thinking about those Civil War bodies, you see. I'm wondering how much notice the family would've had that trouble was on the way. After you went to bed, I was thinking about those Covenantors again, and how odd it is that it's the soldiers we've found buried there, not the family. Without being morbid, you'd expect it to be the other way round, wouldn't you? So I'm wondering whether the family had enough warning to make an attempt at defending the place, and did better than they might have hoped."

"Then let's go for it! Sod it, what else have we got to do!" Drake exclaimed with surprising abandonment, winding the window down and giving two startled farm-workers trimming a hedge a resounding chorus of *Pretty in Pink* as they shot past. For a second, Robbie wondered whether Drake had got hold of some form of drug and was on a high.

"Are you all right?" he asked cautiously, and was astonished to hear Drake give a belly laugh and chortle,

"Never better!"

"Oh?"

Robbie drove on with an increasingly worried look on his face until Drake noticed. Fishing into the inside pocket of his jacket he produced an official looking envelope and waved it in the air with a grin of satisfaction.

"Williams gave me this when you were getting him his second coffee last night. He'd partly come to ask you for my address because this got forwarded from London. It's been chasing me around every place I've been on the way from there to here, because there was no home address left for it to go to, and no permanent working phone number either. The three witches decided that I wasn't paying up enough – I'd got into arrears even before I was in hospital – and so they clubbed together to sting me for more cash, except that they came unstuck! Must've come as a bitter blow to learn that the gravy train has come to an end!

"In a court hearing held in my absence on account of being stuck back on the cardiac ward with a drip in my arm for my op', the judge decreed that I'd forked out enough, and that I was entitled to have enough of my wages left to live on. Which despite the drop in pay I've had in coming out here, now means that ironically, I'll have more money than I've had in years! I'm still going to be pretty broke because I can't live in your spare room forever – and don't you dare offer! You've done more than enough to help me, Robbie. I need to start standing on my own two feet again. But at my age it's going to knock a big hole in my funds to rent and kit out a place. It's not like I've got any savings hidden away to fall back on. It'll be worth it though!"

"So you're not paying alimony anymore?"

"No! All gone! Angie'd finally lined up another sap, just in case, and is now going to marry him! I reckon she was getting fed up of having only a part share of the honey pot anyway. I'm sure this was a last stab at seeing whether it was worth holding out any longer, and that she'd already made up her mind to call it a day. I just wish she'd done it sooner!

"Number Two witch is still wittering on, but rather did herself no favours when she was seen outside the court by the judge after the first day's hearing being greeted by her kids. Kids brought along by the bloke she's been shacked up with for years! Even one of our upstanding justices could do the maths and work out that they were hardly likely to be mine when they're three and five and we've been divorced for over twelve.

I'm free of her at last, thank God, because she was the really grasping one!

"And they've done that tart Lucinda for tax evasion, because she's been claiming that she paid the rent on the shop instead of me. I knew something was up by the time they scheduled the hearing, but not what it was. But this says she was done just days before my hearing. Ever serve her right! I went upstairs last night expecting to hear that I was going to be screwed even harder, and hardly daring to open the envelope. I've been waiting for the result to catch up with me for weeks, and I've been worried sick about what it would be, and then instead I'm free at last!"

Robbie gave a laugh of relief. "Thank God for that!" Although his relief was more that his fears were unfounded.

After a few minutes he ventured to ask about the rest of Drake's past since he was in such an expansive mood.

"Did you ever go to that big New Romantic nightclub in London, then? ...You know, since you seem to be a bit of a fan? Given what we've been listening to and all that. You know what I mean, the famous one?"

"What? ...Oh, you mean Blitz? The one where Steve Strange and Boy George hung out?"

"That's the one."

Drake sighed. "Sadly no, I didn't turn eighteen until '82 by which time it was all fading a bit anyway. Besides, my mum and dad were living in Harrogate from the late '60s, which was hardly a hotbed of alternative culture!"

"Sorry," Robbie apologised, realising that he'd miscalculated how far back he'd been thinking and had got his times all wrong. But then was horrified to realise that Drake was much closer to his own age than he'd come to believe, despite what he'd been told at the start, and that there couldn't be more than a handful of years' difference between them. This was the music of his younger days too, and he didn't even recognise the fact! What an old fart he must have been in his own early twenties!

"It's okay," Drake was carrying on, oblivious to Robbie's internal turmoil. "Mind you, I'd have given a lot to see all that back then. Apparently, there was a club called Billy's in Soho that did Roxy Music nights. God, that must have been something! The nearest I got was seeing The Human League in Sheffield, because that was closer to home. And one time I got a real belting off my dad was for buggering off to Birmingham alone on the train when I was sixteen. Worried Mum sick. I wanted to see Duran Duran at the Opposite Lock club there."

"And did you?"

He laughed again. "Nah! I was a bloody shrimp at that age! Looked about fourteen instead of older! The bouncers took one look at me and told me to sod off. I spent most of the night creeping round the outside trying to hear the bits that escaped through the walls. When I got home the next morning, I was frozen stiff and had scared myself silly! I got propositioned by some drunken old queen on New Street Station at about three in the morning while I was waiting for the first train back! Mind you, after my dad had finished, I couldn't sit comfortably for a week – so maybe the old queer wouldn't have been any worse! I was grounded for what seemed like forever," and he laughed wryly at the memory of his naïve younger self.

"Oh..." Robbie paused, then admitted, "...I don't know why, but I thought you were reliving your bachelor days in the Met. Of course that must've been much later on."

Drake smiled and nodded. "Oh yes, much later. This is more like my lost teenage years. At this time I was a big fan of Bowie, and Paul Weller back in the days of The Jam, but Roxy Music most of all. I used to sit huddled over an old record player doing my homework trying to figure out a way to get out of that bloody house."

Robbie's mental image made a surprised jump to an imagined dilapidated miners' terrace in the back of a northern town, and made an assumption. "Rough?" He wouldn't have put Drake down as coming from a poor family – especially not with that name! That spoke of people who had the time to read, but then maybe he'd been totally wrong. But Drake snorted with amusement at Robbie's new leap in the dark.

"No! Just the opposite! A big post-war detached effort that my mom used to scrub from top to bottom every day. You couldn't move in the bloody place. The minute you got out of a chair she was plumping the cushions up."

"Did they pick your name for its ...erm ...aspirations?"

Drake rolled his eyes. "Fuck knows! It's pretentious enough, isn't it. Alaric, for Christ's sake! They couldn't have had a Tom, Dick, or bloody Harry, could they!"

"Who picked it?"

"Probably Mum, she always had her nose in a book at night, trying to escape from everything else." He looked at Robbie, paused, and then seemed to decide to go on. "Dad worked high up in a local bank. He was the total control freak, and there was no need for Mum to work, so she took out her frustrations on the house.

"Outward appearances were everything to him. We had to have the perfect house, the perfect garden, and the perfect family as far as anyone outside was concerned. He assumed that I would follow him into finance. Never bothered asking me if I was even interested. When I said I'd joined the police Mum cried for a week non-stop, and he didn't speak to me except to tell me to pack my bags.

"God, this is the first time I've ever talked about this with anyone except Angie! ...I didn't understand why Dad did it at the time. It hurt like mad to be chucked out like that when I hadn't done anything to warrant it. I might've hated the house with a passion, and it was certainly no home, but it was the way it came out of the blue which shook me. That and the speed with which he got me out. I'm not kidding Robbie! I came home the very next day and all my stuff was in bin bags on the lawn and the locks had been changed!

"I staggered off to a B & B for the night, then found my first bed-sit and toughed it out as far as the outside world could see. I kept ringing Mum to try to find out why, but all she did was wail at me that I should have obeyed him and should resign from the police. Eight years later we did one of the local big-time villains, and it turned out that for years Dad had been cooking his books for him! That's where the extra money came from for the posh house and stuff, and that was why he'd booted me out so bloody fast. It was his guilt which was the problem all along."

"What about now?"

Drake gave a sigh and a shrug. "Mum died of breast cancer before the scandal came out, and before I really made it in the force. In one way I wish she'd seen me get my first commendation, but in another I'm glad she didn't have to go through Dad's exposure. All the tittle-tattle from the neighbours, and having to sell the house to pay the massive fines and the overdue taxes, let alone the time he spent in an open prison. It would've killed her as quick as the cancer. We were never really close because she never stood up for me when I was on the end of one of Dad's random beltings, but I wouldn't have wished that on her.

"Dad died a few years ago and I didn't even bother going to the funeral. Didn't seem any point. We'd had nothing to say to one another when he was alive, so his death didn't change anything. The last time we'd exchanged words was back at his trial, so he'd been out of my life for years. I know you're supposed to regret that sort of thing later on, but I never have."

Robbie was horrified. "God, I've never stopped missing my mom and dad! They did so much for me, even when they couldn't really afford it – and I was the only one, so there weren't any brothers or sisters to drain the family kitty before me, we were just bloody poor. And I don't know how I'd have survived losing Jean and the kids if it hadn't been for them. They were golden back then, and they were getting on at that point and not in the best of health, but it didn't matter to them – I was still their lad and that was that.

"Because my house was only fit for demolition, they moved me in with them and kept me there until they were convinced I was safe to be on my own again. You can't put a value on love like that, and these days I appreciate more and more what I had with them. I wouldn't even have made it into the police if they hadn't made real sacrifices to let me stay on at grammar school and get the qualifications. I owe them everything.

"I can't imagine having your kind of home-life. It sounds so cold. So detached! No wonder you're so rebellious at times. You wouldn't have had any choice. Me, I had nothing to rebel against! ...Did you have an older brother or something? Someone who was the cherished older child? Someone you were always in the shadow of?" Robbie was still trying to find some way of understanding why Drake's parents had behaved the way they did.

"Two much older sisters, who did what was expected of them and who've spent years on antidepressants as a result," he snorted in disgust. "Bored shitless in middle-class domesticity, married to grey men in suits they don't even like anymore! I've never even seen my nieces and nephews. Dad forbade it once he'd kicked me out, and being good daddy's girls, they did as they were told. No chance of them helping their kid brother! Then afterwards – when he'd been sent down – the gap was too large to bridge. They blamed me for Dad's fall from grace. The oldest even called me a spiteful little shit, like I'd forced him into being bent!

"These days I think they'd had their eyes on the profits the house would bring when they inherited after mom and dad were dead for years before it happened. When I got kicked out, they just saw it as more for them, but then suddenly there was no inheritance to split anymore. So they never spoke to me after the shit hit the fan, and I wasn't exactly worried by the absence.

"...And later I guess I blamed him for the break-up with Angie. We'd married not two years before it all came out, and she was none too happy at having people gossiping about how the copper's dad had just been sent down. No-one in the force questioned whether I was bent, but it certainly put my next promotion on hold for a while, and she hated that as well. All we did was row, and I was having a hard enough time coping as it was – I didn't need to come home and start fighting the fight back there as well.

"I guess a psychiatrist would say that I hadn't dealt with the whole issue of being kicked out when it happened. All I know is that it came back and hit me with a vengeance when Dad got sent down. I could have done with a bit of sympathy when I got home, not more of what was bugging me. So I blamed the folks even more, because Dad's actions hadn't just messed up my past, they were fucking up my future as well!"

Robbie said nothing as they drove on with the music filling the silence, but couldn't help thinking that it explained much of why Drake's marriages had been such disasters. It also made him feel that at least if fate had stolen his family from him, he'd been infinitely more fortunate than Drake in having them in the first place.

His reverie was broken by Drake asking, "What's up?"

"Up? Why do you say that?"

"Because on a lovely day like this you're driving along with a face like someone who's been asked to collect for Christian Aid in Mecca!" Robbie couldn't help but smile. "That's more like it, but you're still brooding over something. Come on, spit it out!"

Robbie sighed. "I think I'm finally having a middle age crisis!"

Drake gave a barked laugh. "You? Haven't you always been middle aged?"

"Yes," Robbie snapped back, "that's the trouble!" Then stopped himself as Drake's face registered total astonishment. It was unfair to take it out on Drake just because he was the one who'd highlighted the problem, and especially when he'd just found something to be happy about.

"Sorry. ...It's just that I was daftly imagining you as the eighties party animal, and it brought it home to me how I've not had a single landmark event in the years since I lost Jean and the kids. I might've been wrong about you, but until today I'd never looked too hard at myself, and now I don't like what I've done to me. It's no wonder everyone calls me a wizard. Monk more like it! I've made a religious cell out of my files. I couldn't have become more of a hermit if I'd locked myself in some hut in the woods and thrown the key out of the window. And now it's too late to go back and relive the time I've missed."

Drake sat bolt upright. "Oh no you don't! Stop it! Stop that right now!"

Startled, Robbie glanced sideways at him with a puzzled look. "Stop what?"

"Blaming yourself! Jesus Christ, Robbie, I've never met a nicer bloke than you, but do you know what? That bastard Williams takes advantage of that! You might think he's Mr. Nice-guy, but he uses you!

"Did it never occur to you that by keeping you chained up in that little office he saves himself having to move you up the pay scale? You're one of the most able officers I've met in a long time, and it's bloody criminal that you're shut up in an office instead of putting your talent to use. If you'd worked for me, I'd have dragged you kicking and screaming back into the outside world, because that's where you'd be most use, and you'd have got more out of your work. Do you know why I was never made up to DCI permanently?" Robbie shook his head.

"It was because I told the Chief Constable of the Met that my Superintendent was a total wanker! And why? Because the Super' was going to drag one of my younger lads over the coals for a mistake. A mistake, but an honest one which any of us could've made under the circumstances. One where there was no justification for taking him down a rank, except to allow that bastard to drop his pay so that he could afford to promote one of his chosen few.

"The lad kept his rank, but I buggered up any chance of further promotion. But do you know what? I don't regret it for a minute because I did the right thing, and I never let anyone mess with one of my men unless I was totally outranked. And if you'd worked for me, I'd have made sure you had your chance at the promotion you deserved, and sod the office politics!

"And while we're at it, don't you dare do too much on those modern cases! The tight-fisted bugger is trying to get you to solve them while you're on leave so he doesn't have to pay you the time. The crafty sod's worked out that it's you, and not Hobson, whose made most of the connections. So if he leaves it to Hobson, the chances are that the clear-up rate will be less than if you stay involved, so to get it solved and have the success at his door without paying for it suits him just fine.

"And Lord does he like getting all the ends tied up! He's just too penny-pinching to stand up and argue for the money to do it properly, 'cause he's probably got his eye on getting even further up the tree and is trying to look like he's the man to balance the force's books in the future. Williams – the man who gets results on a tighter budget than anyone else! Ha! Don't you dare help him! He doesn't give a shit what might happen to you if you never get a break. If you fell sick, he'd wave you goodbye and never bat an eyelid. But he needs you more than you need him, so make him sweat. Williams is a selfish and self-serving tosser!"

"Thanks," Robbie said weakly, realising that Drake had seen a side to Williams' which had never even crossed his mind.

Then Drake gave a little chuckle. "And who says you're wrong and that I wasn't the party animal, even if it was a bit later on?"

"Were you?"

"Robbie, I wasn't *a* party animal, I was *the* party animal! In between wives, I had more sex than hot dinners! There were whole weeks when I went into work from a different direction every day! I never had any problem attracting women, I just never got the knack of relationships. ...But fucking hell, I had some fun!" He turned and grinned wickedly at Robbie. "Tell you what. When this thing is over, what about we have a weekend up in London and I show you the sights?" and he gave a salacious wink.

"I'm not sure I could survive your idea of a weekend out!" Robbie protested nervously, feeling faint just at the thought. "Just remember I'm not simply out of practice, I need the 'beginners start here' course!" Then he remembered the arson attack on Drake's flat which Williams had told him about. "Anyway, isn't it a bit dangerous for you to be gadding about the capital after someone tried to bump you off by torching your place?"

Drake shrugged. "Wasn't the first time someone tried to do for me. Daft bastards were always trying something on."

"And you lived with that? Christ you're either braver than I thought or barmier!"

Another shrug. "Strange though it sounds, you get used to it."

"You're a bloody adrenaline junkie! That's what you are," Robbie said in mock despair, and just for once Drake simply smiled and refrained from saying what he was thinking – which was, 'yes, but at least I knew I was alive!'

At Weord School they walked to the low garden wall which edged the gravelled driveway in front of the Georgian wing. Perching on the wall's stone coping they shared a coffee from the flask Robbie had brought with them and contemplated the view.

"It's stunning scenery," Robbie observed, "but I don't think it would've been that easy to see anyone coming. I'd mistakenly remembered the view from this side as more like the east side of the Malvern Hills where you get a panoramic view of the Severn Vale. But we're not high enough here. Although we're above the trees in the valley they still obscure the roads. Look, that red car's visible in that little gap but we won't see it again until..." he paused tracing a line in the distance with his finger, "...here. You'd have to be really lucky to spot a small troop of horsemen, even accounting for the fact that there might've been fewer big trees then. And at that distance how would you have been able to tell which side they were?"

"What about uniforms?" Drake asked.

"There were differences, but most ordinary soldiers were in un-dyed leather jackets and breeches, and the identifying insignia wouldn't be visible from a great distance. Remember most hostile encounters took place face to face. We're not talking about snipers picking people off from the distances modern rifles can operate at. Even the guns had a limited range."

"Well that scuppers the theory that the family were well prepared."

"Yes, unless someone saw the soldiers beforehand and made it up here to warn them in time. So how on earth did they manage to turn the tables on so many armed men?"

It wasn't that warm outside in the brisk wind and so they retreated inside, but that too was chilly without a fire. So they opened the back door to the courtyard to be able to sit on the porch seats of the old manor house, which were nicely sheltered and still in the morning sun. Robbie dug the thick cardboard file out of the plastic carrier bag he'd brought it in, and they sat sifting through notes and photocopies. They'd already agreed that the Orlando Edwards who'd sold the place in 1678 must've been the son of the Samuel Edwards who received the manor in reparation after the Restoration.

"It's interesting that there's this oblique reference to the suffering of the family when Samuel received the estate," Drake observed. "That must be connected to the buried soldiers, but God knows how."

"It sounds like the mother's acting on this Orlando's behalf," Robbie added. "So I think we can assume that Samuel is dead by then. It's worded oddly, you know, almost like this Orlando isn't a kid anymore but isn't capable of handling his own affairs. Maybe he was a bit simple and his mother did the real running of affairs in his name, even though he inherited the estate. And this is interesting. The hiring of a new farm manager in 1670 is undertaken by Mrs Katherine Edwards, so I reckon she's already a widow by then, because otherwise her husband would've been in charge of that sort of thing."

"Hang on, what year did you say they first got the manor back?"

"1660 ...no, early 1661. In the aftermath of the Restoration."

"Because there's this odd entry in the parish records of a 'cleansing' of the 'old house' in November 1666. What would that mean?"

Drake handed Robbie the piece of paper, and Robbie poured over it for a minute. "I'd almost say it sounds like they thought the place was haunted. Cleansing would be the sort of thing the parish priest did to exorcise a house. 1666, hmm, not a notable year in these parts for any other particular reason. The year of the Great Fire of London, of course, but that was hardly making waves out here. That finally did for the plague which had kept coming back since the previous year, but I don't think the plague really came out this far either. Oh!" he tapped the paper, "here it is – 'relating to the events of 31st of October'! We're back to Sabbats again!"

Drake sniffed in disgust. "So how many of these events do we have now that coincide with these Sabbat things?"

"Too many is the short answer! But the trouble is, I can't see how the connections could've continued despite the changes of ownership."

"Pity we couldn't have been here on one of them to see what went on. ...Anyone got a Tardis we can borrow?" Drake added facetiously.

Robbie suddenly looked up into Drake's eyes. "Good grief, we're in luck! The next Sabbat is next Tuesday! Beltane is otherwise known as May Day."

Drake stared back in amazement. "You're kidding! Next week?" He paused, too bemused to speak for a second. "Well how many Sabbats are there? And what does the observance of one involve then? My only contact with the paganly inclined has been the local London Goth scene, and a bunch of over-enthusiastic white witches we rounded up once for dancing starkers on one of the commons and frightening the resident drunks! And somehow, I don't think either of those is quite what we're talking about here."

Robbie shook his head even as he chuckled at Drake's description.

"How many Sabbats? Well there's Yule, which is Christmas to you and me – a good old fashioned pagan festival for the solstice which the Church conveniently took over! Imbolc, which is the beginning of February. Then Easter, of course, but in this case it's fixed at the spring equinox, so it's around the twenty-first of March.

"Beltane, is on the first of May – hence our May Day festivities. Followed by the midsummer solstice – when all the pagans dance around at Stonehenge these days. After that Lughnasadh is at the start of August, then the autumn equinox in late September, and then the really big one is Halloween. That's properly called Samhain if you're a pagan, but again it got hijacked by the Church and made into All Soul's Eve. So eight in all.

"But I don't think we have to be the ones making the observances if you're actually talking rituals," Robbie pointed out. "After all, we've just been saying that the families who lived here were hardly what you might think of as the local wiccan coven. So they almost certainly did nothing to provoke things. I reckon we should just turn up and wait to see what happens." Then he had another thought. "Let's not forget that whoever killed Timothy Wiggins is still on the loose and might be drawn here on that night."

That really made Drake perk up.

"Right! A proper stakeout!" he enthused. "That's more like it!" He topped up the coffees, then asked. "What are we going to do before then? I know what I'd normally do, but I don't think the likes of Hobson are going to let us go hunting for info' on Wiggins – and that current case stuff is bound to be with him. I'd love to pull this one off and rub Williams' nose in it by bypassing him completely. But I can't see him being any too thrilled if we go into the office to use the computers just when he thinks he's wrung a few more pennies out of the budget."

Clearly Drake was less worried by the political negatives with the scent of the chase in his nostrils, although Robbie wondered whether Drake might yet pull some trick so that any arrest didn't go down on Williams' books. However, he wasn't about to quiz Drake and instead went along with him.

"Mmm. ...I think we need to get these events clearer in our own minds. We've been so busy dredging up information for all and sundry we haven't really bothered to organise it for ourselves. It's what I'd normally do with an old file, and this scattering of information which goes on is usually the culprit when something's been missed."

"Okay. Then I have a question. Why did this Georgian thing we're looking at the back of get built to make such a funny shape?"

He pulled out the copies of the plans and held them up to the light but in doing so Robbie noticed something new. Seeing the shapes from the back and without the detail he was only seeing the rough outlines, and what he saw made him gasp.

"What is it?" Drake asked, peering round the paper.

"The shape!" Robbie exclaimed excitedly. He grabbed the felt pen and the A4 pad. "You've been working with me long enough on this to know that the old house forms the peorth rune. ...But look at this Ric! If you just draw the house as simple lines see how when you add the Georgian wing in it forms another one! ...See? ...The front of the Tudor manor is a straight line. Make that the one angle. ...Then the Civil War house makes a bar across the top. ...But the way the Georgian wing starts at the Civil War house, and goes not only down to connect with the bottom of the old house, but carries on a bit like a tail... What have you got?"

Drake squinted at it for a moment and then suddenly it leapt out at him. "Bloody hell! It's that wynn shape you were talking about, isn't it! Not exactly another rune, but still connected to the house names."

Robbie's huge grin was confirmation enough, and he quickly corrected Drake's assumption. "The wynn might be a letter used in with ordinary writing in Old English, but it is a rune too! That's where I got the meaning from about 'joy'. Those kinds of double meanings really only go with runes, not ordinary Roman letters even back then."

Drake shook his head in bemusement and stared about him. "So this old place had its name changed from Peorth to Weorth sometime before the Restoration, and the original rune shape was broken up by having the new house built at right angles to it. Then someone takes it back to being a rune shape by sticking the Georgian wing onto it, ...and then it gets another change of name but all the time we keep coming back to the Old English. ... That's *really* weird! And that surely can't be all coincidence!"

Robbie gave a grunt of irritation and got up to wander across the courtyard and look at the Georgian brickwork before giving it a small kick. "That really is a puzzle, isn't it? I wish I *could* say that it's coincidence just for once, but all my instincts say it isn't."

He stood staring up at it hoping that something would provide him with a clue, but instead found his mind wandering until he was brought sharply back to earth.

"Robbie!" Drake suddenly exclaimed.

Thinking that maybe Drake was in pain from his heart by the urgency in his voice, Robbie spun round and dashed back to the porch, especially as Drake seemed to be on the floor. But when he got there, he saw that Drake had simply got down in order to be able to spread the papers out on the floor.

"Look at this!" Drake said enthusiastically. "The person who arranged that cleansing of the house was a Miss Jemima Harrington, described as the companion to that Katherine woman. Now look at the later bill of sale to the Phelans! Mr Jacob Phelan, attorney at law, and his wife *Jemima*! We've got our connection! We should dig up more on the Phelans."

With a new lead to follow they drove back home, this time with Robbie joining in the singing, and on the next two days they returned to the record office and library at Hereford. By the time the weekend came round they had a clearer idea of the sequence of events and the people involved, although not necessarily the motivations.

As best they could tell Jemima Phelan really was the companion and governess formerly employed by Katherine Edwards. Jacob Phelan seemed to have been quite a catch for someone of her station, even though he was far from aristocracy, and then the couple had got lucky. Phelan had made quite a name for himself with a couple of big cases, and the money he'd earned had been sufficient to buy Weorth – as it still was then – and contemplate restoration. There seemed to have been some altercations with the builder over the shape of the addition, since joining the new wing to the two older houses at such odd angles was hardly an easy job, but Mrs Phelan had been insistent.

"Interesting that it's her who wants it that way," Drake observed as they were collating the notes they'd made. "It sounds as though he would've let the builder do it his way, but she won't budge. And she's the one with the connection to the previous family, ...curious and curiouser."

Yet the Phelans had had little chance to enjoy their new home. Jacob had seemingly spent more time in London than on the borders, and the house seemed to have been signed over to his younger brother in late 1679. Although the records were sparse, what remained gave a tantalising glimpse of a dissolute younger brother who was a completely different man to his industrious brother. The detectives couldn't say for certain, but it seemed possible that Jacob had taken his family abroad, maybe to the East Indies, since they disappeared from view, and by the time Jacob's father died at a venerable age only the younger brother had inherited.

"So this is the chronology as we see it," Drake said, fighting the flip chart as it danced in the warm breeze coming through the open windows of Robbie's front room. "We think that Jacob and Jemima already had children by the time they decided to build the extension at Weorth, but we have no idea who they are or even how many of them there were."

"That's right. I think we can assume that Jemima and the children would probably have spent most of the time in London while the building work was going on anyway. But I'm staggered that they only built a single storey range to create stables and the like. I was quite sure the Georgian wing would've gone up all of a piece. This means that it was actually a two-stage development, and done by two different lots of people.

"On the other hand, maybe if they were already expecting to be moving abroad that would explain why the Phelans didn't want to spend vast amounts of money on the place. It makes Jemima's insistence even more peculiar – why worry if you know a move is on the cards? But I don't think we can unearth what that was about. So what's next?"

Drake tapped the next name on the list. "Well Jacob's brother Raymond takes over and moves his family in. I think we can be pretty sure that the reason Jacob gives him the house is because 1679 is the same year that Raymond's son Rupert is born. And if Jacob and Jemima were never intending to come back, maybe they thought they were providing for a younger brother who wouldn't inherit anything otherwise. Either that or they gave it him under some kind of conditions which we've no record of anymore. Maybe to keep the place in good repair against the time when they or their children came back, and it was his if they didn't? ...Aach well...," he gestured in frustration to a separate pile of papers weighted down by a large glass paperweight.

"It's lucky for us that Raymond snuffs it in difficult circumstances when his father's estate is still in probate. His son, Rupert, isn't of an age to inherit although not by much, so we get all the legal records. By the time the lawyers have had their say, young Rupert gets both his father's and his grandfather's estates. Without that legal wrangle we'd never have kept track of them. But young Mr Rupert Phelan takes over in 1701, a year after his father's death.

"God knows where he buggers off to for the first few years, but he must be back at Weorth by 1727 because that's when we find him marrying his second wife in the local church. Lucky sod gets an eighteen-year-old bride, and the kids come along at two-year intervals for the next six years. We have his death recorded in 1734 at just fifty-six. She must've worn him out – lucky sod!"

Robbie shook his head at Drake's flippant assessment. "I think people died of a good many other things as well in those days," he chastised his partner with mock severity.

"Well why ever he snuffed it, we have another one of those merry widows. Bloody hell, why can't I ever find some young rich widow who's a secret nymphomaniac?" Drake complained with humorous disgust.

"Maybe because you don't move in the right circles and there aren't that many of them in the first place!" Robbie chuckled, and was treated to a theatrical rolling of the eyes by Drake. "Anyway, it's our golden couple of Rupert and his second wife, Pamela, who put up the big fancy frontage which now makes the Georgian house. However much of an old lecher he was in getting a young bride, he clearly knew what he was doing with the pennies, and made the most of all the money he inherited from both estates. About 1730 would fit for that extension in terms of style as well, although I'm sure it took longer to build than just one year. Poor old stick didn't get much chance to enjoy his fancy new place, though, did he?"

"Humph! ...Well he might not have done, but she did! Pamela Phelan remarries to this bloke called Esmond Jameson in 1735, just one year after Rupert's cold in his grave – a bit callous don't you think? And lo-and-behold, there are even more little Jamesons in 1736, 1739 and 1745."

"The last one killing her in childbirth along with the baby," Robbie added.

"Right. ...Bloody hell, it's like a precursor to what happened to the 1920s family, isn't it? Like history keeps repeating itself in this damned mansion! Man inherits house then dies, young widow remarries, but finds she's picked a bad 'um and loses everything within a few years! ...Only this time the new man actually gets to inherit when she dies." He snorted derisively and added witheringly, "...So then Jameson carries on alone until he dies in 1753 in a hunting accident!"

"Falling off his horse."

"Bloody daft pastime! Jumping hedges on horses!

"Townie!"

"Humph! And *you'd* get on something that big that doesn't have any brakes? ...I think not! ...However, ...we then have a younger brother of Jameson's acting as guardian for his oldest son Richard, who's the one born in 1739, who's still only fourteen at that stage."

Suddenly he began scrabbling through the papers with a frown of concentration. "Which raises the question of what happened to the kids from Pamela's first marriage to Rupert Phelan? Surely *they* should've inherited? It was their *father's* estate not their step-father's, and while I can imagine their mother having the use of the house in her lifetime, why did no-one claim it when she died, even before Jameson has his mishap with the nag?

"And there were two sons, for goodness' sake, so you'd think one of them would still be around," he said tapping the names on the chart. "We've got no parish record of them dying. They would've been young men by then, well able to defend their right to inherit their father's land."

"I think we can only assume that they'd died somewhere else," Robbie said with a dismissive wave of his hand. "We'll be here forever if we try to trawl through the whole country's records looking for them. The youngest from Rupert and Pamela Phelan's family was already twelve by the time his mother died, so he and the others could well have left home some years before the estate came up for grabs. Especially if they didn't like Jameson.

"Young lads like that could've ended up in the army or navy, or died of an illness or in an accident. Midshipmen were almost considered too old if they went in over twelve years old, you know, so they could have been shunted off to sea, or to the army, as early as when their mother died and wasn't around to watch out for them. Life was more precarious in those days.

"There would've been no obligation for Jameson to actually look after them personally. And some might've thought him generous if he bought them commissions, and never questioned his motives. Personally, I think it's more telling that there isn't so much as a whiff of scandal over who inherits. Very different to our 1920s family, despite still being in such a close community. And back then they certainly had newspapers – or broadsheets as they were called – as we've found. Therefore the means to broadcast dirty doings to the general public were there all right. That, more than anything, makes me think that it was something quite every-day and normal."

Drake nodded. "You're probably right. I was just remembering the way our twentieth century boys to all intents and purposes disappeared. Too creepy for words that we keep getting these echoes all the time! ...So here we are, then, in 1753 with a fourteen-year-old heir, Richard Jameson, and an uncle in charge. All legit' and above board. Or as near as we'll ever be able to tell. Except that this Richard dies heir-less himself, having been murdered ten years later in 1763 by some bloke who looks like he was his lover or some eighteenth-century rent-boy. Did they have cottaging back then?"

"I think they had pretty much everything back then! This is hardly the most prudish period in British history! The Georgians were pretty liberal even by modern standards, and I've got prints in a book over there of some of the old etchings showing the effects of over indulgence in gin and the like if you need further convincing. But it is a bit more unusual to have it so openly referenced in legal documents, the way it is in the accounts that we have.

"I mean, normally, our lad would've been buried in the family grave at the church, and money would've exchanged hands to hush up his indiscretions. To have the vicar refuse point blank to have him in his churchyard means that there must've been something pretty extreme going on. Homosexuality on its own wouldn't warrant that! Burial on un-consecrated ground is ...well, nearly unheard of for someone of that status. The desperately poor might bury children close to the churchyard wall if they couldn't afford the burial fees, and things like that, but not someone from a known family."

"So do you think we have a whiff of dodgy dealings rearing their heads again?" wondered Drake. "Because then Richard's younger sister, Camilla, inherits – that's in 1764 – and her husband, Wesley, is none other than a great-grandson of our Orlando Edwards from a different line. Then these poor buggers seem to bury child after child. Admittedly all seemingly legally and without any doubt about how they died, but nine does seem a touch high even for the eighteenth century."

"And the two who survive aren't exactly robust or normal are they?" Robbie commented. "Daughter Beatrice finally takes herself – or is sent – into a convent in 1794, and the son, Algernon, seems to take ages before he can find any woman willing to marry him. Forty is very old to be marrying for the first time in that age when there's a decent estate's interests to protect. He inherits in 1789, and moves in with his wife and sister Beatrice, prior to her taking herself off."

"But yet again, no kids. And Algernon is the bloke we found the later reference to, about him being committed to an asylum in 1808 for hearing voice and supposedly talking to the fairies! He's the one who changes the name from Weorth to Weord too! I mean, come on Robbie, if the poor sod's a few sandwiches short of the full picnic, he's hardly going to be an expert in a dead language! So where on earth does he get the idea from?

"Even weirder," Drake tapped the next name down on the chart, "our lecherous 1815 squire, Osgood – the one we were talking to Carol about and who took over in 1808 – is actually another, utterly separate son of Wesley, the man who married the 1764 heiress, Camilla. Clearly this Wesley must have been married before Camilla, because Osgood is his son from a previous marriage, not her son – but it still makes this lad another descendant of Orlando Edwards. A great-great-grandson, in fact! How the hell he manages to wangle it so that he gets his mitts on the estate is beyond me."

"And marrying someone who in effect is his cousin at that! No wonder they didn't manage to breed. The gene pool must've been getting pretty muddy by that stage with everyone marrying back into the family. You know, Osgood, was entitled from both his father and mother's sides – that's through Camilla (née Jameson) connecting back through to Pamela Phelan, and through Wesley back to Orlando Edwards." He stopped and thought, then shook his head, coming to stand and look at the chart of the family tree just as Drake mentally caught up with him and muttered,

"Oh I see what you mean! Camilla is Pamela Phelan and Esmond Jameson's descendent, not Pamela and Rupert Phelan's. So there's no direct bloodline to Orlando, although anyone would be forgiven for not seeing it that way. Bloody hell, they must have had records which would put the Kennel Club to shame to keep this lot sorted out!"

Robbie laughed. "I know what you mean! But if there was no-one else left, Osgood would probably have inherited on the strength of those connections. It's amazing how far down the lines the lawyers had to go sometimes in order to find a surviving male to saddle with some estate in the back of nowhere. Somewhere close to London usually got snaffled up by someone in the know with a suitable exchange of cash – the inns of court were notoriously corrupt – but out in the farther flung counties there was less competition."

Drake nodded sagely. "That was what Dickens was getting at with that court case he did in one of his books wasn't it? The one with Jarndice versus Jarndice in it. Everyone so corrupt that by the time it got settled there was nothing left to inherit because it had all gone in lawyers' fees."

Again, Robbie found himself surprised by Drake. He would never have guessed that he'd even pick up a book, much less be reading some of the classics of English literature. "That's the one."

"And look at this family tree! It's got crossing lines and double connections like I've never seen the like of, even away from the main line of inheritance! God Almighty, Robbie! It's a wonder they weren't all cross-eyed with the brains of newts the amount of interbreeding that went on from when our lady Jemima disappears in 1679, up to the squire who gets lucky in 1808."

Their contemplations were interrupted by the sound of Robbie's neighbours again desperately trying to start the car. Leaning out of the window Drake looked out then called,

"Hang on a minute, love," and went towards the door. For a minute or so Robbie heard the murmur of voices and then Drake appeared at the open window.

"Let me have the keys to the Honda, will you? The battery on this thing's as dead as a dodo. I'll run Mandy to the garage down the road and get a new one for them."

Handing the keys over Robbie reminded him,

"Just be careful, eh?"

"Tsk! ...Don't worry! I'll bring the Honda back without blowing a gasket!"

It's not the Honda's gasket I'm worried about! Robbie thought as Drake disappeared into the distance, and he went to inspect the contents of the fridge for that night's meal. When he'd first asked Drake about whether he had a car, he'd been given a terse response that parking was so hard to come by in London he'd just used the force's cars when he'd needed one. Given that Robbie, by his own admission, knew nothing about the workings under the bonnet of his car, it hadn't occurred to him that Drake might not be the same.

However, even in the short time Drake had been lodging with him, Robbie had realised that this was another of Drake's fictions. Far from being indifferent, Drake clearly loved cars and was extremely knowledgeable about them, leading Robbie to wonder whether his straightened circumstances had deprived him of something else he had loved.

The Honda reappeared on the drive with a good deal more élan than when Robbie was at the wheel, Drake removing a new battery from the boot and disappearing with it next door. His curiosity getting the better of him, Robbie went out to join them. Again, Drake was expertly dealing with the girls' Peugeot, taking the dead battery back to the Honda with some quip about it belonging with the relics, which earned him laughs and groans at the pun from the girls. Only as he turned back did they all become aware of a young man weaving his way rather drunkenly across the front lawn towards the girls, two of his mates trailing in his wake.

"Got yourself a sugar daddy, Mand?" he slurred sulkily. "Does he know what a rotten shag you are?"

"Bit early in the day to be in this state, isn't it?" Drake asked evenly. The girls clearly picked up nothing in his tone, but then Robbie had heard Drake telling them that he'd moved up to Worcester with his job and was lodging with Robbie while he found a place. He'd made no mention of what his job was, making more of a joke of the fact that they'd wondered if he was gay, and for his own part, Robbie hadn't got to know them before Drake's arrival. Consequently Kirsty, who'd wheedled it out of Drake that he'd moved on health grounds, was more worried for Drake than of what he might do.

"Oh, give it up, Josh," she groaned. "He's just our neighbour helping us with the car. Keep him out of it and leave Mandy alone."

"Piss off!" Josh's friend hiccupped. "You keep outta it! 'S all your fault! You an' that Sandra, there! You set Mand against Josh, you bitches!"

"No, they didn't," Mandy said, tears welling up in her eyes. "You did it to yourself. All I asked was for you to not be pissed every day. You were the one who said you'd had enough and left."

"Fuck off!" the other lad said swaying forward with a bottle in his hand.

He may well have lost his balance, but whatever the cause he swayed and then broke the bottle against the Peugeot but tottered forward, still holding the bottle by the neck as if he was intending to glass Mandy. Robbie had rarely seen anyone move as fast as Drake did. In a blur of motion, he was around the back of the Peugeot and pounced on the lad, wrenching his arm backwards and smacking him into the side of the car. The bottle clattered to the floor as the lad screamed in pain.

"You bastard!" Josh yelled. "I'll get the police onto you!"

"Yeah! Fucking assault, you old sod!" his mate screamed, fumbling with a mobile phone but too drunk to operate it quickly.

Drake had no such problems. Still pining his charge against the car with one-armed professional ease, he reached to his back pocket with the other and produced his warrant card, which he flashed at the boys.

"Police, is it? I'm Detective Inspector Drake and that man over there is Detective Sergeant Roberts!" He let go of his charge and stepped menacingly up to Josh. He hardly towered over the lanky youngster in height, but he certainly had more muscle than the willowy younger man. "Now, if you three pathetic specimens don't want to spend the night in a cell sobering up, I suggest you leave and don't come back! I don't care how pissed you get in your own hovel, but I will not let you come around here threatening these girls!"

Robbie had moved to Drake's side and was putting on his most severe expression, surprised at how easily he could fall back into the ways he'd learned years ago as a young constable on the beat. Maybe Drake was right, he should have got back to active policing after all. The three lads, whom Robbie guessed were probably fellow students with the girls, suddenly lost all their bravado and slunk away down the street, the shock of Drake's actions having sobered them up considerably.

As soon as they were out of sight the tension evaporated.

"Oh God!" Mandy sobbed, as Sandra turned to hug her, "I thought Jack was coming for me with that bottle again!"

"Again?" Robbie was horrified. "When did this happen before?"

"About a month ago," Kirsty answered as she joined in the three-way hug.

"God Almighty! Why ever didn't you call me?" an appalled Robbie asked them.

Kirsty shakily smile down at him. "We thought you were just some old bloke next door. We thought you worked in an office somewhere – we never dreamed you were a copper!"

"I told Mr Drake about it just when we were out in the car," Mandy confessed, which explained why Drake had reacted so fast when Robbie hadn't even registered the full danger.

As Robbie shook his head – less in despair at the girls' assumptions than at his perceived ineffectuality – he suddenly realised that Drake was leaning back against the car and very pale.

"Oh shit! Ric? Are you OK?" Robbie immediately went to his side and allowed Drake to drape an arm over his shoulder for support.

"Yeah, ...I'll be all right once I've sat down for a minute. ...A bit out of practice with the old moves!" he tried to joke, but there was no disguising the fact that he didn't feel well at all.

The three girls' eyes opened wide at the sight of him.

"What happened?" Mandy squeaked. "You look awful!"

Drake waved a hand in denial at her, and squeezed

her arm in reassurance going past as Robbie helped him back towards his house.

"He had a heart-attack under a year ago," Robbie explained in passing. "That's why he isn't working vice in London anymore. He's right, he'll be fine. He just forgets he can't quite do what he used to do, and it knocks him about when he tries."

Kirsty's "Oh bless him!" at least made Drake snort with amusement, and once he was sat in the armchair by the front room window both he and Robbie could hear the girls' continued conversation. Clearly Drake was quite the hero!

"Incredible!" Robbie teased him, bringing him a strong cup of tea as a restorative and to take his medication with. "You hijack three young women and flirt with them, knock the crap out of an ex-boyfriend and his scabby mates, and you're a hero! Me? I get written off as the ineffectual old git who can't even be called upon to dial 999, let alone help! Bloody marvellous! How do you do it?"

"The old Drake charm, Robbie boy!" Drake answered with a wink. "At least that hasn't gone yet!"

Robbie snorted a laugh. "No, it hasn't gone. ...It might kill you, but you still can't stop trying! ...Incredible!" And he shook his head and went back to the desk. "Do you feel like carrying on?"

Drake was still massaging his chest, but managed a wry smile. "I don't think there's any untoward excitement there which is likely to bump me off yet, somehow!"

For a few minutes Robbie recapped where they had got to until Drake had an idea.

"Robbie? Do you think that the bits of bones that your mate Carol said had been disturbed by the Victorian gardeners might be one of those nine eighteenth-century children or babies who died? And that maybe there were more of them which got destroyed? Small bones would easily get overlooked once they were all messed up, wouldn't they?"

"What makes you think that?"

"Well it strikes me that at any given time from the Civil War onwards things only get strange when there are children in the house. It's like something there specifically targets them. Look at the dating Carol and Sylvia gave us for the bodies. There's not a thing going on when that nutty bloke Algernon has the house in the late eighteenth century. Well at least not unless you think there was something in his strange visions and voices. And if you look at our body count it coincides with the times when we have children in permanent residence."

"And given the coincidence with the Sabbats it does begin to look as though the children are regarded as some kind of sick sacrifice," admitted Robbie reluctantly. "I don't know much about the belief systems which go with this, but I do remember reading something somewhere that virgin sacrifices were thought to be the most potent. The more innocent the better, if you follow. Dear God, it's like something is trying over and over again to make something happen by getting people in this rotten house to give up their kids to it."

"Then we're going to put a stop to it!" Drake said with great firmness. "I don't give a rat's left swinging knacker if this is a family thing – some sick tradition – or some cult which gets handed on some other way. There's too much evidence piling up that there's something seriously dodgy going on at that old manor, and whatever it is it seems to corrupt anyone who comes into contact with the place. Bloody thing wants bulldozing not restoring, but I don't think we'd get away with doing that! So the next best thing we can do is track down whoever's currently feeding this sick chain of events and stop them. We go there on Tuesday, we stake the place out, and we nail any dirty sod who comes snooping round. And if Williams doesn't like it he can stuff it where the sun doesn't shine! No more kids are dying on my watch!"

Chapter 12

The present day

On Tuesday the first of May they set up camp in the old hall, having booked two additional days' leave from an incurious Williams the day before. They had gone into the office for the Monday, but had concocted a story for Williams' benefit about going to a concert in Birmingham on the Tuesday night, which would result in a late return home. However, his utter disinterest had had Drake wagging a finger at Robbie to mark his words over the Superintendent's ulterior motives. He didn't say so to Robbie's face, but Drake dreaded the thought that if his health forced him to retire – or worse, he died – then Robbie might go back to being Williams' unquestioning underling once more. If he left no other legacy, Drake wanted Robbie to wake up and really start living his life again.

On Saturday they'd gone on a shopping spree in a local army surplus store and bought several lanterns, the lights of which were now dimly illuminating an area of the hall. A mini heater powered by Calor gas was also taking the chill off the corner where they'd set themselves up, and the two new camp chairs were draped with unzipped sleeping bags for when it got even colder in the early hours. Robbie's car was hidden in a disused gateway down the hill now that it had been offloaded, and they were waiting for any sign of activity. It had been a slow day, for they'd got to Weord first thing in the morning, and with even Hobson's lone guarding PC now withdrawn for other duties, they'd been all alone. Not even a tractor had appeared in the neighbouring fields, and despite regularly taking binoculars to the upper floors of the various buildings they'd been unable to see any signs of anyone lurking nearby.

It was now approaching midnight and Drake was obviously bored stiff.

"No-one's going to show, you know that," he said in disgust, and dug out Robbie's old portable c.d. player. "If they were ever planning anything for tonight, they should surely have been here hours ago and setting up shop by now. We might as well have some music on to pass the time until midnight, but if nothing happens then we'll admit failure and go home. Whoever did for Wiggins is obviously long gone, but then – given the police presence here over the last week or so – I was stupid to think he would show.

"God I'm losing my touch! I'd never have been so blind when I was on form. Any felon capable of arranging such a murder, with so few clues for us to work on, isn't going to be dumb enough to come waltzing back into a place only days after it's been crawling with the force." He grunted. "And even some of the thicker ones I've known over the years have had a bit better sense of self-preservation than to do that!

"The best thing we could do is clear off and come back here for the next one of those feasts. Give him time to be lulled into a false sense of security. He won't come now. We'll just wait and see if there's something telling lit by the moon at the witching hour, or whatever, but I don't hold out much hope. I think there's some very human hands behind all of this."

He dug in his own pack and brought out a 70s' & 80s' compilation c.d. and put it on. For a while Robbie sat listening while Drake prowled restlessly around the hall, both of them disappointed but neither willing to admit how much.

"What exactly is or was the Strand?" Robbie suddenly demanded in response to the Roxy Music track playing. "I mean I can tell it was a dance, but..."

Without a word Drake began to dance across the floor, black coat swirling as he strutted his stuff, giving Robbie the chuckles then reducing him to helpless mirth, which only prompted Drake to further antics. Even as he laughed, Robbie felt secretly relieved that Drake had taken no lasting harm from his tussle at their neighbours'. An incident he couldn't shake a feeling of responsibility for – for had he been more the policemen at the time of the first incident, he could've warned the boyfriend off before Drake had needed to step in.

"A few disco lights and a decent sound system and you could have a good nightclub in here," Drake said, by now having dismissed the idea of any malevolent influence as he struck a pose at the end of the track. "Come on, you! Let's see if you look any better up here! If we're going to have that wild weekend in London you need to get into practice. Come on! Show me what you can do on a dance floor, so you don't embarrass us both when the gorgeous women start falling at my feet!"

He gave Robbie a wicked grin and a wink, robbing his words of their arrogance. Then gesturing to Robbie to join him as the next track started, Drake turned to work his way back across the floor.

"Nothing lasts forever ...of that I'm sure," he sang lustily, if tunelessly, in time with the track. "Now you've made an offer, I'll take some more!" Then turned to face Robbie, stretched, and said, "and if it doesn't last, then at least it's been nice getting out of the office and up off our bums for a while!"

"So maybe there's something still left worth doing

even if it wasn't what you expected?" Robbie called across hopefully to the still-dancing Drake.

What the response would've been he never found out, for a strange voice from back in the gloom by the stairs suddenly said,

"What in God's name is that noise?"

Drake spun to a halt and Robbie pounced on the stop button of the c.d. player. Both of them began to run towards where the voice had come from. only to see a teenage girl walk through the doorway from the stairs towards them, with a slightly older young woman behind her.

"Hello," she said uncertainly.

"Hello," Robbie replied cautiously, holding out an arm to halt Drake's dash. "Does your mom know you're out here, love? It's not safe, you know. We've had reports of someone hanging around here. Can you get home easily or should we call for someone to come and take you home?"

However, the girl ignored his question to ask one of her own. "Who are you? Why are you here?"

Brushing Robbie's hand aside Drake snapped, "Police!" instantly the professional again, marching forward and pulling out his warrant card. His manner was less brusque than it had been with the young men, but the girls' appearance at this time and in this place made Drake very wary, his tone of voice carrying a warning not to mess him around. "DI Drake! And this is DS Roberts. So how about you answer my colleague's questions and tell us what you're doing here! Why are you here and what's your name?"

"The police?" she said instead in surprise.

"Yes, the police! This is the site of an incident we're investigating," Drake said firmly, "and we're asking the questions here. So once again, who are you?"

The girl looked timidly up at Drake who by now was looming over her. "I'm Suzanna Fisher."

Drake staggered back as if he had been struck. It was one of the few things which could've rattle him out of his professional calm under such circumstances, and he reacted sharply. "No fucking way are you Suzanna! If you are, you haven't aged a day since you disappeared seventeen years ago, and I'm not so bloody stupid as to believe that! So stop pulling my pisser, young lady. Who the bloody hell are you?"

The girl's eyes began to fill with fear at the proximity of the furious Drake, who was once more right in her face.

"I really am Suzanna, sir. Honestly!"

"Bollocks!" Drake roared, causing her to flinch and retreat back with the other girl behind her. "Who sent you? You aren't old enough to remember the original investigation. There's no way you could know enough to pass for her by yourself. So who set you up? Who's playing games with us? What about Carrie Lewis? Did you know her? Did you know Timothy Wiggins? Is that the connection? Did you help set him up to be killed for what he did? Answer me!"

"Stop it, Drake!" Robbie remonstrated, hurrying to him and trying to grab his arm again. "You're really frightening her! She's gone as white as a sheet! Look at her! She's only a kid!"

"Yes and I've had kids her age attack me with broken bottles! And I don't just mean the three drips we met last week! You might still think the best of everyone, but some of the kids I've met of her age have been a dab hand with knives and guns. They can be more vicious than the older felons. Don't turn your back on them for a second!" Drake snapped, while reaching out to ready to grab her arm in his turn.

But before he could say any more there was a savage scream and a young man, also barely out of his teens, came hurtling through the doorway from the stairs brandishing a sword, and made a wild swipe at Drake. A startled Robbie just had time to think it was no wonder Drake had avoided the broken bottle so easily if he'd experienced far worse weapons, for Drake never batted an eyelid as the blade whistled past his head, simply dodging backwards and then diving in again. With an ease revealing years of practice, Drake avoided the weapon again as it swung back at him, and then pounced on its wielder, flooring him with professional thoroughness, and disarming him on the way down by the simple expediency of breaking his arm.

"Little bastard!" he snarled, whipping handcuffs out from his back pocket, and securely cuffing the lad, ignoring the cries of pain from the broken arm. "Attack a police officer, would you? You're going away, sonny! You have the right to..."

"...No!" the girl called Suzanna cried. "Please sir, no!"

"He should've thought about that before he tried to brain me with that thing," Drake snarled unsympathetically.

Suzanna sobbed. "No! You can't take him away from this house! If you do, he'll die!"

"Don't be daft love. Prisons are a cushy number these days," Drake dismissed her plea.

"Oh please, sir, help him!" she begged Robbie. "I don't know what year it is now, but if it really is seventeen years since I left, then it's nearly eighty years since he came over. He won't be able to go back into the real world without it catching up with him. He will die!"

And suddenly Robbie thought he could guess who the young man was. "Hold it Ric," he said putting a restraining hand on his colleague's arm. "What if this lad is one of the kids from the 1920s family?"

Drake looked at him as if he had lost his mind. "Don't be fucking stupid, mate! How old is this little toe-rag? That lad would be an old codger in his nineties if he was still alive."

But Robbie held up a silencing hand asking Drake, "So where did they appear from?" before turning to the girl again. "We know all the outside ways in are locked tight, so why don't you show me where you've just come from," he said gently.

The two girls looked at one another doubtfully, but seemed to come to some unspoken agreement.

"It's this way," the older companion said in an odd accent, which Robbie now identified as the first voice which had spoken, and turned to the stairway.

With Drake hauling the whimpering young man along with him, they followed the two girls to the stairwell and up to the first landing. As they got there another female figure suddenly stepped out of the solid wall to stand in front of them.

"Jesus *fuck*ing Christ!" Drake yelped in shock, and to Robbie's horror in one swift movement he'd produced a compact automatic pistol from the inner pocket of his coat, which he pointed in a rock-steady hand at the woman. "Fucking hold it right there, lady!"

"Christ Almighty, Ric!" Robbie also yelled, appalled. "Where the hell did that come from? Are you mad? A *gun*?"

Yet before he could remonstrate further with Drake, there was a soft sound of movement on the stairs above and behind them, and Robbie looked up to see many men all aiming wicked-looking barbed arrows straight at them. The clothing was distinctly odd, and they all looked like a good bath wouldn't go amiss. Whether they were re-enactors or something else, there was no doubting the proficient way they were also handling the weapons.

"I think you'd better put the gun down, Ric," Robbie said, holding his own hands up to show that he wasn't armed. "We're a bit outnumbered here, gun or not!"

With great reluctance, the still snarling Drake placed the pistol on the stairs, but well away from the young man whom he continued to hang on to.

"Now then," Robbie said very carefully, taking a measured step towards the new older woman who'd just appeared. "Could you please tell us what's going on here?"

Instead the woman looked to Suzanna. "These are those police you spoke of?" she inquired. "They are not as I imagined! You said they protect people yet they act violently towards you."

"That's my fault," the boy in Drake's grasp cut in weakly. He looked up at Drake. "Please sir, will you let me go? I only attacked because we thought you were with the one who came here at Easter."

"At Easter?" Drake exclaimed, now totally wrong-footed and confused.

"That would have been back in March?" Robbie queried, mentally dissociating the Sabbat from the more recently celebrated modern Easter, and got a nod in confirmation. "But we only found the bodies a few of weeks ago. What happened in March?"

But now the newcomers looked worried and only had more questions in response to his own.

"Bodies? Weeks ago?" the third woman asked. "What did you find?"

"You know bloody well what we found!" snapped Drake, patience at an end. "The mangled body of seven-year-old Carrie Lewis and her pervert of a stepfather stuck with so many wounds he could've been used as a bloody tea-bag, that's what! And besides that the remains of Helen Fisher!"

The youngest girl gave a sob and buried her face in her hands. "Another girl dead? No! The Elfael killed the man who murdered my sister and tried to kill me!" she cried. "He's dead. He couldn't have hurt anyone else!"

"No, he didn't," Robbie said, coming forward to place a comforting arm around her shoulders despite drawing all the aimed arrows towards himself, and making Drake take a sharp intake of breath at his friend's unconscious courage. "We've found his body buried in the garden. We know it wasn't Albert Walters this time."

"Albert Walters?" Suzanna said, this time with outright shock. "Was that him? Is that Emily and Julia's father? Was he the man who tried to kidnap me? Oh poor Julia and Emily! And he's dead? They must be so upset!" She sounded very confused. "But he went away. He couldn't have been the one who attacked Helen."

"Yes, it was him," Robbie confirmed. Then it suddenly occurred to him that she'd spoken as if the girls were still alive. "You'd better sit down, love," he said gently, gesturing to her friend to come closer. As she sat down on the stairs, with a worried frown Robbie crouched down to look her in the eye. "I'm terribly sorry to have to tell you this, sweetheart, but he killed Emily and Julia the Christmas after you disappeared from here. He faked taking them away from school, but in reality they were dead, and their bodies were left here. And sometime before then he'd killed his other daughter, their half-sister Rita, although a lady scientist we know thinks he brought her body to join Julia and Emily later on.

"That was all before he did what he did to Helen. Maybe she even disturbed him bringing Rita's body here, we don't know. But it's pretty certain he was responsible for the deaths of all of them. I'm so sorry to have to tell you this, but it's better that you know you're safe from him now. You're the only one we've found who escaped from him alive."

The poor girl gave a howl of dismay and dissolved into sobs. Robbie moved back to allow the other two women to come forward and comfort her.

"How do you know all this?" the older of the two asked. "You just told us that it's seventeen years since Suzanna came to us. If that is so, and I confess it is hard to keep track of time on the other side, then the bodies would've been unrecognisable."

"Forensics, love," Drake said tersely.

"What are *...forensics*?"

"Science," Robbie attempted to explain. "We can now take bodies, or even just skeletons, and get our scientists to work on them, and they can prove who was related to who. And we can also check the remains against records of things they had done by dentists and doctors. We can tell what diseases they had, sometimes, and all sorts of other things like what they had as their last meal."

"Good Heavens!" another voice spoke and a fourth woman stepped out of the wall painting.

This time Robbie and Drake were closer and saw how the surface seemed to move like water as she stepped through.

"*Fuck*in' *hell*! That *is* weird!" a badly shocked Drake swore, then looked down at the boy at his feet and reassessed his opinion. "Are you really one of those lads who disappeared in the 1920s?"

"Yes, sir," the youngster replied weakly. "My name's Colin. Me and my brother Bertie got rescued by the Elfael. It was our new father. He killed my brother Edward, and then James disappeared, and Mother got all upset. Then he came into our room and threatened to kill us if we didn't pretend that James had run away with the gypsies. So we were going to run away together, because we were sure he was going to kill us anyway, but the Elfael found us and took us back with them where we'd be safe."

"We know all about your stepfather, Gregory Smith," Drake said dryly. "Nasty piece of work wasn't he!" Colin nodded and Drake bent down to undo the handcuffs. Helping Colin to his feet he took his own belt off to make a makeshift sling for the broken arm. "Sorry son," he said gruffly, having less of Robbie's natural empathy to call upon, "but we found your brother James' body in the same place as her friends. We didn't know his name at the time because we weren't sure which one of the three of you it was."

However this time the recipient of the bad news just nodded sadly, and there were no tears. "I knew James was dead," Colin said sadly. "We both did. There was no way he would've run off without telling us. And he'd left all his things behind. He'd never have gone without his copy of *Treasure Island*."

"So who are these Elfael?" Drake demanded, looking up at the men on the stairs whose guard had never dropped for a second.

"Please would you explain?" Robbie added more gently. He looked down at Suzanna who seemed to have regained some of her composure. "You'll have to excuse DI Drake. You see he never stopped looking for you and your sister Helen. He was the policeman in charge of your sister's case and this is all very stressful for him."

"But you said it was seventeen years ago?" her friend said. "So Helen disappeared not long after that as well. That's a long time ago for you!"

"Yes, it is," Drake said tersely. "But it was my job to find Helen and I failed! So I kept on looking. Not every day or even every week, I'll admit. But any time I got a chance I would check to see if anyone had appeared, or if there was any new evidence, and yes, I really did keep doing that for the full fifteen years since she went missing."

"He doesn't give up easily," Robbie told her with a faint smile, "because despite what you've just seen, he really does care. And now you also know that we're here because someone else got hurt. So won't you tell us who the rest of you are?"

Suzanna got to her feet helped by the girl who had come into the hall with her. "I'm Sophie," the girl introduced herself. "I joined the Elfael in 1815."

"Ah, you're the girl whose father came to find her!" Robbie gasped.

"Yes. Unfortunately, Uncle Osgood had a gun. He loved going out hunting with the horrid thing! The Elfael came through in time to rescue me and my children, but not Father. Bless him, he fought with Uncle Osgood and he turned the gun on Uncle even after he'd been shot. He managed to knock Uncle out with it before he collapsed. Uncle wasn't dead, though, and then my aunt came out and started having hysterics while the Elfael were burying Father, and she got the servants to take Uncle Osgood inside.

"The Elfael didn't want to have to start attacking the innocent servants just to get to Uncle. They said he wouldn't live long with a head wound like that, anyway, but I still left with them just in case. They'd been planning to get me out of the house the previous time the portal opened, but it doesn't open for so long anymore, so they tell me, and my aunt had taken my baby to show him off to some friends. She was passing him off as her own! I couldn't leave without him, and so the Elfael had to come back for us the next time."

"And your children? Are they safe now?" were Robbie's next questions.

"Oh yes! Quite safe!"

"Good!" he turned to the third woman. "And you are?"

"My name is Deb," she said with a smile. "I came much earlier, in 1679." She gestured to the much older woman who had just arrived. "This is my aunt Nancy. She decided to join her friends with the Elfael in 1666, but they in their turn had been with them since 1645."

Both detectives stood in open-mouthed astonishment at this pronouncement.

"Are you telling me that you're ...what? ...Four hundred years old ...give or take a decade?" Robbie asked faintly, as his mind did the maths and then did a double-take. "You don't look a day over forty!"

"Thank you! And in the sense that I've lived that long in a real world, no, it's not been four hundred years for me," Deb admitted. "Time seems to do funny things over in Ffreuer – that's the name the Elfael have given the land beyond the portal."

"As best we can make out," Colin added, now propped up against the wall very white-faced but lucid, "it must've once been a part of what we think of as Powys. But it's like a bit of it got detached a very long time ago and went into some other place."

"Detached? How long ago are we talking?" wondered Robbie.

Colin took a deep breath. "Well hard as it seems to believe at first, we've discovered that the first of the Elfael came here when the Anglo-Saxons were just about getting to the Welsh borders." He managed a wobbly smile. "I loved reading *Puck of Pook's Hill* with Edward and James, so I remembered a bit about early history."

"Heavens!" Robbie gasped. "You're talking about the sixth century?" Then he looked up at the men surrounding them. "So these people are sixth-century Welsh warriors?" Colin nodded. "Good grief! Can they understand what I'm saying, then? I mean, the language has changed immensely since then."

"We understand," replied a male voice with the thickest Welsh accent Robbie had ever heard.

"They understand enough," the woman called Deb qualified, "although you'll lose them with anything more than simple words. I find your modern speech hard enough, and I've been one of the ones monitoring the portal, so I've seen the changes more than most. The trouble is the changes have come very quickly for us. Those of us who've come through the portal have found it easier to learn some of the Elfael's language since there are – or were – more of them than us, and we use it all the time."

"Were?" Drake picked up on the correction immediately.

Deb sighed. "Would you mind coming with us? I think Colin's arm should be seen to, and it would be easier to show you much of this than try to explain."

Robbie and Drake exchanged glances, then Drake shrugged and gestured to Colin to lead the way. With the women keeping them company, and the warriors at the rear, the two detectives walked up to the steps which appeared to come out of the wall to lead up to the edge of the mural, four feet above the floor of the landing.

"I don't bloody believe this!" Drake muttered under his breath, as he made the jump up to what should have been a solid wall. But when he turned back to look at the way he'd come he found Robbie right behind him and looking at him oddly. "What?"

Robbie paused then looked him straight in the eye. "Don't pretend to me that you haven't been having chest pains these last months! So then tell me how you've wrestled a fit young man to the floor, dragged him up a flight of stairs, and coped with the strain of having weapons pointed at you, without you even struggling to breathe once! The last time you did that you were one step away from me taking you to casualty!"

Drake was so astonished he tripped over his own feet. He shook his head as if to clear it, then took his own pulse before looking back at Robbie in wonderment. "Steadier than it's been in years. And no pain! Not even discomfort!" Drake pulled his shoulders back and took a deep breath. "Bloody hell it's been ages since I could do that this easily! I feel well, Robbie, *really* well."

"You've been ill?" Deb asked, having heard their conversation.

"He's been dying!" Robbie said baldly. "His heart is giving out on him and even our advanced medicine hasn't been doing that much good."

"Then maybe he should stay," she said giving Drake a flirtatious glance.

"The old Drake charm, Robbie boy," Drake whispered softly, with an appreciative grin as he watched Deb's swaying skirts as she moved on, "the old Drake charm!"

"Unbelievable!" sighed Robbie trudging in the wake of his friend, who had a new spring in his step and was now quite clearly chatting up this new woman.

The landscape they found themselves in was a direct copy of the one they'd left outside the house, if you discounted a millennium and a half of human interference. The main contours were the same but its appearance was much wilder. No roads or power lines, and few field boundaries. The hills were forested and visible, even at this hour, by a night sky filled with stars no longer masked by light pollution. A short way from the portal, Deb sat down on a grassy meadow and gestured the others to join her. Colin took his leave of them and walked off down a torch-lit route in the direction of what appeared to be some kind of hall built into the very heart of a nearby copse of trees. The air smelt clean and fresh, and everything had a vigour about it as if it was all still very new and had never heard of twentieth-century pollution.

"I daren't take you too far from the portal," Deb explained, as another older woman joined them to sit beside Nancy, "because if it starts to close, we'll have to get you back pretty quickly. To save time, may I ask what you know of Weorth Manor?"

"Over to you," Drake said, gesturing at Robbie, who launched into an abbreviated version of what their investigation had turned up.

When he'd finished Deb breathed a sigh of relief. "Your knowing so much helps greatly. As for the rest," and she then proceeded to fill in the gaps and give them the back story about her grandmother Margaret. "There's a lot more detail, you understand," she admitted straight away, "but given that time is a problem that's the bones of it."

"But there's more," Sophie added. "Deb came over once her friend Jemima told her that she and her family were leaving for India. Aunt Nancy, here, had managed to tell Jemima and Deb that the Elfael's seer, Seithmath, had a theory that if they built the new wing in a particular way it would help to turn the original summoning of Feannag."

"Ah!" Drake gasped appreciatively. "So that's where the funny shape came from! We've been racking our brains trying to work that one out! We couldn't figure out how or why someone in the eighteenth century would have come up with rune shapes."

Sophie smiled. "Yes, it was on the Elfael's instructions. Deb and Jemima used to come to the portal every Sabbat they could. Most of the time together, but sometimes one of them alone. It meant they got the message, and Jemima managed to convince her husband to pay for it. Since then, there's been no sign of the Beast of Battle manifesting itself. They've not seen it in physical form in the real world since they fought it in 1666, and I've only seen it like a ghostly shadow in this world. But the portal also doesn't open for as long at each Sabbat now. It still wasn't enough for Jemima, though. Once she'd had her children she wouldn't set foot in the place, and who could blame her?

"The Elfael hoped that the house's fortune had been fully reversed, but what happened to me showed them that it still pulled the wicked to it like a magnet. If what you say is true about there having been no children in the house for many years up until I had mine there, then that's very disturbing news, because it would mean you're right about the evil targeting children."

"And unfortunately, it makes a lot of sense as to why we've seen a lot more trouble in recent years," Deb admitted. "We hadn't made the connection about the building becoming a school and the sudden increase in the wicked folk we were seeing coming here. We just thought that maybe it had taken time for the evil essence to build up again, although without Feannag's attachment there we couldn't work out how that would happen."

"You see, it's coincided with renewed attacks on our other borders of Ffreuer, by what the remaining Elfael think are the descendants of the Mearcstapan," Nancy added.

"And you think otherwise now?" queried Drake. "Could it be that things are the other way round?"

The other older woman who had been introduced as Anne spoke for the first time. "In what way?"

Drake was clearly in full investigative mode now. "Well instead of these Mearcstapan ...is that what you called them? ...and this beast Feannag over *here* in these other worlds summoning the evil on our side – because that's the way you saw it before – could it really be that it's been the evil on *our* side which summoned *them*? You said that these earlier Elfael thought the peorth rune was an invitation. Well who was inviting who? How could the evil in another reality reach through to our time and space *before* the portal was built?

"...Because the way I see it, no matter how wicked and evil this Feannag was, it never managed to do a thing to reach you or us for the best part of a thousand years on its own after the Elfael arrived here. But something changed in 1575, and that change was in our world, not over here. As someone who's had his fair share of dealing with the ungodly over the years, I would say that most out and out villains don't change their basic personality, no matter how much you try to reform them.

"Now you've said this Doctor Parker was just such a man. So the evil was on our side to start off with. If there are any of the old Elfael left you might want to ask them if they'd ever seen the Mearcstapan before the portal was opened in 1575. Because my money would be on the answer being no, and it being them who were irresistibly drawn to the way into our world, and therefore to the Elfael's beyond it.

"If that rune's some kind of arcane invitation, it's bugger all use on humans who don't even know what a rune is for the most part. But pretty good if it's something from that distant time you want to drag out into the world again! And that's why the doorway stayed even though you defeated the ...Beast of Battle did you call it? The invitation remains because it's on our side, not yours! Except that now it's less directed on our side. While the beast Feannag was stuck in the chimney's brickwork the connection was very strong, but even doing what you did wasn't enough because the house itself is pulling its essence back to it all the time."

The four women exchanged worried looks with two more women who had just walked over to join them and were introduced as Hope and Milly.

"Oh dear," Anne said. "That is a possibility we had not considered." Her speech was more archaic than that of the others, except Nancy, and she was clearly speaking slowly in the hope that Drake and Robbie would understand.

"What about Colin's other brother?" Robbie suddenly thought to ask. "Where's he?"

The women's demeanour became sad once more.

"He's dead," Nancy said sadly.

Suzanna took up the story since she could tell it

faster. "They keep a close watch on the portal since the brothers arrived, and half a dozen boys were brought over in the time between them and me for safety's sake. Well they always did watch before, but it can be hard when time moves more slowly here than in what I still think of as the real world. Before, they would miss whole years, and sometimes several. The trouble is, this place doesn't make you immortal. Even here people eventually age and the Elfael have begun to die. Too many of the warriors were killed in the big battle when Nancy and Deb were involved, and then over the following years even more of them have gone. The hall here is half empty now, and how long we'll be able to defend the borders of Ffreuer we don't know.

"Because of that, when we saw through the portal someone pursuing a child, back at Easter, Bertie said that he would go back across the divide instead of one of the warriors. He was the oldest of the brothers and the other boys, but he was still a very young man here. He said that he would just go across for the time between Sabbats to see what happened and to try to protect the child, whoever it was. I think he was trying to find out if we could go back as well – just in case Ffreuer got overrun and we had nowhere else to go."

"The person you saw chasing her," Drake asked. "Was he medium height, reddish hair with freckles, about twenty-five years old?" The nods confirmed it. "That was Wiggins. He's dead."

"Then Bertie succeeded," Sophie sighed. "At least poor Colin will have that consolation."

"But where's Bertie's body now?" Robbie still wanted to know. "You said he died?"

"We saw him briefly at the portal," Deb told them in a choked voice. "He'd already aged far faster than we had feared he would. He was an old man clawing at the wall as if he was trying to force his way in. Then he just crumbled to dust." She had to stop to dry her eyes. "We think the trouble was that he left the house. From the portal we can see out through the landing window on a good day, and those on guard reported seeing him out in the garden walking towards the lane. You two will be all right because you've only been here an hour or so and when the two worlds are aligned. But that's why Suzanna was so worried when you said you were taking Colin away. She knew he would die like Bertie did."

Drake was still thinking about Wiggins. "He must've tried it on with someone else," he said to Robbie. "A trial run, or maybe the child got away and he had to make do with Carrie? Or more likely he'd brought Carrie here once before, but something got in the way that time and he had to come back."

"When did Bertie die?" Robbie asked. "Would it have been about four weeks ago in our time?" When he got confirmation from the others he added, "then that ties in with what we found. Bertie must've had a grave already prepared for Wiggins and shot him. His last act must've been to bury Wiggins but he didn't have time to bury Carrie before his strength ran out."

"Or Wiggins had dumped Carrie's body where Bertie didn't get chance to search, perhaps?" Drake theorised.

"The Elfael have buried the ones they killed out in the garden," Sophie confirmed. "It started with the builder, Dr Parker, and was only ever meant to help Margaret start a new life. But when the soldiers attacked Anne's family, they had to make it a permanent set of graves. After that they kept going because it seemed too dangerous to bring the bodies of the evil ones back through the portal. We had no idea what might happen. At least in the real world they were dead."

"What? You think they might have come back to life here?" Drake asked in blatant disbelief.

"Not life, no," was Deb's instant response. "We never thought that! But we did worry that the evil force which had attached itself to them might use them as a way of getting into our world here. Sort of like using the body as a box in which to hide and come here without us knowing."

This Drake could accept more easily, although of the two he was clearly having more of a problem accepting what he was seeing than Robbie was. He was already thinking ahead, though.

"So what happens now?" he asked. "Do you believe that the house is finally safe?" Quite clearly he didn't.

The women exchanged worried glances and once again Deb spoke for them.

"I wish we could say yes. ...And if you were to ask me what proof we have to say that, I couldn't produce anything."

"But your gut instinct is saying there's still a danger," Drake said. "I can understand that. There've been times when that's stood me in good stead in an investigation, even when the evidence said otherwise."

Anne took a deep breath and Robbie could see that she found it hard to join in the conversation but felt she had to. "We have talked of this often," she said slowly, enunciating clearly so that they would understand her. "We have been forced to the conclusion that Seithmath was right. The only thing left to do is to demolish the chimney breast or even the whole house. From what you've told us tonight it looks like the only way to ensure no more children are targeted for Feannag's sacrifice." She sighed. "I hate the idea of the old place being gone forever, even though I can never go back and live there again, but it has to be done. Especially if what you say is correct and the continued existence of the peorth rune shape, albeit added to and altered, holds the doorway open."

"You might get your wish," Robbie said giving her hand a consoling pat. "The last I heard there was a builder interested in buying the place. I think he wants to turn it into some kind of conference centre and health spa, so he'd be ripping the inside out of it."

Then he looked at their blank expressions. "Ah... You haven't a clue what a conference centre and health spa is, have you? Oh dear! Put it this way. Very rich people will come to talk about business and will live like noblemen while they do it. So the man who's going to change the place will have to do a lot of building work on the three houses to make them luxurious enough."

The women clearly thought the twenty-first century must be a very mad place to live in, but were willing to accept that he knew what he was talking about. However, something different was preying on Drake's mind.

"What's this threat you've been talking about? The one on your other border? And how far is this border?"

A pale-faced Colin with his arm now strapped into a proper sling, even if it was hardly standard hospital bandaging, had just walked across to them, and he now replied to Drake as he handed him his belt back.

"To the west we seem to have no boundaries. Or at least none that we've discovered. We may be able to go all the way to the sea – if the sea is actually there in this world. To the north and south we have a pretty clear run too. What worries the old Elfael is that the eastern boundary of Ffreuer is barely half a day away now and it's getting closer. It appears like a shimmering at first. Like a heat haze. The Elfael's leader, Elfan, tried a desperate attack on it before I came here and it cost him his life. It didn't kill Elfan outright, but it was as though something had sucked all the strength out of him and he just faded away until his death was just a foregone conclusion.

"The men who fought with him think that Feannag finally got him. That in some way the portal enabled Feannag to insinuate part of himself across the divide, even if he can't come fully into either our world or yours any more. They think that Feannag's need for the blood of innocents is somehow linked to it being able to come and fight across the divide into our world. As if the blood makes a bridge for it where one wouldn't otherwise be. They call Feannag a Beast of Battle, and certainly its essence is there whenever our warriors have to fight the Mearcstapan. Who knows, maybe if it ever completed whatever ritual it wants to do, it would be able to appear at will and take our warriors by surprise. It's certainly drawn to any kind of conflict.

"Seithmath thinks that only something that strong could have killed Lord Elfan they way it did. Their lady, Ferylt, pined away within a few years. Since then, the remaining Elfael have been doing the best they can, but it's getting harder to repulse the attacks when they come."

"And what are these attacks like?" Drake queried. "Who makes them? And in what kind of numbers?"

Colin sighed. "They're never made in great numbers since I've witnessed them, and the figures are like deformed people. These Mearcstapan descendants are like some corrupt version of human beings – maybe they originally always were – as if someone made them out of spare parts from a graveyard. ..."

"...Inbreeding? Vicious, congenital idiots?" Drake wondered sotto voce to Robbie, as Colin continued.

"...The trouble is, only iron seems to work against them and we're running out of that. The Elfael came with plenty of arrow heads, and have carefully recovered as many as they could after each battle. But time has worn and corroded many, and they never found any iron to mine here, although admittedly they never seem to have had any miners amongst them."

Deb chipped in. "Seithmath thought that the fact that there's no iron naturally occurring in these worlds outside of the real world was the reason why it was so effective against the monsters. It wasn't just the sharp edges and the physical damage. It's like it's a poison to them as well."

"But the real problem," Colin continued, "is that each time they drive us back and stop us from resettling the land, the border moves up to where they stop."

"How fast does this happen?" Drake wanted to know. "Is it as the battle is happening or afterwards? How long do you have?"

"Not instantly," Colin was adamant. "It's more like we get driven off and then night comes, but in the morning there's that haze about the area where the Mearcstapan – or their successors or whatever they are – have stopped overnight. If we can't drive them back that day the haze is even thicker the next day, and the next until the border is fully present at the new spot. The border completely blanks out anything beyond its edge.

"So it's like a grey wall runs across the countryside for as far as the eye can see. If you go close to it you start feeling dizzy and sick. Elfan's the only one who's ever managed to touch it, and when he did it went clear again for a moment and those with him could see the countryside beyond, like the rest of Ffreuer is still there but out of reach. But it also summoned the

Mearcstapan so fast they must have it patrolled at all times."

Drake gazed off into the distance, thinking. "Do you think that if you could drive these monster things back that the border would follow them? Could it retreat if the countryside is still there beyond this wall thing?"

This time Anne answered. "Maybe, but we cannot know for certain. Whilst Elfan led them, the Elfael simply maintained a status quo they had found when they came here, even if it got harder. Since then, despite immense bravery and determination by the warriors, we have only lost ground. If, as you say, that was because of Dr Parker, then our future is bleak indeed, because we can't undo his actions and we're running out of men to fight for us."

And suddenly Robbie knew that Drake had found himself a new battle to fight. If he could no longer fight evil in the real world, he would come and fight here. However, the guard by the portal suddenly began to gesture to the group and Deb got to her feet.

"I'm sorry, but you have to go back now or stay until midsummer. The portal is closing."

They hurried to the entrance point and Robbie stepped through. However, Drake paused.

"Be here at midsummer!" he said firmly, then bent and placed a kiss on Deb's lips before stepping through to join Robbie.

"Why?" an astonished but clearly pleased Deb wanted to know.

"Because I'll be back," Drake replied, "and that's a promise!"

The two of them stood in the darkness of the stairs as the mural slowly returned to its solid state, and they saw the figures turn and walk away. Once Deb had turned to go, Drake led the way back to the hall without a word and began packing their things up. Robbie left him be and let him pick his own time to say what was on his mind, but Drake was silent right up until they got to the car. As Robbie started the engine and turned the Honda towards Worcester and home, he could finally stand the suspense no longer.

"I thought you might stay there right away," he confessed. "I wouldn't have blamed you. Over there it's blindingly obvious that you can have a much longer life than you'll be able to have here."

"And I'll have it," Drake assured him. "But there's something I have to do here before I can go."

"I'm rather glad about that," Robbie told him. "I hope that includes giving your resignation to the force, because I don't want to have to try to explain your disappearance to Williams. He might end up locking me in a padded cell!"

Drake laughed, then cautiously asked. "Would you consider coming too? It'd be good to have you along."

"I don't know," Robbie admitted. "There's not much to keep me here, but it's not such an urgent choice for me. I'll have to think about it." Then he thought of something else. "Do you think we could let Suzanna come back into this world? She would only be in her late twenties by now? That's not so much time to make up, is it?"

Drake rubbed his tired eyes and took a ragged breath. "I don't think so, Robbie. ...I know you! You're thinking that if you stay, she could live with you until she adjusts back to the real world. And I'm not saying you wouldn't make a damned good job of being a surrogate dad to her." He had to pause to get his breath, worrying Robbie who could hear his laboured breathing even over the car engine.

"But, mate, I feel crap! I really do! I'm struggling like mad to breathe here and I've only been away an hour or so. It feels like all the wear and tear I should've had in that time has caught up with me in one go! If you bring Suzanna back her body might not be able to take the sudden changes." He paused and gasped for another couple of breaths. "It's the difference between being fourteen with all her hormones going loopy and being a mature woman of ...what ...thirty-one? I reckon the strain would kill her."

Robbie sighed morosely but couldn't argue with what Drake had said, and then worried whether his friend had been done lasting damage too. He had to manage to live for another seven weeks in the real world if he was to make it through the portal at midsummer.

By the time they got back to Worcester all they wanted to do was sleep, and come the morning Drake was more his normal self. For the next couple of days, they were busy back at work in the proper office, sorting out the paperwork which had stacked up on their desks in their absence. Little of it had any urgency, though, most of it being requests from other areas as to whether Robbie had come across old case with particular features which would shed light on old cases elsewhere. Nothing with anything like the interest of Weord School.

The following Monday Drake handed his notice in, explaining his change of heart as a desire to go and live abroad where he could just forget the past altogether. No-one made any attempt at trying to persuade him to stay, which saddened Robbie. It was as though none of the others could see what they were losing, if only in terms of the experience Drake brought to the job. He also had the feeling that although Drake had offered four weeks' notice, if he'd said he wanted to go immediately, Williams would've had him clearing his desk that same day.

There was no love lost there, and, with the new insight Robbie had gained by rubbing shoulders with Drake, it made him wonder whether Williams was worried over what the talented DI might have spotted, or might decide to report on over his head. Drake hardly had anything to lose in the way of a career if he was to make trouble for Williams, and Robbie suspected the Superintendent knew it. It also made him realise that although Drake was the newest of his colleagues, he was also the only one he thought of as a friend.

As soon as his month's notice was worked Drake began packing, and then announced that he had to go to London. Despite much probing he refused to tell Robbie what he was going for, but he willingly accepted the offer of a lift down there and then of being collected. The weather had turned to chilly and damp again, for which Robbie was very grateful. He wasn't happy about Drake going back to a place where there were those who might hold a very long grudge against him, but at least his heart wouldn't be struggling fighting a heat-wave too. With all the scepticism of a born countryman, Robbie believed every breath of polluted London air would lessen Drake's life. If had been baking hot he was convinced that the fumes would do what all the villains had failed to do as yet, and that the next call he got would be to fetch a body back for burial.

When Robbie dropped him off outside a seedy hotel near Soho in the early hours of a grey morning, Drake leaned back in through the window.

"Don't worry. I'm not going to do anything daft, but there's something that I *really* need that I can't get in such an out of the way place as Worcester."

"I'm sure the locals would be thrilled to hear you say that," Robbie said with forced humour. "You take care of yourself! And if you're not here next week when I come back, I shall start taking the place apart brick by brick to find you."

Drake smiled. "I'd better be here, then! I don't think the Met would be any too happy at the prospect of a country cousin coming in and showing them up." And with that he turned and walked away.

For Robbie the next week was one of anxiety and dread. At every ring of the phone his heart was in his mouth, as he anticipated the call telling him that Drake had been killed by someone he'd crossed in the past. The only thing which saved his sanity was being informed that Hobson's investigation had been formally closed as far as Weord School was concerned, and that the sale of the place was now clear to go ahead. Robbie made it his business to find out who the competing builders were and what they were like, for he had a budding plan of his own.

Yet before he had chance to take his own plans any further, he received a phone call in the early hours of Friday morning. Waking to the sound of the phone ringing, he rolled over and looked blearily at the bedside clock. Three a.m.! He snatched up the phone knowing that only Drake would be calling at that hour.

"Can you come and get me?" the familiar voice said wheezily without any preamble.

"Of course," Robbie said, still slightly sleep befuddled. "Ten o'clock at the hotel."

"No! Now!"

Robbie sat up in bed, fully awake now. Drake wasn't sounding at all well and this didn't sound good. "Ric are you ok? Do you need an ambulance?"

"No! But I fucking will if you don't get me out of the capital before morning!"

"Oh God! What have you got yourself into?"

"Never mind that! Meet me at Victoria Coach Station as soon as you can. Six o'clock would be good!" and the line went dead.

Struggling out of bed and into his clothes, Robbie ran downstairs and brewed a flask of coffee so strong he could've put it in the Honda's fuel tank, and then dashed to the car. Thankfully he'd kept the tank full just in case of needing to do an emergency run back down to London, and within minutes he was heading for the M5. Once on the motorway he urged the Honda up to seventy and beyond, and then risked pouring himself a mug of coffee in the spill-proof mug he'd grabbed in passing too. He hated abusing the old car like this, but at least it had a big two litre engine and had been well looked after and could take it. At the last minute he'd picked up a police radio he'd sneaked out of work the previous evening, and now turned it on to listen for any bored colleague spotting him breaking the speed limit. The last thing he needed was to have to stop and argue the toss with some keen young constable.

However, no-one even gave him a passing glance, and as the summer dawn broke, he enjoyed a clear run into the heart of London. A stranger to the city, he had to trust to road signs to get to the coach station, but eventually found himself kerb crawling along outside it trying to spot Drake. Suddenly a familiar figure detached himself from a shadowed spot and hurried towards him.

"Good man!" Drake said as he got in.

"Jesus! You look awful!" Robbie gasped, taking in Drakes dreadful colour and the way his breath was coming in gasps.

"No time for that! Turn left here!"

"What are you doing?" Robbie demanded, as Drake's hand went for the door handle as he gestured Robbie to pull in at the kerb only a few yards on.

"Going to 'Left Luggage'."

"Oh no you're not!" Robbie said firmly. "Not breathing like that! You sit with the car and I'll go and get whatever it is," and held out his hand for the key.

Instead of one, Drake handed over a handful. "It'll take a couple of trips and you'll have to be quick. Keep your eyes peeled as well! Someone might be watching you!"

Robbie looked aghast at what Drake was implying, but hurried away without another word. For the next few minutes, he lugged incredibly heavy sports bags out to the Honda with his suspicions growing with every trip. A couple of extremely heavy bags went in the back foot-well to try to distribute the weight more evenly. It was only as he got back in the car that Drake noticed that he'd donned latex gloves and raised an eyebrow.

"If whatever it is that you've got me into is dodgy enough to have *you* looking over your shoulder," Robbie said with some vehemence, "then I'm not leaving my prints and DNA all over the place to add me to the list of suspects when your old mates from the Met come looking. I thought you said you weren't going to be up to anything *daft*?"

"Well you'd only have worried and argued if I'd told you the truth!"

That was true, but it did nothing to calm Robbie's fears of what Drake had spent his time doing. He pulled away and headed into the already rising rush hour traffic. "Where to now?"

"Back to Worcester," Drake replied, already

seeming to breathe a sigh of relief. "And Robbie? Thank you!"

However, Drake didn't fully relax until they were past the M25, often directing Robbie down back streets to avoid one hold up or another. Sometimes Robbie wondered whether the assumed congestion ahead wasn't really Drake wanting to double back and weave to make sure no-one had followed them. Unused to such things, Robbie wouldn't have had a clue as to whether that was happening unless whoever it was was being downright obvious. But Drake had the sun visor down to use the vanity mirror, and was clearly watching behind them by the way he repeatedly checked the mirror, and once or twice turned round to look backwards.

Once they were free of the capital, though, he went out like a light and Robbie had to wake him when he pulled onto the drive at home. Mumbling something inaudible Drake tottered into the house and up to his room, and when Robbie went up it was to find him crashed on the bed without even having undressed, deep in sleep but at least breathing steadily.

For Robbie the first task was to ring into work and concoct some excuse for why he hadn't appeared that morning. The last thing he wanted was a visit from an inquisitive colleague. Then he put the Honda in the garage and shut the door and locked it. Only then did he open the boot and look at the bags. Pulling on another pair of gloves he opened the zip on the top bag and gasped in shock. Worried, he opened another and then another until he had to sit down on the back seat because he was starting to shake badly.

In all of his life he'd never seen so many guns or so much ammunition. Of course, he had seen training videos and other such things on the rise of gun crime, and how to respond to certain circumstances, but in his world such things had always seemed very far away. Now he was looking at enough firepower to start a war.

Not only that, but he knew that Drake could never have bought them, whether legally or illegally, given the state of his finances. Which meant that Drake had somehow cheated some very nasty characters. No wonder he'd been desperate to get out of London in a hurry! But where to put the bloody things? He could guess that Drake intended to take them through the portal with him, but midsummer was still days away and he could hardly drive back and forth into work with the damned things rattling away in the back.

Luckily his excuse for work had been putting his back out trying to change a flat tyre, and so now he decided to expand on that. The Honda would have to develop some major fault which required it to be taken into a garage as far as work was concerned, and he would hire a cheap car for a few days. That way Drake's cache could stay in the Honda, hidden away ready for the big day, without exciting any comment.

Locking it all up, he went into the house and dialled the local rental place he had used before and arrange for a hire from Monday. He could walk down to fetch it, he told them, and then went to finally get some breakfast although he had little appetite. He'd nodded off on the sofa when Drake emerged in the late afternoon, and was woken by Drake tapping him on the arm and handing him a mug of tea.

"I'm sorry you had to do that," were Drake's first words. "Things got a bit complicated quicker than I expected."

"Where did they all come from?" Robbie asked the dreaded question.

"I'm not going to tell you," Drake said gently. "You're a crap liar, Robbie. If someone asks you about guns from one of the places I got them, the answer will be written all over your face even if you don't say a word. I don't want you to get into trouble ...that is unless you're coming with me in five days' time?"

But Robbie shook his head. "No." Then saw Drake's disappointment. "Not yet, anyway," and saw him perk up at the thought that it wasn't final. "Now do you want to tell me why you want all that 'stuff'?"

Drake stretched out in the armchair and took a long drink of tea. "It was what they said about iron. Deb and the others. It struck me that the Elfael they were talking about had fought one to one with those monster things. Now I'm not daft enough to think that one man in my state is going to make much of a difference under those circumstances. But I reckon it's a fair probability that those things haven't got modern weapons. If they had, I reckon they would've used them already to complete their conquest of our little band of survivors."

And suddenly Robbie saw where he was going with this. "But you're thinking that steel will be as good as iron!"

"Exactly! With automatic weapons I can take on far more and without ever getting close enough for it to become physical. I wonder if the enemy have become depleted in the same way those Elfael have. In which case, if I can finish them off then at least the last of the survivors can live out their lives in peace in Ffreuer. They've nowhere else they can go now!"

"But you have to take enough ammunition to last you because once the portal goes you won't be able to come back for more."

"Exactly! I'm afraid I've pissed off some very nasty characters, Robbie – and some of them supposedly on our side! But the consolation is that I shall be a very long way from any place that they can find me, and I want you to be safe too. Which is why I won't tell you who or where I got them from."

For the rest of the weekend they kept a very low profile, and it was only on Monday, when Robbie came home in the hired Fiesta with a bundle of papers, that Drake got curious as to what his friend had planned.

"What's all this?" he asked.

"The dirt on the builders putting in bids for the house," Robbie said. "This one here wants to make it into executive apartments. This one wants to do the conference centre. And this bloke is after it for a country club, restaurant, and golf course. We certainly don't want anyone putting in apartments! That might mean kids for a start off.

"But also it would mean the least disruption to the fabric of the building. I was thinking of having a word with him before the sales auction. Point out to him just how many bodies were found in the house and in the surrounding grounds. This bloke loves to maintain his image. The flash local magnate! And he'd hate bad press! So I'll liken the goings on to Fred West's killing spree – but going on for longer and how the press will just love that! Spell it out to him that it might not prove such a popular place to live, and that he might have more trouble selling his developments than he thought."

Drake received the idea with enthusiasm, even adding a few ideas of his own. However, he had certain things to get before he went away for the last time, including a good many spare clothes, for Drake had no intention of swapping his comfortable modern underwear for woollen homespun. On the Thursday evening, they put his bags of clothes and belongings into the Honda and set off for the house. For a heart-stopping moment they thought they might be defeated by a large padlock which had been used to close the gate to the drive, but it proved no match for Drake's skill.

By the time midnight approached they had everything piled up on the landing ready and waiting, and as soon as the mural began to shimmer Robbie called "stand back!" and began to throw the lighter bags of clothes through to the other side. Minutes later men from the Elfael came through and began helping with the heavy bags until there was nothing left on the stairs. Once there was only Robbie and Drake left, they went through and were warmly greeted by the others.

"Are you staying?" Anne asked Robbie hopefully, earning him a wink from Drake who already had one arm draped around Deb's shoulders.

"Yes, do stay, please," Nancy added her plea. "It would be so nice to have you here."

"Oh Robbie, boy! You've got an incentive to come with me now!" Drake teased giving him a lascivious wink.

"Maybe at the next opening," Robbie consoled them. "You see someone has to cover our tracks. The last thing we want to do is have the other police wasting time looking for us, because we just went missing, especially when they could be doing much more important work. And besides, I want to make sure that this time the house really is put to sleep. Ric, here, has brought some things with him which should help with your problems, and make up for having fewer men to defend the place. You won't need me for that. And I still have some things of my own to do."

"Only we've been thinking while you were gone,"

Deb said with the air of someone who was unsure of how her words would be received.

"Oh yes?" Drake responded with curiosity. "What about?"

"You," Deb said, earning her an, "Oh good!" from Drake in a tone which made her blush.

"Not just Deb," Nancy chipped in to save her niece from explaining her blushes. "You said to us that the house was an invitation, and that you thought it was drawing people to it. Well what about you two? You seem to have been drawn here more than any others of your time, but far from being of evil intent you seem bent on stopping it. So how does that work?"

Robbie gave a startled gasp. "My word, that's a thought, isn't it! ...But you're right! We've been absorbed by all of this far more than any of our colleagues. Perhaps whatever force drew the evil here has a counterpoint which drew someone like Drake. Someone who had nothing to lose by leaving our world and would act to balance things. Good grief Ric, maybe you were always meant to do what you're doing!"

"Come off it, Robbie! That's too spooky and weird for words," Drake sniffed.

"And you, Robbie?" Anne asked. "Have you got nothing to lose?"

Then Drake broke into a broad grin as he said triumphantly. "Oh he's got plenty to lose, but he's got something I haven't! One of his ancestors was involved in the building of the manor!"

"Who?" Anne gasped.

"The glazier. Moses what's-his-name?"

"Jones?"

"That's him! So there you are, Robbie! Maybe I'm only here because you are! If you want to believe in all that kismet stuff, maybe you are the one to break the spell, because you're the one left who has the connection back to the earliest days. *Now* tell me you won't come with me!"

Robbie shook his head. "I will, Ric, just not yet! Whatever the reason is for me being the last one here, I have to make sure things are done properly so we don't cause even more chaos."

Nonetheless it was still hard for him to walk away when his time ran out. As he descended to the landing, Drake stood on the edge of the portal to say farewell.

"I'll be watching for you," he said warmly. "Don't you dare not come, Robbie! If you don't, I might have to come back just to find you, and you don't want to be responsible for what that might do to me!"

"Blackmailer!" Robbie protested, even as he felt himself choking up. He had no idea whether it would prove possible for him to join Drake, because a lot would depend on how fast the builders moved in once the sale had gone through. If the house was ripped apart before the next Sabbat, he could find the portal inaccessible, and he would've lost the first real friend he'd made in years. "You take care Ric. Don't go tilting at too many windmills like Don Quixote, will you! You're supposed to be extending your life over there, not shortening it!"

"I won't! See you on the other side soon!"

The drive back to the house was almost unbearably empty, and had it been possible to turn the car round and get back to an open portal Robbie knew that he would've done it.

The next day he walked in to find a fresh-faced constable sitting at Drake's desk and that almost finished him off. It made no difference that Williams had recognised the value in what he was doing, and had given him an extra pair of hands again. This youngster lacked Drake's experience and had none of his personality, and Robbie found himself struggling to find anything to say to the man.

He managed to somehow get through the next week, but by the Friday could stand it no longer. The building was awash with gossip about someone ripping off an evidence store in London, and how also some gangster down there was accusing the police of breaking and entering into his warehouse. The Met were apparently holding their collective breaths, waiting for an outbreak of gang warfare and the appearance of some new, but as yet unknown, drug baron. Robbie kept quiet and did his best to pretend he knew nothing of either matter, despite wondering what Williams would say if he knew that Drake was the anonymous 'drug lord'! But more than anything it only reminded him of Drake, and how much more fun life had been with the awkward, acerbic character around.

So it was with relief that he managed to make his excuses to get out of the office for half a day and head for the auction of Weord Manor, which was taking place in a local country hotel. As he circulated through the room, he spotted the first builder who wanted to create a small housing development on the site, and engaged him in conversation, expanding on the gory details of what they'd found until the man was looking distinctly pale. He went even paler when Robbie expressed the opinion that it would all come out in the press as soon as Carrie Lewis' case went to the coroner's court, along with that of Timothy Wiggins. After all, Timothy's unknown murderer was, as far as the police knew, still on the loose.

The man took Robbie's bait hook, line, and sinker, and by the time the bidding opened on the manor his heart wasn't in it. The golf club entrepreneur had been more put off by the prospect of how much it was going to cost to turn the surrounding landscape to billiard table smoothness, and of diverting natural springs, and so he hardly bothered to bid at all, turning his attention to a more profitable bid earlier in the proceedings. That left the builder who was Robbie's favourite to win with a clear field.

As everyone began wandering out of the room at the end when all the lots had gone, Robbie loitered until the builder had completed his business and sidled up to him at the door.

"Hello Robbie," the man greeted him cordially. "Long time no see."

"Indeed. How are you, Roger? Have you got time for a drink? I've got something I need to tell you."

"Not here on official business, are you?"

"Not the kind you're thinking of, no. But you do need to know this! It's more of a friendly bit of advice, but you're going to be glad you've got it!"

Epilogue

The present day

Robbie created a storm in the offices surrounding his when the news broke that he'd tendered his resignation. Williams summoned him to his office and sat staring at the piece of paper as if he couldn't quite believe his eyes.

"Why, Robbie?" was all he could seem to think of to ask. "You seemed to be so happy here."

The small detective felt a load lifting from his mind as he sat looking across the desk at his superior. Drake had been right, Williams had hardly noticed him as a real person.

"I wouldn't say happy," Robbie replied carefully. "I think it was more a case of not being *un*happy. It took Drake coming here to make me see how much I allowed myself to be buried away." He let the word 'allowed' sink in and watched Williams avoid his glance.

"Well I'm not going to let the rest of my life slip away! I've only got a few more years until you shunt me off into retirement anyway – and I have no illusions that you'd be begging me to stay on when you're trying to balance the wages budget." Williams looked even more uncomfortable. *No, you sod! How did I never spot it before?* Robbie thought. *Drake was right through and through, wasn't he? You'd soon have me out of my office when it works in your favour, and you wouldn't give a shit about what happened to me after that, would you?*

"So," he carried on, not giving Williams enough time to bluster his way out of the situation. "I've had a postcard from Drake. He's up in Dumfries and Galloway at the moment, drinking the local pub dry of Guinness and whisky, and he's asked me to join him."

"I thought he was heading for Marbella or somewhere on the Costas?" Williams said suspiciously.

However, Robbie had had more time than Drake to think of his cover and he was fully prepared. Anything requiring passage through customs would be checkable, and he didn't want that. He and Drake would have to disappear somewhere much closer than Spain.

"Oh it sounded great at first, but it turned out that he wouldn't have been able to afford to buy a place out there. You know how broke he was! On the other hand, he didn't want to rent from some dodgy Spanish landlord, and then find himself homeless in a foreign country.

"So Drake's renting a cottage in the back of beyond where there's no work, so the rent's cheap enough for even his limited wallet. On the other hand, he wouldn't object to having someone to split it with. It would give me time to do more of my history stuff – Wigtown has more bookshops than even I'll be able to deplete – and there's loads of good walks and wildlife to watch."

"Doesn't sound much like Drake's cup of tea," Williams said dubiously.

"No, it isn't," Robbie countered. "But Glasgow's near enough for the odd trip and he's not stupid. He knows he can't go anywhere in the south-east. He made one trip down there while he was with me, when we went to check on the records for Hobson's case." There! Robbie thought. If you hear of Drake having been in the capital in the time since he's been up here, you'll associate it with the case, and not the missing weapons!

"I think he realised that it was one thing to stand up to the thugs as DI Drake, with the force behind you and in good health, but that as Ric Drake, police pensioner, and with a dickey heart, he was a walking target. He finally woke up to the fact that the countryside was a damned side safer even if it lacked the excitement of the Smoke, and anyway, he was really starting to enjoy the walks I'd drag him out on. I think he's trying to make the best of what he has left. Let's face it, sir, with his heart in the state it's in he hasn't got that long. I'm not selling my house – my cousin's going to look after it for me because her daughter is going to uni' this year, and if she can use my place, it makes sense for her to come to Worcester."

That was all perfectly true, and allayed any suspicions Williams might have had of it all being out of character for Robbie to act impetuously. His cousin really did have a daughter who'd included Worcester university amongst her choices. However, it had been Robbie dangling the bribe of the house which had sealed the arrangement. He knew he couldn't just walk away from that without ringing a lot of alarm bells, and now there were timed letters left with his solicitor to be passed on as per his instructions.

In three years' time the house could be sold when his colleagues had forgotten all about him, and it would provide a nice retirement nest egg for his divorced cousin, who'd struggled to bring up three kids as a single mum. Robbie was a great man for the details, and he'd thought long and hard about what would happen after he'd gone even before Drake had appeared.

By the time the end of July came round Williams had resigned himself to the fact that there was little he could do if Robbie was determined to walk away from the job, and had given up trying. With more than a hint of sadness Robbie drove the Honda up to the manor and hid his many bags in the arboretum, out of sight of the builders who were already hard at work on the fabric of the place. He explained his presence by going to see Roger, who was inspecting his latest venture.

As he walked round to the old back door, he was heartened to see that the two single storey arms which had made the peorth shape were now nothing more than lines in the dirt. The old oak beams were stacked over to one side, clearly waiting to be reused to keep an air of authenticity to whatever Roger's plans included. However, Roger's builders lacked the imagination and literary know-how to ever recreate the complex invitation pattern with them.

The two of them stood in the hall watching three men dismantling the fireplace – the chimney having already been brought down to single floor height.

"I would never have known those hiding places were there if you hadn't said," marvelled Roger. "That upper one only made sense once we measured the place up and, to be honest, I would've put it down to the old builders just over-engineering the thing."

One of the workers came over with a piece of wood. "Look at this," he said holding it out. "It's a funny colour even accounting for the soot."

"That's where the dead girl's blood soaked into it. Hers and her baby's," Robbie told them, pulling no punches. He wanted the full horror of this place to sink in so that no-one would doubt him once he had gone away. "Dr Whitmore found the skeleton of a new-born child amongst those of its mother. She must've bled to death up there."

"Oh fuck! That's horrible!" the man said, and threw the wood into the wheelbarrow as though it had burned him, rubbing his hands on his brick-dusted jeans as if that would remove any taint.

"I'm glad you told me, Robbie," Roger said. "I'd have hated to discover all this – or even worse for it all to come to light in the press – after we'd finished."

"What are you going to do here?" asked Robbie with studied innocence.

"Oh, we'll have to put another fireplace in. We'll probably keep that nice piece of stone which made the lintel and the two side pieces, but it'll sit further back, and the chimney breast itself will be made out of some matching stone we found in a reclamation yard – at least on this side, it'll be recycled bricks on the outside. It won't need to be so big, though, because it doesn't have to take fires from upstairs, and this will only be lit for show once the central heating goes in. When we come to rebuild it we'll have to find some matching coloured bricks, because these ones we're taking out have had it. They're completely rotten! We'll probably use them for hard-core somewhere – that's all they're fit for."

"Not like the beams out the back?"

"Oh no, they're lovely aren't they! All nicely blackened and rugged! Those tatty outhouses had to go, of course. Neither use nor ornament they were."

"So what's going out there?"

"Oh, on the right, nearest to the drive we're putting in a complete new, modern kitchen. We'll need it for the conferences and things, and I want decent extractors and the like in there – which the planners just won't let me do in the old buildings. We're going to take all the right-hand two-storey down too and tack it onto the left-hand one to make a big wing looking out over the views. We'll reuse the salvaged original timbers so that the extension to the left wing matches completely."

Robbie felt a glow of satisfaction at this. It was exactly what needed to happen, the whole thing needed to be broken up and dispersed. No more invitations of any kind, and the only possible rune shape left would now be the wynn – and Robbie could cope with nothing more taxing than one meaning 'joy'. However, he noticed Roger wasn't looking terribly happy.

"Is there something else?" Robbie asked him.

"Oh it's the bloody planning people – again! I wanted to put an indoor pool in the basement of that Georgian wing, but it would mean all sorts of work on the foundations and they just won't let me do it. It's a bugger, though, because I really wanted a pool in this complex. It really ups the profile of the place."

"Why not put it in the triangular courtyard?" Robbie suggested. "You could cover it over with a conservatory type thing, and being in the middle of the buildings it wouldn't be too cold. If you put the pool by the timber-framed bit which won't have deep foundations, and have a wider pool-side on the Georgian side, I don't see that they can object. In fact, if I remember right, most of these big timber places sit on a foot-plate of big timbers. They often don't have foundations at all, or at most a couple of feet. It shouldn't be too expensive if you aren't shoring up the building, so the planners might not bat an eyelid at that, and after all, it won't be visible from outside the place."

"Robbie, you're a bloody genius! Yes! We could do that. It wouldn't matter if we had to go down ten feet at this end to put all the pipes and stuff in. Oh yes! I can see it now! We'll have conservatory plants and a Roman tiled floor to the pool and a cocktail bar serving olives with the wine and nibbles. We can market it as the whole history experience!"

"Mmmm!" Robbie murmured noncommittally. Roger's idea of 'historical' was clearly closer related to Hollywood than reality, but if it got the contaminated earth out of the courtyard and carted away, Robbie wasn't about to correct him.

"You can come and have a complimentary jacuzzi and massage when the place opens," Roger offered him, but Robbie declined.

"Thanks but no thanks. I think I've seen enough of this place. Anyway, I won't be around here much longer, I'm off travelling, making up for lost time in my old age."

"Good for you," Roger replied, clearly taking little notice now that he had a new plan to be putting into motion.

"I'd better leave you to it," Robbie said and moved away, getting only a wave of the hand as Roger got his mobile phone out and began more wheeling and dealing with the planners.

Out of the hall, Robbie checked to make sure that no-one was watching and then went upstairs to make sure that the loft hatch into the roof was still there. Having confirmed it, he slipped out and drove the Honda to the dealer who was buying it. With great sadness Robbie handed the keys over and climbed into the taxi he'd called for. He hated selling the old car, but to have left it rotting in the garage would've caused more comment, for his cousin knew he went everywhere in it. Having been dropped at the bottom of the lane to the manor once more, Robbie crept up to the house, and while the builders ate lunch on the other side, slipped into the hall, up the stairs and hoisted himself into the roof space.

Once everyone had gone home that night, he undid the security locks from the inside and lugged his bags up to the landing on the stairs. What on earth he was going to do if the portal failed to appear he had no idea. It was too late to go back now. Already nervous over this impulsive action, he became even more agitated as his watch ticked closer and closer to midnight without any sign of the mural changing its character. By the time quarter to twelve came round he felt a nervous wreck, not least because there'd already been one pass around the building by a security guard with a dog, no doubt employed by Roger to stop thefts of his supplies and equipment, rather than anyone getting into the building itself. As it was, the guard dog had spent a good minute sniffing around the trees where Robbie's bags had been hidden.

Consequently, Robbie had no idea how he would get all his things back out if the portal failed to appear. He could hardly leave all these bags sculling around for a whole day and expect them to go unnoticed. The quiet time when he'd brought his bags in was around seven in the evening, for the guard and his dog had only appeared at eight, but now Robbie was keyed up waiting for the man to do a midnight patrol.

He tentatively prodded the wall and felt nothing but chalky plaster, but then suddenly he heard a faint voice.

"Robbie! Can you hear me?" It was Drake's voice, no doubt about that, but Robbie could only see something which looked like a faint outline or shadow on the face of the painting. "You'll have to be very quick! The portal may only be open for a minute or two! Throw the most important bags first and be prepared to leave some of it behind if necessary. You might have to jump for it."

Robbie immediately changed the order of the bags and waited with bated breath. At ten-to the texture of the mural had become definitely soggy, although nothing like as fluid as before, and Robbie decide to take a chance.

"I'm going to push one of the bags through," he called to Drake, and hefting a good solid bag filled with useful books onto his shoulder, rammed it hard into the wall. The front end went in but then it was hard going until the end when it shot out of his hands, maybe because Drake or someone was pulling from the other side. "Is it intact?" he asked.

"Yes!" he heard the faint reply filtering through to him.

Without further ado he began stuffing more of the bags through. At first they were as hard going as the first, and took over a minute each to get through, because Robbie had to get them almost halfway in before there was enough for Drake and the others to pull from the other side. In his mind Robbie was beginning to panic. Everything he'd sent through would be of use to Drake and the others even if he wasn't there himself, but how was he going to get through if there was no-one to push him from this side? However, after five-to came around it got easier, and when the last but one bag shot through, nearly pitching him on his nose when there was no resistance, his hopes rose. Lifting the last bag, he threw it at the wall and was relieved to see it slip through without any effort.

"Now Robbie!" Drake's voice said above him, and looking up Robbie saw his friend as clear as day staring down at him. "Quick!"

Backing up the half turn of stairs Robbie ran and leapt at the dado rail with all his might. As he flailed through the air, he felt a hand grab him and pull him up, then suddenly he was through and landing in a heap on the grass beside Drake.

"It's gone!" Deb's voice said from beside him.

Staggering to their feet Robbie and Drake looked at the place where the portal had been. The outline of the edges of the mural still stood between two mighty oaks, but within them there was nothing but more of the new world. There was an opaque texture to the air, but the view of the hall's staircase which Robbie had seen when he'd been here before had vanished altogether.

"Well that rather settles it," Drake said, but with little regret in his voice. "God, I'm glad to see you! For a horrible hour or two I thought you hadn't come. It was only in those last few minutes that we could start to see you moving about on the stairs. Then I was worried stiff in case pulling you through did something horrible to you!"

"No, I'm intact ...as far as I can tell!" Robbie said with a grin. Suddenly he felt lighter-hearted than he had in many a year. All the past was left behind on the other side of the closed portal. There was nothing holding him back now. He was starting with a clean slate, and with the chance to build something worthwhile instead of mouldering away.

Now that the crisis had passed, Robbie also had time to inspect Drake and was amazed at what he saw. His friend appeared to be brimming with health and looked a good ten years younger than he ever had back in the real world. Moreover, the bitter cynicism seemed to have melted away, and the harried look in his eyes was gone.

"Come on," he said to Robbie, "you've got to see this hall of theirs! It's bloody amazing!"

He turned and draped an arm over Deb's shoulder and began to lead the way across the green sward.

"What about the hall, though?" Anne asked as she linked her arm through Robbie's. "Will it be safe or are we just cut off from it and unable to help anymore?"

"I think the reason I just had so much trouble is because the chimney breast is almost completely demolished," Robbie told them with a triumphant smile.

"What? All of it?" asked Nancy coming to his other side.

"All of it," Robbie confirmed, getting a grin of approval from Drake. "Once I'd finished with the builder, he couldn't wait to get rid of it – especially when they found that inside that lower priest's hole the wood was indelibly stained with Agnes' blood." He gave Anne's arm a squeeze. "She was buried in a proper graveyard, and her baby with her, once our people had finished the investigation," he told her, knowing how he'd felt about losing his own children, and how much worse it would've been if he'd known they had remained unburied.

Anne gave a little sob but smiled up at him, her face showing her gratitude without the need for any words.

"And it gets better," Robbie went on, unable to resist the chance to be smug for once. "The two low wings have gone, so the peorth rune floor plan is no more, and because they've gone there aren't any more runes in the frame of the place now. Not so much as a crossbeam out of place! It's just a normal old half-timbered farmhouse, as it should've been in the first place. It's no invitation to anything anymore!

"And that builder who's bought the place wanted to put a swimming pool in inside, but now it's going to be in the courtyard. From the old porch, which will be the way into it, they'll be digging down maybe ten feet to put pipes and heaters in for the pool, so all the earth where you swept that monster's remains to will be dug up and carried away to be spread on fields. There'll be nothing of the contamination left by the time the next month is out. Poor little Carrie was the last kid who'll ever have to fear this place. There's nothing left to pull at the other worlds with. Even the line of runes running round the hall have been taken away to a local museum – they don't fit with the builder's new decorative plans!"

"Then Feannag has been truly wiped from the place," Nancy sighed with relief. "Oh I'm so glad! I just wish Elfan and Ferylt could be here to see it happen."

"Ah! Speaking of them," Robbie said with an even bigger grin. "They found immortality of another sort, you know."

"You've been digging again haven't you," an immediately suspicious Drake said, unable to resist teasing his bookish friend, but infinitely glad that he was here again. "What have you been up to and what have you found?"

Robbie pulled a piece of printed paper from his jacket pocket. "I knew that name, Elfan, rang a bell from somewhere but I couldn't remember where. But it's from this poem or should I say poems. They're in early Welsh and are about the battles between the native Britons and the Anglo-Saxons. The big one is something called the *Gododdin*, but there are others and one of them is a lament for fallen heroes. And guess what? Elfan of Powys is among them!"

"Well you shall have to read that out in the hall tonight!" Anne told him. "The remaining Elfael will be delighted."

"I never really saw myself as the bard," Robbie confessed to Drake, as the group led him away towards the hall clutching the bags between them.

"And you're not bloody well going to be, either!" Drake told him firmly. "We've got a job to do before you sit on your arse being all Celtic and inscrutable.

There are some nasty folks out there on the border to get rid of for a start!"

* * * * *

"What do you think?" Roger asked the man from English Heritage, who was standing looking up at the mural.

"Oh it's splendid! Quite splendid!" the man enthused.

"Yes, but can you move it?" Roger pressed him. "It's going to be a nightmare if it has to stay here, because then we'll have all sorts of trouble keeping it preserved."

"I don't think there's any doubt that we can deal with this, do you Melissa?" The man turned to the woman on his left who was the conservator he'd brought with him.

"Absolutely," she replied. "With the way this plaster was held together with what looks like some kind of hessian backing, we should be able to take it off in nearly one piece. It'll take some restoration, of course, but we've had to cope with others in a far worse state than this."

"And it'll go to some museum then I suppose?" queried Roger.

"Oh no," the man said quite emphatically, "we have somewhere much more appropriate lined up for this little beauty! And we'll certainly take that carved dado panelling from the hall too! There's a lovely old mansion house up on the Scottish border which we've been restoring stage by stage over the years. At first it was just a shell, but now we're getting it back to its former glory, and the Georgian plaster has just had to come off the walls because of damp rotting it away.

"Underneath we found evidence of a scheme which must've once been like this one. Only faded hints on shards of plaster, unfortunately. This will have pride of place as its replacement! Wonderful setting! The house isn't quite as early as this medieval fresco masterpiece, of course, but this will help create the atmosphere for an exhibition we want to put in to draw the school parties in. It's just marvellous that you've got all these Anglo-Saxon-looking figures in it!

"You see, the house is just over the border of what was then the kingdom of Northumbria, in what was the native Briton's territory back in Anglo-Saxon times. We've already got a lot about that period in Bede's World over in Jarrow, so this will put our house firmly on the same tourist trail, as well as the educational things going on. There's even a poem about one of the battles they fought! It's very important because the poem's so early, and this mural could almost have been commissioned to illustrate it, they fit so well together. All terribly romantic, of course, it's called the *Gododdin*, have you heard about it? No? Well, it's all about the heroic stance of the local Britons when ..."

Historical Notes

Around 1550-1600 beautiful half-timbered houses with elaborate woodwork were still being built along the Welsh Borders, the supports of the main structural timbers being used to make intricate patterns. A huge example is Little Morton Court, but there are many across the Hereford border as complex if not quite so big. In this period, the earliest antiquaries were starting to look into the Old English writings and runes, and as early as 1575 a transcription of a runic text was made, the copy of which still survives – albeit not with arcane instructions!

On 17th Feb. 1575 Marcle Hill began to move, and according to contemporary records kept on moving for three days. About 25 acres of soil and rock shifted, uprooting trees and hedges, killing sheep and cattle, and burying the small chapel at Kinnaston whose bell was only found centuries later. The cause of the convulsion, which moved the hill about 400 yds., remains unexplained. Marcle Hill is named in several parts of a long ridge. However, the part which slipped seems to be a detached hillock rising to 163m a little over a mile west of the centre of Much Marcle. The church of St Bartholomew at Much Marcle has a 1,000-year-old yew with a split trunk, and the medieval house of Hellens is across the road. However, I am not aware of any real major house on Marcle Hill itself – built in the shape of a rune or otherwise.

From late July to early August 1645, the Scottish Covenanter Army swept down through the border counties on a circuitous march from Worcester to

Hereford. On the way they caused chaos at Hartlebury, Tenbury Wells, and Castle Frome, and ravished their way through many farms and homesteads. Hearing of the royalist advance on their position, the Covenantors then marched again heading south-east for Gloucester – their route must therefore have taken them over the high ground and near to Much Marcle, if not through it. At the time, the men of the area right across to the Malvern Hills were part of a local militia, the Clubmen, desperately trying to stop the armies of both sides from despoiling their homes. Of all the various factions on both sides, the Covenantors were the most feared, and they had an evil reputation for cruelty born out of their fanatical beliefs.

Around this time there are houses like Packwood House being built – nearly three storeys high in stone with almost mullioned windows, not as grand as the Georgian houses which were to follow but still significant family homes. The practice of tacking a new Georgian frontage onto a much older farm building can still be widely seen in rural areas.

The *Gododdin* can be read in translation in several compendiums of early poetry, as can the poems from the *Heledd Saga* which includes the poem called *Ffreuer* which refers to Elfan's death.

Thank you for taking the time to read this book.
I hope you would like to read other books like this, and the fastest way to do that is to sign up to my mailing list. I promise I won't bombard you with endless emails, but I would like to be able to let you know when any new books come out, or of any special offers I have on the existing ones.
Go to ljhutton.com to find the link

If you sign up, I will send the first in a fantasy series for free, but also other free goodies, some of which you won't get anywhere else!

Also, if you've enjoyed this book you personally (yes, *you*) can make a big difference to what happens next.

Reviews are one of the best ways to get other people to discover my books. I'm an independent author, so I don't have a publisher paying big bucks to spread the word or arrange huge promos in bookstore chains, there's just me and my computer.

But I have something that's actually better than all that corporate money – it's you, enthusiastic readers. Honest reviews help bring them to the attention of other readers (although if you think something needs fixing I would really like you to tell me first!). So if you've enjoyed this book, it would mean a great deal to me if you would spend a couple of minutes posting a review on the site where you purchased it.

The Room Within the Wall

A Roman shrine with a curse, a man accused of a murder he did not commit, and an archaeologist who holds the key to saving his life.

The Rune House

When archaeologist Pip comes across Cold Hunger Farm and the ancient Roman shrine to Attis embedded in its wall, it rakes up demons from her own past. Yet as she digs deeper into its records, shocking revelations come to light of heroic Georgian-era captain, Harry Green, accused of a vile and brutal murder – but who is the sinister woman manipulating his fiancée into making those claims? She sounds frighteningly like someone Pip knew, so how did she get into the past? And can Pip follow her to put things right again and save Harry's life before he gets hanged?

Time's Bloodied Gold

Standing stones built into an ancient church, a lost undercover detective, and a dangerous gang trading treasures from the past. Can Bill Scathlock save his friend's life before his cover gets blown?

DI Bill Scathlock thought he'd seen the last of his troubled DS, Danny Sawaski, but he wasn't expecting him to disappear altogether! The Polish gang Danny was infiltrating are trafficking people to bring ancient artefacts to them, but those people aren't the usual victims, and neither is where they're coming from. With archaeologist friend Nick Robbins helping, Bill investigates, but why do people only appear at the old church, and who is the mad priest seen with the gang? With Danny's predicament getting ever more dangerous, the clock is ticking if Bill is to save him before he gets killed by the gang ...or arrested by his old colleagues!

Printed in Great Britain
by Amazon